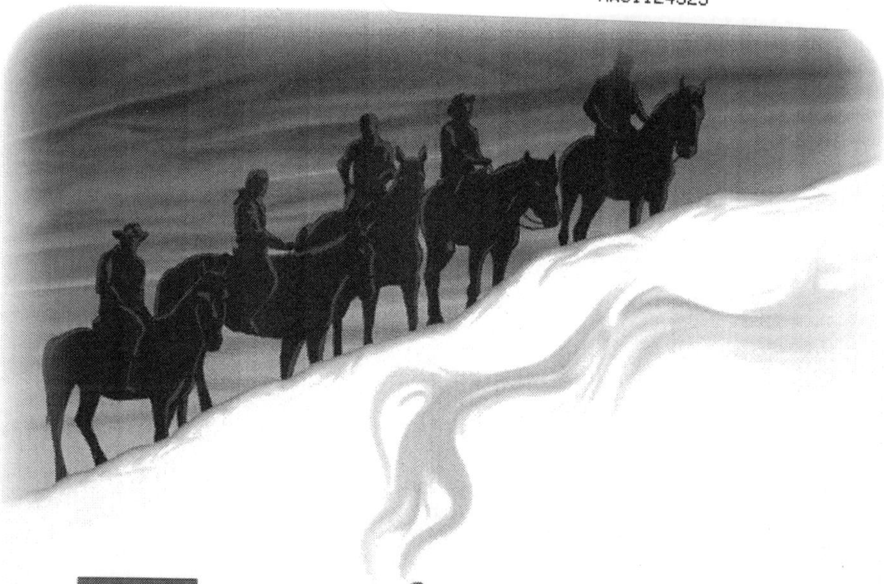

Five Dark Riders

The Nazi Plot To Kill President Roosevelt - A Fact-Based Novel

BILL SLOAN

Bill Sloan

Zipp City Press
3603 Urban Ave.
Dallas TX 75227

Front cover illustration by Mike Motz.

Author photo by Gus Gustovich.

ISBN: 1475031416
ISBN 13: 9781475031416

Library of Congress Control Number: 2012904995
CreateSpace, North Charleston, SC

In memory of my friend Jimmy Kerr, a brilliant investigative reporter who vividly remembered Roosevelt's trip to Texas and gave me the original idea for this story.

PROLOGUE

The boy could tell by the position of the moon that it was almost midnight – later than he'd realized – and he felt the need to hurry. Just over three weeks ago, he'd turned eighteen, and he considered himself a man now, but he knew his mother would be worried because he was out so late.

Carefully, he tied a knot in the end of the burlap bag containing the two bullfrogs he'd caught and slung the bag over his left shoulder. Then he hefted the pole of the fork-shaped frog gig in his right hand, and made his way down the bank of the pond in the direction of his house, a twenty-minute hike away. He'd gone less than a dozen steps when he saw two shadowy figures emerge from a patch of woods to the south and start toward him across the nearby meadow.

The boy paused, sensing instinctively that the figures didn't belong here on the farm where he lived and worked. His grip tightened on the pole of the frog gig as he gingerly placed the burlap bag containing his catch on the ground.

Trespassers, he thought. Maybe from across the river.

"Que paso?" he shouted. "Who are you? What are you doing here?"

The figures said something to each other that the boy couldn't hear, then quickened their pace until they were only about fifty feet away.

"Friends," one of them said then. "Amigos. We seem to be lost. Can you help us?"

The boy relaxed a little. "Where are you going?" he asked.

The figures made no further reply until they were within a dozen feet of the boy. Then the larger one whipped a pistol from under his belt and pointed it at the boy.

"To kill you, of course," the bigger man said. The boy stood there stunned as both of them grabbed him at once, knocking the frog gig from his grasp. He tried to yell, but the smaller man clamped his hands over his jaws so tightly that the only sound the boy could make was a stifled grunt, and the larger one forced him to the ground, smashing his face into the dirt. Then, as he sat astride the boy's back with his victim struggling beneath him, the man with the gun calmly produced a bottle from his pack and took a long swig from it. The boy tried desperately to squirm away, knowing that the men were going to shoot him and wondering why, but the man who held him was too strong.

"Don't fight it," the smaller man told the boy quietly, almost sympathetically. "It will all be over in an instant."

The last thing the boy heard was the larger man's chuckle. The last thing he felt was the cold nose of the pistol pressing against his head just behind his left ear. The last thing his nostrils detected, a split-second before the shot, was the scent of tequila.

The boy's senses had ceased to exist by the time the two men dragged him to the edge of the pond and rolled his body into the water.

ONE

Reál County, Texas
May 9, 1936

Adam Wagner knelt in the shade of a liveoak tree, staring at the corpse of his young friend, Julio Hernandez, and even in his grief, he was struck by the gruesome oddity that stared back at him. Adam had known Julio ever since the Mexican teenager was in diapers, and this was the first time he could remember seeing the kid without a grin on his face. Sometime during the night just past, that perpetual grin had been erased forever by a bullet that left a neat, round hole in Julio's skull. Now his bloated body lay on the bank of a small stock pond while a handful of onlookers kibitzed nearby.

Adam had seen more than his share of dead bodies in his time. He'd been only a little older than Julio when two of his closest friends were killed within a few feet of him in France during the World War, but even those deaths hadn't wracked him as hurtfully as this one. Wars were full of horror and hellishness. People were expected to die in wars, but violent death seemed grotesquely out of place beside this placid pond on the farm where Adam had spent most of his life.

Indistinctly, the voices of other bystanders drifted to him from a few yards away, and Adam felt himself shaking inside. Then a wave of dizziness gripped him, and the scene beside the pond abruptly dissolved as his mind swept him back into the distant past and halfway around the world.

It was an awful autumn morning in 1918, and he was in the dark woodlands along the Meuse River. The pond, the bank, and the liveoak tree were gone, replaced by the stench and smoke of a shell-blasted forest glade. And instead of staring down at Julio's lifeless body, Adam was leaning over the mangled remains of another aways-smiling Mexican boy of about the same age and build.

The eyes of Private Francisco Lemos were wide with shock, and a spark of life still lingered in them. But Lemos's belly had been ripped open seconds earlier by a canister round from a German 75, and his intestines spilled onto the ground through a gaping, foot-long wound. Lemos tried to speak, but all Adam could hear was his own hoarse plea echoing in his ears:

"Cisco! Cisco! Hang on, amigo, I'll get help. Stretcher bearer! Stretcher bearer!"

Only when Adam tried to lift Lemos in his arms did he feel the knifing pain in his legs and look down to see his own blood saturating his shredded leggings.

Then he lost his balance and fell beside his dead buddy.

Adam choked off the scream that formed in his throat as the forest glade faded into nothing, and the bank, the pond, and the liveoak tree re-materialized around him. He rubbed at a solitary tear on his cheek and flung it away.

Former Sergeant Adam Wagner of the U.S. Army's First Infantry Division had learned to understand death on a battlefield. It was just as terrible and final there, but it happened so often that it became almost routine, whereas the kind of death that confronted him now was beyond his comprehension.

"Damn it, Julio," he whispered. "Who the hell did this to you?"

A fence-rider had found Julio's body about sunup that morning. The youngster was floating face-down in the pond, one of a dozen watering holes for the sheep and goats on the Wagner Farm. There was a single bullet hole behind the boy's left ear, and an empty tequila bottle lay on the bank nearby. From the look of the body, it had been in the water most of the night.

Now several vehicles were parked along the narrow trail nearby, and a small cluster of men stood farther along the bank of the pond. A gnarled cedar frowned down at them, its dark-green shadow reflected in the still water against a cloudless sapphire sky. Recently sheared sheep and new lambs, their wool still almost black, grazed in a nearby meadow. A slight chill clung like mist to the rugged landscape, but the temperature would climb well above 80 degrees by mid-afternoon.

"Could've been wetbacks that did it," said George Wagner, Adam's father. "A good many of 'em been coming up from the Rio Grande this spring." The old man's labored breathing and brittle voice gave evidence of his failing health. He was still the recognized bossman of the farm, but Adam had actually run the place for years.

"Maybe so," said Sheriff Wilfred Streicher around a plug of tobacco. "But from the looks of things, he could've just been fighting with some other *muchacho* over that bottle of tequila."

Adam walked slowly along the bank toward the sheriff and the others, pausing to rest his damaged knees and scratch the ears of "Lobo," the grizzled collie at his side. The sheepdog was going on eleven years old and, like his master, he wasn't quite as sharp or nimble as he'd once been, but he was still a damn sight smarter and more reliable than some people Adam knew.

"Bullshit," Adam snapped, spitting into the dust at his feet and forcing the Sheriff's eyes to meet his. "He was out here frog-hunting. I found his gig and the two frogs he'd caught over there by the bank. Whoever killed him took him by surprise."

"Could be he came out here with somebody else, though," the Sheriff said. "You know, two amigos hunting frogs and sharing a little tequila."

"Look, Sarge," Adam said, "I've known Julio for a good sixteen years, and I've never seen him touch a drop of hard liquor. Maybe a beer once in a while on a hot afternoon, but getting in a fight to the death over a jug of hooch? Not a chance!"

Adam and Julio had spent countless hours together doctoring sick lambs, shearing sheep, hauling wool to market, stalking deer and turkey, and fishing in the Frio River. Julio was as steady and responsible as any kid his age Adam had ever known – Latino, Anglo, or otherwise – and his irritation at Streicher's remarks was plain in his voice.

"Well, don't get your bowels in an uproar, old buddy," said the Sheriff mildly. "I just mentioned it as a possibility."

Adam had also known "Sarge" Streicher for a long time. They'd gone to high school together, lettered on the same football team, enrolled as roommates at the University of Texas, and joined the First Infantry Division on the same day in 1917. They'd made buck sergeant within a week or two of each other, and both had ended up as rifle squad leaders. For months, they'd huddled together in the same muddy trenches and charged together across the same godforsaken no-man's lands. They'd shared a barrel or two of French wine and cognac and generally been as close as any two brothers-in-arms could get.

But when the war was over – especially after Streicher had been elected the county's "Doughboy Sheriff" in 1922 and Adam had gone back to his father's farm as a sheepherder with a permanent limp – things had changed. On the surface, they still got along fine most of the time, but deeper down, a gap had formed between them and gradually widened. Adam didn't always agree with Streicher's concepts of law, order, and "equal justice," particularly where Mexicans were concerned, and he was disturbed by the Sheriff's coziness with the county's richest, most powerful family. Sometimes he had to bite his tongue to keep from telling Sarge so to his face.

❖

Following his father's first heart attack eleven years ago, Adam had taken over the day-to-day operation of the family farm. Since then, as Julio had grown up, the Mexican boy had become Adam's co-worker and a substitute for the younger brother Adam never had. Now the kid's body lay on the ground, covered by a horse blanket that somebody had thrown over it.

"Maybe he shot himself," suggested Sam Lehmann, the balding, heavy-jowled justice of the peace, who'd just made the twelve-mile car trip out from Leakey (pronounced "Lake-ee"), the county seat of Réal County.

Under Texas law, it was the JP's responsibility to establish the official cause of death – even if the JP happened to be a semi-literate lummox like Lehmann. Adam stood up slowly, motioning for Lobo to stay.

"But he was right-handed," Adam said, pushing back the brim of his sweat-stained hat. "How's he gonna shoot himself in the left side of the head with his right hand?" He used his own right hand to demonstrate how awkward this would be.

Lehmann stared at him, then shrugged. "Well, maybe he just decided to use his *left* hand for some reason," he said with a sour smile. "You know, just for fun."

Somebody in the small crowd snickered, and Adam felt a momentary urge to push Lehmann into the pond and hold his fat head under the water.

It would've have been a ludicrously easy thing to do, even with two gimpy legs. At nearly two hundred pounds, Adam weighed about the same as Lehmann, but at six-three, he was half a foot taller. And twenty-three months in the Army, followed by eighteen years of mending fences, wrestling goats, fighting rattlesnakes, and clawing a living from the unforgiving hills had left him considerably leaner and tougher than Lehmann could ever imagine being.

On the other hand, Adam didn't want to do anything to put a strain on his father's weak heart. He didn't want to end up in Sarge Streicher's friendly jail, either. So he forced himself to calm down a little.

To Adam, telling Jake and Maria Hernandez that their only son was dead –and seeing the look in the eyes of Julio's little sister, Juanita, when she heard the news – was almost as bad as Julio being dead in the first place. But with his father's frail health, there was no one else to handle it. Irene Wagner, Adam's mother, would lend her quiet support later on, but conveying the initial shock would be solely up to Adam.

"Julio was murdered, and you know it as well as I do, Sam," he told Lehmann. "Trouble is, you don't give much of a damn, do you?"

George Wagner laid a frail hand on Adam's shoulder. "Take it easy, son. I know how much you liked Julio. I liked him, too, but now we just have to stand back and let the Sheriff and Judge Lehmann do their job."

"We'll do our dead-level best to get to the bottom of this," Streicher told Adam solemnly, clapping him on the shoulder. "You've got my word on that, buddy."

Adam clenched his jaw and nodded. Wagner men didn't show emotion where anybody could see it. His father and grandfather had made that clear as far back as Adam could remember. He snapped his fingers at Lobo, then turned and walked slowly away from the body and the small cluster of men. The old dog followed at Adam's heels, his tail curled jauntily over his back.

Even if they were Mexicans, the Hernandezes were like part of the Wagner family, and they'd all had high hopes for Julio. Jake and Maria's dream was for their first-born to go to college after his graduation from Leakey High School next month, and Julio was in line for a full scholarship that could've made the dream a reality. Now the only place the kid was going was into a hole in the rocky ground at Rio Frio Cemetery.

The whole damned mess seemed inconceivable. Except for a few hunting accidents, there hadn't been a fatal shooting in Reál County in over ten years, and it was just hard to imagine anybody getting mad enough at a boy like Julio to kill him in cold blood. Robbery wasn't a very likely motive, either, since Julio never had any valuables to speak of, and three soggy dollar bills and some change were still in his pockets when he was pulled from the water. Besides, the wetbacks George Wagner had mentioned almost never had guns, and they usually went well out of their way to avoid trouble.

So why had it happened? There had to be a reason – even for something as unreasonable as this.

In the distance behind him, Adam could still hear the men around the stock pond talking among themselves.

"What kind of gun you figure it was, Sheriff?"

"Probably a small-caliber pistol at close range," Streicher said. "Definitely wasn't a deer rifle. If it was, it would've blown his skull wide open, but there's not even an exit wound as far as I can see."

"Where you reckon the gun is?"

Streicher shrugged. "Chances are, the killer took it with him. Or it could be at the bottom of the pond, I guess. Any of you men want to volunteer to jump in there and search for it?"

There was another brief ripple of laughter, and Adam felt another flash of anger. He knew from experience that the authorities in Reál County weren't inclined to go to a lot of trouble locating evidence in a case like this. Most likely, there wouldn't be much of an investigation at all, and an autopsy was out of the question.

At the moment, this was the only significance that Adam attached to Sarge's remarks about the gun. Later, though, they would take on added meaning.

TWO

Adam plodded through the lingering coolness of the morning while Lobo ranged a dozen yards ahead, his ears and nose alert and his tail busy. They walked until the empty ache in Adam's gut eased a little and the misery in his knees also subsided. At first, the Army doctors had said he'd never walk again without crutches or at least a cane, but Adam had proved them wrong. The pain – sometimes slight, sometimes more severe – was a constant companion, but he'd made up his mind long ago not to give in to it, and he'd worked hard to build up his leg muscles and keep his knees limber through regular exercise.

About two hundred yards from the pond, the man and the dog stopped at the eight-foot-tall, deer-proof fence that marked the boundary between the Wagner Farm and its massive neighbor to the north, the 73,000-acre Radke Ranch, the largest in the county. Adam hadn't consciously realized until now that the pond where Julio had been found was so close to the fence line. The realization pricked his curiosity.

The Radkes and the bastards who worked for them were as predatory as coyotés. Kurt Radke, who'd been lord of the manor since old man Gus

Radke's death, had once been a friend of Adam's – sort of – but in a way the two of them had always been adversaries as well. Kurt was about a year older than Adam, and he'd been bigger and stronger when they were in high school. He'd also had a mean streak in him a yard wide.

Their first serious clash had come on the football practice field one fall afternoon. Kurt, the team's star fullback, had intentionally tripped a clumsy young lineman named Wagner, sending him to the ground, jolting his helmet loose, and splitting his lip. Adam had bounced up with an egg-sized rock in his right fist and punched Kurt squarely in the eye, giving him a shiner that lasted over a week.

The coach had shoved them apart and threatened to throw Adam off the team if he pulled a stunt like that again. Tension remained high between the teammates until the day Adam threw a key block that set Kurt free on a fifty-yard touchdown run. After that, the two of them started hanging out together and spent a year or two trying to out-drink, out-ride, and out-womanize each other.

Then something happened that first drove a wedge between them and later became a permanent barrier. In the years since, they'd been reasonably civil to one another when they occasionally crossed paths, but they definitely weren't friends anymore.

The Radke forebears had come originally from the same part of Germany as the Wagners, and many other early settlers of Reál County had, but there was no love lost between the Radkes and their neighbors. Hardly anybody in the county claimed to be friends with them, but still fewer had the nerve to buck them publicly on any issue. Even George Wagner sometimes accused them of "thinking they own the whole damned county instead of just half of it."

The Radke Ranch had always been one of the most private places in Texas. It had become even more so when Kurt and his neurotic sister, Karla, had taken charge of the place after their father died. They did their socializing in Austin, New York, Washington, and other places beyond the reach of the rest of Reál County, and they rarely showed up at local functions. It was an unwritten law that outsiders never ventured uninvited onto Radke property. Adam had once moved freely in and out the Radkes' main gate, but his father claimed he could count on the fingers of one hand the times in his seventy-four years when he'd been inside the Radkes' two-story fieldstone mansion.

Radke fence-riders rode big palomino stallions with the distinctive RR brand on their rumps. Armed with saddle carbines, they were ruthless enforcers of the no-trespass law. Over the years, they'd shot several game poachers, but only a couple had actually been charged with a crime, and those charges were eventually dropped, probably because the district attorney was Kurt's uncle – a fact that had kept Kurt himself out of trouble more than once.

Through the barbed-wire fence, Adam could look across a wide, hill-fringed valley and down a gentle slope to a grove of gray-green liveoaks, interspersed with darker scrub cedars. The valleys between the hills were capable of producing rich stands of grass and grain, but it took two or three acres of hillside to support the grazing of a single sheep or goat. It was hard country to wrestle a living from.

Beyond the intervening valley, Adam could make out a tin-roofed limestone house and several shearing sheds. Still further away, the blades of a lonely windmill slowly revolved in the breeze. He could see for more than half a mile at this vantage point, and there was no hint of human activity anywhere on the other side of the fence.

But in the lush spring grass directly in front of him, Adam noticed a set of faint tracks crossing the near pasture. He saw no signs of hoof prints in the soft earth, only a double trail where the grass was flattened and its natural uniformity disturbed. The tracks came right up to the edge of the Wagner property, then seemed to vanish, but since sheep had recently been grazing on Adam's side of the fence, the grass was simply too short to show tracks.

Adam would've bet a month's pay that two people had crossed the Radke pasture on foot sometime within the past twelve hours or so. If they had, they could easily have been in the vicinity when Julio was shot.

When he got back to the stock pond, the Sheriff's black Ford sedan and Sam Lehmann's green Buick coupe were gone. George Wagner had apparently gotten tired of waiting and hadn't felt up to looking for his son because the trail-worn Chevy pickup in which they'd driven out to the pond was gone, too. Adam was all alone.

He sat down on the earthen dam above the waterhole and stared at his reflection in the water: He saw a battered hat, a mane of sun-bleached hair the color of cornsilk, an untrimmed mustache, dirty Levis, faded work shirt, and worn brown boots encasing legs still studded with the

Kaiser's shrapnel. Nothing visible remained of the cocky young infantryman he'd once been. He was, by his own definition, a mildly disabled, 38-year-old nobody headed for nowhere – and in no big rush to get there.

Lobo drank noisily from the pond, then flopped down beside him. It was about a mile back to the house over a twisting trail studded with prickly pear and bluebrush, but Adam didn't care. The walk would be good therapy for his legs when he eventually made up his mind to go. Right now, he needed a while to think.

Adam had never returned to the University of Texas to continue his education after the war. His messed-up legs had been a primary factor. He'd come close to losing his right one to gangrene in a French hospital, and it had been mid-1919 before he even made it back to the States. After that, there were stints in other hospitals in New York and San Antonio and six months on crutches that ate up another chunk of his life. Then, after he finally got home to stay, the bottom had dropped out of the wool market, and there'd been no money for college.

At one point, he'd dreamed of being a lawyer, a journalist, or some other kind of professional who wore a suit and tie to work and lived somewhere interesting and exotic. He still regretted that none of that had been in the cards he was dealt, but he didn't waste time fretting about it. He shared his father's and his grandfather's love for Reál County, and fate apparently intended him to spend the rest of his days there. So, in trying to forget what he'd seen and suffered in France, he gradually withdrew into the simple life of an outdoorsman, roustabout, and loner. Yet now that it seemed too late to change course, he still thought sometimes about moving somewhere a thousand miles away and never looking back. This was definitely one of those times.

When the sudden heart attack had hit his father in the spring of 1925, there was no one else available to keep the farm functioning. Adam's baby sister, Carolyn, had still been in high school, and his older sister, Christine was living in Houston, working as a registered nurse, and had zero interest in managing a struggling South Texas stock farm.

Then, three years ago, George Wagner had almost died of a second seizure, leaving Adam with the entire burden of running the 5,600-acre farm and tending to more than 1,800 head of sheep and angora goats. From the fifth grade through his college and Army years, his ambition had been to witness important events and live in exciting places. One of the songs he'd heard people singing when he finally got back on the homeward side of the Atlantic had hit the nail squarely on the head:

How you gonna keep 'em down on the farm
After they've seen Par-eee?

For Adam, though, memories of Paris consisted mostly of nurses and doctors, who drifted past his bed shaking their heads; pain that refused to end; and imaginary conversations with Lieutenant Earl Garrett, his dead company commander, who kept promising him that everything would be all right. Although Adam had no rational explanation for it, he remained convinced, even after all these years, that it was Garrett's delirium-induced encouragement that had somehow kept him from dying there.

Postwar life might have been better if he'd found a woman he cared about, and, God knows, he'd tried, but a man's choices in Reål County were strictly limited. The county seat of Leakey was only a wide spot in the road with a population of 650 people, and Camp Wood, the only other town in the county, was even smaller. Most of the girls he'd known in high school were long-married by the time he got home from the war – and it was easy to see why those that weren't were still unattached.

Occasionally, he drove the forty-odd miles down Highway 4 to Uvalde, the nearest good-size town, and made small talk with the barmaids in the beer joints there. Now and then, he even took a few of them out. He'd once been sufficiently attracted by a busty blonde at the Nite Owl Tavern to get in a fistfight over her with a cowhand from LaPryor. Adam had won the fight, but after three or four dates with the blonde, he wondered why he'd bothered.

There *were* some very attractive Mexican women around, but sons of respectable Anglo families weren't supposed to get involved with "those girls." Sometimes they did, but not openly. For Adam, there was also the constant matter of money, or, more correctly, the lack of it. The sixty-five dollars a month he earned as his father's top hand didn't cover a whole lot of heavy dating.

Adam wasn't much of a Franklin Roosevelt fan, but whether you liked the New Deal or not, the country was moving steadily away from the narrow norms and close-minded prejudices of other days – most of the country, anyway. But in Reál County, with people like the Radkes, Sarge Streicher, and Judge Lehmann in charge, the "dark ages" seemed to go on and on.

He stood up and tossed a stone into the quiet pool where Julio Hernandez's body had floated some three hours earlier. It was time to go to the cottage where Julio's family lived and do what he could to console them. He'd postponed it as long as he could. But as he started along the bank of the pond, his eye caught a glint of sunlight on something near the water's edge, and he paused for a closer look.

It was the empty tequila bottle, still lying where it had been when Adam, his father, and the sheriff first arrived. Surely, he thought, if Streicher seriously believed Julio had fought with somebody over this same bottle, it should've been taken as evidence. It should've been tested for fingerprints – or something.

Surely.

Yet there it lay, steadfastly ignored like everything else pertaining to the calamity that had befallen a good Mexican kid last night.

Adam searched around until he found a sizable twig, then inserted it into the neck of the bottle and picked it up. Removing the stick and holding the bottle with his bandana handkerchief, he passed the neck of it under his nose and sniffed. It was tequila, all right. There was no mistaking the unique odor.of the fermented juice of the agavé plant. Tequila was dirt-cheap – as little as fifteen cents a liter – in towns on the other side of the Rio Grande like Nuevo Laredo, Piedras Negras, and Villa Acuña. But a state tax offset that bargain by imposing an additional twenty-cent-per-liter charge before the liquor could be brought legally across the river. And the real cost of a tequila drunk usually came the next morning.

This bottle bore no tax stamp, however, so it had obviously been smuggled into the United States.

Adam thought back to the tracks in the grass, his father's observation about wetbacks, and Streicher's half-joking remark about where the murder weapon might have wound up. He stared into the depths of the pond, but after the first two or three feet, the water became impossible to see through. There was very little mud at the bottom, though, and certainly none of the oozy variety into which a heavy object could sink and be lost. Like every pond on the place, the bottom here was mostly rock, and the water was only six or seven feet deep at its deepest point.

He cradled the bottle in his arms and trudged slowly toward the farm's distant main house with Lobo trailing along behind. Before he'd gone a dozen steps, he knew he'd be back that night to do some diving.

THREE

Jake Hernandez stood on the narrow front porch of his cottage and lit his hand-rolled cigarette with a kitchen match. Behind him in the darkened house, Adam could hear the sound of weeping women, but except for two small streaks of wetness under Jake's eyes, his weather-beaten face betrayed no emotion whatever.

"*Mil gracias* for coming, Señor Adam," he said softly, exhaling a mouthful of smoke. "You cared for my son as much as we did, and I know it is very hard."

"You and Maria take as much time off as you need," Adam said, aware of how inadequate and empty the words sounded. "And don't worry about the funeral expenses; they'll all be covered. You pick out whatever kind of coffin you want, and we'll see it's taken care of."

There was no funeral home in Reál County, but Boren's Store on the courthouse square in Leakey kept an ample supply of coffins in stock, and many of the Mexican women were skilled in preparing a body for burial. Only the county's wealthier families utilized the services of the big mortuary in Uvalde with its shiny Cadillac hearse and limousines.

"I am most grateful, Señor," Jake said. "There is one other favor I would ask. I pray it is not too much."

"Of course not," Adam said. "What is it?"

"My wife's sister is Rachel Velasco. If you recall, she and her husband, Ramon, operate a small store in Leakey – the Mercado Velasco."

Numb as he was, Adam felt a peculiar, tingling sensation pass over him at the sound of the name "Velasco." It was a word he hadn't heard spoken in a long time – one that brought vivid images to mind.

"I know the place," he said. "Do you want me to go and tell them about Julio?"

"It is a terrible thing to have to ask, Señor Adam, but Maria is not up to going, and I . . . "

"It's all right. I'll take care of it."

As he retraced his steps back toward the main house and the double garage behind it, Adam's head was suddenly whirling with memories of Rachel and Ramon Velasco's two daughters – Luz and Elena. Not that he'd ever forgotten them in all the intervening years. Forgetting them would have been impossible, but he usually kept their images locked away in a special, secret place in a back corner of his mind. Now Jake's innocent remark had released them.

Like most of the teenage boys who hung around the drugstore on the courthouse square, Adam had lusted after sexy Luz Velasco, but also like the others, he'd never quite found the nerve to ask her out. After dropping out of Our Lady of Guadalupe Catholic School, the only local educational institution open to Mexican children, at age fourteen, Luz had found a job behind the soda fountain, making and serving sandwiches and iced drinks. By the time she was seventeen, she was the drugstore's main attraction, and her lurid reputation had made her very name an off-color joke. In Spanish, Luz was pronounced "Loose," and Luz Velasco was indisputably the loosest teenage siren Leakey had ever known.

But Elena Velasco – or "Ellie" as she liked to be called when she was in her early teens – was as different from Luz as a mountain sunrise from a midnight hailstorm. Except for an age difference of close to five years, the two girls could've been twins, but where Luz was fiery and flamboyant, Ellie was studious and subdued. She was only in the seventh grade at Our Lady of Guadalupe when Adam was a senior at Leakey High, and the truth was, Elena was so overshadowed by Luz that Adam hardly noticed her when she first started showing up at the drugstore in the afternoons to pass the time with her older sister.

Several of the town boys claimed to have scored with Luz, but Adam had a feeling they were making it up. No one else had ever caught and held Luz's roving dark eyes the way Kurt Radke had, and half the town knew that something hot and heavy was going on between them that spring of 1916. Adam had known it better than anyone, since he and a girl named Teresa Sanchez often double-dated with Kurt and Luz. Teresa wasn't a bad looker, but she was no Luz Velasco. Adam would've traded places with Kurt in a second.

Then the whole thing turned incredibly ugly.

One dark Saturday night, Luz was killed in a one-car crash on a winding mountain road east of Leakey. She was driving a Cadillac touring car owned by Gus Radke, Kurt's father, and when word got out about the accident, the town rumor mill had gone crazy. One story claimed that Luz had committed suicide and was carrying Kurt's child when she died. Another said she killed herself in a jealous rage after she caught Kurt messing around with her kid sister. Others claimed she was merely drunk or full of loco weed when the car left the road and rolled end over end into a 200-foot canyon.

For his part, Kurt first denied even knowing Luz and claimed the car was stolen. Ray Baughman, the elderly sheriff at the time, supposedly looked into a complaint by Ellie that Kurt had assaulted her that same night, but nothing ever came of it.

For reasons Adam couldn't explain, he'd felt compelled to go to Luz's funeral, and the sight of Ellie sitting in the church, her bruised face a mask of grief and guilt, had burned itself indelibly into his brain. He'd seen a similar look on her face at the Radke Ranch a few weeks earlier when Kurt had torn her blouse half off and Adam had had to wrestle him away from her. All during the funeral service, Adam had ached to reach out and touch Ellie, to comfort her somehow, to say something that might make a difference.

In reality, he'd done nothing, yet for weeks afterward, he couldn't get the girl off his mind. Several times he'd gone out of his way to stop at the Mercado Velasco, hoping to see her, but whenever he'd had a chance to say something to her, he could feel her retreating into a defensive shell. Finally he'd given up and quit trying.

When that summer was over, Adam and his high school friend Wilfred Streicher headed off to college in Austin. Just over a year later, he was aboard a troop ship bound for France. And that had been the end of it – or so he thought

But two years ago, Ellie had slipped so quietly back into Adam's world that he didn't even realize she was there for a long time. After graduating as valedictorian of her class at Our Lady of Guadalupe, she'd earned an education degree at Southwest Texas State Teachers College in San Marcos, then taught in San Antonio for several years. Finally, someone had casually mentioned to Adam that Luz Velasco's sister had been hired as a first-grade teacher at the Leakey School. One or two members of the school board had supposedly opposed hiring a Mexican for the job, but the superintendent had talked them into it.

In all the time since, Adam had never once seen Ellie face to face. Now perhaps he would. The thought filled him with a mixture of apprehension and boyish excitement.

FOUR

Hyde Park, New York
May 10, 1936

From a distance of about ten feet, Colonel Edmund W. Starling kept a wary eye fixed on his boss, the President of the United States, and what he saw touched off vague but all-too-familiar feelings of unease. In this unguarded moment, slumped in an armless wheelchair with his legs covered by a lap robe, Franklin Delano Roosevelt bore little resemblance to the confident, robust persona he displayed in public. As he gazed pensively toward the Hudson River through the windows of the small cottage known as the "Hilltop," the President looked older, wearier, and more fragile than Starling could remember..

In short, he looked more *vulnerable* to Starling. As chief of the White House detail of the Secret Service, it was the Colonel's job to think that way. It was also his job to counteract that vulnerability by any and every conceivable means.

Starling had accompanied FDR to the cottage from the crowded main house on the Roosevelt estate this Sunday afternoon in search of a quiet place where the President could deal undistracted with matters that wouldn't keep until he returned to the Oval Office on Monday. Besides Starling and Roosevelt, the only other people present were Marguerite "Missy" LeHand, the President's personal secretary, and Stephen Early, his trusted press aide, who had taken on a broader role as a key White House adviser in recent months. One purpose of their meeting was to discuss upcoming travel plans – a prospect that always made Starling's stomach churn.

"The last time we were here, it was still winter," Roosevelt mused, turning back from the windows. "Now it's suddenly spring. Where does the time go?"

"It flies by because you're always so busy," Missy said. "You need to slow down a little." Starling watched her lean down to straighten the President's lap robe – one of many small, unconscious mannerisms that revealed how closely personal their relationship was.

"No rest for the wicked, Missy," FDR said, fitting a Camel into his cigarette holder, then allowing her to reach around and light it. "War threats are popping up in every corner of the globe. I have nightmares about what our friend Hitler may be plotting next in Europe, not to mention Mussolini in Africa and the Japanese in Asia – which reminds me, I've *got* to meet with Secretary of State Hull on the China situation as soon as we get back to Washington. On top of that, the national convention will be here before we know it, and then we'll be in the thick of another campaign with no time for anything but speeches and trains and parades and hoopla. Do we really have to go to Texas in June, Steve? It's so blasted far!"

"It'd seem a lot closer if you'd fly instead of going by rail," Early said. He sat at a small, drop-leaf mahogany desk just to the President's right and kept a memo pad at his elbow as he leafed through a sheaf of papers and scribbled notes on a planning calendar. "A Navy plane could have you from D.C. to Texas inside six hours."

That was a terrific idea, Starling thought, and it would make everything so much less complicated. With modern aircraft, the hazards of flight were minimal compared to those a president could face on the ground, but Starling had no illusions about FDR taking Early's suggestion. Roosevelt hadn't been on a plane since flying out to Chicago nearly four years ago to accept the 1932 Democratic nomination, and he made no bones about his dislike of air travel.

"I prefer looking up at clouds, not down," he said, waving his hand as a signal to drop the subject and move on.

"Then I guess we'll be living on the train for a week or more," Early said. "The Texas thing's almost a must at this point, Boss. It'll be priceless exposure in a part of the country where you really need it, and it's also a golden chance to steal some thunder from Alf Landon and the Republicans. Their nominating convention's in Cleveland about that same time, and Landon looks more and more like a cinch to be your opponent in November."

"I know," Roosevelt sighed, drawing on his cigarette. "Besides, I've already promised Vice President Garner that I'll show up at that Texas Centennial Exposition of his. He wants me there for the opening on June sixth. Can we manage that, Steve?"

"It's possible," Early said, studying the calendar, "but the following week looks a lot better for diverting press coverage from the Republican convention. It also depends on what else we want to do on this trip."

"Well, as long as we're going that far, we may as well make a real to-do out of it," FDR said. "We could schedule five or six major events along the way and maybe twice that many stops in smaller towns where I can say a few words from the train."

"I've got off-the-train events penciled in so far in Little Rock, Houston, San Antonio, Dallas, Fort Worth and Vincennes, Indiana," Early said. "Sound about right?"

The President smiled and blew a smoke ring. "It sounds perfectly horrible, but I guess it'll have to do."

"Of course, that doesn't include a possibility we discussed several weeks ago. The idea of going on down to the Mexican border to meet with President Cardenas, I mean."

Roosevelt frowned. "I'd almost forgotten. Maybe I *wanted* to forget. What's the status of that?"

"Our embassy's pitched the idea informally to some top Cardenas aides, and they're pretty receptive. They think a meeting could help his image and make it easier to sell his reform programs. Trouble is, the last thing the *Cardenistas* want is for their man to risk losing face with the

Mexican electorate by coming to Washington hat in hand. If you two met on the border during the Southwestern trip, they could make it look more like you came to him."

The drift of the conversation sent sudden red flags flapping in Colonel Starling's head.

"I've got no problem with that, Steve," FDR was saying. "It's just that – "

"I hate to butt in, Mr. President," Starling said, standing up abruptly, "but going into Mexico isn't a good idea right now – and that means any part of Mexico. The situation's too volatile and unpredictable. We'd need at least a battalion of U.S. troops for security if you went across the Rio Grande, and frankly I'd still be sweating blood."

Roosevelt snorted. "I doubt the Army could spare us a battalion as shorthanded as it is right now," he said. "Our military's in deplorable shape, and our head-in-the-sand Congress is too tightfisted to do anything about it."

"Don't worry, Ed," Early said. "If the Cardenas meeting comes off, we'll insist it be held on our side of the river. Probably in Laredo, Texas, a couple of hours by train from San Antonio." He turned back to Roosevelt and added, "Even so, we'd be looking at a good four thousand miles of travel, and that may be stretching us a little thin."

Missy Lehand had been standing at the windows, looking down at the river while the three men talked. Now she moved up behind FDR's wheelchair, laying one hand lightly on his shoulder.

"Let's leave the door open for now," Roosevelt said, absently patting Missy's hand. "I want to talk to the Mexican ambassador when we get back to Washington, and I'd also like to hear what our ambassador in Mexico City has to say before we make a final decision. At this point, all we're doing is exploring the matter, and nothing's firm. Let's not let anything out to the press yet."

"Right, Boss," Early said. "What about the date for your visit to Dallas? Shall we leave that open, too?"

Roosevelt nodded. "You can tell Garner I'm coming to his pesky centennial," he said, "but I can't commit to June sixth, and I may have to let Commerce Secretary Roper fill in for me at the opening. Oh, and as long as you're talking to Garner, ask him what he thinks about the Cardenas meeting."

"I doubt if he'll be very excited about a meeting with any foreign leader, Boss," Early said. "Garner's about as much of an isolationist as Governor Landon."

"I know, but he's pretty close to the Mexico situation – geographically, anyway – and he's always miffed because I never consult him about anything."

"I'll contact him as soon as we get back to D.C.," Early said. "Anything else?"

FDR stared again out the windows toward the Hudson, and there was a noticeable pause before he answered.

"Matter of fact, yes," he said. "If you'll have my car brought around, I think Missy and I might take a little drive down by the river. It may be a good while before I get a chance to do it again."

As they waited for the dark blue, four-door Ford phaeton with the special hand controls that enabled FDR to drive it, Ed Starling looked down at Roosevelt's dead and useless legs. As always, the severe physical limitations of the most loved and hated man in America made Ed wince inwardly. At the same time, though, he marveled at how adroit the President was in minimizing his dependence and concealing his infirmity from everyone, including himself. Even after more than three years in office, the average American had no idea that Roosevelt was unable to take a single step without considerable assistance.

Something in Roosevelt's demeanor told Starling that right now the President wished above all else for a brief interlude of peace and privacy, where he could forget about pretense, pressures, and politics. But the instincts born of twenty-plus years of protecting five different occupants of the White House prevented the senior Secret Service agent from granting that wish.

No matter how much he might want to, Starling could never allow FDR and Missy to drive off alone. Not even the friendly confines of the Roosevelt estate could be considered totally risk-free. No place on earth could.

So, instead, Starling stepped briskly ahead of the President as the car eased to a stop, then opened the door on the driver's side while Missy helped Roosevelt guide the wheelchair up beside it.

"I'll just sit quietly in the back seat, Mr. President," Starling said, feeling the bulk of the pearl-handled .45 Colt revolver pressing against his ribs beneath his jacket as he helped FDR from the wheelchair into the seat. "You'll never even know I'm there."

The President glanced at Missy LeHand. "I somehow doubt that, Ed," he said.

FIVE

Real County, Texas
May 11, 1936

Julio Hernandez's funeral at the Iglesia de Jesús in the tiny community of Rio Frio was attended by virtually every person of Hispanic descent in the county, plus nearly a hundred Anglos. They shut down the high school in Leakey for the service, and most of Julio's classmates and teachers were there.

The Wagner family was well represented, but its members were scattered among the congregation. George Wagner sat stiffly with other white farmers, ranchers, and merchants at the rear of the church. Adam's mother sat with Julio's parents and kept her arm around Maria Hernandez's thin shoulders. Adam, meanwhile, positioned himself just one row behind Elena Velasco and stole furtive glances at her through most of the service. He kept trying to direct his gaze somewhere else, but every few seconds his eyes invariably crept back to her dark head.

By Adam's calculations, the younger Velasco daughter was about thirty-three years old now, although she actually didn't look much older than she had when he was in college. The main difference was that her jet-black hair, which had fallen to her waist back then, was now only shoulder-length, and instead of a girlish pastel cotton dress, she wore a schoolmarmish navy blue suit. Despite its long skirt and conservative cut, thc suit failed to conceal the arresting figure beneath it.

If she was aware of Adam's presence, she gave no indication. She tried to comfort Julio's thirteen-year-old sister, Juanita, even as silent tears wet her own cheeks. Adam fervently wished to be sitting next to her and that he could find some way to ease her grief. As unlikely as it seemed after all these years, he desperately wanted to know her better. But after what had happened between them the previous Saturday, he doubted that he ever would.

It had been close to seven hours since the discovery of Julio's body when Adam had stepped warily into the cool, spicy-smelling interior of the Mercado Velasco. When his eyes adjusted to the dim light and he saw Elena behind the counter, his pulse quickened sharply. Despite the images that had played in his mind as he drove toward town, he'd never honestly expected to find her in the store.

"Hello . . . Ellie," he said, twisting the brim of his hat in his hands and trying to decide how to say what had to be said.

She regarded him blankly at first. Then a hint of recognition slowly dawned in her eyes. "Adam Wagner," she said quietly and with no discernible warmth. "What brings you here?"

"I've got a message from Maria and Jake Hernandez. It's about your cousin Julio, and I'm afraid it's bad news."

Their eyes met as she leaned toward him across the counter. Hers were as dark and deep as two brown wells. He caught the flicker of apprehension in them.

"What's happened?" she whispered.

Subtlety had never ranked very high among Adam's limited verbal skills. The only way he knew to convey the terrible message was just to spit it out – so he did.

"Julio's dead," he said. "We found him this morning in one of our stock ponds. He was shot once in the head. He probably never knew what hit him."

He tensed, waiting for her reaction. When something like this happened in the movies, women always seemed to faint or scream or burst into tears or throw themselves face down onto something – sometimes all the above. But for a long moment, Elena neither moved nor spoke, and her expression remained impassive. Finally, he saw her set her teeth hard against her lower lip, much as he sometimes did himself in times of pain. She shook her head slowly and made the sign of the cross.

"Oh, my God," she said, covering her eyes with her hands. "I've had a bad feeling all week – like some kind of premonition. This must be what it meant."

Adam had never put much stock in such things, but the suggestion made him feel even spookier than he did already.

"I'm awful sorry about it," he said. "I wish there was something I could do."

"Why should you care?" she said, wiping her eyes. "What's another *muchacho* more or less? What could it possibly mean to you?" There was no real rancor in her tone, only emptiness.

"It means a lot," he said. "Julio was like a little brother to me."

Elena stared at him with an expression he couldn't decipher. "Who did it?" she demanded.

"I don't know," he said, "but I've got a couple of ideas, and I aim to find out."

"Oh, sure. And then what? What would you do if you did?"

"I don't know," he said again, "but if I find whoever shot that boy, I just may kill him myself."

Her cold eyes studied him for a long moment. "That's pretty big talk," she said. "What if it happened to be another Anglo? Are you saying you'd kill one of your own kind over some insignificant wetback boy?"

"Julio wasn't a wetback," he said. "He was a native-born American."

"I never knew you people made a distinction."

Now it was his turn to bite his lip. "Sorry you feel that way," he said, taking a backward step toward the door. "I can't speak for anybody else. All I know is what's in my own heart."

"Well, if I were you, I'd just forget it," she said. "I'm sure our diligent local authorities will do one of their usual thorough investigations and come to the conclusion that nobody was killed after all."

"I've known Sheriff Streicher for a long time," he said. "He's not really such a bad guy. Besides, I'm not going to let him forget about this."

"What does he care?" she said tonelessly. "What do any of you gringos care?" Then she turned and walked away from him to the other end of the counter.

❀

The church was filled with the sick-sweet smell of flowers and sweat and the droning sound of the priest's voice as he recited the closing prayer.

Adam had been somewhat surprised to see Sarge Streicher and his two deputies at the church just before the funeral began. They hadn't come inside but remained among the overflow crowd on the front steps and sidewalk during the service. Later, as Adam filed out with the crowd, he saw them still hanging around, eyeing the mourners as they made the two-hundred-yard walk under overcast skies to the small graveyard.

Such a high-profile gesture was pretty much out of character for the sheriff, but maybe Streicher considered it part of the "thorough investigation" that Elena had derisively mentioned.

Adam wondered what Sarge and his men would do if he showed them what he'd retrieved Saturday night from the stock pond where Julio's body had been found. Probably not much, he figured, not that it mattered. For the time being, Adam had no intention of sharing his discovery with them anyway. He'd trusted Sarge like a brother once, but that had been before Adam came to realize that the Réal County Sheriff's Department meted out two entirely different brands of justice. The gentle, forgiving kind was reserved for white, upstanding "solid citizens," and a harsher variety was dealt to Mexicans and other "undesirables," regardless of how many generations of their families had been U.S. citizens.

A few minutes later, Adam stood beside the open grave beneath a grove of liveoaks. Twenty feet or so away, Elena and Juanita sat in folding chairs and listened to Father Hidalgo reading the Scriptures. The priest spoke in Latin, but the words registered in English in Adam's mind:

"I am the resurrection and the life. Whosoever believeth in me, though he were dead, yet shall he live . . ."

The words were almost drowned out by the questions still gnawing at Adam's thoughts: Who had Julio encountered the night he was shot? Where had the killer come from? Where had he gone?

And how had the strange pistol wound up in the Wagner stock pond?

SIX

The air had been chilly on Saturday night after the sun went down. As Adam peeled off his Levis and laid them beside his boots, the only sound was a cricket chirping persistently from the opposite bank. The ink-black water was like ice at first, but at least it washed away some of the numb depression that had gripped him ever since he'd left the Mercado Velasco that afternoon.

An uneasiness lingered in his chest as he started diving, and even after his body adjusted to the cold, the inner discomfort remained. He stayed under for a minute or two, then lunged to the surface gasping for air. After the first half-hour and about fifteen groping explorations along the bottom of the pond, his feelings of futility were steadily mounting. This was all a fool's errand, he told himself. The gun that killed Julio could be a thousand miles from here by now, so why waste all this time and energy?

Less than fifteen minutes later, at a point when his arms were heavy, his lungs burning, and his brain telling him to give up, Adam's left hand touched something that was definitely out of place on the rocky bottom.

It felt smooth and metallic, but before he could grasp it, he had to surface for air. Then, as he caught his breath, he became slightly disoriented, and it took several additional dives to locate the object again. Finally, though, he managed to grasp it with his right hand, and he knew instantly that he'd found what he was looking for.

He pulled himself onto the embankment above the pond, panting and hugging a towel and his flannel shirt around him. He shivered as he stared in the yellowish glow of a flashlight at the nickle-plated pistol in his hand. It had an almost delicate design, with a long, slim barrel; a distinctive, knob-shaped mechanism just above the butt, and the name "Mauser" stamped into its side. The eight-shot clip still held seven live rounds of ammunition, meaning it had probably been fired just once, twice at most. Neither the gun nor the unspent bullets inside it had been in the water long enough even to tarnish.

He felt certain that no more than a handful of Réal County citizens had ever laid eyes on a gun like this, but such weapons had been common on the Western Front in France in 1918. Many German officers had carried them, and Adam himself had once taken one as a souvenir.

Adam knew beyond any reasonable doubt that he was holding the gun that had killed Julio, yet the discovery brought him no relief or satisfaction. On the contrary, the mere touch of its cold metal against his fingers gave him butterflies in his stomach.

It was a 9-millimeter German Luger, and sight of it transported him back to an afternoon in April 1918, as his infantry platoon charged a French village called Cantigny. The weapon had been gripped in the hand of a wounded German major crouched in the corner of a blown-out doorway amid the ruins of the village – and it had been pointed squarely at Adam's chest.

"Welcome to France, Yank," the major said quietly in flawless English. "You really should've stayed in America and minded your own business, you know, because now I have to kill you."

As the German's finger tightened on the trigger of the Luger, Adam realized that he'd already fired the last shot from the clip in his rifle, leaving the bayonet affixed to its barrel as his sole defense – his only hope. But before he could jab the blade at the fallen officer, a burst of fire roared from his right, and the German slumped dead in the doorway.

His heart pounding in his throat, Adam glanced over his shoulder and saw Private Francisco Lemos grinning at him and clutching the smoking '03 Springfield with which he'd just killed the enemy officer.

"You okay, mi amigo?" he heard Lemos ask. Then the voice trailed away into the distant past. "You okay-y-y-y . . . ?"

Adam had intended to keep the major's pistol as a souvenir, but a few weeks later, he'd lost the Luger when the Huns broke through the Allied lines at St. Mihiel. Now, incredibly, he'd acquired another Luger almost identical to the first – a weapon as strikingly out of place in the middle of Colt .45 country as a rocket from Mars. No handgun in the universe seemed less likely to find its way to the bottom of a pond on a remote farm in Southwest Texas or to be a prime piece of evidence in the murder of a Mexican teenager 5,000 miles from where it was made.

As he examined the weapon closely in the dim light, Adam noticed something else – something that chilled him worse than the cold water. He switched off the flashlight and held his breath, listening warily to the muted night sounds around him.

On each of the pistol's grips was a symbol that had been unknown in Europe in 1918 but which the whole world had come to recognize since Adolf Hitler had come to power in Germany three years ago. Adam had seen it often in newspapers, magazines and movie newsreels. He'd seen it emblazoned on Nazi flags and armbands and the uniforms of steel-booted Nazi storm troopers, but he'd never before confronted it at such close range.

Embedded on the butt of the Luger were two small, silver swastikas – the trademarks of Hitler's menacing new Third Reich.

After drying himself and pulling his clothes on in total darkness, Adam wrapped the gun carefully in the damp towel, then carried it back to the Chevy pickup and stashed it under the driver's seat. He took the .30.30 carbine from the rack behind the seat and took it with him as he slowly retraced his steps back to the point on the Wagner-Radke fence line where he'd noticed the disturbance in the grass that morning.

Even in the moonless night, he easily found his way to the exact spot. His eyes had adjusted well enough to the darkness that he could clearly see the high grass on the Radke side of the fence waving gently in the breeze. He could even make out the faint remains of the twin tracks that bisected the pasture. Far across the valley, a quarter-mile or more away, a faint light was visible in the window of the small limestone house he'd noticed that morning. The fence, the house and the shearing sheds adjacent to it were the nearest man-made structures to where Adam stood at this moment – and to the pond where Julio's body had been found.

He squatted behind a clump of sagebrush and watched the distant light intently, wishing he'd brought his binoculars. On an impulse, he raised the carbine and fixed its sights on the faraway window, wondering if the sound of a gunshot would carry that far.

Probably so, if it came from a rifle, he decided. But from a pistol, maybe not.

Adam had never paid much attention to the little house before, but now he seemed unable to get it off his mind. Such outbuildings were generally unoccupied except at the height of the shearing season, when crews often stayed there around the clock to reap the annual harvest of wool and mohair, or during deer season, when wealthy hunters sometimes leased the houses and a few hundred surrounding acres to ply their sport.

Judging from the lights, someone was inside the house at this very moment, and Adam could only wonder what the occupants – whoever they were – had been doing at this time last night? For a minute, his curiosity almost overwhelmed his common sense. He caught himself calculating how long it would take him to cross the valley, take a look through the lighted window and make his way back to his own turf.

Seconds later, though, he realized the potential folly of this idea. The sound of hoofbeats approached rapidly from his left, and he huddled lower into the brush as a Radke fence-rider and his huge steed pounded past on the opposite side of the fence.

When Adam was sure the horse and rider were gone, he took a final glance at the distant lights, then stood up and retreated quickly to the pond and the waiting pickup. As he drove back toward the Wagner farmhouse, he knew he'd done the sensible thing, but he still itched to know what was going on behind that lighted window.

SEVEN

The Reichschancellory, Berlin
May 14, 1936

It was just after 9 a.m. when Major Ernst Dietrich of the Gestapo's ultra-secret Foreign Espionage Unit strode into the anteroom outside the private office of S.S. Commandant Heinrich Himmler.

Dietrich was eager to present the status report Himmler had requested on the mission called "Operation Pegasus." With the rearmament program now in full swing and the streets of Berlin bustling with activity, the Major's confidence was running high He'd felt exuberant enough this morning to walk all the way from his flat in the Wilhelm Strasse instead of using the staff car that was always at his disposal.

The sights and sounds along his route conveyed a clear, uplifting message: Germany was on the move again, and nothing could stop her now. He could read it in the faces of university students rallying in the Unter den Linden. He could see it in the strong bodies of the girls of the League of German Maidens as they marched smartly toward their daily assignments in their white blouses and blue skirts. He could smell it in the exhaust fumes of trucks filled with uniformed Hitler Youth as they rumbled past the Brandenburg Gate en route to their Labor Service jobs.

Dietrich even had a smile for Hagen, Himmler's dour aide, as Hagen saluted and ushered the major into the presence of one of the most ruthless, powerful men in the Third Reich.

"Good morning, Herr Reichsfuehrer," Dietrich clicked his heels and extended his right arm in a rigid Nazi salute. "Heil Hitler!"

"Ah, greetings, Major Dietrich," Himmler said. He made no effort to rise from his chair and returned his visitor's salute with a perfunctory, half-bored gesture that only a member of the Leader's closest inner circle would dare use these days. "Come in. I've been eagerly awaiting your arrival."

Himmler stared coldly through his pince-nez at the black-uniformed aide who continued holding the door after Dietrich had passed through it. "You may go, Hagen," he said. "Close the door behind you, and see that I'm not disturbed for the next half-hour."

"Very good, sir," Hagen said, departing quickly.

Himmler smiled at Dietrich and gestured toward a heavy leather chair. "I trust you bring good news, Major. As you know, our Leader is keenly interested in this project of yours."

As Dietrich sat down, Himmler studied the handsome officer in front of him. In many ways, Dietrich seemed the ideal person to lead this mission. He was intelligent, resourceful, and impeccably Aryan. He was also fanatically loyal to the Fatherland and had proved himself totally merciless toward its enemies. If it benefited the Nazi cause, no act was too violent or bloody for Dietrich, and he had nerves of solid steel.

There had been times, however, when the Major had indulged in certain excesses. Himmler had come across a half-dozen troublesome incidents in Dietrich's dossier. They were well-documented episodes involving young, dark-skinned females, and in another type of society, they could have landed Dietrich in prison for rape – or worse. Fortunately, the women had all been gypsies, Jewesses, black Africans, or others considered "non-persons" by the Reich. Since Dietrich had broken no German law in victimizing them, nothing had ever come of any of his misadventures.

Still, the Major seemed to have an obsession about such women, and in light of the mission at hand, it raised a worrisome question. Dietrich's assignment would take him to Mexico, which was filled with seductive women with dark skin. Could he maintain the self-discipline necessary for the mission's success, or would his compulsion overpower him?

"I'm honored, Herr Reichsfuehrer," Dietrich said, "and I'm pleased to report that our mission is on schedule and proceeding as planned. Our first two-man team – Becker and Hauptmann – have arrived safely at our base in Texas and made contact with our American associate. Our second two-man team – Reinhardt and Lutz – will depart by U-boat for Mexico next Monday."

"Good. Then all our planning is beginning to pay dividends. You've done a great service to the Reich by establishing and cultivating this Texas connection. Your rewards will be great when the mission is successfully completed."

"I'll make every effort to justify your confidence, Herr Reichsfuehrer."

"And what of your own travel plans?" Himmler asked. "Have all the arrangements been made?"

"Yes, I leave to take command of the mission just four days after the departure of the second team. Once in Mexico City, I report to our embassy for any last-minute instructions, then join the others at the Texas base no later than May 30, giving us well over a week to complete our preparations."

"You foresee no difficulty traveling alone in Mexico and the U.S.?"

"None whatever," Dietrich said. "I've visited both countries several times, including two lengthy stays with our American associate in southern Texas. All those selected for the mission speak fluent English and are well-versed in American customs and mannerisms."

"I hesitate even to bring this matter up, Major," Himmer said, fixing Dietrich with a cold gaze. "But in the past you've been involved in – how shall I put it? – in some rather untidy business with women. I must warn you, nothing of that nature can be allowed to endanger this operation. Do I make myself clear?"

"Yes, Herr Reichsfuehrer," Dietrich replied smoothly. "My total and constant attention will be focused on our objectives. I will let nothing interfere."

"Excellent. Your dedication, courage, and resourcefulness have always been commendable, Major. Have you determined when and where you will strike?"

"At the moment, we're prepared for several contingencies," Dietrich said. "Our American friend has a reliable contact in the office of Vice President John Garner, and this source says that Herr Roosevelt plans to meet with Mexican President Cardenas at Laredo, Texas, on or about June tenth. I've been to this place called Laredo, and in my opinion it would be an ideal place for the culmination of Operation Pegasus."

"Really? Why is that?"

"For one thing," said Dietrich, "Roosevelt will be in unfamiliar surroundings and as far from his heavily protected power bases in Washington and New York as he's been since assuming the presidency. For another, Laredo is on the international border with Mexico – an *open* border, I might add, where citizens of both countries cross freely with little supervision. Many Mexicans dislike Cardenas's penchant for reform and Roosevelt's meddling 'Good Neighbor Policy,' so dissident groups could easily be blamed for any incident involving Roosevelt."

Clearly warming to his subject, Dietrich quickly continued: ""As we now know, Roosevelt is severely crippled and virtually helpless without constant physical assistance. Once he leaves his special train, he'll be personally guarded only by a small detail of Secret Servicemen and military aides, and his disability will put him at an added disadvantage. All in all, our American associate believes Roosevelt will never be more vulnerable than during his stopover in Laredo."

Himmler nodded. "It sounds like an ideal situation for what we have in mind," he said.

"I wholeheartedly agree, Herr Reichsfuehrer. Am I to assume then that we have the Leader's final approval to proceed?"

"Yes," Himmler said, toying thoughtfully with his pince-nez. "Our operatives in Washington report that Roosevelt is assuming an increasingly anti-German stance. They say he's committed to building up the U.S. military and determined to rescind his country's Neutrality Act in order to actively aid the enemies of National Socialism."

"But under American law, doesn't he lack the power to act without the approval of his Congress?" Dietrich asked.

"That's true. But if he should be re-elected this fall, he may well pick up support in Congress. Meanwhile, our Foreign Ministry has obtained a copy of a letter from Roosevelt to William Dodd, the American ambassador in Berlin. In it, Roosevelt clearly indicates that he foresees war with Germany."

Dietrich frowned. "Because of our move into the Rhineland, no doubt."

"Precisely," Himmler said. "In the letter, Roosevelt compares the situation to the early summer of 1914. This time, he says he refuses to be lulled into a false sense of security by experts who say there will be no war. This time, he vows to be ready, 'just like the fire department.' This is why our Leader has concluded that we should act now, before Roosevelt can marshal his forces."

"I couldn't agree more," Dietrich said. "From what I know of the American electoral system, this would also be an ideal time from a political standpoint."

The Major had learned a lot from his American cohort about the way U.S. Presidents were chosen. It was a confusing system, but Dietrich had eventually come to see how it could work to the Reich's advantage. Roosevelt's Democratic Party was to hold its national convention in late June – just two weeks after the President's trip to Texas – to re-nominate him for a second term. But if something happened to Roosevelt, Vice President Garner would automatically become President Garner, and with such a short time left before the convention, the Democrats would have little choice but to give the nomination to Garner, a strict isolationist who wanted nothing to do with Europe and its crises.

Meanwhile, the opposing Republican Party would almost certainly have nominated Alfred Landon, the isolationist governor of Kansas, as its presidential candidate, so the November election would pit one isolationist against another. Regardless of which of these novices in international affairs should win, the danger of active U.S. interference in Europe would no longer exist. And, unless Dietrich missed his guess, the election of either Garner or Landon would give the Americans enough social and economic problems to worry about at home to keep their minds off Germany for quite a while.

"This Garner," mused Himmler. "You say he is a former congressman from Texas, and our American associate is quite well acquainted with him?"

"That's correct," Dietrich said, "and although Garner is Roosevelt's second-in-command, there's much underlying animosity between them.

This is one reason we were able to make such a reliable contact in Texas. Our American comrade would like nothing better than to see Garner in the White House."

"In less than a month, if all goes well, he may see exactly that," Himmler exulted. "A backward old hillbilly from Texas will be President of the United States. Think of it, Dietrich."

"I'll do all in my power to ensure our success," the Major assured him. "Each man was handpicked for this mission, both for his total devotion to our cause and the special strengths and talents he can contribute. None will shirk his responsibility. All are ready to die for the Fatherland, and no man among us will ever betray the trust of the Reich by allowing ourselves to be taken alive."

"You have the Leader's and my deepest respect, Major," Himmler said. "All Germans everywhere will owe you a debt of gratitude if you succeed."

"Thank you, Herr Reichsfuehrer."

A small smile played briefly across Himmler's lips as he walked to the door and prepared to dismiss his visitor. He turned to Dietrich.

"Since Garner is *from* Texas, what are the chances of making it appear that he and his supporters are somehow involved in this Pegasus operation? If this should happen, it could only add to the chaos and confusion in America – and to the glory of our ultimate triumph."

Dietrich nodded, thinking of the wealthy Texas rancher and Garner supporter whose hatred of Roosevelt had first set this chain of events into motion.

"An intriguing idea," he said. "I think we just might be able to arrange it."

EIGHT

Reál County, Texas
May 15, 1936

All week long, Adam had tried to keep Elena Velasco out of his thoughts, but by Friday he could tell it was useless. He'd dreamed about her Monday night, and by mid-day on Tuesday, he was barely aware of the fences he was mending or the lambs he was doctoring for screwworms. That night, he lay awake until after midnight thinking about her. By Wednesday, he was grouchy and prone to frequent fits of swearing.

He wanted to tell her what he'd seen and what he suspected – about the suspicious twin tracks in the grass of the Radke pasture, the pistol at the bottom of the pond, and the lights in the little stone house. But that wasn't the only reason he wanted to see her. When he closed his eyes, he could hear the long-ago sounds of Kurt Radke making love to Luz Velasco just a few feet away. He could see Kurt manhandling a terrified young girl in the backseat of a fancy car. He could see himself watching Elena, first at Luz's funeral, then at Julio's . . .

By Thursday night, he knew he couldn't stand it any longer. Damn it, he told himself, there came a time when a man had to take the bull by the horns – even if it gored him to death in the process. He had to see her. The worst she could do was tell him to go to hell.

So on Friday morning, he'd pushed his venerable Model A roadster out of the dusty shed where it reposed most of the time these days. He'd checked the oil, water and tires, and cranked it up to make sure it would still run. He'd even driven it down by the creek and given it its first real wash job since sometime the previous fall. Except for his infrequent beer-drinking excursions to Uvalde, he rarely used the car nowadays, but the well-worn Chevy pickup that he usually drove simply wasn't suitable for what he had in mind.

The gray roadster with its red wheels and trim was still a pretty spiffy machine, although it was eight years old and, like its owner, beginning to show its age. The engine was still reliable, so long as you kept a sharp eye on the oil level, and the tires were good enough. The clutch tended to slip a little, even in dry weather, and the windshield wipers were the old-fashioned kind that usually swamped in a heavy downpour.

Because of the wipers, the ominous clouds in the western sky only added to Adam's tension as he parked in front of the two-story limestone building that housed all eleven grades of the Leakey School. It was about 3:25 p.m. on Friday. Minutes later, he heard the dismissal bell, and thirty seconds after that, the first of several score pupils began pouring out of the building.

When the exodus subsided, he got out of the car and started up the sidewalk toward the school. The unfamiliar slacks and sport coat that had replaced his usual work shirt and Levis were stiff and scratchy as he walked.

He couldn't remember being inside the school since his sister Carolyn's graduation, but the main hall looked much the same as when he was a student. The same pictures of George Washington and Abraham Lincoln still hung in the same familiar locations. The trophy case containing mementos of the Leakey Eagles' infrequent athletic and Interscholastic League accomplishments still occupied the same spot in the foyer. The dark, oiled oaken floor felt as slippery as ever under his feet.

Directly ahead of him was the office where he'd been sent on several occasions to receive a paddling at the hands of Mr. Bradford, the principal. He paused at the door, feeling some of the same trepidation he'd felt back then, but he finally stuck his head inside. He saw a large woman behind a small counter.

"May I help you?" she asked.

"Yeah," he said. "I was looking for Miss Velasco's classroom."

"Down the hall to the left. Third door on the right."

At first glance, the room reminded him of his own first-grade classroom, only it was more colorfully decorated. Bright cutouts of butterflies and birds were pasted on the windows, and childish drawings of trees and flowers adorned most of the rear wall. A bulletin board displayed baby chicks, ducklings and rabbits underneath a hand-lettered sign that said, "Spring Means New Life."

Except in Reál County, he thought, where it meant sudden death.

Miss Velasco sat at her desk, wearing a suit almost identical to the one she'd worn at Julio's funeral, except that this one was brown instead of blue. She was deeply engrossed in a stack of student papers and didn't immediately notice Adam as he paused in the open doorway. A few strands of her tightly braided hair were loose and askew. When she smiled at one of the papers, the whole room seemed to brighten.

"*Buenas días, Senorita,*" he said softly, hating to break the silence.

She glanced up and jumped slightly when she first saw him there. Then she surprised him by smiling again. It was a wry, not altogether cheerful smile, and it lacked much of the warmth of the other one, but it *was* a smile.

"You mean '*Buenas tardes,*'" she said. "It's afternoon, not morning."

"Oh, yeah. I forgot."

"What are you doing here?" she asked, her smile slowly fading. "You're a little old for grammar school, aren't you?"

"I wanted to see you . . . Ellie," he said. It was all he could think of to say.

"Nobody else has called me by that name in a long time," she said. "It sounds odd to hear it again after all these years."

"Do you mind if I call you that?"

She frowned for a second. "No, I guess not. I liked the name when I was young because it sounded more . . . *American* than Elena. Now I don't know how I feel about it, but it's okay. Why do you want to see me, Mister Wagner?"

"Because I need to talk to you about. . . some stuff."

"What kind of 'stuff'?"

"Stuff about Julio and what might have happened to him. Things I don't feel comfortable talking about to anybody else right now – not even my own family." He paused. "Stuff I thought you might want to know about. But if you don't, then I apologize for bothering you."

She shook her head. "You don't need to apologize. If anyone should apologize, it's me. I was rude when you came to the store the other day, and I'm sorry." She stared out the window for a moment, chewing her lip. Then she shrugged. "I just react that way sometimes when something hurts me really bad. It was kind of you to come all the way to town to tell us about Julio."

"Forget it. I can understand how you felt."

She shook her head again, then stood up from the desk, walked to the windows and laid her forehead against one of the glass panes.

"I doubt it," she said. "I don't think anyone in the world really knows how I feel."

"Well, maybe you ought to tell somebody."

"They wouldn't care," she said in the same expressionless tone he remembered from the previous Saturday.

"They might if you'd give them a chance," he said, wishing that he could find the words to tell her that *he* cared. Not just about Julio, but also about what had happened so long ago. "Look, couldn't we just go someplace and talk for a while? Maybe we could get a Coca-Cola down at the cafe on the square?"

"They don't serve my people in the cafe," she said. "It's whites only."

It was incredible, he thought. She could hold the futures of a roomful of six-year-olds – Anglo and otherwise – in her hands. But she couldn't drink a lousy Coke in a greasy-spoon cafe. It didn't make sense.

"Then how about just going for a drive?" he said. "We can talk on the way."

She offered no response, except to walk slowly back to her desk and stare down for a moment at the stack of papers she'd been reading.

"I really don't think so," she said hesitantly. "I've, uh, got a lot of work to do." She looked at him as if she were waiting for him to say something else. He had no idea what it might be, but he decided it was time to play his ace in the hole.

"I think I've found the gun that killed Julio," he said, "and I think I know where the killers are hiding. If you're not interested, just say so."

He watched as she carefully placed a paperweight on top of the papers and picked up her purse.

"I'm interested," she said. "Let's go."

He drove south on rough, dusty Highway 4, not really knowing where he was heading. By the time they were two miles out of Leakey, the western sky was crisscrossed with lightning bolts, and claps of thunder were rolling across the hills. Moments later, the first fat drops of rain spattered the roadster's windshield, and a hundred yards farther on, the clouds opened up in torrents.

"The sky looks terrible," Elena said. "Maybe we should just find a big tree and stop till the storm blows over."

He forced a smile. "I think you're right," he said, "but I warn you, this ragtop may leak a little in spots." A moment later, he eased under the protective boughs of a massive liveoak..

"I don't mind the rain," she said above the muted clatter of the idling engine. "I think I could stand out in it and not even know I was wet. I feel so numb and empty, like part of me got buried with Julio the other day. He was such a good boy, and he would've been such a great example for the other Latino kids."

He nodded. "That's why I can't let whoever killed him get away with it."

"I saw you sitting behind me at the funeral," she said. "I wanted to say something to you, but it just wouldn't come out."

"I wanted to say something to you, too," he told her. "But sometimes I get kind of tongue-tied when I try to say something serious."

"I never would've believed it," she said. "I always thought you were such hot stuff in the old days. You were a big football player and one of the rich Anglo kids from the big ranches, and I heard you were voted 'most likely to succeed' or something. You hung around with guys like Freddie Brunner and Charlie Shuster and our current noble sheriff . . . " She hesitated noticeably. "And Kurt Radke, of course."

"Kurt and I drank a lot of beer and moonshine together," he said, "but we had our share of fights, too. I never really knew what was wrong with him – just that *something* was."

"I remember one of those fights," she said, her voice barely audible. "I was there."

"I know," he said as their eyes met. "I remember it, too, Ellie. I remember it like it was yesterday. I'll never forget it.

She lowered her head and, for the first time today, she seemed to be withdrawing back into the old, protective shell he remembered. "I don't want to talk about him," she said. "I'm sorry I mentioned his name."

He decided it was time to change the subject. "Julio was your first cousin and you knew him pretty well. Did you ever see him drinking booze or hear him talking about it? I mean hard stuff like tequila?"

"No, never," she said. "Except for communion wine, I doubt if Julio ever touched alcohol in his life. What makes you ask?"

"There was an empty tequila bottle lying near his body," Adam said. "The sheriff thinks maybe Julio was fighting with somebody over the bottle, and that's how he got killed."

"Anybody who knew Julio knows how stupid that is."

"Sure, I totally agree," Adam said, "but that's just the way Streicher and everybody else in authority around here thinks about Mexicans."

He winced even as the words came out of his mouth. He hated it when he was so outspokenly tactless, but when he caught his breath and looked closely at her to see if she was offended, he was surprised to see another wry smile on her lips.

"That's what I meant about 'all gringos' the other day," she said. "Believe me, I know how they are."

"To hell with them," he said. "Look here, I want to show you something."

He reached carefully under the seat and pulled out the old towel in which he'd wrapped the gun from the pond, then slowly folded the towel back. Her eyes widened as he withdrew the shiny, nickle-plated weapon and held it out to her.

"I've never seen one of these before. What is it?"

"It's a German Luger," he said. "I found it at the bottom of the pond where Julio's body was. You're the first person I've showed it to."

She took the pistol gingerly but with a certain air of familiarity. "I don't like guns, but my Papa taught me how to shoot when I was little. He made me practice until I could hit a target, and he taught me not to be afraid. He always keeps a pistol under the counter at the store, and I know I could shoot a robber if I had to. I wouldn't like it, but I could do it."

Her voice was calm and dispassionate. Adam had no doubt that what she said was true.

"See the insignia on the pistol grips?" he asked. "Do you know what it is?"

"Of course, it's a swastika – the ancient symbol the Nazis stole from the American Indians. Does that mean Julio was killed by a Nazi?"

"I don't know," he said, "but I'm almost sure whoever shot Julio and threw the gun in the pond is hiding out on the Radke Ranch."

"I wouldn't be surprised at anything Kurt Radke might have on his ranch." Her voice was low and trembling. "As far as I'm concerned, he's worse than Hitler himself. Are you going to tell the sheriff about this gun?"

"I'm not sure," Adam said above the sound of the rain drumming on the roadster's canvas top. "What do you think he'd do if I did?"

"Nothing," she said, laying her head against the back of the seat and closing her eyes. "The only thing he and the others who run the town and the county ever do is look the other way – just like they did when Kurt Radke killed my sister."

NINE

From a regal office suite on the ground floor of his sprawling ranch house, Kurt Radke ruled a dozen square miles of the Texas Hill Country with an iron hand. In addition to the 30,000-plus head of livestock that grazed his land, he had numerous other business interests scattered across North America. They ranged from oil and natural gas to banking and real estate development to imports and textile manufacturing, virtually all inherited by Kurt five years earlier on the death of his empire-building father, Gustaf Radke.

His fleet of automobiles included a Packard, a Duesenberg, and a Mercedes. He kept a 40-foot motor yacht anchored in Corpus Christi Bay, and he owned the only private airplane in Reál County. He spent at least three months of the year traveling – to the East and West Coasts, Mexico, South America, and Europe. He hobnobbed with some of the world's richest, most powerful people.

By every visible measure, Kurt Radke had it made. His only major unmet aspiration was winning a seat in Congress. But he was young yet as politicians went, not quite forty, and he had realistic hopes of achieving that goal within the next eight years. Meanwhile, his immense wealth, opulent lifestyle, and political clout in Austin and Washington made him the envy of many men and drew the attention of countless women, although he still remained one of the state's most eligible bachelors.

Yet within the past two weeks, Kurt's whole world seemed to have gone as crazy and out-of-control as his sister Karla. His life was suddenly filled with such turmoil that he couldn't sleep nights. For the first time since his early childhood, he wasn't sure how to cope with the events swirling around him.

Worse, he was forced to admit to himself that the whole mess was his own doing. He was the one who had invited the German agents here in the first place, arranged for the phony papers they used to slip into the country, supplied them with American money, maps, and directions on how to reach the Radke Ranch, then provided them food, weapons, and a discreet place to stay once they got here. But he'd failed to anticipate the trouble and anxiety that accompanied them.

And worse yet, only two of the agents were here so far. Two others were on their way, and he dreaded the thought of having to deal with all four of them until their commanding officer arrived to take charge.

The older and more stable of the first pair was named Rudolf Becker. He was quiet, efficient and well-disciplined, just as someone in his business should be. But Otto Hauptmann, the younger one, had the build and manners of an ox. He was a boisterous bully with an unpredictable temper – and an alcoholic to boot.

The problems had started before dawn the previous Saturday, moments after Hauptman and Becker showed up on Kurt's doorstep.

"Unfortunately, we encountered a nosy Mexican just before we reached your ranch, Herr Radke," Becker said just after two fence-riders had found the Germans and escorted them to the main house as instructed. "He came upon us unexpectedly and overheard us talking. We had no choice but to dispose of him."

Becker was a compact, muscular man whose eyes were as hard and black as onyx. His tone was so matter-of-fact that he might have been discussing the weather.

"What do you mean?" Kurt asked with a frown. "What did you do?"

"I shot the *schweinhunt*," Hauptmann said with a faint smile. "You needn't worry. He won't be telling any tales out of school now."

"How long ago did this happen?" Kurt demanded. "And where?"

"Perhaps an hour ago on the adjoining farm," Becker said. "We were only a short distance from your property line when he saw us."

Kurt's eyes moved from Becker's face to Hauptmann's as he tried to digest what they were telling him. Apparently, the shooting had taken place on the Wagner Farm, which lay immediately south of the Radke Ranch. Anyone traveling due north from the border on foot would have to cross the Wagner place to reach the ranch. Several Mexican families worked for George Wagner, but Kurt doubted that he'd recognize any of them if he met them face to face.

"You're absolutely sure this Mexican's dead?" he asked.

"He's dead, all right," Hauptmann said, leaning close enough for Kurt to detect the sharp, unmistakable smell of alcohol on the man's breath. "I shot him once, very neatly, behind the ear and left him floating in a pool of water."

"No one else saw or heard anything," Becker assured his uneasy host. "Within five minutes, we were across the fence and on your property, Herr Radke, and I'm quite sure there were no other witnesses."

"What did you do with the gun?"

"I made Hauptmann throw it into the pond, in case someone else came along," Becker said. "Since it was a Luger with our National Socialist emblem on it, it didn't seem prudent to keep it."

"It was my favorite pistol, too," Hauptman said sourly. "I'll never forgive you for that, Rudi."

Kurt glared at Hauptmann. "If you'd brought that gun onto this ranch, you'd be a dead man right now. I can tell you've been drinking. Quite a lot, too, unless I miss my guess."

"It's no concern of yours," Hauptman said tauntingly. "I don't answer to you, but I'll tell you this: I'm worth any ten Americans, drunk or sober."

"Shut up, Otto," said Becker. "I apologize, Herr Radke. Hauptmann's a good man, and his strength and courage will be a great asset to our mission. But during our brief stay in Mexico, he became infatuated with a certain type of Mexican liquor. I think it's made from some sort of cactus."

"I'm not happy about what you've done," Kurt said. "It could jeopardize the entire outcome of our mission. The last thing we need right now is for the county sheriff to come poking around out here."

A look of concern crossed Becker's face. "What should we do, Herr Radke?"

"Just keep out of sight as much as possible," Kurt said. "I've had a small house fixed up for you to use as living quarters. It's well isolated out in one of the southwest sections, and I want you to go there immediately and lie low. If anybody asks who you are, tell them you're wool buyers from Pennsylvania. Is that clear?"

"Yes," Becker said. "We will do our best to make no further trouble."

Kurt's face was burning as he turned to Hauptmann. "When Major Dietrich arrives, I intend to give him a full report on your lunatic behavior. In the meantime, you'd damned well better lay off the tequila and stay out of trouble. Otherwise, you may not live until the major gets here."

Hauptmann stared back at Radke. There was still a slight smile on his broad face, but his pale blue eyes were full of malice.

"You talk big, *Amerikaner*," he said. "One day, perhaps, we will see just how big you really are."

The first time he'd visited his ancestral homeland, Kurt had been nine years old, and he'd traveled to Germany with his father. It had been the summer of 1908 – only a few months after Kurt's mother had gone away for good. The journey had been therapeutic for both of them, but it had also been anything but easy. It had begun in the horse-drawn carriage that took them to the railway station at Uvalde. From there, the train trip to New York took five days, followed by an eight-day steamship voyage to Hamburg and another long train ride to the small town south of Stuttgart where many of Kurt's distant relatives still lived.

Karla, only three at the time, was too young to go along, and Kurt had been glad. He'd never cared much for his little sister. She was peevish and whiny even then, and at times, he was sure she was the real reason his mother had left. At other times, though, he was equally sure that *he* was the reason. In his nightmares, he'd regularly relived the terrible day when Henrietta Radke had packed her bags and disappeared forever.

Mama, Mama, please come back! Please don't leave me alone! I'll be good, I promise!

What's all this noise, boy? Why are you making such racket in the middle of the night?

I want my mama. I want her to come home.

You hush your mouth. She's never coming back here, and I call it damn good riddance. Someday you'll understand.

Only Kurt *didn't* understand, even now. He later came to recognize his father as a domineering tyrant and his mother as a spoiled socialite from San Antonio, but he'd never fully grasped what precipitated their breakup. In the years afterward, he'd seen a half-dozen Mexican hired girls slip in and out of his father's bedroom, and once he'd stumbled in on the old man in the act of humping one of them. But Gus Radke had gone to his grave without a word of explanation about Henrietta's abrupt departure from their lives. After that fateful day, Gus had never spoken her name again as long as he lived.

Kurt had loved Germany from the beginning. Its quaint towns, picturesque countryside, rousing music, and old-world charm temporarily soothed the pain of being deserted by the woman who'd given him birth. But the legends of the Lorelei, the beguiling female spirits that allegedly haunted the Rhine's treacherous shoals, somehow reminded the boy of his mother. He hadn't known then what the term "abandonment" meant, but he was all too familiar with the feelings it left in its wake: guilt, anger, alienation, and bewilderment.

He'd almost succeeded in talking his father into going back to Germany for a second visit a few years later, but by then it was the summer of 1914, and Europe was at war. Another decade would pass before Kurt was able to return, alone this time, and he was shocked to find a far different Germany – a defeated, depressed, desperate place, where life had become a day-to-day struggle for survival. Everything was in short supply. The currency was next to worthless. Crowds of destitute men and women roamed the streets. Hope itself seemed to have died.

But some people were determined to return Germany to greatness. One of them was Ernst Dietrich, a handsome young man about Kurt's age and the first hard-core Nazi Kurt had ever met. By the end of Kurt's visit, they were close friends, and after that, Kurt returned at least once a year. He witnessed the growing commitment of Dietrich and other young Germans to Adolf Hitler. He watched the Nazi movement revitalize Germany's spirit, and he applauded openly as Hitler grew stronger and stronger.

In the early 1930s, three events coincided to bring Kurt to Germany with increasing frequency. His father's death in 1931 made Kurt the sole owner of one of the richest ranches in Texas. It also relieved him of many of the duties delegated to him by Gus and left him ample time for travel. When transatlantic airline service was inaugurated on a regular basis, he could fly from San Antonio to New York to Berlin in a matter of three or four days. And when the Nazis gained control of the Reichstag in 1933, Kurt sensed a key opportunity. The friendships he had cultivated with Dietrich and others might now open up a lucrative new market for the tons of wool and mohair produced annually in Southwest Texas.

Simultaneously, Kurt had watched the Democrats come to power in the U.S. with two total opposites as their top elected leaders. Kurt disliked Franklin Roosevelt from the start, but he greatly admired Vice President John Nance Garner, who was both a neighbor from adjacent Uvalde County and a right-thinking man who shared many of the values and ideals that Texans and Germans alike held dear. Garner and Gus Radke had been friends for forty-odd years, and Kurt had known Garner all his life. When Garner became the powerful Speaker of the House, Kurt began to see the huge advantage of Garner's influence if Kurt should decide to enter politics. When Garner sought the '32 Democratic presidential nomination as a favorite son, Kurt gave him his all-out support. Even after FDR was nominated, Kurt stayed solidly behind the ticket, becoming one of the campaign's largest financial contributors.

By the end of Roosevelt's first year in office, Kurt's initial disappointment had given way to alarm at the left-leaning policies of the New Deal. Even more disturbing was Garner's inability to exert any control over those policies in his figurehead role as vice president. Yet Kurt could see that incredible power lay right at Garner's fingertips if he could only grasp it. If Roosevelt were out of the way and Garner were in the White House, everything would be perfect. The country would be back on the proper course, and Kurt would have the personal friendship and political support of the President of the United States himself. With assets like these, there was no limit to how far a rich, ambitious man could rise or how much power he could claim.

On his trips to Germany, Kurt often voiced his feelings openly, and Ernst Dietrich always lent a sympathetic ear. By now, they'd known each other for more than ten years, and Kurt had twice arranged for Dietrich to visit his ranch and see some of the rest of the United States. They were utterly candid with each other where political philosophies were concerned, and the fact that Dietrich now sported the black uniform of an S.S. major and was a rising star in the Gestapo made no difference to Kurt.

One evening just over three months ago, the two friends had met for dinner at a picturesque resort at the foot of the Bavarian Alps. Their talk had turned predictably to politics, and after a few brimming steins of beer, the tycoon from Texas grew even more outspoken than usual.

It was here that the groundwork had been laid for the unnerving scheme in which Kurt now found himself entangled.

"If America minds its own business, it has nothing to fear from National Socialism," Ernst Dietrich was saying. "Actually, our countries have much in common. They should be natural allies."

"Not as long as that pig Roosevelt's in the White House." Kurt finished his beer and set the stein heavily on the table. "He's leading the country straight down the road to Marxism. If he serves another term – and God knows I can't see any reason why he won't – my ranch may end up as a damned commune."

"So why doesn't your friend Garner do something to stop him?" Dietrich prodded. "Surely, a tough Texian like your 'Cactus Jack' could overcome a paralyzed New York dandy like Roosevelt."

Kurt shook his head. "If only it were so," he said. "The problem is, the vice presidency has no power of its own, so the only power Garner has is what Roosevelt delegates to him – which isn't any. They don't even like each other. The only reason Roosevelt put old Jack on the ticket was to persuade the South to vote Democratic."

"Doesn't Garner have friends in the Congress? In the military?"

"Sure, he's got friends all over," Kurt said, "but there's no power base for him to operate from. I talked to him in person when he came home at Christmas, and you know what he said? He told me, 'Son, the whole dang vice presidency ain't worth a bucket of warm spit.' Those were his exact words."

Ernst laughed and waved to the waiter for two more beers.

"You must be very close to the vice president," he said, "for him to confide in you this way."

"I am," Kurt said. "He and my father were lifelong friends, and one of his top aides is an old college chum of mine. I worked my tail off for Garner's nomination in '32, but he never really had a prayer against a slicker like FDR."

"Yet if something should happen to Roosevelt," Ernst mused, "then your Cactus Jack would instantly ascend from a bucket of spit to the most powerful position in America, right?"

"Absolutely," said Radke. "If Roosevelt should die in office – or even if he was too incapacitated to fulfill the duties of President, Garner would be top dog."

Ernst remained silent until after the waiter brought two fresh steins of beer and departed. Then he leaned forward on his elbows, glancing quickly from left to right to make certain that no one else was in earshot.

"Suppose for a moment that Roosevelt had, uh, an unfortunate accident of some sort," he said quietly. "Have you ever considered that possibility?"

"Yeah, I think about it a lot," Kurt said.

"Well, such things *do* happen, you know," said Dietrich, staring straight into his friend's eyes. "With the right kind of coordination on both sides of the Atlantic, perhaps something could be arranged – if you were willing to become totally committed to such a project, I mean."

Kurt Radke felt a chill rise within him, half of elation and half of apprehension. He thought of the vast implications of where this conversation was leading, and for a second, he hesitated. Then he swept his misgivings aside like so many dry leaves.

"If you're truly serious," he said, "consider that commitment made."

"Excellent," said Dietrich. A slight smile tugged at the corners of his mouth as he raised his stein in a toast. "To the next President of the United States."

En route back to Texas, Kurt had dropped by the vice president's office in Washington to visit Arthur Wayland, a former college classmate and now one of Garner's most trusted aides. During lunch, a chance remark by Wayland suddenly started all the pieces falling into place.

"You'll be thrilled to know the boss is trying to get your favorite President to come to Texas for the Centennial celebration in June," Wayland said. "If he comes, I know you won't want to miss a single minute of his visit."

"You know I'm no fan of FDR's, Art," Kurt said smoothly, "but I would like to see how people react to him in Texas. What's this Centennial thing you're talking about?"

Wayland looked mildly shocked. "Hell, Kurt, what kind of Texan are you, anyway? It's been a hundred years since Texas won its independence from Mexico, and we're going to celebrate like crazy. There's going to be a World's Fair in Dallas and lots of other stuff across the state. It's a hot deal, man."

Suddenly, Kurt's mind and his pulse were both racing at once. It had never occurred to him that Roosevelt might actually come to Texas – not in his wildest dreams. It all seemed so perfect, so tailor-made for what he and Dietrich had discussed.

It was as though the fly were about to blunder right into the lair of the spider.

TEN

The White House, Washington
May 21, 1936

Agent Nathaniel Grayson had been in law enforcement for almost eighteen years, but he still considered himself a novice at his present job. He'd joined the White House Detail of the U.S. Secret Service less than two and a half years ago, and he was still its most junior member. But that hadn't kept his boss, Colonel Ed Starling, from tapping Grayson six months ago to become the detail's second in command, passing over several more experienced agents.

Grayson had attracted the service's attention because of his courage and quick thinking as a Chicago cop during the assassination attempt against President-elect Roosevelt in Miami in February 1933. Chicago Mayor Anton Cermak had been fatally wounded in that attack, and FDR might have died, too, if not for Grayson.

Nat was average size – five-ten and a hundred and seventy pounds – but a lot of people said he didn't look that big. He was average in appearance, too, with an easy smile and gentle hazel eyes that women liked. Yet nothing about him stood out in a crowd, and he'd always considered that one of his major strengths as an agent. He knew he had the nerve, instincts and stamina to handle the White House job, but sometimes he was still caught off guard by the abrupt twists and turns that came with the territory.

This afternoon, for example, Starling had called Nat into his office and told him that FDR's planned trip to the Mexican border and his scheduled meeting with Mexican President Cardenas were about to be cancelled.

"Something's come up, and we're just asking for trouble if we go ahead with the Mexico thing," Starling said. "Of course, we've still got to convince the President, and that may be easier said than done."

"But it's barely three weeks away," Grayson said. "What happened?"

"We've got a serious problem," Starling said. He glanced at the closed door of the office, then added softly. "The very worst kind of problem."

Nat frowned. "Another assassination attempt?"

"That's how it looks. If I had my way, we'd scrap the whole Southwestern junket, but this fellow we're trying to protect would never hear of it. I'm meeting with him in an hour to go over the situation, but my guess is we'll have to settle for dropping the part at the border."

Colonel Starling worried a lot because worrying was an inseparable part of his job. No detail was too insignificant to merit his notice, no straw in the wind too obscure for him to chase down and examine. He'd been doing it for so long that it had all become second nature, a reflex that was almost as automatic as breathing. Yet Nat had never seen his boss over-react to a situation, much less panic, so the message was clear: When the Colonel acted as worried as he did now, it was time for everyone else to start worrying, too.

Tall, courtly and past sixty, Starling looked more like a grandfatherly banker than a G-man, but he was still as tough and unflappable as anyone Nat had ever met. He carried a pearl-handled Colt .45 in his shoulder holster and a hammerless .38 Smith & Wesson in his oversized watch pocket, and Nat had witnessed first-hand how quickly and accurately Ed could still draw and fire either weapon. His slate-gray eyes had an uncanny way of penetrating anything they encountered. His voice was often as soft as a whisper, but it always commanded attention.

Actually, the Colonel had never risen above the rank of sergeant during a brief military career, but like his father before him , he'd been designated a Kentucky colonel by the governor of his native state. He'd started out as a rural deputy sheriff, then built a reputation as a tough railway detective. Since joining the Secret Service in 1914, he'd personally guarded the lives of five Presidents – Wilson, Harding, Coolidge, Hoover, and now Roosevelt. All in all, he was the last person in Washington whose concern could be taken lightly, especially if you happened to be his assistant.

"Where's the information coming from?" Nat asked.

"It originated in Germany," Ed said. "British intelligence picked up on it three or four days ago and passed it along through unofficial channels in London. Our counter-espionage people checked it out thoroughly. They say we need to be damned careful."

"But it specifically mentions the border and the Cardenas meeting, right?"

"More or less. The message was relayed by radio from a British agent in Germany, and it was very sketchy. Now the British have lost touch with the guy and think he may have run into trouble." Starling pulled a scrap of paper from his pocket and laid it on the desk. "Here, take a look for yourself."

Nat picked up the paper and stared silently at the seven-word message:

"Warn U.S. . . plot against FDR . . . Mexico . . . June . . ."

"We can't be sure who the plotters are," Starling said, "but there are several possibilities. Since the message specifically mentions Mexico, it could be a dissident Mexican faction hoping to embarrass the Cardenas government or sour U.S.-Mexico relations. Or it could be some rabid element in Texas that's hell-bent to see Garner in the White House. Then, of course, there's always a third possibility . . . "

Nat stared quizzically at his boss, waiting for him to continue.

"It could be the Nazis themselves," Starling said.

Nat shook his head. "But what could they possibly hope to gain that justifies the risk of war with America?"

The Colonel smiled tightly. "Oh, I think they know they're going to have to fight us sooner or later, but they also know we're nowhere near ready for a war at this point – not with them or anybody else. The thing is, though, they may think the only way *not* to end up fighting us is to get rid of this fellow Roosevelt right now."

"So what happens next?"

"Let's assume Roosevelt's smart enough to call off the Cardenas meeting, but too stubborn to scrap the whole trip. He figures he's promised too many people he's coming to Texas to back out now. Besides, he can't stand the thought of the Republican convention getting all the uncontested press attention that week."

"Then the biggest part of the trip could still be on" Nat mused, "and the assassins could try to hit the Chief somewhere else."

"Exactly. All we can do is beef up security and stay on our toes. I'll be going down to Arkansas and Texas next week as advance man for the trip, and without getting into specifics, I'm going to tell the military units and local police along the route to have every available man on duty and take every precaution possible. I'm also asking permission to double our usual complement of service personnel on the train."

"When do you expect a final decision on the trip to the border?" Nat asked.

"Within twenty-four hours, but I've already talked to Steve Early, and he's agreed to hold off announcing the cancellation until just before the train leaves Washington. There was never a formal announcement, anyway, so we can probably just deny the Mexico thing was ever scheduled."

"That should throw at least a temporary hitch in the plot," Nat said.

"We can hope so," Starling said. "But the big question is, if the Cardenas deal was never officially scheduled, how the hell did somebody in Germany find out about it in the first place?"

ELEVEN

Réal County, Texas
May 23, 1936

Except for vaguely persistent thoughts about Adam Wagner that kept distracting Elena from the papers she was grading, it was a fairly typical Saturday at her parents' store – until the two strange men showed up. She'd never seen either of them before, and when they came, everything about the day changed with startling suddenness.

Elena minded the store every Saturday to give her parents a break from their twelve-hour-a-day grind. Since Sunday was devoted to morning and evening worship at the Iglesia de Jesus, with a period of rest in between, Saturday was the only time Mama and Papa had to do their personal chores. They'd been going through this same drudging routine since long before they immigrated to the States and came to Leakey to be near Mama's sister and her family. They were proud to be among the few Mexican-born Texas citizens to own their own business, and they'd struggled for twenty-eight years to keep it operating.

In their younger days, before Elena and Luz were born, Ramon and Rachel Velasco had run a similar store in a village in northern Coahuila. Life there had been much harder for small merchants. It had been more dangerous, too, mainly because of raids by Pancho Villa's "revolutionaries" and other outlaws. In the winter of 1908, the family had fled the country.

Elena's Saturday stint usually began about 10 a.m., after most regular morning customers had come and gone, and lasted until around 4 p.m., when her parents returned in time to catch the bulk of the evening trade. She didn't look forward to her six hours behind the counter, especially when she was tired from the demands of the long school term. But she never failed to be there. Papa and Mama had made great sacrifices to allow her to finish college, and she considered this chore part of her repayment. It also helped to fill what would otherwise be a bleak, empty day for her. Saturdays and Saturday nights were times when she had to struggle harder than usual to keep from brooding about how lonely she was.

During her years at the Teachers College in San Marcos, she'd gone out with a half-dozen young men, including two she'd dated regularly for several months, but none had been Anglos. Ever since Luz's death, she'd avoided gringo males and reacted to them with instinctive suspicion. Yet the Hispanic men with whom she became involved inevitably disappointed her or lost interest when she refused to become a subservient wife or mistress.

Not once since she'd returned to her birthplace had she had a real date – not on Saturday night or any other time. Eventually she'd admitted to herself that only a miracle could keep her from living out her life as an old maid schoolteacher, but the realization still stung. Much as she loved teaching, she hated the idea of never having children and a home of her own.

Her world seemed drab sometimes, but it was at least orderly and predictable. Besides, it was better never to find love at all than to be used and abused as the mere object of some man's lust. She was convinced of that much – and steeled to the likelihood that she would never marry. The sudden re-appearance of Adam Wagner had done nothing to change her feelings, either about the present or the future. But for more than a week, the thought of him had nagged at the back of her mind.

Since he'd first shown up at the school just after the dismissal bell that Friday, he'd come back three more times. She'd done nothing to encourage him, but he didn't seem to need encouragement. He made no demands on her, either physical or emotional, but his very presence tore open the scar tissue on the old wounds inside her. Every time she saw him, the wounds turned raw and painful again. She knew that none of the wounds were really his fault, but it was impossible to keep from associating him with them.

Once, when she was in the seventh grade and Adam was a senior in high school, star-struck little Ellie had secretly idolized him. But after what had happened with Kurt, Adam had taken on another identity in her mind as Kurt's friend and partner in crime. Adam had done the same things with her cousin Teresa that Kurt had done with Luz. In fact, he was probably doing those very things somewhere with Teresa the night when Kurt raped Ellie and triggered the rage that had sent Luz to her death.

Both Kurt and Adam were cast from the same mold, she'd decided. They were arrogant Anglo boys who amused themselves with Mexican girls, then tossed them aside or trampled them in the dirt. In some inexplicable way, she still blamed Adam along with Kurt for the lingering agony inside her. The occasional evidence that Adam displayed of courage, integrity, even gentleness, couldn't change what he was. It was all a sham, another deceitful gringo trick.

❋

It was a few minutes past two, and the road in front of the store had been quiet and deserted for an hour or more when Elena heard the rumble of an engine and the sharp crunch of tires on the caliche driveway. She looked up from the papers she was grading to see a dusty, dark-blue pickup truck bearing the "RR" trademark of the Radke Ranch lurch to a stop under the wooden portico that shielded the two red gasoline pumps. The sight surprised and unsettled her. Not once since Luz's death could she recall a Radke vehicle stopping at the Mercado Velasco.

The last time Elena had seen Kurt Radke face to face had been less than two weeks after Luz was buried. She'd been walking to school with a small group of classmates when he'd driven up at the wheel of a big open car. He'd shooed the others away like so many chickens, then turned to her.

"I won't lie to you," he said. "Luz was one helluva woman, but she was only a diversion for me. It was always you I wanted, and now that Luz is gone, I want you more than ever. I'm leaving for college at Georgetown tomorrow. If you'll go with me and be my girl, I promise you won't be sorry. You can have anything you want – clothes, jewelry, money, you name it. What do you say?"

"I'd rather be dead like my sister," she said. "I hope I never see you again."

"Well, it's up to you," he said, "but I only make this kind of offer one time, *chiquita*. If you change your mind, I'll be passing by this way again tomorrow morning on my way to the train station in Uvalde. After that, you'll just be shit out of luck."

"I hate you," she said and walked away.

In all the years since, she'd been within view of Kurt no more than three or four times. As far as she knew, he'd never come anywhere near the Mercado Velasco, and neither had anyone who worked for him. But it wasn't necessary for her to see him for the old revulsion and fury to rise up inside her. Anything that reminded her of him had the same effect.

Without ever confronting her in person, Kurt had done everything possible to stop the Leakey School Board from hiring her as a teacher. Only Superintendent Isaac Blair's respect for her and his refusal to kowtow to Kurt and two of his lackeys on the board had enabled her to get the job.

She watched as two men got out of the truck, slamming its doors loudly behind them and kicking up little motes of dust with their boots as they crossed the driveway. One of them was small-framed and muscular with black hair and piercing black eyes. The other was a bear of a man with a broad, ruddy face and a shock of pale yellow hair.

Elena could smell the mixture of alcohol and sweat the instant the big man stepped through the door. It was clear from his gait and demeanor that he was half drunk, but something else about him bothered her even more. His body movements and the thump of his boots against the wooden floor conveyed an aura of barely restrained violence.

"I'm hungry, Rudi," he said. "Let's see if there's anything fit to eat in this place."

"All right, but make it quick. We promised to get the truck back in an hour."

The big man laughed. "Radke will never miss it. He has a dozen trucks."

While the big man prowled around the store, the smaller one came over to the counter. His lips formed a tight smile, but Elena could feel his eyes boring into her.

"Camel cigarettes, please." His voice was surprisingly soft as he laid a quarter on the counter.

She reached back into the slotted wooden cigarette holder against the wall, then turned and handed him the cigarettes, avoiding his eyes as she opened the ancient cash register and made change.

"Hey, Rudi, look here," the big man shouted from across the room.

The small man glanced irritably at his companion. "What is it, Otto?"

"Look what I found. It looks like wurst. Let's get some."

Elena turned to see the big man gazing admiringly at the loops of dry smoked sausage hanging at one end of the counter. The sausage was made by an old farmer named Adolph Mueller, and everyone knew it was composed mainly of illegal venison mixed with a little beef. The store's only refrigeration was a large oaken icebox, so it didn't stock fresh meat, but Papa always kept a supply of Mueller's mesquite-smoked sausage on hand. Like jerky, it would keep indefinitely at room temperature. But Elena had never heard anyone call it "worst" before.

"Just shut up and get it if you want it," Rudi said, opening his cigarettes and moving toward the door. "Hurry up. You talk too much."

Otto pulled four of the links down from the metal hooks on which they hung and slapped them down on the counter.

"How much?" He grinned broadly, seeming to notice Elena for the first time.

"Thirty cents a link," she said. "That's a dollar-twenty total. Anything else, sir?"

Even as edgy as the two men made her feel, she was hardly prepared for what happened next.

Still smiling, Otto laid two dollar bills on the counter. Then suddenly and with amazing quickness for a man of his size, he reached out and grabbed her arm in one of his huge fists.

"You can keep the change as a tip if you'll give me a little kiss," he said, winking at her.

Before she could react, he pulled her close to him across the counter, lifted her chin with his hand – much as Kurt Radke had once done – and kissed her soundly on the mouth.

"Umm, very nice," he said as she jerked away. "Tell me, what's a sweet girl like you doing in a pigsty like this?"

Rudi was almost to the door when he whirled around and saw what was happening. To Elena, the look in the smaller man's eyes was far more unnerving than Otto's clumsy pass at her. She'd never seen anyone look so angry, and she wondered if part of the anger was directed at her.

She shrank back, her hand feeling instinctively along the shelf under the counter until it found Papa's long-barreled .45 Colt revolver. Her fingers closed around the cold wooden grips of the pistol, her thumb pulling back on the hammer.

She held the fully cocked gun in both hands, just out of sight behind the countertop, as her heart pounded in her ears. If either of the men came toward her . . .

"Get away from her, you imbecile!" Rudi snarled, grabbing Otto by the shoulder and shoving him so hard that he stumbled halfway across the room. "I apologize for him, Miss. He's just trying to be cute."

The big man seemed totally unperturbed by Rudi's anger. He paused just inside the front door and removed a sheath knife from his pocket. Then he carved off a large chunk from one of the sausage links and popped it into his mouth.

"Want a bite, Rudi?" he asked. "It's not as good as wurst, but it's not so bad, either."

Elena puzzled over this last remark even as relief flooded through her at the realization they were leaving. When they slammed the screen door behind them, she could feel the tension draining away, but she kept a tight grip on the .45 while the two men went down the front steps, and a question formed in her mind.

Not as good as worst, but not so bad, either. What could that possibly mean?

She could still hear the men's voices from outside.

"Just get in the truck and be quiet, you ass," Rudi said.

Otto laughed around a mouthful of sausage. "Relax, Rudi. She's only a Mexican wench, right?"

She couldn't see Rudi's coal-black eyes as he turned to stare at Otto. But she had no doubt that if looks could kill, Otto would be dead in his tracks.

When the men were gone and she sat shaking behind the counter, hrt first thought was of Adam. She wanted desperately to talk to him. Regardless of what thorny old barriers might stand between them, she needed to tell him about the two men. He had confided in her about the gun and the mysterious happenings on the Radke Ranch, so it was only fair that she tell him what had just happened.

The big man's chance remark about the sausage took on added significance when she remembered a film she'd shown her pupils at school not long ago. Part of each Friday afternoon was set aside for "audio-visual education," which basically meant showing movies on the school's new projector. Among the regular features was a series of ten-minute films called "Famous Foods of Other Cultures." It included segments on cheese production in Switzerland, catching and canning sardines in Norway, the coffee harvest in Brazil, and so forth.

But it was her recollection of a film on German sausage-making and the colorful "Wurstfest" in Munich that triggered a burst of recognition.

The big man hadn't been saying "worst" at all. He'd been comparing Adolph Mueller's smoked sausage to something he was obviously very familiar with – something called "wurst."

Something that was clearly German in origin.

Could that be the real reason for the smaller man's burst of anger? Was it because the big one had let something slip in his woozy state that could connect the two men in the Radke truck with Nazi Germany?

It wasn't nearly as damning a piece of evidence as the gun Adam had found in the pond, but the more she thought about it, the more impossible it was to shake it from her mind. If Germans – Nazis – were being harbored on the Radke Ranch, they had to be considered prime suspects in Julio's murder. But that was only part of it. Obviously, they hadn't come all this way merely to gun down an innocent boy. Their long journey had to have another purpose.

It was still two days until the school dismissal bell would ring on Monday, bringing with it Elena's first chance of seeing Adam again. Maybe he'd show up at the door of her classroom again on Monday afternoon, the way he'd done before. Maybe. Maybe.

The thought did nothing to console her. She wanted desperately to see him,

She wanted to see him *NOW*.

TWELVE

Dallas, Texas
May 29, 1936

Ed Starling yawned and stretched as he strapped on the shoulder holster with the pearl-handled Colt revolver that had been part of his everyday attire since the spring of 1912. Then he lit a cigarette and gazed down from the window of his eighth floor room in the Adolphus Hotel, surveying the intersection of Akard and Commerce Streets.

Directly below him was the epicenter of Dallas, a vibrant young city that took pride in its many tall buildings – most of which were clustered within a few blocks of where Ed stood at this moment. It was 7:30 on a Friday morning, and the streets below were filled with cars, trucks, crowds of hurrying pedestrians, and the hum of business.

It was to this same hotel at this same busy intersection that the President of the United States would be coming to lunch exactly two weeks from today, following a parade through the city and a speech at the Cotton Bowl Stadium some two miles east. Hence, every inch of the scene below Starling's window was of intense interest to the chief of the White House Secret Service Detail.

Dallas was anything but a regular stop on presidential itineraries. In fact, the last President to visit here had been William Howard Taft in 1909. Ed had never been here before, either. Yet he'd decided soon after his arrival the previous afternoon that he liked Dallas. It was a prosperous, orderly community that seemed to know exactly where it was going and how to get there. It had reaped an economic bonanza from the recent discovery of vast oil reserves in East Texas, yet it had none of the boomtown atmosphere of Houston, where he'd spent the day before yesterday, or the Latino-flavored lethargy of San Antonio, where he'd breakfasted yesterday morning.

Fortunately, Ed had always enjoyed traveling. He was refreshed by the constantly changing panorama from the window of a Pullman coach and relaxed by the muted *click-clack* of the rails as the miles rolled by. He enjoyed the wide range of local customs, cultures and dialects in the cities and towns he visited. He appreciated the fine hotels and restaurants he was able to patronize at taxpayer expense (the Adolphus, with its grand Italianate architecture and opulent French Room being prime examples) and he relished meeting and comparing notes with other law enforcement professionals across the nation.

Although Roosevelt traveled more than any American president in history, Ed normally thrived on the hectic here-today-there-tomorrow schedule. But for several reasons, Starling's current swing through Texas to lay the groundwork for FDR's Centennial tour had been more stressful than most of his trips as the official White House "advance man."

For one thing, Ed had recently married for the first time in his 60 years. This was his first extended absence from his bride of four months, and even a long phone conversation with her each night was no antidote for his loneliness. For another thing, trying to anticipate the infinite possibilities for trouble during a full week and four thousand miles on a train with the fiercely independent Roosevelts could be downright maddening.

In his lighter moods, FDR seemed to take a perverse delight in ditching his Secret Service protectors and striking out on his own. Just last year, on a jaunt through the West, Roosevelt had given Ed the scare of his life. He'd eluded the agents assigned to him, taken off up a narrow mountain road in a car with Federal Relief Administrator Harry Hopkins and Senator Key Pittman of Nevada, and finally gotten stuck after dark on the edge of a precipice. The President had apologized personally to Ed, but he gave no indication of changing his tactics.

If anything, Mrs. Roosevelt was an even worse offender. She'd told Ed and the rest of the White House contingent in no uncertain terms to leave her alone, and she adamantly refused to let Secret Service personnel go with her when she was traveling separately from her husband.

At one point, Starling had been concerned enough about the First Lady's safety to storm into the office of the late Louis Howe, the President's top aide, and demand that Howe "do something" about her flagrant security violations.

"What do you expect *me* to do?" Howe had grumped. "If Eleanor won't listen to you, she sure as hell won't listen to me. Basically, the lady does what she damned well pleases."

Normally, Ed wasn't inclined to theatrics, but he'd whipped out a small, short-barreled revolver and slammed it down on Howe's desk.

"Well, if she's too hardheaded to accept protection from my men and me," he fumed, "she damned well better carry this. It's better than nothing – and it just might save her life one of these days!"

To Starling's surprise, Mrs. Roosevelt had readily accepted his heavy-handed suggestion. From that point on, she carried the little pistol in her purse on all her travels, and even went to great lengths to learn how to shoot it accurately by practicing regularly at the Secret Service pistol range. It was small comfort to Ed, but it was better than nothing.

One of the White House advance man's more frustrating tasks was locating a suitable seven-passenger open car for FDR to use in each city he visited. The major automakers had quit producing such limousines in the early '30s, and they were increasingly difficult to find, but Roosevelt would settle for nothing less. The make of the car was unimportant. It was the jump seat in open seven-passenger vehicles that was indispensable to the President, who used it to pull his crippled body into the position he always occupied in the rear of the car.

Consequently, Ed had had to settle for an ancient Marmon in San Antonio, and he'd almost given up finding anything suitable in Dallas until someone finally located a presentable enough Packard. Unfortunately, it was bright red and had "Dallas Fire Department" printed in large gold letters across its side, but it was being repainted a proper presidential black at this very moment, so it would fill the bill nicely.

Now, on top of everything else, there was this nebulous threat seeping out of Europe. Starling's boss, Chief Moran, had been warned by British intelligence that the danger was very real. Moran wasn't fully convinced, but he was considering increasing the number of agents on this trip beyond the usual five or six, and he'd strongly emphasized the need for extra security arrangements.

"Because of the reference to Mexico," Ed had told Agent Nat Grayson just before leaving Washington, "we may be looking at higher risk levels in south Texas. I won't breathe easy till we've got maximum security at every stop."

Now Ed buttoned the jacket of his gray pinstriped suit over his shoulder holster and checked the.38 derringer in his watch pocket. It was time to walk the two blocks to City Hall for his 8 o'clock meeting with Police Chief R. L. Jones and his command staff. As he took one final downward glance, he realized that the tidy little city outside the hotel troubled him more than any of the others on this trip.

Mostly it was because of all the tall buildings. Dallas had a resident population of just 230,000, but it had more skyscrapers than Houston, San Antonio and Little Rock put together. Like open cars, tall buildings always put Ed on edge. A hundred feet away on the opposite corner of the Akard-Commerce intersection, for example, rose the brown-brick facade of the Baker Hotel, where Mrs. Roosevelt would be a luncheon guest on June 12. And just to Starling's left jutted the tallest skyscraper in the city, the 29-story headquarters of the Magnolia Petroleum Company, topped by a huge revolving reproduction of its "Flying Red Horse" trademark.

For several blocks along the Commerce Street route over which FDR's open limo would bring him back downtown from State Fair Park, site of the Centennial Exposition, Ed could see a string of other multi-story buildings against the pale blue prairie sky.

If Ed could have his way, Roosevelt would eat a box lunch amid the unthreatening low-rise surroundings of the Exposition grounds and ride around town in an armor-plated truck. But that wasn't the way it worked with presidents. They always had to be in the big-ass middle of everything, and those who guarded them had to make the best of it. All told, Ed could stand here and count thousands of windows overlooking the street that FDR would travel in that once-red open car two weeks hence. And behind every last one of them he could envision a potential sniper lurking.

As he strode down the air-conditioned hallway toward the elevator, he felt himself start to sweat.

THIRTEEN

Reál County, Texas
May 30, 1936

The three of them – Adam, Ellie, and Lobo – had been huddled for more than an hour behind the Christmas tree shapes of a small stand of cedars, exchanging only a few occasional words as the day faded around them. Now the sun was sinking noticeably beyond the ridge of hills to the west, and the temperature was starting to drop. The smell of cedar sap was faint but pungent in the air.

It was an odd way to spend a Sunday afternoon, Ellie reflected. She was sitting close to Adam, watching him peer intently through a pair of binoculars and listening to the soft, measured panting of Adam's old sheepdog.

Until twenty-four hours ago, Ellie had never worn a pair of men's jeans in her life, but Adam had insisted on lending her a pair of his – which were six inches too large in the waist and had to be turned up three times at the cuff – because they were hiking into rough, brushy country.

She'd felt slightly strange when she first put on the well–worn Levis, but twenty yards after leaving the parked pickup yesterday, she'd realized what a necessity they were. Within minutes, she was wishing for some boots like Adam's to go with them.

It was now the third day in a row that they'd spent several hours together, and she was adjusting to the idea of being near Adam, but her conflicting feelings about him were still like oil and water. Her cynical side had taken full control when he'd failed to show up at the school on Monday afternoon – or Tuesday or Wednesday, either. This only confirmed his duplicity, she thought. It meant he didn't really care about Julio or bringing Julio's killer to justice – or probably anything else he pretended to care about. It was just a charade, part of the same old gringo game.

By Thursday, she told herself she didn't care if she never saw him again. She wouldn't waste any more time waiting and wondering about him. If he did finally come, she'd tell him to go away. Then, on Friday, she looked up to see him standing in the doorway of her classroom.

"Where have you been?" she blurted. "I've been looking for you all week."

Surprise crossed his face, closely followed by a sheepish smile. "You have?"

She wanted to bite her tongue off. "Well, sort of," she said.

"I'm sorry," he said, and somehow she sensed that he meant it. "I've been shearing ten hours a day all week and playing 'I-spy' for two or three hours every night. But if I'd known . . ."

"Forget it," she said. "I just thought you might like to know I saw your two mystery men from the Radke Ranch last Saturday. In fact, I came pretty close to shooting them."

"Good God!" he said. "What happened?"

She swallowed her pride long enough to give him a fairly detailed account of the encounter at the store. When she finished, she wasn't miffed anymore, only curious about his reaction.

"That was really perceptive of you," he said. "To remember that 'wurst' means sausage in German, I mean."

"I'd never have realized it if I hadn't just seen that film."

"Well, what I've seen in the past few days was a lot more obvious," he said. "For one thing, there's four of them now. Two others showed up

Monday while I was watching the house, and I could see them all giving each other those 'heil Hitler' salutes. It gave me the shivers."

"Then there's no doubt about it, is there? They really are Nazis."

"Sure looks that way," he said. "Question is, are they here just to eat sausage and kiss pretty girls, or do they have something else in mind?"

❋

Now Adam sat inches away from her as motionless as a statue, keeping his eyes glued to the glasses for several minutes at a stretch. She was starting to wonder if he'd ever move again when he finally lowered the binoculars and handed them to her.

"Take a look, and see what you think," he said. "When they leave, they usually go on horseback, although I did see a pickup out there a time or two. There aren't any horses in the corral right now, so my guess is they're all gone."

She rested the unfamiliar weight of the glasses against her cheekbones and squinted through them. At first she saw nothing but blackness, but then a distant section of the valley floated into focus. It was amazing, she thought. The house looked no more than forty or fifty yards away, and every detail of it was sharp and clear. As Adam had noted, the corral was empty.

"There's some towels or something hanging on the porch," she said. "But except for that, I don't see any signs of life, either. Could they have left for good?"

"I don't know. This is the first time I've noticed them all being gone at once. I'm not sure what it means, but I think . . . " He paused and looked at her. "I think I'm going over there and have a look around."

She turned and met his gaze. "I don't think that's a very good idea." A chill ran down her backbone.

"Maybe not, but it's the only way to find out what's inside the damned place." He picked up the rifle propped against one of the cedars and laid it across his shoulder.

"But it seems so far," she said. She lowered the binoculars and gazed across the distance that actually separated them from the little house. "How long would it take us to get there?"

He looked at her levelly. "It'd probably take Lobo and me about ten or twelve minutes. I never said anything about 'us.'"

She frowned. "Well, if you think you're leaving me sitting here to worry about you while you go off over there, you can just forget it. I'm going, too."

"I'd rather you didn't," he said. "I'm afraid you'll just slow us down. Besides, what if we have to run for it?"

"You're the one with the bad knees!" Ellie flared. "If it weren't for these baggy jeans, I could probably run faster than you. Are you saying you trust your dog more than you trust me?"

"I know what my knees can stand, and I also know what Lobo's capable of, that's all. He can create a nice diversion sometimes when he goes crashing through the brush, and he's as fast as greased lightning." Adam smiled. "Besides, he'll bite the hell out of somebody if I tell him to. Can you do all that?"

She'd always hated being teased, and she felt a flash of anger for a moment. Then she smiled in spite of herself. "Maybe," she said. "It depends on who you want bitten. I'm going, and that's final."

"But why?" He seemed genuinely puzzled. "I never intended for you to take risks like that when I asked you out here."

For some reason, Ellie found it extremely difficult to look him in the eye right then, so she looked at Lobo instead. "Because I want to," she said. "And because I don't want you to go without me."

Adam knew from repeated observation that the Radke fence-riders made their rounds on an average of every hour and a half, give or take five or ten minutes. Theoretically, this was ample time to reach the stone house, take a look around and get back across the fence without encountering one of Kurt's mounted marauders.

But there was no way to know when the men from the house might return, and that was a significant danger in itself. Besides, Adam had learned through hard experience that everything took longer than you expected. Unforeseen problems always arose. It was an inescapable fact of life – and death.

Part of him drew comfort, even pleasure, from Ellie's closeness as he held up the barbed wire and allowed her to slip through the deer-proof fence. But as Lobo scrambled through the gap between the strands of wire and Adam followed, guiding the .30-30 Winchester ahead of him, worry nagged at the rest of him about what her presence could mean in case of trouble.

Still, she'd already proved she was tougher than she looked; he had to admit that much. Most of the "town girls" he knew would've played out on him long before now and demanded to be returned to the safety and comfort of civilization. But this one had stayed with him every step of the way, asking no favors and clearly expecting none.

Two decades ago, he'd thought of her as a helpless child who needed protection, but a lot had changed over time. If her account of the confrontation with the two men at the Mercado Velasco was accurate, she could be a formidable ally.

Nevertheless, Ellie had trouble from the outset keeping pace with Adam and Lobo, who would have ranged far ahead if Adam hadn't frequently clucked his tongue at the collie, signaling him to stay close. After crossing the fence, they skirted the high grass of the pasture – although it represented the shortest route to their destination – to avoid leaving the same sort of telltale tracks Adam had spotted the morning after Julio was shot. This led to further delay, and it actually took more than twenty minutes of darting across open spaces, clamoring up and down hills and through rocky ravines, and taking maximum advantage of each bit of cover to reach the clearing where the small stone house stood.

Finally, though, they threw themselves to the ground where the rear wall of the house backed up to the hillside, and from where they were concealed from anyone approaching along the trail. They spent the next sixty seconds or so catching their breath, and for a few seconds, Adam's thoughts drifted back to some of the patrols he'd led in France. Then he reached out and touched Ellie lightly on the shoulder.

"You okay?" he asked.

"I guess so," she puffed, "but I keep asking myself if we're really doing this.'"

"We're doing it, all right," he said, "and we'd best get it done in a hurry. Those four goons could decide to come back any time."

Ellie crossed herself. "You don't have to remind me. What do we do now?"

There were no windows on the rear of the house, only a blank stone wall. That made it an advantageous hiding place, but it offered no clue to what was inside.

"I'm going around there and check the windows," Adam said, pointing around the corner to his left and holding the rifle out to her. "Hold onto this while I'm gone. You ever shoot one of these things before?"

"A few times," she said. "I'm more comfortable with pistols."

"It's easy enough," he said. "All you have to do is release this catch and pull the trigger, then crank the lever to eject the shell and you're ready to fire again. But only in a matter of life or death, okay? One gunshot could bring every Radke fence-rider within five miles down on top of us."

"I'll be careful," she said. "Now what do you want me to do?"

"Go down to the other corner of the house and keep an eye on the trail."

"And if I see something? What then?"

"Just make a noise like a mourning dove," he said.

"Oh sure," she said, "and how am I supposed to do that?"

"Like this." He vibrated his tongue against the roof of his mouth in a series of low but high-pitched whirring sounds. "It's simple. Go ahead and try it."

She made a face, then produced a fair imitation of the sounds he'd just made.

"Good," he said. "Now sit tight and watch close. Stay, Lobo."

As he turned away, their eyes met for a second and he was tempted to say something else. Something like how pretty she looked in his ill-fitting jeans and drab khaki work shirt and that he'd never met a woman quite like her. And maybe even that, damn it, he was glad she was here.

But in the end, he merely winked at her once as he ducked around the corner.

The first window Adam came to was partially open, and it was a simple matter to raise it far enough to slither into the cool, dark interior of the house. But as he discovered a moment later, it would've been simpler yet to walk a few more feet and enter through the unlocked front door.

There were three rooms in the house, one equipped with a half-dozen bunks and another with a large table and assorted benches and chairs. The other was a kitchen with a potbellied iron stove, a tin sink, a wooden icebox and an oak cabinet with a porcelain counter. Off to the side of the kitchen was a bathroom with a sink, a flush toilet and a corrugated washtub that were its only furnishings.

The place was an untidy mess – the kind easily created by several men residing for days under the same roof with no one but themselves to do routine housekeeping. Two of the bunks held only bare mattresses, but the other four were a disarray of wadded pillows, twisted blankets and dirty clothes. Unwashed dishes, empty bottles and scraps of food littered the table and cabinet counter. Other dishes and utensils were piled in the sink. A greasy skillet and several blackened pots and pans dominated the top of the stove.

"Sportsmen" often left such a scene behind after a week or two of silliness on a deer lease, but it wasn't hunting season, and even drunken deer hunters seldom left such an arsenal lying around.

Along one wall of the bunkroom was enough weaponry to slaughter every deer in Reál County. Three high-powered rifles with telescopic sights stood in a row, flanked by a pair of Thompson sub-machine guns, their ammunition drums fully loaded and in place. On the floor nearby was a compact leather case containing yet another rifle, this one unlike any Adam had ever seen. It was disassembled and its various components were packed neatly into the velvetized compartments of the case. Hanging from the end of one of the bunks was a holster with a semi-automatic pistol similar to the one Adam had found in the stockpond, only this one was blued steel, not nickle-plated, and it had no swastikas on the grips.

"Judas priest," Adam whispered. "Are these guys planning on starting another damned war?

He tiptoed back into the kitchen, although there was no need to keep quiet, and his eyes roamed over the cluttered surfaces of the room until they came to rest on a newspaper lying on the dark wooden table. It was the front section of the previous Friday's *San Antonio Express*, stained with spilled coffee and folded to reveal the lower left-hand portion of the page. Someone had penciled brackets around one particular article and the headline above it, which read:

President Gets Preview
Of Texas History As
Centennial Trip Nears

Below the headline was an Associated Press dispatch datelined Washington. It began:

"A miniature replica of the San Jacinto Monument and copies of various Texas historical documents were presented to President Roosevelt Thursday by members of the Texas congressional delegation as the President prepared for his upcoming visit to the Lone Star State, scheduled for June 10-13.

"During the trip, Roosevelt will make major speeches in San Antonio, Houston and Dallas in observance of the 100th anniversary of Texas independence.

"The White House announced this week, however, that the President will be unable to officiate at opening ceremonies of the Texas Centennial Exposition in Dallas on June 6, as exposition organizers had hoped. Because of pressing commitments in Washington, he has asked Commerce Secretary Daniel C. Roper to preside at the opening in his stead."

Adam shook his head as he replaced the paper on the table. The pencil marks framing the article and headline were heavy and deliberate, but what significance did the maker of those marks place on this particular story – and why? Despite being a native Texan, Adam had only the most peripheral interest in the Centennial and the President's upcoming visit. If the occupants of the untidy little house were, in fact, Germans – as all evidence collected thus far indicated – why should they care one way or the other? Unless . . .

His thoughts jumped back to the assortment of guns in the next room.

My God, could they be – ?

Before he could finish the thought, he heard the soft call of a mourning dove from somewhere outside.

FOURTEEN

Ellie crouched as low as she could, her face only a foot from the ground, and peered intently around the corner of the house. Her heartbeat was loud in her ears, and she pressed her hand tightly against the ruff of long hair at Lobo's neck, the way Adam had shown her to keep the dog quiet and still. She was panting as if she'd just run a mile, but she managed to give the dove call again.

Less than a minute earlier, she'd been staring toward the point where the trail disappeared over a ridge a hundred yards away when she heard the distant clatter of horses' hooves. The sound grew steadily louder as several riders approached at an unhurried gait. When they topped the rise in the gathering dusk, she could see each of their figures distinctly for a moment before it descended below the ridge line and into the cover of a small grove of trees.

She counted the figures as they came. There were five of them now – five dark riders silhouetted against a pale-orange sky.

The dog tensed and whimpered low in his throat.

"Hush, Lobo," she whispered.

Increasingly alarmed, she was about to risk giving the signal one more time when Adam suddenly materialized beside her. She sighed with something like relief as he took the rifle from her.

"Five of them," she said.

He put his lips close to her ear. "I know, but just stay put. They're too close and it's still too light to make a run for it. We've got to wait till they put away the horses and the sun goes down. Otherwise, we'll be buzzard bait tomorrow."

Every cell in her body urged her to break and run, but she knew he was right. The horsemen were only fifty or sixty yards from the house now, and it was useless to try outrunning them on foot. Even with the carbine, they'd be hopelessly outgunned, she thought, remembering Adam's warning that any shot would bring heavily armed Radke fence-riders on the double.

She closed her eyes and held her breath.

Barely a minute later, the five riders reined up in front of the house. One of the horses snorted, followed by the sound of creaking leather and low, gutteral voices. Then Ellie heard the booming, unmistakable voice of Otto, the big man who'd kissed her at the store:

"*Wilkommen, Oberhaupt! Wilkommen tu unser demüitig gasthaus.*"

There was laughter and a jumble of other voices, obviously in assent.

"*Danke, kameraden,*" a crisp, authoritative voice responded. "*Danke schön.*"

As the men's boots clumped against the wooden porch, Ellie reached across Lobo's motionless form and touched Adam. "I'm scared," she said.

He clutched the .30-30 and looked down at her in the dying light. "So'm I."

"What're they saying? Can you tell?"

"My German's real rusty," he said, "but it looks like the big boss has arrived."

*

Lieutenant Becker hurriedly lighted two lanterns against the encroaching darkness as Major Dietrich unpacked his gear. At the side of the house, Lutz, Reinhardt and Hauptman were unsaddling the horses and putting them in the corral, and the mission commander and his adjutant were alone inside.

"I understand that the men are hungry for the sound of our mother tongue," Dietrich said. "This is why I decided to let them speak German just for this evening. But after tonight, only English will be allowed, even when we're alone out here. Is that clear, Lieutenant?"

"Yes, sir. I couldn't agree more. We can't afford any slip-ups."

"No, and from what Radke tells me, Hauptman's already had some. You know that's why I sent you along with him – to keep him under control. I thought I could count on you, Rudi."

"Otto really had no choice but to shoot the Mexican," Becker said, his cold black eyes meeting Dietrich's. "In fact, if Otto hadn't shot him, I would've been obliged to kill him myself."

"What else has Otto done?"

"There was a minor incident involving a Mexican *fraulein* in town," Becker said. "I haven't allowed him to go back since, but it's hard keeping him confined out here. He grows very restless."

"I know, I know. Too bad we can't give the men leave for a day or two, but it's much too risky. Absolutely nothing must be allowed to jeopardize this mission, Rudi. There's far too much at stake here."

As Dietrich spoke, he was actually thinking as much about himself as about Otto. He'd been shaken by the emotions that ran through him during his three days in Mexico. When he was surrounded by dark-skinned people – especially women – his emotions turned ugly and potentially vicious. They were more than mere sexual urges; they also filled him with the desire to strike out and inflict pain, and he felt trapped and fearful when he tried to resist them. It was almost as if he were an innocent teenager again and at the mercy of the damned gypsies.

"We'll all be amply rewarded later," Dietrich said, "but for now I have to depend on you to keep the men focused totally on the mission. In two days, I leave by automobile to reconnoiter Roosevelt's major stops in Texas – first to Laredo to study the situation, then to other cities on his route in case we have to shift our focus elsewhere."

"But I don't understand, Oberhaupt," Becker said. "I thought Laredo had been definitely selected as the target site."

Dietrich smiled tightly. "When I left Berlin, that was my understanding too," he said. "But Radke has new information from Vice

President Garner's office suggesting that Roosevelt may not be going to Laredo on this trip, after all."

Becker cocked an eyebrow, but his eyes remained impassive. "What does this mean, Oberhaupt? Could he have been warned somehow?"

"It's possible," Dietrich said. "But all it means to me is that, if necessary, we may have to kill him in San Antonio or Dallas or somewhere else. It doesn't matter where, as long as he dies."

FIFTEEN

Adam and Ellie had been pressed against the wall by the open window for what seemed an eternity when he laid his hand lightly on her arm. She turned and saw him holding his forefinger to his lips.

"When I count to three," he said in a barely audible whisper, "head for the fence as fast as you can, and don't look back. I'll be right behind you."

"But . . . but I'd feel better if you led the way."

"Don't argue," he said. "I've got the rifle, so I'll cover the retreat."

"What if I go the wrong direction?"

"Then I'll catch you and get you pointed right. One . . . "

The sky had faded to deep lavender while they crouched outside the house, listening to the voices inside and holding their breath. There was still a hint of light above the hills to the west, but it would soon be full dark, and Adam knew they couldn't afford to wait any longer. Unless they made it back across the fence in another twenty minutes or so – which was doubtful at best in the darkness – the risk of running head-on into a Radke fence-rider rose sharply. The only alternative was another hour or more in enemy territory, and he doubted if either of them could stand that.

Adam knew for sure that he couldn't. Not with everything now buzzing around in his head and trying to get out.

" . . . two . . . "

He had no idea if Ellie had understood any of the conversation between the Nazi commander and his aide. There'd been no way to translate for her, but Adam had picked out enough words to grasp the enormity of the plot they'd stumbled onto.

The Nazis had mentioned three places that any Texan would recognize – Laredo, San Antonio and Dallas – but they'd said much more in German.

Hundert-jährig meant Centennial; *präzident* meant Roosevelt. *Enmorden* meant assassination. But there was no time to talk about it now.

He gave her arm one final squeeze, followed by a push.

" . . . three! Heel, Lobo."

She was off like a shot, hugging the too-large Levis around her and sprinting across the open meadow that separated them from the line of trees marking the first of several ravines and dry creekbeds they would have to cross. He moved quickly after her at a distance of about twenty feet – enough, he hoped, to prevent any single shot from felling them both. The collie trotted effortlessly a half-dozen steps behind him.

Adam glanced back once, fearful of seeing pursuing figures or hearing shouts of alarm. But there was only silence from the house and no indication that any of its occupants had noticed their departure. The pain in his damaged legs had grown from light to moderate, and he noticed that the limp in the left one, where the German shell had made sausage of the cartilage, was getting more pronounced.

Seventy-five yards later, they ducked into the trees. They tried to make a minimum of noise as they slid down the rocky slope to the bottom of the five-foot creekbank and scrambled up the other side. At the top, they paused to rest.

"We should be pretty much out of earshot of the house by now," Adam said, taking advantage of the break to massage his knees. "Let's take it at a fast walk from here. We'll be less likely to trip or run into a prickly pear that way."

"Also less likely to collapse from lack of oxygen," she gasped. "Maybe we should've run their horses off like they do in the movies."

"I'm not too worried about the Germans," he said. "They'd be after us by now if they were coming, but they're too busy buttering up their 'Oberhaupt' to pay much attention to anything else. What bothers me is Kurt's fence-riders. They move like the wind, and they're crack shots. They know every inch of this ranch, too."

"Then let's go," she said, shivering a little.

"I'll stay a little farther back this time and watch our flank," he said. "If anything happens, give me a dove call. I'll do the same." He pointed straight ahead, to where two low hills rose side by side against the horizon. "Just keep walking toward that gap between the hills. In fifteen minutes or less, we should be at the fence."

They moved up a slight incline into another semi-open area studded here and there with small cedars and sagebrush. The slope soon steepened, sending sharp pains through Adam's knees, and he could tell that Ellie was tiring. Her pace slowed so much that he had a hard time keeping enough distance between them. Unless he stopped every minute or two, he found himself practically stepping on her heels.

Although they'd come about three-quarters of the way, Adam was starting to worry. Every passing minute put them deeper into the time frame when the fence-rider assigned to this section would be making his rounds. To complicate matters, the last hundred yards before the fence offered only a few small clumps of brush for cover.

As they approached the last ravine separating them from the fence, Adam again closed the distance between them to a few steps. He glanced quickly in all directions as Ellie started her descent into the shallow arroyo. As it turned out, it was a good thing he was so close.

She was using a small tree sprout as a handhold to lower herself over the edge while she reached down with her right foot for a rocky ledge about halfway to the bottom. But before she could plant her foot on the ledge, the sprout suddenly snapped. He heard her gasp in alarm and he lunged at her, but he was a second too late. She clutched in vain at the rocky bank and tumbled sideways into the gulch. By the time Adam reached her, she was sprawled at the bottom. He could see a bleeding scratch on her cheek, and her left foot was doubled under her.

He squatted beside her, lifting her until her head and shoulders were resting against his knee. She seemed dazed, and he thought he saw tears on the rims of her eyelids, but she didn't cry.

"Oh, God," she said. "I feel so clumsy."

A mild panic gripped him as he dabbed awkwardly with his shirt-sleeve at the blood on her face and willed himself not to dwell on the misery in his legs. "Are you all right?" he asked. Can you get up?"

"Are you hit bad, soldier?" a faint voice from the Argonne Forest echoed inside Adam's head. "Here, let me help you. Can you make it back to the trench?"

"It's my ankle." Ellie's voice said, jerking him back to the present. "It's sprained or something. I don't think I can walk."

Oh damn, he thought, *now both of us are crippled.*

Between them, they managed to work her injured foot out from under her. The ankle was swelling fast, and Adam was barely able to get her shoe off without cutting it. The bone could be broken, he thought, but more likely it was only a bad sprain. He'd seen several of those during his football-playing days, and he knew the pain was excruciating at first.

"The first thing we've got to do is get out of this damned ditch," he said. "Luckily, it's the last one we have to cross. Come on, I'll give you a boost."

Gritting his teeth, he lifted her to a ledge about two-thirds up the opposite bank, where Lobo was watching the proceedings with a puzzled look. Then he cupped his hands under her good foot and pushed until she could get a hand on Lobo's collar and haul herself the rest of the way. Finally, Adam scrambled up beside them.

"What now?" she asked.

He handed her the .30-30. "You carry this," he said, "and I'll carry you. We've got to get the hell out of here."

She was silent and subdued as he scooped her unceremoniously into his arms. He'd taken a dozen plodding steps before she finally found her tongue.

"You were right, Adam. I should've stayed behind. You're limping because I'm so heavy."

"We'll patch up those knees the best we can, son," said the doctor at the battalion aid station, "but I wouldn't advise trying out for the track team when you get back to college."

"Don't be silly," he said. "I'm limping because of some old war wounds, and you aren't heavy at all. If you hadn't been there, those guys probably would've caught me red-handed inside their house."

"What makes you think so?" she asked.

"A little dove told me," he said.

Even at their painfully slow pace, they almost made it safely back across the fence without further incident. Almost but not quite.

They were only about fifty feet from Wagner property when Ellie heard the thud of hoofbeats. Over Adam's shoulder, she saw a huge pale horse and a shadowy rider pounding toward them from a hundred yards away and closing fast.

"Adam–"

The warning froze in her throat, but she knew from the way Adam's whole body tensed that he'd heard the hoofbeats, too. He broke into a stumbling run.

"You there!" she heard the fence-rider yell. "Stop where you are or I'll shoot."

Then they were at the fence line, and Adam was dropping her to the ground, pushing her toward the fence. She lit on her bad foot and winced in silent pain.

"Quick," he said. "You've got to get on the other side. No matter how, just do it."

He pulled up on one of the strands of barbed wire while she pressed down hard on the strand below it. The wires were as taut as guitar strings as she shoved herself between them. They tore at her clothes and she felt the khaki shirt rip. A barb scraped across her back just below her shoulder blades. It hurt, but she pushed herself the rest of the way through, falling to her knees on Wagner soil.

Thank God, she thought. But Adam and Lobo were still on the other side of the fence. "Adam, hurry!" she gasped.

It was too late. The fence-rider was too close. Adam crouched as the lumbering palomino bore down on him.

"Run!" he said. "Get to cover!"

Ellie crawled on her hands and knees toward the nearest tree. She heard the rifle crack and fought to keep from screaming. Even if the bullet missed, the huge horse would surely trample Adam into the ground. She hated herself for not being able to do anything but pray.

God help him! He doesn't have a chance otherwise.

At the last possible second, instead of going for the fence as the rider anticipated, Adam threw himself the other way. As the rider tried to turn the big horse with one hand and hang onto his rifle with the other, Adam grabbed his leg. The rider kicked out savagely, but one of his kicks went awry, catching the horse squarely in the flank.

The horse reared, and the rider dropped his rifle. Clinging with both hands to the rider's boot, Adam dragged him out of the saddle. The man fell hard, but immediately jumped up again and grabbed for the .45 revolver at his belt.

"Charge, Lobo!" Adam shouted.

Without warning, the old collie sprang at the fence-rider and bowled him over before he could unholster the .45. In a snarling fury of fangs and claws, Lobo went straight for the man's throat. The dog would've killed him if Adam hadn't called him off.

"Stay, Lobo."

Adam picked up his own rifle and kept it trained on the stunned and prostrate fence-rider while he lifted the barbed wire to let the collie jump through. Then Adam climbed over the fence himself, using a post as support and keeping the .30-30 at the ready as he did.

The fence-rider got to his feet slowly. He touched the lacerations left by Lobo on his chest and throat. The big palomino stood nearby, grazing contentedly on the lush Radke grass and oblivious to his rider's distress.

"You wetback bastards," the fence-rider said. "You'll pay for this."

"Just get on your horse and go," Adam said. "If you're still here in thirty seconds, I may let my old dog finish chewing your damned head off."

Ellie watched from behind the trunk of the tree while the fence-rider retrieved his rifle and remounted his horse. As he rode away, relief flooded over her, and she began to shake. She felt like kissing the ground on the Wagner side of the fence.

She could have kissed Adam, too – and she probably would have if he'd given her the opportunity. But as he dropped exhaustedly to the ground beside her, his thoughts were obviously on other matters.

"We've got to do something fast," he said. "Trouble is, I don't know how to start."

She took a deep breath and tried to compose herself. "Relax," she said. "I'm just thankful we're both safe."

"But we have to stop them, and we don't have long to figure out how. I never had a chance to tell you what I saw in the house or what I heard those guys saying, but there's a lot more than Julio involved in this thing. I know that now."

She drew back a little, studying him. "I don't understand. You know *what?*"

"You'll think I'm crazy if I tell you," he said.

"I'll *go* crazy if you don't. Talk to me, Adam."

"They're Nazis, all right, and they're here on a special mission. The one that showed up today looks like their commander, and Kurt Radke's bound to be mixed up in this whole thing, too. I figure he helped smuggle them into the country somehow."

"But why? What's this 'special mission' all about?"

He turned to face her. It was too dark to see his eyes, but she could imagine how they looked as he spoke.

"President Roosevelt's coming to Texas in less than two weeks," he said. "When he gets here, they're going to kill him."

SIXTEEN

The White House, Washington
June 1, 1936

Secret Service Agent Roland Stewart pushed away his empty lunch plate, lit a cigarette, and tried to stifle a serious case of spring fever. It was warm and sunny outside 1600 Pennsylvania Avenue, too nice to be cooped up indoors. He could almost hear the largemouth bass calling to him from every stream in northern Virginia.

He considered the cardinal sin of putting his feet up on his desk and taking a short nap. Even the thought felt good. His main boss, Colonel Starling, was still out of town, and his other boss, Nat Grayson, was at an all-day briefing at headquarters. No one else was in the office this afternoon, so who was going to know the difference?

Before he quite got up the nerve to try it, though, he heard the door open, and he turned to see Malvina Scheider, Mrs. Roosevelt's prim personal secretary, standing there with a puzzled look on her face.

"I've got a phone call from a man someplace in Texas," she said. "I don't know how he ended up on my line, and I can hardly make out what he's saying, but he seems to think the President's in some kind of danger. I'm going to have the operator transfer him over to you, okay?"

Stewart reluctantly straightened his lanky form in the chair. "Oh, sure. Nothing like listening to a long-distance loony to spice up a quiet afternoon. Thanks a lot."

"Actually, he doesn't sound crazy at all," Malvina said. "He keeps trying very patiently to explain, but the connection's so bad I'm losing about every other word."

"I'll see what I can do," Stewart said. "Go ahead and have him switched over."

He stubbed out his cigarette and stretched. After a minute, the telephone on his desk rang, and he lifted the receiver.

"Secret Service, Agent Stewart. How can I help you?"

At first, he heard only a burst of static, but after several seconds, he made out a faint, tinny voice on the line. Malvina was right; the connection was terrible.

" . . . is Adam . . . ner. Can . . . hear me?"

"No, you're not getting through," Stewart said. "Where are you calling from?"

" . . . key, Texas."

"Okay, you're calling from Texas. What information do you have?"

"Five . . . plan to . . . Presi . . . Roosev . . . when he . . . down here."

"Sorry, I didn't get that. Say again."

" . . . going to . . . him."

"Listen, this just isn't working," the agent said. "I can't hear what you're saying. Tell the operator to call me back on a better line. Do you understand?"

"Can't . . . a . . . ter line," the voice protested. " . . . trying . . . day."

After that, Stewart heard only the stutter of static, followed by a series of metallic clicks, then a dial tone. When he was sure the connection was broken, he rang the White House switchboard.

"This is Stewart in the Secret Service office," he said. "I was talking to a man in Texas, but we had a bad line. If he calls back in, don't let him get away. If *anybody* from Texas calls in the next few minutes, just put them through to me."

He waited ten minutes, then fifteen. After twenty minutes, he walked down the hall to the small office occupied by Gus Gennerich, the President's personal bodyguard. Gennerich had been with Roosevelt since FDR's days as governor of New York, and most of the agents in the White House Detail considered him a nuisance and/or a joke. But Gennerich was very close to the Chief, and he had a lot of influence with him. Besides, unless Stewart wanted to go out and talk to the uniformed guards at the White House entrances, there was no one else to tell about the call from Texas.

Gus was puffing a stogie and reading a magazine when Stewart opened the door. The air in his office was blue and acrid with cigar smoke.

"Aw, hell, don't worry about it," Gennerich said after Stewart recounted the fractured phone conversation. "Chances are, it was just some crank. We used to get calls like that all the time in Albany, and none of 'em ever amounted to fly shit. Besides, anybody who tries to do anything to the Boss'll have to get past this." He patted the .38 revolver under his suitcoat.

Stewart nodded. He could see why so many of his fellow agents thought Gennerich was a clown. The guy acted as if he'd never heard of electronic time bombs or snipers with high-powered rifles or other ways of striking at a public official that didn't involve walking up and grabbing him by the throat. Stewart also knew that nobody had bothered to fill in Gus on the threat out of Europe. What good would it have done?

"Starling's on his way back from Texas himself," Stewart said. "Guess I'd better write up a report for him on this."

"That's all you federal guys know how to do – make out reports," Gennerich jibed. "Look, if this jerk's on the level, he'll call back. Otherwise, forget it."

There was no way to forget it, Stewart thought. He kept visualizing Ed Starling's face when he heard about the informant Stewart had let slip away.

It wasn't a pretty sight.

Reál County, Texas
June 1, 1936

"Sorry, Mr. Wagner," said JoNell Joiner, chief operator for the Leakey Telephone Company. "All those trunk lines are still busy. The San Antonio operator says she'll try again in thirty minutes."

Her tone was patient and apologetic, but Adam felt a growing sense of frustration as she turned back to her switchboard. She'd repeated the same bad news five or six times so far today.

The idea had seemed simple enough when he and Ellie first talked about it: Just call Washington, and tell the Secret Service what they'd found out. Only it wasn't simple at all. Nothing was simple anymore. Meanwhile, time was slipping away. Adam's surveillance of the house on the Radke Ranch had been cut short for the past few days, but he was fairly sure the head Nazi had left again, only a day or so after his arrival. The other four Germans had still been visible this morning through Adam's binoculars. The Oberhaupt, however, was conspicuously absent.

"Okay," he told JoNell. "I'm going over to the drugstore for a cup of coffee, but I'll be back in plenty of time."

The towns of Leakey and Camp Wood had had phone service for over fifteen years, but there were still fewer than 200 crank-type phone sets in use in the whole county. Except for the Radke Ranch, which had run its own line, there was no service outside the two towns. George Wagner couldn't abide being disturbed by a ringing phone anyway, but Adam hated having to drive all the way to Leakey to make a call.

Ellie, still limping on her sprained ankle, was confined to the schoolhouse until the spring term ended today, but Adam had been slipping off to town whenever he could. The shearing was about over, and he'd left Jake Hernandez to oversee the windup. He'd made the twelve-mile trip to town four times since Monday and spent close to seven hours all told at the small telephone building on Mountain Street.

JoNell's switchboard was old and primitive, but it offered dependable enough local service, and callers normally had little trouble reaching parties in Camp Wood and Uvalde. Calling San Antonio was usually possible, too, except during busy peak periods. Beyond that, the lines of communication were swallowed up in a vast, frustrating maze. It took forever just to reach a Washington operator. Then the main number for the White House was often busy for hours. Even getting the call routed to the right extension could be tricky. Twice, Adam and JoNell were accidentally disconnected and had to start the whole exhaustive process all over again.

Yesterday, they'd come agonizingly close to success. His request to speak to "someone in the Secret Service" was misunderstood, and he was connected instead with a secretary named Shyler or Snider or something. Then, when he finally got a real, live federal agent on the line, the agent couldn't hear what he was saying because of some kind of interference.

"Just call me back on a better line," the agent had said matter-of-factly before the line went dead, but this, of course, was much easier said than done. To add insult to injury, Adam still had to pay six dollars for the aborted call. JoNell was very sympathetic, but it was a company rule, she said.

Now Adam sipped his third cup of stale drugstore coffee and scanned one of the day-old editions of the *San Antonio Express* that had come in on the Wednesday afternoon mail truck from Uvalde. He and Ellie had been watching the papers closely all week for any news of Roosevelt's approaching visit. It would've been nice to be able to check the Houston and Dallas papers, too, but the *Express* was the only major daily the drugstore carried. It wasn't quite as anti-FDR as the other San Antonio paper, the Hearst-owned *Light*, but it came close.

Yesterday's edition was fairly typical. The top spot on Page One was devoted to a story on Republican leaders trying to keep Kansas Governor Alf Landon from winning the party's nomination on its first ballot. Japanese troops, fresh from the conquest of Manchuria, were reported poised to invade North China. The French Chamber of Deputies was debating a series of social reforms while widespread nationwide strikes continued. One of Adam's old college acquaintances, Tim Spurlock, now the *Express*'s top criminal courts reporter, had a bylined story on a murder trial on the local news page. The President of the United States apparently wasn't doing anything worth mentioning, however.

When Adam got back to the telephone building, it was almost four o'clock. Down at the school, a lot of excited kids would be heading home after the final day of classes, and Miss Velasco would be tidying up her classroom for the last time this semester. He could close his eyes and see how she would look, the way she would move, the expression on her face.

"Any word from the San Antonio operator?" he asked.

"No sir," said JoNell, "but you know what? By the time she calls back, I bet those offices up there are gonna be closed. It's about five o'clock Washington time right now."

Adam shook his head. Hell, he'd forgotten all about the time difference. "You're right," he said. "I guess we might as well forget it for today."

"I'm sure sorry, Mr. Wagner," she said, "but I'll be glad to try it for you again tomorrow. It's kind of exciting, you know. Calling the White House and all, I mean. What exactly is it you're trying to tell them about, anyway?"

Her gaze was wide and innocent, but he would've bet a month's pay that JoNell had heard at least part of his conversation with the Secret Service agent. She was always looking for choice tidbits for the town gossip mill, and everybody knew she listened in on private calls whenever she got a chance. The question was, how much had she heard, and who would she tell about it?

"Oh, something they probably wouldn't believe anyway." Adam said. "Maybe I'll just forget it and write them a letter."

SEVENTEEN

Slater Tillman had been riding fence on the Radke Ranch for five years. He rode hard all week and played hard on his nights off. He'd never quite managed to drink all the Southern Select beer in Uvalde, but that didn't keep him from trying. He didn't win every fight he was in, either, but he never backed down to anybody. He was known for his rough treatment of rustlers, poachers, and illegal aliens, and most of his fellow ranch hands went out of their way not to cross him.

Tillman was no crybaby, but the dog bites he'd suffered on Sunday evening had brought him as close to real tears as he'd been since he was nine years old. The punctures and lacerations on his neck, upper chest, and left shoulder were still as sore as boils.

"If I ever see that ornery mongrel again," he swore as he examined the affected area in a mirror, "I'll kill the bastard too damned dead to skin."

Ordinarily, Tillman would have just kept his shirt collar buttoned and his bandana in place and never said a word to anybody about the wounds. But as he was getting ready to bunk down last night, some cowpoke had made a casual remark about rabies, and Slater had started to worry. If it hadn't been for the wrangler mouthing off about "mad dogs," he wouldn't have told a soul about the incident with the trespassers. It was fear that finally prompted him to go up to the big house, tell the bossman what happened, and let him decide if Tillman needed to see a doctor.

But Kurt Radke seemed a lot more interested in the dog and the two people with him than in Tillman's pain or the threat of hydrophobia.

"If all this happened just after dusk on Sunday, you ought to be docked for not reporting it sooner," Radke said. "You say it was right at the Wagner fence line?"

"Yes, sir, Mr. Kurt. They was trying to get over the fence when I rode up. The woman was definitely a Messkin, and I was pretty sure they was wetbacks. But then I seen the man had light hair, so he could've been Anglo. That was one mean son-of-a-bitch of a dog, I can tell you that."

"What kind of dog was it?"

"Big, long-haired. Mostly black with some brown and white on it."

Radke nodded. "Sounds like a collie."

"Yeah, some kind of collie or shepherd, I'd say. Might've been part coyoté, too, from the name the guy called it."

"What name was that?"

"He called it 'Lobo.' Last thing I heard before the dog jumped me. The guy says, 'Charge, Lobo,' and that son of a bitch was on me like a damned mountain lion."

Radke looked closely at Tillman. "Describe the man again for me."

"Fairly tall, pretty well built. About thirty-five or forty, I reckon. Dressed like a regular ranch hand. His hair was light, like I said, and kind of long. Had a bushy mustache, and he was carrying a carbine. Walked with kind of a limp, too."

"Have you ever seen the man who runs the Wagner farm?"

"Can't say as I have," Tillman said, "but I hear he's an old coot with a bad heart."

"That's George Wagner, the landowner. I'm talking about his son, Adam. He's been in charge over there since the old man got sick."

Tillman shook his head. "I could've seen him at a distance, but I don't reckon I ever met him face to face."

Radke stood up and walked to the built-in gun cabinet at one end of the spacious office. He studied the collection of expensive weapons behind the glass doors.

"Well, that's damned odd," Kurt said, "because you just described him to a tee."

Kurt had been pacing the floor for almost an hour by the time Becker and Lutz reached the office. He'd specifically told Tillman to bring only these two. Both Hauptman's nerve and brute strength and Reinhardt's expert marksmanship would doubtlessly be important assets later. But of the four Gestapo agents remaining during Dietrich's absence, Becker and Lutz were the most dependable and disciplined. They would best understand the need for decisiveness and caution – as well as a plan of action.

"This won't be nearly as simple as getting rid of some curious teen-ager," Kurt said. "I've known Adam Wagner a long time. He's a tough, smart war veteran, who killed a dozen or so of your countrymen in France in 1918, and he's one of the most tenacious people I ever met. When he gets hold of something, he's like a goddamn Texas terrapin; he won't turn loose till it thunders."

The regional reference seemed lost on Wilhelm Lutz. His dour, hawk-nosed face remained expressionless. "We will be glad to kill this killer of our Aryan brothers, Herr Radke," he said. "But what of the woman who was with him?"

"At the moment, I have no idea who she is," Kurt said. "But my guess is that she'll be less of a problem than Wagner. According to Tillman, she's a Mexican. Wagner's not only a white man; he's also from a prominent family, and he's well-respected in this county. We have to be very careful how we handle this."

"But how can you be so certain he knows about us?" Lutz said. "What makes you think he's been watching us – or that he may even have been at the house where we stay?"

"I don't know where he's been or what he's seen, but he damned sure knows *something*," Kurt said. "There's no other reason he'd sneak onto this ranch like he did."

"Couldn't he simply have been looking for lost sheep?" Becker suggested mildly.

"Lost sheep, my ass," Kurt said. "If it was anything like that, he would've come through the front gate and talked to me personally about it, not slipped through the fence and set his dog on my fence-rider. I've been worried about something like this ever since Hauptman shot that Mexican boy. The kid obviously worked for Wagner, and from what I've heard, so does his whole family. They've been there a long time. I'm guessing Wagner got upset about the kid and started snooping around."

"But why should he care so much for some meaningless Mexican boy?" Becker's black eyes were puzzled. "Surely, the boy could be replaced with no difficulty. It was my understanding that these Mexican farm laborers – these waterbacks, as you call them – are always plentiful and cheap. A dime a dozen, yes?"

Kurt shook his head. "You'd have to know Adam Wagner to understand," he said. "He's always been different that way. Stubborn as a fence post and with all these damned principles roaring around in his head."

As he spoke, Kurt wasn't thinking of the boy Hauptman had killed. He was remembering a night nearly twenty years ago.

❁

Kurt and Adam had just arrived home from different colleges for the Christmas break that early December of 1916, Kurt having finished his fall semester at small, exclusive Southwestern University in Georgetown, Texas, and Adam the first term of his freshman year thirty miles south of Georgetown at UT. They were both full of smart talk and bravado and overflowing with hormones. They were double dating with two of the hottest *chiquitas* around – Adam with Teresa Morales, who had breasts the size of cantaloupes, and Kurt with Luz. Damn Luz. So beautiful and full-bodied. So utterly, totally crazy.

They'd had a jug of moonshine, and they'd driven Gus Radke's almost-new Cadillac touring car along a dusty trail to a line shack out on the far northwest corner of the Radke Ranch. Adam and Teresa. Kurt and Luz. For some reason, Luz's little sister, Elena, was there, too.

They'd left Elena in the car while they went in the shack. Adam and Teresa in one room; Kurt and Luz in the other. It was a drunken orgy that went pretty much as planned at first, until Luz got soused and passed out cold, long before Kurt was finished. He tried to wake her up, but she was like a zombie.

After a while, Kurt had wandered outside for a smoke and seen Elena sitting in the backseat of the car by herself. Pretty little thing. Quieter than her sister but about as well-built. Maybe as good between the sheets, too. Hell, maybe better.

For a moment, he made himself turn away. After all, she was only about fourteen, and he sure as hell didn't have to stoop to robbing cradles for kicks. But then, in his mind's eye, he caught a glimpse of the Mexican hired girl he'd caught in bed with his father a year or so after his mother left. He froze in his tracks, feeling anger and confusion and something else.

He floated over to the car and smiled at Elena. "Hi, baby sister. Feel like some company?"

"No thanks," she said. "Just go on back to Luz."

"But old Luz conked out on me. Say, I bet you wouldn't conk out on me, would you, honey?" He opened the car door and got in. She retreated to the far corner of the seat, but he slid over beside her and draped his arm around her.

"Stop it, Kurt," she said. "Leave me alone."

"Aw, hell, don't be so standoffish." He took her chin in his hand, turned her face toward him, and kissed her roughly on the mouth. She shoved and slapped at him with both hands, but he caught her and threw her down in the seat. Her yelling and struggling only excited him more. He caught the fragile fabric of her blouse and ripped the whole front of it open.

For a moment, she managed to wriggle away from him and lurch across the seat, grappling for the door handle, but he caught her and pulled her back.

"You're not getting away from me," he panted. "You're staying right here, and we're gonna have ourselves some fun."

The sound of his own shrill words echoed in his ears. For some reason, they took his mind back to the worst day of his life – the day his mother had deserted him.

Mama, come back! Please don't leave me, Mama!

Maybe Henrietta Radke could get away with running off and leaving a helpless seven-year-old boy, but things were a whole lot different where this little Mexicali twit was concerned. The only place this bitch was going was on her back. Kurt laughed at the thought.

He was still laughing when Adam suddenly appeared from somewhere, got him in a headlock, and dragged him out of the car. Next thing Kurt knew, he was sprawled flat on the rocky ground with Adam was sitting astride him, screaming at him.

"You drunk bastard. What're you doing?"

"I was just playing around with her, damn it. Let me up."

"Only if you promise to stay away from her. You hear me, Kurt? I mean it."

"Who the hell are you, somebody's mother? Why should it make a big rat's ass to you?"

He couldn't actually see Adam's eyes in the darkness, but he could feel them boring into him. He could feel the outrage in them.

"She's just a kid, for Christ's sake," Adam said. "You leave her alone, or I'll break your damned neck."

They hadn't seen each other again that holiday season, but Kurt heard the following spring that Adam had joined the Army, which only provided more proof to Kurt that Adam was some kind of idealistic fool. Now that war had been declared, a lot of Kurt's fellow students at Southwestern were also volunteering for military service, but no son of Gus Radke's would ever put on an American uniform to fight against the German fatherland.

Kurt and Adam had never double-dated again.

EIGHTEEN

Indianapolis, Indiana
June 1, 1936

Ed Starling was tired, worried, impatient, and smoking too much. Ordinarily, he tried to limit himself to twenty-five cigarettes a day. But it was only 9:30 a.m. – still over an hour until his flight was scheduled to take off – and he was already working on his seventh Lucky Strike.

He was also still six hundred miles from home, although he had only himself to blame for that. He'd finished up at Vincennes, Indiana, the day before yesterday, and he could've been back in Washington by now if he hadn't decided to make a quick trip to Kentucky. But it wasn't often that he came so close to his native state these days, and he wanted to visit his mother's grave. No telling when he'd get another opportunity.

Until Ed had met and married Flora, his mother had been the only important woman in his life. He'd written her each day as long as she lived and sent her mementos and trinkets from everywhere he went. The pain of losing her had been dulled somewhat by passing time, but he thought of her every day, often several times. He still remembered the jesting lines he'd written on a picture he'd mailed her from Paris when he was there with Woodrow Wilson for the Peace Conference after the World War.

"See your son marching with all the great men! Doesn't he look noble, or is he just hungry?"

The detour to Kentucky had consumed an extra day, but he didn't feel guilty about it. That was only a small part of the time off he was owed, and Flora would understand. Besides, he'd be able to make up half the lost time by taking a plane from Indianapolis to D.C. instead of riding all the way back on the train.

A lot of people had come to Indianapolis for the big 500-mile race at the Speedway this past weekend, but fortunately not many were flying out, so Ed had been able to get a seat on this morning's only scheduled eastbound flight. It was an added bit of luck that the plane was a modern ten-passenger Boeing 247 instead of a rickety Ford Tri-Motor. The 247 had a top speed of 180 miles an hour, and the only scheduled stops between here and Washington's National Airport were in Columbus and Pittsburgh. If they didn't hit rough weather, he could probably nap a little on the plane. It would be a breeze.

What awaited him at the White House, on the other hand, was an entirely different story. From all indications, it was going to be anything *but* a breeze.

Ed almost regretted calling Nat Grayson this morning. In the space of five minutes, Nat had bombarded him with one piece of bad news after another.

"Moran's not going along with our request for a dozen agents on the Texas trip," Grayson said. "We can take seven instead of the usual six. Some concession, huh?"

Ed tried to hide his chagrin. "Well, Moran's got his reasons, I guess. For one thing, if we took twelve agents like I wanted, we'd have to add another car to the train. That could cause problems and slow us down."

"Yeah, but that's not the main reason," Nat said. "I hear Moran's been talking to some commander in Naval Intelligence who thinks the whole story about a Nazi plot's just a ruse by the British to scuttle the Neutrality Act."

"You don't believe that crap, do you?"

"I might've," said Grayson, "if it hadn't been for the call Stewart got from Texas the other day."

"What call?"

"Some guy down there claimed to have information on a plot against the Boss," Nat said. "There was a bad connection, and Stewart couldn't hear him. He asked the guy to call back, but he never did."

"What did the guy say?"

"Stewart couldn't make out much. Malvina Scheider said he told her a bunch of men with guns were hiding on a ranch someplace in South Texas."

"Oh, that's really great. Well, you can start the paperwork right now to get Stewart transferred, and I don't want him on this Texas trip, either."

"I hate to bring it up, but there's something else I better tell you, too."

Ed stuck a Lucky in his mouth and dug for his lighter. "Go ahead. Spit it out."

"Steve Early's putting out a press release for tomorrow's newspapers about the cancellation of the Cardenas meeting and the trip to the Mexican border."

Ed inhaled deeply from the cigarette and closed his eyes. He didn't like to swear, but he felt like swearing. "Damn it, Steve promised to hold up on that. He told me the story wouldn't be released till the President's train was ready to leave Washington. That's still four and half days away. What's the big rush all of a sudden?"

"Steve says the Mexican government was getting upset about our silence on this thing. The Mexican ambassador even complained to Secretary Hull about 'embarrassing reports' that were circulating about the meeting. The Cardenas people always seem to be looking for something to get insulted about, so the President decided to go ahead and issue an official denial to try to make everybody happy."

Starling sighed heavily. What in God's name was this fellow Roosevelt thinking about? Didn't he know his life was in danger?

"Well, it sure as hell doesn't make *me* happy," Ed said. "The whole idea was to keep potential plotters in the dark as long as we could. Since when are the Mexican ambassador's feelings more important than our own national security? To hell with the Mexican ambassador. I want you to go to the President yourself, Nat. Reason with him, plead with him. Tell Steve Early I'll have his ass in a sack. Do whatever you have to, but make them hold up on that release till I get back there tonight, understand?"

"I'll do what I can, sir," Nat said. He didn't sound hopeful.

Now Ed sat in the nearly deserted Indianapolis Airport terminal and fidgeted. He glanced at his watch, then reached compulsively for another cigarette and his lighter. It wasn't quite ten o'clock, and his mouth already tasted like a coalscuttle. He'd only been gone from Washington a little over a week. How could everything get so totally screwed up in such a short time?

That press release had to be delayed at all costs, he thought. The mythical meeting between FDR and Cardenas was their only ace in the hole. They couldn't afford to throw it away. In a high-stakes game like this, showing your hole card too soon could be fatal.

NINETEEN

Reál County, Texas
June 1, 1936

Shortly before 6 a.m., a crowing rooster catapulted Adam back to consciousness from the depths of the most horrific nightmare he'd had in years. He sat up in a cold sweat, barely managing to stifle the hoarse cry lodged in his throat. For a few seconds, he didn't comprehend that he was safe in his own bed and not cradling the bullet-riddled body of First Lieutenant Earl Garrett in his arms.

Adam had had virtually the same dream dozens of times while languishing in various military hospitals after the war, but the last time before this morning had been at least a dozen years ago. Despite all that elapsed time, the dream was as searingly real as ever:

Dawn was just breaking on October 4, 1918, and the entire First Infantry Division was jumping off as part of the last great Allied offensive aimed at ending the worst war in human history. With Adam a few paces behind him, Lieutenant Garrett was leading an advance patrol through dense woods, when a concealed

German machine gun suddenly opened up. The dedicated young officer – who had become Adam's closest friend and mentor in the months since they'd met on the University of Texas campus – was cut down instantly by a half-dozen 20-millimeter rounds.

Adam was the first man to reach him, but Sergeant Billy Birmingham was close on Adam's heels.

Garrett's voice was faint and halting but surprisingly calm considering the blood seeping from multiple wounds across his mid-section. A hint of a smile even played across his lips as he spoke:

"Looks like I'm shot, Adam, but you and Billy . . . can handle this. Send two or three men as decoys to the right . . . to draw the Huns' attention. Then the rest of you . . . hit 'em hard on the left flank . . . Grenade the hell out of 'em, and you'll break their backs . . . I promise you."

"But, God, Earl," Adam said, "we can't leave you here like this. We've got to get help for you."

"I'm done, buddy, so don't waste your time." By now, Garrett's voice was only a rasping whisper. "Just do like I say and trust me, Adam . . . trust me . . . "

Moments later, faced by a half-dozen furious American soldiers, the survivors among the twenty Germans in the machine-gun nest raised their hands and surrendered. When they were disarmed, Adam left Billy Birmingham in charge of the prisoners and made his way back to the spot where Earl Garrett lay. Garrett's eyes were still open, as if he'd been watching the whole thing, but the lower half of his uniform was drenched with glistening, dark-red blood, and he was as dead as a man could be when Adam lifted his limp body and stumbled with it toward regimental headquarters.

Adam and Garrett had first met early in 1917, when Garrett had just returned to his law studies at UT after serving with a National Guard unit in General John J. Pershing's "Punitive Expedition" to Mexico in pursuit of Pancho Villa's bandits. Garrett was twenty-three years old and the son of the county judge in Kerrville, a sizeable town sixty miles northeast of Leakey.

"I understand you're from Leakey," Garrett had said as they shook hands. "Distances being what they are in our part of the world, I guess that practically makes us neighbors."

Adam had grinned. "I think you're the first person I've met here that ever even heard of Leakey," he said. "How long were you down in Mexico?"

"Close to a year," Garrett said. "Sorry to say we didn't catch Villa, but I think we got our message across to some other border troublemakers. Anyway, it's good to be back in Austin. I hope I get to stay a while."

That hope had been dashed a couple of months later when President Wilson asked Congress to declare war on Germany in retaliation for the Kaiser's threat to unleash "unrestricted submarine warfare" against American ships venturing into the European war zone. Garrett didn't seem to mind. He applied for a spot at a special officers' school before the ink was dry on the declaration.

"I'm going after a commission in the new First Infantry Division, and we'll be leaving for France in a few weeks," Earl told Adam when they bumped into each other a day or two later. "General Pershing's looking for all the able-bodied Texas volunteers he can find, and you ought to consider going over there with us, Adam. We'll be the first to fight the Huns, and, trust me, you'll never find a nobler cause than this."

At the time, joining up had seemed like a fine idea. Adam was nineteen years old, consumed with patriotic fervor, and filled with such admiration for his new friend that he'd done exactly as Earl suggested. He'd even talked his hometown friend and roommate, Wilfred Streicher, into enlisting along with him. Now Earl Garrett lay buried in a field of white crosses in Flanders, never having had the opportunity to wear the Distinguished Service Cross he'd been posthumously awarded or to know that one of Kerrville's major streets had been named in his honor.

Meanwhile, Adam Wagner limped through life in Réal County, and Sheriff Sarge Streicher played lackey to the county's power structure, including the latter-day Huns who owned the Radke Ranch. Nothing about any of it made much sense anymore – least of all the nightmare that had left Adam in a cold sweat. It seemed incredible that after so many years, he'd picked today of all days – when he and Ellie were planning to drive to Uvalde on a trip that might change their lives forever – to have the dream again.

Was it merely an eerie coincidence or one of those omens that Ellie talked about? Adam had no answer to his own question, but in less than half an hour the significance of his dream would be clarified with crushing force.

A pot of vegetable soup was simmering on the kitchen stove, and Irene Wagner was putting away the last of the breakfast dishes when Adam rushed through on his way out of the house.

"I'll be gone the rest of the day, Ma," he called as he passed. "You need anything from Uvalde?"

"Nothing I can think of, son," she said. She looked him up and down, noting that he was wearing slacks, not jeans; shoes, not boots; a "Sunday shirt," not denim, flannel, or khaki. His battered, sweat-stained old hat was nowhere in sight. "What in the world are you going all that way for today? I thought all the wool was taken already."

"It was. I've just got some stuff I need to do. Be back soon as I can."

"Is, uh, Miss Velasco going with you?"

He paused with his hand on the screen door and turned back to look at his mother. She invariably raised her eyebrows, and her tone always changed when she spoke Ellie's name.

Clearly, Ellie's several visits to the farm and the recent frequency of his own trips to town hadn't been lost on Irene Wagner. She knew something was going on; she just didn't know what, and Adam had no intention of trying to explain it to her. But at the same time, he didn't want his mother to think he was merely bushwhacking again. It wouldn't be fair to Ellie.

He couldn't resist rubbing it in a little, though. "Matter of fact, she is. School's out now, you know. She's got the whole summer off, and with the shearing done, I may take a little time off, too."

His mother didn't say anything else, but her eyes darkened slightly. It was hard for Irene Wagner to imagine anything worse than her son gallivanting around in public with one of "those girls." What *would* she do, Adam wondered, if she'd known that five Nazi assassins were hiding next door, preparing to murder the President of the United States?

Worse yet, the plotters just might get away with it unless he and Ellie managed somehow to interfere and quit running into telephonic brick walls.

Today, though, things were going to be different. Adam was sick of obstacles and delays, fed up with disappointments and frustrations. Today, by God, he was going to see some results or know the reason why.

Lobo was napping comfortably under the big liveoak tree by the driveway as Adam trotted toward the garage. But sensing that something special might be about to happen, the old collie jumped up and followed along, wagging his tail. If Adam had been bound for the south pasture or the big barn, Lobo likely would've dozed on, but he could always guess when his master was going someplace *interesting* – and the old mutt loved nothing better than jumping in the back of the truck and going for a ride.

"You want to go to Uvalde, boy?" Adam asked, jingling the ignition keys at him.

Lobo barked softly as Adam lowered the tailgate.

"Get in then. Ellie'll be glad to see you. She thinks you're a damned sight cuter than I am, anyway."

It was just after 10 a.m. when the truck clattered across the cattle-guard at the main gate of the Wagner Farm. The sun was already uncomfortably warm as Adam turned south toward town and kicked the speed up to almost forty. The road was bumpy, winding, and pocked with chuckholes, and Adam usually didn't drive that fast. His father always said it was hard on the truck, but today Adam felt a dire sense of urgency. Even if he picked up Ellie between 10:30 and 11 as promised, they still wouldn't get to Uvalde until noon or after.

The two of them had put their heads together yesterday and made a decision. The only way to cut their losses and get something done was to make the eighty-mile round trip to the larger town. From Uvalde, their odds of getting a phone call through to someone in Washington who could help would be much better. While they were there, they could go to the big news agency on East Main Street and buy copies of all the major state newspapers. Sometimes the agency even had a recent Washington or New York paper in stock. Surely, by now, some reliable information about FDR's upcoming visit to Texas was being published somewhere.

Beyond that, Adam was also excited at the prospect of having Ellie by his side for a full day and actually taking her *out*.

"While we're there, we'll have lunch at the Elite Cafe," he'd told her. "They've got the best chicken-fried steak in the whole country."

"Are you're sure they'll let me in?" she'd asked.

Such a possibility had never crossed his mind. But when he stopped to think about it, he couldn't distinctly remember ever seeing any Mexican customers in the place. Like most other eating and drinking establishments in South Texas, the Elite had a sign posted in the lobby that said, "We Reserve the Right to Refuse Service to Anyone."

"Sure, don't worry about it," he'd assured her, then spent the next few hours doing exactly that . What would he do if they refused to serve her? Complain to the manager? Punch somebody in the nose? If he did, she'd be so embarrassed she'd never speak to him again. Maybe he'd just take her to Casita Blanca for some Mexican food instead.

He'd driven less than a mile along the narrow, unpaved ranch road when a blue pickup appeared in a small cloud of dust in his rearview mirror. He thought nothing of it at first, but then he noticed that the pickup was closing the gap between them in a terrific hurry. It looked like a Radke Ranch truck, but there was nothing unusual about that. Radke crews passed this way often, and some of them drove like bats out of hell. This guy was doing close to sixty and coming up fast on Adam's back bumper.

Having no interest in getting run over and not being in the mood for a race, Adam moved over as far to the right as he could when the other pickup was still about two hundred feet behind him. He also slowed down a little because there was a slight curve coming up, and he wanted to give the driver of the blue truck plenty of room to pass.

The other truck was barely forty feet behind him now, and through the dust from his own wheels, Adam could see two figures in its cab. The face of the man behind the steering wheel was impossible to make out, but when the sun caught the other man's features, they looked strangely familiar.

The pursuing pickup was already moving to the left and preparing to pull alongside him. Adam could smell the chalky caliche dust from its grinding wheels. Then he saw the barrel of a rifle jutting from the window on the passenger side of the other truck.

At that same instant, he realized why the face of the man holding the gun looked so familiar. It was one of the Nazis. The big one named Otto. The sausage lover from the Mercado Velasco.

For the briefest instant, Adam's eyes caught the image of Lobo in the mirror. The old dog was stretched out in the bed of the truck, blissfully unaware of what was about to happen.

But Adam saw exactly what was coming. He hadn't come under small-arms fire in close to eighteen years, but the knowledge and experience he'd gained in France was still with him – rusty with disuse but still there – and it helped him stay calm and maintain his concentration. Lieutenant Earl Garrett had been an excellent teacher.

Swerving and bouncing, the blue pickup drew abreast of him. He glanced toward it. Not five feet away was the muzzle of Otto's rifle.

A split-second before Otto opened fire, Adam threw himself flat in the seat. As he did, he hit the brakes as hard as he could and jerked the steering wheel sharply to the right. The Radke pickup flashed by, and he felt his own truck plummet off the roadbed, bounding over rocks and cactus.

Adam heard three shots, and his truck's windshield exploded into a snowy mass of shattered glass. He felt the fragments of it raining in on him. He slammed violently into the door on the right side of the cab and felt his shoulder and arm go numb. Then, just as he bounced back to the left, the right front wheel of his truck crashed into a bathtub-size boulder. The impact flung Adam forward again, driving him into the right-hand door and almost hurling him out the window.

He felt blood on his face. In a daze, he heard Lobo howling from somewhere. His eyes weren't focusing right, but he thought he saw the blue pickup slowing down.

My God, they're coming back, he thought.

Adam turned, grasping with fingers he couldn't feel for the .30-30 in the rack across the back of the cab. His head was swimming, but the carbine was there, and somehow he got it down. He pushed the right-hand door open and eased out behind it, kneeling on the running board with one knee and resting the gun barrel on the top hinge in the crevice between the door and the cab.

The blue pickup had come to a full stop. Now it slowly began backing up.

He waited until he calculated it was less than a hundred feet away. Then he aimed the .30-30 as well as he could at the fuzzy image and squeezed the trigger.

He couldn't tell if he hit anything, but when he fired a second shot, the Radke pickup immediately changed gears and sped away. Adam stared in the direction the pickup had gone until his vision cleared a little and most of the dust had settled. All quiet on the western front. The bastards didn't like it when he returned their fire.

His first reaction was relief, but it lasted only a few seconds. *Uh-uh, it was too easy. They had me dead to rights, and they knew it. Why didn't they stay and finish the job?*

The answer to his question came in the sudden, staccato roar of an aircraft engine. He saw a silverish monoplane streaking in low from the north. It was flying almost at tree-top level and casting a shadow like a giant vulture.

The ground troops had done their job. They had put Adam's truck out of commission and left him stranded, stunned and vulnerable, far from any source of help. Now they were turning it over to the air corps. In the time it took the realization to sink in, the plane was almost directly overhead. He looked up and saw someone leaning out the side of the cockpit. Someone extending his arm. Dropping something.

A baseball-size object hit the ground no more than two yards from Adam's feet, then bounced miraculously in the opposite direction. Many years had passed since he'd dodged a hand grenade, but he took the defensive against this one with surprising dexterity, considering how much he was hurting. He heaved himself onto the floorboard, drew himself into a tight ball, and wrapped his arms around his head a split-second before the explosion.

If the grenade had gone off two seconds earlier, it undoubtedly would have killed him. As it was, it rolled about a dozen feet away from the front of the truck, and he was partially shielded from the blast. But he knew some of the fragments had hit him from the sharp stinging sensation across his legs and backside. The blast showered the truck with dirt and rocks and knocked out what was left of the windshield.

Adam was dizzy and disoriented, and there was numbness and pain in every inch of him from his head to his toes, but he knew he had to move fast if he ever intended to move again. The disabled truck was poor protection from grenades, and it made too good a target. If one of them should explode inside it, he thought, he'd be mincemeat for sure.

His only chance was to get away from the truck – but where? His attackers had picked their spot well. It was one of the most barren stretches of road between the Wagner Farm and town – mostly open, windswept terrain, dotted with a few low patches of brush and stunted trees.

The plane was already banking sharply and swinging around for another pass. The nearest cover of any kind was a small stand of scrub cedar and sagebrush twenty or thirty yards away. He grabbed the .30-30 and stumbled at a crouch toward it. The high-pitched whine of the approaching plane intensified behind him.

Inside Adam's head, he heard a British officer shouting shrilly across the years from a trench near the Marne River:

"Air attack! Jerry up! Jerry up! Take cover!"

Then Adam heard another kind of whine and glanced around. Lobo was limping toward him. There was blood on the old dog's ruff and one of his front legs was doubled up under him.

Without thinking, he dropped the rifle and lifted the collie in his arms. It was a bad trade – abandoning his only weapon for a gimpy, old dog that weighed over sixty pounds, but it was impossible to carry them both, and Lobo would've been safe at home right now if not for his master's thoughtlessness. There was no way Adam was going to leave him.

"Easy, boy," he said. He gasped for air and felt a stabbing pain in his ribs, but he managed to stagger on toward the patch of green ahead.

They made it to the cover of the scrub cedars with no time to spare. The cedars' sticky boughs threshed across Adam's face as he plunged into them. He tumbled to the ground with Lobo under him.

Lobo whimpered softly an instant before the second grenade went off. The roar was deafening, and it kicked up a cloud of stifling dust, but this was much less of a close call than the first grenade had been. It exploded at least twenty feet away, and the thick foliage of the cedars blunted its force. As nearly as Adam could tell, it did no further harm either to himself or the dog, but this was small comfort. They probably wouldn't be so lucky next time.

He heard the plane banking again as he stripped off his blood-spattered white shirt and wadded it into a ball under one of the cedars. Otherwise, the shirt was bound to stand out like some kind of beacon from the air. A dozen or so yards beyond the cluster of cedars where he crouched, Adam could see a denser stand of trees, including some larger cedars mixed with a scattering of small liveoaks that would offer more protection. At the far edge of the trees, the land sloped sharply downward toward a distant ravine. It was clearly a better hiding place than his present location, but Adam seriously doubted his ability to get himself and Lobo that far.

As he paused, panting and lightheaded, trying to decide if he dared to risk it, Adam thought he heard a soft, calming voice close beside him.

"You can't stay where you are, Adam," the voice said. *"There's not enough cover here, and the Jerries will get you for sure unless you can make it to those larger trees. If you've got enough stuff left to get there, you'll be safe, I guarantee."*

In Adam's rational mind, he knew that no one was there with him among the scrub cedars, that he was utterly alone except for the wounded dog, and that he was very likely slipping into shock. Yet the voice seemed so real – and so familiar – that he turned instinctively toward it, expecting for the ghost of a second to confront a misty image in a steel helmet and a bloodstained khaki uniform. There was nothing there – nothing visible, at any rate – but Adam still sensed a strong presence of some sort.

"Earl?" he muttered. "Lieutenant Earl Garrett? My God, is that you?"

"Trust me, Adam," the voice said. *"You have to trust me one more time."*

"Damn it, Earl, I did trust you. I trusted you more than I ever trusted anybody, and look where it got us. You're as dead as a doornail, and I'm not far behind."

"Run, Adam. Run for the big trees. Do it now, and you'll understand why when you get there. I give you my word."

"Earl . . . "

"Trust me, Sergeant Wagner. Trust me . . . "

If he lived to be a hundred, Adam would never understand how he found the strength to heed the voice, but somehow he managed to scoop Lobo up in his arms and obey his late company commander's order.

When he reached the larger cluster of trees, he found that the voice in his head had indeed kept its word. Beneath one of the cedars lay a dark, round hollow left by the dislodgement of a large boulder that had rolled downhill into the ravine at some point in time. The hollow was four or five feet deep, and it curved back into solid rock under the roots of the tree. It was exactly the right size for a man and a dog to huddle into. In this burrow, if they could stay quiet and still enough, they would be totally undetectable from the air. It was a godsend.

Now the plane was almost back. It was very close, very low.

"Dead dog, Lobo," Adam whispered, pushing the collie ahead and dragging himself after it into the hole. "Dead dog."

Lobo had done the dead-dog trick hundreds of times since he'd first learned it as a pup. Sometimes he did it so well it was hard to tell he was even breathing. Right now, he lay perfectly motionless, but Adam could feel the old collie's heartbeat, so he knew he was still alive.

The next grenade didn't even come close, and the second and third ones missed by even wider margins.

"Thanks, Earl," Adam muttered faintly as the plane roared away.

TWENTY

When noon came with no sign of Adam, Ellie was slightly miffed, but it never occurred to her to worry. It was just some unavoidable, unexpected delay, and he would be there soon. When he told her he was coming, he always came. He'd gradually proved his dependability in that respect. Up to now he'd never been more than a few minutes late. Never as much as a whole hour and a half. It wasn't like him.

She grew steadily more irritated as the early afternoon dragged on. By 2 o'clock, she was angry. She'd begun to trust him again, and that had been a mistake. He'd probably forgotten the whole thing.

By three o'clock, she was ready to scream. She would never speak to him again, much less go anywhere with him. No matter how much he grinned at her. No matter how sheepish he looked, or how much he tried to joke and cajole her. No matter if he begged and pleaded. By four o'clock, she was scared to death.

Something had happened. She could feel it in her bones. There was no way he wouldn't have come by now if he was physically able. She felt a lump the size of a garlic pod in her throat. What if he'd been in an accident?

What if the same thing had happened to Adam that had happened to Julio?

At 4:20, she went into the store where Papa was filling jars with three-for-a-penny candy.

"I have to borrow your car, Papa," she said. "There's something important I have to do."

The car was a stovepipe blue '34 Chevrolet four-door with black fenders. It was the first brand-new car Papa had ever owned, and he was very proud and possessive of it. Ellie often drove it when the three of them went somewhere together, but she'd asked to borrow it for her own use only twice – both times to go to Uvalde to buy teaching materials.

"*Qué paso?*" he said. "Where do you have to go?"

"Out to the Wagner farm. Adam and I were supposed to go someplace, but he never came. I've got to check on him. I'll be very careful. Don't worry."

Her father's look was plainly disapproving. "Should young ladies go checking on young men who don't keep their appointments?" he said. "That isn't the way it was when I was young, *hija*."

"I don't need a lecture, Papa. I need the keys to the car. I don't ask many favors, but I'm asking one now. Please."

He shook his head, but it was a gesture of resignation, not denial. When she used a particular tone with him, he knew better than to press her or try to interfere.

"The road up that way is very bad in places," he said, handing her the keys. "Promise me you won't go over thirty. *Comprendê?*"

"Okay, I promise." She grabbed the keys and bolted for the door.

*

With every passing minute, Ellie found it more impossible to keep her word about not speeding. After ten miles, the Chevrolet was whipping along at close to fifty on the straightaways.

When she rounded the gradual curve and saw the truck sprawled beside the boulder, her heart leapt at first. Maybe it was a simple breakdown and nothing more. Then she recognized the scarred gray shape for what it really was – a distress symbol as obvious as a flag flying upside down. The right front wheel was crumpled under it. The doors hung askew and the windshield was gone. A litter of rocks and debris covered the hood and front fenders.

She pulled carefully to the side of the road and stopped. When she switched off the engine of the Chevy, there was no sound except the faint howl of the wind. She held her breath, listening intently, turning in a slow half-circle, looking for some sign of life. Anything.

"Adam!" Her voice sounded small and lost in the emptiness. But she called again, trying to make it louder. "Adam, are you out there?"

As she passed the open door of the truck's passenger side, she noticed a small spot of blood on the seat. Then she saw Adam's .30-30 carbine lying on the ground a few steps away. Her heart froze in her chest.

Hail Mary, full of grace. Blessed art thou . . .

He'd never have left the gun behind if he was able to carry it. He would've died first. Kurt Radke and the Nazis had caught him in an ambush and killed him. It was true. It had to be.

Pray for us now, and at the hour of our death.

She stooped down to retrieve the gun. There were still three unfired rounds in it. She saw drops of blood on the ground, now brown and dried by the sun. He was dead. She knew he was dead, but she couldn't stop herself from running in the direction the rifle pointed and screaming his name.

"Adam! Adam! Please, answer me."

She heard a soft threshing sound at the edge of a small strip of sage and cedar just to her left, and she wiped her blurring eyes and whirled to look. Lobo struggled slowly out of the undergrowth and stood there on three wobbly legs. When he saw her, he whimpered and wagged his tail.

Then she heard Adam's voice. It was faint and far away, barely audible above the whine of the wind. At first she was afraid it was only her imagination playing a cruel prank, but when she heard it again, she knew it was real.

"Over here! I'm over here!"

Her knees were quaking, and her stomach was churning. Tears of relief ran down her cheeks, but she didn't care. She clawed her way toward him through the cedars.

TWENTY-ONE

Nuevo Laredo, Mexico
June 2, 1936

The taxi was waiting when Dietrich stepped out of the building into the shadowy side street. It was a battered Overland sedan that belched blue smoke into the morning air, but the important thing was that it was there on schedule, just as Umberto had promised. It was two minutes past 8 a.m. on a Tuesday, and the narrow street was deserted. The cabdriver himself was the only visible witness to Dietrich's departure. That was good. He felt relieved.

He opened the taxi's rear door and slid across the worn seat, setting his leather attaché case on the floorboard beside him.

"Take me across the bridge," he told the driver.

The driver nodded, keeping his eyes averted from his passenger – probably on Umberto's strict instructions. As the taxi picked up speed, Dietrich glanced back at the faceless, two-story structure where he'd spent most of the past two days. He touched the white triangular scar on his left cheek and smiled.

The young prostitute named Veronica still lay in a heroin stupor in the room on the second floor. It would be at least an hour before her latest dose of the drug wore off, but he'd left her securely tied to the bedposts in case she awakened before Umberto came for her. By then, Dietrich would be miles away in another country.

He'd come within an inch of surgically removing the lobe of the whore's left ear while she was passed out and keeping it as a memento of his trip. It wouldn't have taken more than a few seconds with the razor-sharp knife he always carried. But in the end, he'd managed to fight off the urge, realizing the element of risk involved, even with an illiterate street girl who might well have cut off her own ear for a fix if she was forced to go forty-eight hours without one.

The taxi pulled to a halt along with a trickle of traffic at the customs checkpoint at the north end of the international bridge. A black Ford sedan bearing the insignia of the U.S. Border Patrol was parked beside the station, but there was no one in it.

"Are you an American citizen?" the uniformed federal officer asked, leaning in the taxi window toward Dietrich.

"Yes, sir," Ernst said, trying to match the guard's disinterested monotone.

"Did you purchase anything in Mexico?"

"Only food, drink, lodging and entertainment. Nothing I'm bringing back with me." He felt a lingering twinge of regret at the truth of his statement.

He would've been more than willing to leave Umberto an extra twenty dollars to pacify Veronica about her missing ear lobe, and if she was smart, she'd allow herself to be soothed. If not, she'd end up in the river. But Umberto himself might've posed a much more serious problem. American agents in Mexico would pay handsomely to learn of Dietrich's presence there.

"Then you have nothing to declare for customs?" the officer asked.

"No, sir, nothing."

The guard gave Dietrich a look designed to intimidate tourists. To Ernst, it was almost comical. He knew more about intimidation than these silly Americans would ever know. After a second, the guard nodded to the taxi driver and motioned for him to move on.

Ernst had crossed and re-crossed the border six times on this trip, always with ridiculous ease. It wasn't even necessary to show the bogus driver's license identifying him as Earnest W. Dickerson of Reading, Pennsylvania, or any of the other forged papers.

In downtown Laredo, people were hurrying to work, and seeing numerous Anglos on the streets made Ernst feel more at ease. He despised being surrounded by dark-skinned people, and he feared the feelings they aroused in him. Mexicans reminded him of the filthy gypsies who'd beaten and robbed him as a boy. In the quarter-century since, he'd never fully trusted any member of the dark mongrel races, including Umberto and the taxi driver.

A block from the bridge, he left the taxi and walked the rest of the way to the parking area where he'd left the four-door LaSalle provided by Kurt Radke. It would've been much more pleasant to drive the luxurious sedan across the bridge, instead of taking one of the rattletrap Mexican taxis, but Radke had warned him to leave the car on the U.S. side of the river. Too many unfortunate things could happen to an expensive automobile left unattended in Mexico.

Dietrich had no regrets or apologies about lingering longer than necessary in Nuevo Laredo. He'd resolutely put the needs of the mission first, blocking everything else from his mind until those needs were satisfied. Only then did he allow himself to yield to the old compulsion that had gripped him periodically for nearly twenty years.

He'd been a naive youngster of fourteen when it happened. If he closed his eyes, he could still see the voluptuous gypsy woman luring him into the old warehouse in the St. Pauli district of Hamburg. The exciting bulge of her half-exposed breasts and the suggestive motion of her hips beckoned him deeper into the shadows. Her hands were deft and electrifying inside his trousers.

"Come on, sweet boy. I'll show you delights beyond your wildest dreams!"

He was on his back with the woman astride him when the three gypsy men suddenly materialized out of the gloom. The men beat him with clubs and fists while the woman's weight held him down. During the melee she bit a chunk of flesh the size of his thumbnail out of his cheek. He was still semi-conscious but unable to move when they took his trousers, shoes and money, leaving him with three broken ribs, a hundred cuts and bruises and a concussion. He'd almost starved to death before he regained enough strength to earn a subsistence living. Dietrich touched the scar on his cheek again as he slipped behind the steering wheel of the LaSalle. The whore named Veronica deserved a scar of her own, he thought. All the mongrel bitches deserved scars.

With Umberto's help, it had taken less than forty-eight hours to work out a simple, practical plan and walk through it. Two stolen U.S. Army uniforms would allow Reinhardt and Becker to get close to Roosevelt with their weapons as he left the train. It remained unknown where the Cardenas meeting would be held – if, indeed, it was to be held at all. But the site would have to be near the local railway station, perhaps at City Hall or Laredo College, and an auto caravan was a certainty, since Roosevelt couldn't walk more than a few steps. Clearly, it wouldn't be a closed, private meeting aboard the train. Both Presidents would want all the public exposure possible. Politicians were like that.

If the two men in uniform could escape from the area in the confusion after the strike on Roosevelt, a car and civilian clothes would be waiting for them at a safe house a few blocks away. They would leave Laredo immediately, drive south and east along the Rio Grande to McAllen, Texas, then cross the river to the Mexican town of Reynosa. After the excitement died down, Umberto would guide the other three across the river. With luck, all five would be heading home aboard a U-boat in the Atlantic inside a week.

Laredo offered near-ideal conditions for the success of Operation Pegasus and a clean escape afterward. But Ernst had done all he could in the border town at this point. Until Roosevelt's official itinerary was announced, other options would have to be explored.

The first of these was San Antonio, although it had several disadvantages. Traffic congestion would be a major problem in the city's narrow, always crowded downtown streets, hampering both the stalking of the prey and the getaway. It was also expected to be late in the day when Roosevelt arrived, possibly near nightfall by the time he left the train. This would make even a crack marksman's job far more difficult.

The second option – Dallas – seemed better in several respects. Unlike much of the rest of the trip, the Dallas schedule had already been made public. Roosevelt would arrive at early morning, stay until mid-afternoon and travel back and forth across the city by car. It would be his final major public appearance in Texas, the end of a grueling week of travel, and everyone would be a little tired. Possibly a little lax. Even the Secret Service. The one liability was Dallas' location. It was more than four hundred miles from the network of Nazi sympathizers and German agents in Mexico. Over that distance, escape for all five members of the team might well prove impossible.

Dietrich had never been to Dallas, but he'd seen pictures of the city. There were many modern skyscrapers there – each of them a potential sniper's nest – and Radke had a contact at the tallest Dallas skyscraper of all. It was called the Magnolia Building, and it overlooked two of the routes that Roosevelt's entourage would be using.

It also had a "Flying Red Horse" emblem on its roof. A Pegasus, no less.

Except for Radke, no one had known of this coincidence when the name for the mission was selected. At the time, the choice of Operation Pegasus had seemed fanciful, yet appropriate: Roosevelt riding an "iron horse" to his doom in a land of legendary riders and steeds. The fearless warriors of the Reich striking swiftly and vanishing as if they had wings. The culmination of their feat standing as a German victory of soaring, mythical proportions. But now, if Dallas became the target site, the name would take on even greater meaning – as if it were chosen by fate itself.

Traffic was light on the two-lane highway as the LaSalle left Laredo and sped north into flat, desolate brush country. Ernst was still more than two hours from San Antonio, where much checking and observation remained to be done. It would be the next day before he reached Dallas, but he was already excited at the prospect.

From a purely logistical standpoint, it would be best to complete the mission in Laredo, but if that proved impossible, Dietrich fully expected Dallas to be the chosen locale. Having to shift the mission so far to the north had worried him at first, but now he welcomed the challenge. Whichever way it happened, he was confident of success. The building with Pegasus on top was like a positive omen.

Fleetingly, he thought of Veronica. He wondered what special souvenir might be waiting for him in Dallas.

TWENTY-TWO

Uvalde, Texas
June 3, 1936

Adam's own muffled shouts jerked him awake. As he struggled to a half-sitting position in the bed, their echo was still ringing in his ears.

"Dead dog, Lobo! Here they come again."

Then he realized there was no attacking airplane overhead. It was early on a Monday morning and he was in Cottage No. 8 of the Leona Motor Courts on U.S. Highway 90 at the eastern edge of Uvalde. He'd been there since about nine o'clock the night before. Among the last things he remembered about arriving at the Leona was Ellie's arm around him as she helped him from the car to the room. He recalled her filling a glass with water, poking a couple of aspirins into his mouth, then looking back at him from the door while he'd sagged in a chair tugging at his boots.

"Will you be okay?"

"Sure, if you'll stay for a while."

She'd shaken her head. "You've had a hard trip, and we have lots to do tomorrow. I'll be next door. If you need me just pound on the wall."

"Would you come if I did?"

She'd looked at him impassively, then shut the door firmly behind her.

She hadn't left him totally alone, however. Lobo was still stretched out on the floor beside the bed, where he'd fallen asleep last night long before Adam had. The collie's injured front leg was swathed in a dirty-white bandage, but his tail was drumming steadily against the worn carpet.

"Knock off the noise," Adam warned, "before you get us thrown out of this high-class place."

Lobo yawned, and his tail continued to thump. He'd been petted and fussed over more in the past few days than in all the rest of his life put together, and he liked it. Adam couldn't blame him, especially when it was Ellie doing the petting and fussing.

They both owed her a lot. When Adam had opened his eyes and seen her leaning over him in the rocky burrow under the cedars, it was like seeing an angel. And when she'd lifted his dizzy head and cradled it in the softness of her arms, he'd thought he was in heaven for sure.

He closed his eyes, letting his thoughts drift back.

Every bone and muscle in Adam's body had protested as Señor Velasco's Chevrolet bumped and bounced toward Leakey on the afternoon following the air attack. Even as weak and groggy as he was, it was all Adam could do to keep from moaning out loud. He and the car were a perfect match, he'd thought – both black and blue.

"It doesn't make any sense going all the way to town," he mumbled. "We could've been at my place in ten minutes or less."

"It *does* make sense, and if your brain wasn't scrambled, you'd know it," Ellie told him, keeping her eyes on the road. "You need a doctor, and so does Lobo. And what about your father? He'd have another heart attack if he saw you like this."

"Are you saying I don't look so hot?" He tried to laugh, but it hurt too much.

"You look terrible," she said, "but I think you'll live."

Less than an hour later, the doctor had pretty much confirmed her diagnosis. Adam had a moderate concussion, a cracked rib, a dislocated right index finger, and cuts in his scalp that took a total of ten stitches to close. He also had a half-dozen grenade fragments embedded in him from his shoulders to his thighs, including a pair of small ones just above his damaged knees, plus three loose teeth and various scrapes and bruises. None of the injuries was life-threatening, but in combination they left him feeling more dead than alive. After Doc Kendall had patched him up, it took all the energy Ellie could muster to put him to bed in the spare room behind the Mercado Velasco.

"I really should go home," he groaned. "I don't think your Mama and Papa understand what I'm doing here."

"I'll explain it to them," Ellie said. "I'll explain it to your parents, too. I don't know what I'll tell them, but I'll think of something."

"The truck . . ." He was so tired his mouth wouldn't work anymore.

"I'll ask Jake Hernandez to see if it can be fixed and get it towed to Klinger's Garage if it can. Go to sleep. I've got to go to the vet's office and check on Lobo."

He'd felt her fingers touch the side of his face and tried to say something else, but his tongue was thick and everything around him was spinning and fuzzy. He'd felt nothing else for close to thirteen hours.

When he'd awakened, Ellie was sitting beside his bed, reading a book. Raising his head to look at her made everything about him hurt, and it had been hard to focus his eyes, but he was glad he'd looked anyway. It had been like that first afternoon at the school when he'd come into her room unnoticed – as if he could see inside her for a few seconds.

She'd finally glanced up and caught him watching her.

"*Buenas dias*," he said.

She'd smiled. "I'm afraid it's *buenas tardes* again. It's almost two in the afternoon."

"God, you mean I've been asleep all this time? How's Lobo?"

"His foreleg's broken, like you thought. The vet cleaned the wound and splinted it. He'll be fine. How do you feel?"

"Sore as hell all over. What about my folks? Did you tell 'em what happened?"

"Of course not," she said. "I told them you had an accident in the truck, but nothing about you being hurt. I said you were staying in town till the truck's fixed, and you sent me to pick up some clothes and things."

"That didn't strike them as odd?"

"Probably, but they didn't say anything about it. The truck *can* be fixed, by the way, but it'll take up to a week to get all the parts. I told Jake what really happened, but I made him promise not to let anybody know where you are. They're bound to figure out sooner or later you're not dead, but they might not think to look for you here."

"You think they'll try it again?"

She looked at him as if he were a pupil with a severe learning disability. "I *know* they will if they get a chance. Next time, they may do a better job."

"Then you've been taking one helluva risk running back and forth between town and the farm on my account. I can't let you do that anymore."

"I don't remember asking your permission. Besides, I don't think they know who I am – not yet, anyway. The ones who came to the store don't have any way of connecting me with you, and Kurt's fence-rider may have recognized you, but he never saw me before. As far as he knows, the woman at the fence was just another *chiquita*.."

"But people have seen us together in town," he protested. "Stuff like that has a way of getting around. I don't want anything to happen to you."

"I can take care of myself. You're still safer here than you would be at home. That's the important thing."

His eyes met hers and clung to them. "How about coming over here for a minute?" He patted the mattress beside him.

She closed her book and placed it carefully in her chair. Her hair swirled loosely around her as she moved, its blackness framing her face and spilling down over her white peasant blouse. He could see stray wisps of it against the coffee-and-cream contours of her neck and shoulders. Her eyelashes fluttered as she sat on the bed.

Her fingers touched the stitches in his chin. "What is it?"

He found her hand with his. "You saved my hide out there yesterday. Thanks."

"I owed you one," she said, bending toward him.

It seemed wholly natural when he drew her down to him and kissed her, and just as natural when she returned his kiss. It was spontaneous and easy – not like something they'd never done before. It lasted maybe five seconds, then it was over. She pulled away and stood up, and the kiss evaporated like a puff of smoke. So far, it hadn't happened again.

Afterward, she'd cared for him as diligently as ever, but she'd also held him at arm's length. She'd brought him his meals and pills, tidied his room and made his bed. Over his objections, she'd even washed his clothes. But in the midst of all this, she'd retreated behind an invisible wall and taken her emotions with her. On the rare occasions when she met his gaze, her eyes held a veiled warning. *Don't push it*, they said. So he hadn't.

On the morning after the kiss, Ellie was sitting under the portico and drinking a cup of Mama's strong coffee when she saw the car pull in. Papa had just declared the store open for business, and Mama was baking bread in the kitchen. Adam was still in bed, but Ellie had awakened before daylight, her mind too full of worries for sleep.

The car was a late-model Dodge that she didn't recognize, and she tensed slightly. Then she saw Jake Hernandez open the door on the driver's side, and the tension eased. But when Adam's father got out on the other side, the tension came right back. George Wagner looked drawn and pale as he pulled himself slowly erect while Jake hovered uneasily at his elbow.

"Mornin', ma'am," the old man said. "I'd like to have a word with Adam if you don't mind."

"Come and sit down, Mr. Wagner," she offered. "I'll go find him for you."

Just then, Adam pushed open the screen door and stepped outside. He was barefoot, wearing jeans and a unbuttoned plaid shirt that revealed the bandage around his ribs. His hair was tousled and he had a heavy stubble of beard. Ellie cringed when she saw him.

"Hello, Pa," Adam said. "What's the matter?"

The old man stared at his son and shook his head. "What the Sam Hill happened to you, boy? You look like somethin' the buzzards wouldn't touch."

"I got in a little scrape, Pa. It's nothing for you to worry about. The Velascos are letting me use their spare room while I'm waiting on the truck. I just felt like I, uh, needed a little vacation from the farm, that's all."

His father nodded. "Yeah, you look like you *could* use a few days' rest."

"Well, what'd you come all the way into town for? You don't need to be breathing all that road dust and bouncing around. Doc Kendall says it's real bad for you."

"I got Jake to bring me in early before it got hot," the old man said. "I wanted to make sure you were still in one piece. Your Ma's been fret-tin' about you ever since Saturday. I told her you're a grown man and you can do as you damn please. But I got worried, too, when Kurt Radke came to the house lookin' for you."

Ellie had been standing to one side, trying not to intrude. But when she heard the reference to Kurt, questions began jumping from her lips before she could stop them. "How long ago did this happen? What did Kurt say?"

"He came by last night," said George Wagner. "Him and a couple other fellers I didn't recognize. Said he needed to talk to you about some-thin', some kind of problem with trespassers. He acted like he thought I was lyin' when I said you weren't there. 'Course he didn't have the guts to come right out and say it."

"Where'd you tell him I was?" Adam asked.

His father shrugged. "I knew you hadn't had any dealin's with Kurt in years, and somethin' about the whole thing just didn't seem right. I told him you'd gone fishin' for a few days someplace over on the Guadalupe."

Adam smiled. "What else did he say?"

"Wanted to know were you upset about Julio gettin' killed. I said, 'Yeah, some.' Asked me if you had a steady girlfriend. I said, 'Not as

I know of.' Asked me how old Julio's little sister Rosita was. I said, 'Thirteen, why?' He said, 'I was just wonderin'.'"

Ellie felt a strange, crawling sensation between her shoulder blades. "He's trying to figure out who was with you that night at the fence," she told Adam softly.

Adam's father looked puzzled. "Are you in some kind of trouble, son?"

"Not as much as I could be," Adam said. "Did Kurt say anything else?"

"Yeah, he wanted to know if we'd ever had a telephone put in at the house. I said, 'Hell no, I can't stand those janglin' things.' He said he heard you'd been makin' lots of long-distance calls lately, and he thought it'd be a lot simpler if you could make 'em from home."

Ellie caught her breath sharply. She knew how many hours Adam had spent at the telephone company trying to get through to Washington. She also knew what a notorious snoop and gossip JoNell Joiner was. But until now, she'd never realized what a potentially deadly combination that could be.

She touched Adam's arm. "I've got a very bad feeling about this," she whispered.

"So do I," he said. "What do you think we ought to do about it?"

"Get away from here as fast as we can," she said, "while both of us are still able."

TWENTY-THREE

Uvalde, Texas
June 4, 1936

The past twenty-four hours had been a whirlwind of confusion and urgency.

Deciding on a primary destination had been easy enough. Of the four roads leading out of Leakey, three were dead-ends. Basically, the rest of the country was accessible by automobile only through Uvalde, where Adam and Ellie had been bound, anyway, when disaster intervened. The larger town wasn't far enough away to be totally safe or big enough to lose themselves in, but it was at least outside Kurt Radke's immediate domain.

Beyond that, though, nothing had been simple. Doing everything that had to be done had consumed an entire day and become an exercise in tension verging on panic. Adam had ridden back to the Wagner farm with Jake and his father, despite Ellie's pointed reminders of how close he'd already come to dying on that road. In the end, three key factors had made him go anyway.

First, there was the matter of money. For five years he'd been saving something from each month's wages with the vague idea of needing it one day for something. He'd never gotten around to opening a bank account, but his nestegg of close to $1,000 was in a tin box in the top of his closet, and it was time to make a major withdrawal.

Second, unless they planned to hitchhike, he had to retrieve his Model A roadster from the farm. Adam wouldn't have taken Ramon Velasco's treasured little Chevy on the frantic trip that lay ahead even if Ramon had volunteered it. Meanwhile, what was left of the farm truck was confined indefinitely to Klinger's Garage, and it was pointless even to think about asking to borrow Pa's Dodge. Unless an affordable later model car could be located for sale along the way, the Model A was his only alternative.

Third, Adam had to reassure his parents – without actually providing them very much information – that everything was going to be okay. This would be easier without Ellie being there to whet their curiosity about how she fit into this clouded picture. In the interim, Ellie would also have some private time to explain to her own parents that she wasn't merely running off with a gringo – at least not in the usual sense.

They were bound to each other now by events beyond their control and a secret almost too earthshaking to comprehend. They were the only two people on earth – outside of the plotters themselves – who knew that a lethal trap was being laid for the President of the United States. But something else was also drawing them together. Adam could feel it, and he thought Ellie could, too. He'd longed to nurture and explore it – but there was no time.

Their last stop on the way out of town that afternoon had been Klinger's Garage. The German Luger from the stock pond was still wrapped in a towel under the front seat of the battered truck, and Adam had remembered it at the last minute. They could ill afford to leave the pistol behind. Except for the wounds on his and Lobo's bodies, it was still their only tangible evidence of the Nazi plot.

Adam stared with unveiled disgust at his image in the mirror of the room at the Leona Motor Courts on the morning after their arrival in Uvalde. "You look like a damn scarecrow," he told the image.

The long night's sleep had done him good, however. He was still stiff and raw in spots, but the exhaustion and pervasive sore-as-a-boil feeling were less intense. The stitches in his scalp were hardly noticeable, and his bruises were starting to turn from dark blue to yellow. He was going to be okay, but considering his appearance, it was small wonder that Ellie had insisted on checking into the motel separately last night.

He found his safety razor and got rid of his stubby whiskers. Their abrupt absence made an ugly scratch on his chin stand out more vividly, but at least the rest of his face looked somewhat human, and after letting the spray from the shower pound down on him for two or three minutes, he felt considerably refreshed. He'd just finished drying off and pulling on a clean pair of jeans when he heard a knock on the outside door.

"Just a second," he said.

Before he could finish buttoning his shirt, the knocking came again, more insistent this time, and he could hear Ellie's voice:

"Hurry up, Adam. I've got something to show you."

When he first opened the door, he didn't even notice the newspaper she was holding. For a few seconds, all he could do was stare at her. She was wearing a form-fitting gray dress that he'd never seen before and a red silk scarf tied around her neck. Her hair seemed darker than ever, her eyes larger and brighter.

"You look very nice," she said. "I'm glad you finally shaved."

"You, uh, look good, too." He felt tongue-tied.

"You must be feeling better. May I come in?"

He stepped clumsily aside, awed by her closeness and almost overwhelmed by the feelings surging inside him. Ellie didn't seem to notice. She brushed lightly past him and sat on the bed, spreading the newspaper out on the rumpled bedclothes. It was a copy of the *San Antonio Express* – not yesterday's or last week's edition but dated this very morning and no more than seven or eight hours off the press.

"Look at this," she said. "It's what we've been waiting for."

He eased down next to her and looked over her shoulder. The smell of her hair was distracting, but he forced his eyes to follow her pointing finger to an article under a small headline in the middle of Page One:

☆☆☆☆☆☆☆☆☆☆☆☆☆☆☆☆☆☆☆☆☆☆☆☆☆☆☆☆☆☆☆☆

WASHINGTON, June 3 (UP) – President Roosevelt Wednesday denied reports he would meet Mexican President Lazaro Cardenas at the border during his Texas trip next week. He explained that the itinerary for the trip was all set and that he would go no nearer the border than San Antonio.

"The President is interested in conferring with President Cardenas at an early date about matters of mutual interest to our two nations," said White House spokesman Stephen T. Early. "But regretfully, their schedules will not permit a meeting on this upcoming trip."

☆☆☆☆☆☆☆☆☆☆☆☆☆☆☆☆☆☆☆☆☆☆☆☆☆☆☆☆☆☆☆☆

Ellie's face was close to Adam's as she watched him read, and it took an all-out effort for him to concentrate on the significance of the article. "Well, for whatever it's worth," he said, "I guess we don't have to worry about Laredo anymore."

"But what will the Nazis do?" she asked. "Is there a chance they might just forget the whole thing now that the President's not going to the border?"

"Don't bet on it," he said. "They went to too much trouble to give up that easily. They mentioned San Antonio and Dallas, too. They're bound to try it somewhere else."

"So what are we supposed to do now?" Her breath was warm on his face, and she was tantalizingly close. "Is there any way we can keep it from happening?"

His insides were like jelly. Her lips were only inches away. He couldn't stand it another second. "None that I can think of," he said and kissed her.

This kiss lasted longer than the first one, and there was infinitely more to it. Her arms came up around his neck, and they sank slowly backward onto the bed. They were both breathing hard when they finally came up for air.

She looked up at him. "That's not what I meant," she said quietly.

"I know, but I just couldn't get focused on that other stuff right then. I still don't want to think about it." His lips moved across her face, then aimed for her mouth again. "I don't want to think about anything but you."

"But we have to think about 'that other stuff,'" she said, pressing her fingertips firmly against his lips to keep them from meeting her own. "We can't just close our eyes and let these people kill President Roosevelt. We've got to try to stop them."

"But can't it wait a while? Can't we just stay here the rest of the morning?"

For maybe twenty seconds, she lay silent and perfectly still. He didn't know if she was considering his suggestion or if she hadn't heard it. Then she rolled over in the opposite direction and sat up.

She kept her eyes averted. "I'm just not ready for that, Adam. I don't know if I'll ever be ready."

He forced a smile. It took a lot of effort. "I'll wait," he said.

She chewed her lip for a second, then met his eyes. "Suit yourself. Meanwhile, what do we do about Kurt and his friends?"

With intense reluctance, he loosened his mental grip on what had just happened between them. He didn't know what had shattered the moment, but it was obviously over. Now he had no choice but to confront the enormity of Ellie's question.

He shrugged. "I guess we go get a bunch of quarters and find ourselves a pay phone. Sound like fun?"

"You're going to try calling the Secret Service again?"

He frowned thoughtfully. "I kind of struck out with them before. Maybe I'll try the FBI this time."

TWENTY-FOUR

FBI Headquarters, Washington
June 4, 1936

Helen Gandy pushed open the heavy door without knocking and stepped quietly into the opulent eight-sided inner office of the Director of the Federal Bureau of Investigation. Her boss, J. Edgar Hoover, was sitting alone at his massive mahogany desk in the center of the richly appointed chamber, framed by two American flags on ornate brass standards. At the moment, he seemed deeply engrossed in something he was writing in a large notebook, but Helen knew that in just over an hour, regardless of what business might be at hand, Hoover would stand up, remove the carnation from the lapel of his cream-colored jacket, and toss it into the trash. Then he'd put on his jaunty straw hat and go to lunch at the Mayflower Hotel with Assistant Director Clyde Tolson. It was a ritual that never varied..

"There's a long-distance call on line two that I thought you might want to take personally." Helen's soft, well-modulated tones produced a slight echo in the room.

"Is it somebody important?" Hoover glanced up with a mildly curious expression on his pudgy face.

Relatively few people realized it, but Helen Gandy was one of the most influential women in the entire Department of Justice. She'd been Hoover's confidential secretary ever since his appointment as director twelve years ago, and she'd worked for him even longer than that. No one at Bureau headquarters had more pull with the Director than she did. If she said a call was worth his attention, he listened.

"No, Jay-ee," she said, "just somebody I think you might find very interesting."

In private, Helen still sometimes called the world's most famous G-man by the nickname he'd used when they first met in the fall of 1918, when both were obscure young employees in the government's War Emergency Division. No one in today's Bureau was aware that they'd even dated briefly. Helen had been a strikingly pretty twenty-one-year-old when Hoover first asked her out, and she was still trim and attractive at thirty-nine, but that had no bearing on her special relationship with the chief of the FBI. As she'd long ago realized, Hoover didn't care for women in "that way." It was her efficiency, perceptiveness and unquestionable loyalty that he valued.

He trusted her implicitly. And because of this trust, Helen was among a select inner circle of confidants who knew how much Hoover wanted to be President of the United States.

"It's a gentleman calling from Uvalde, Texas," she said. "He claims he has information about an assassination plot against Mr. Roosevelt."

Hoover pursed his lips in thought and closed the notebook. "Hmm, Uvalde," he mused. "That's the Vice President's hometown, isn't it?"

"Yes, I believe so."

"Did the caller say anything about the Vice President in relation to this plot?"

"No, he didn't mention Mr. Garner," she said. "He says German spies plan to kill the President when he comes to Texas next week."

Earlier in the spring, when the Republicans had seemed stalemated in their efforts to find a strong contender to face FDR, Hoover had envisioned himself being drafted as their party's nominee. Helen knew how much that vision pleased her boss.

By supplying Roosevelt with political intelligence, Hoover had succeeded in worming himself into the President's confidence. As a result, FBI authority to snoop on public figures had expanded significantly. But as Helen and a few others knew, Hoover actually loathed FDR and "his liberal crew" as "a dangerous bunch of Reds." Emboldened by a survey showing him to be the second most popular man in America (with Roosevelt a distant seventh), Hoover was convinced that if he ever got the opportunity, he could unseat FDR.

"I wonder if the caller's a policeman," Hoover said. "How else would he come up with information like this?"

Hoover firmly believed that the support of the nation's law enforcement community could propel him into the White House. That spring, he'd sent a corps of trusted veteran FBI agents out on a secret mission to drum up support for his candidacy among federal, state, city and county law officers. He especially wanted to test the waters in the South and Southwest, where he felt he was most admired. This was the main reason Helen had agreed to talk to the long-distance caller in the first place. Hoover had been disappointed in the level of support his agents found, but a plot against Roosevelt could strengthen Hoover's hand in a variety of ways.

"No, he says he's a sheep farmer named Adam Wagner," she said. "But he sounds sane and sincere, and I've got a feeling that what he claims to know could be important to national security." She paused and looked squarely into her boss's eyes. "It could also prove very useful to you personally."

Hoover nodded. "All right, you can put the call through to me," he said. "But use the surveillance line and make sure the recorder's switched on."

Two minutes later, the phone on the mahogany desk rang, and Hoover sighed and lifted the receiver. He hated being bothered by insignificant people, but perhaps Helen was right about this one. This could be something worth listening to even if the caller was a nobody. Helen had a good feel for things like that.

"Good morning, Mr. Wagner," he said. "This is J. Edgar Hoover."

"Hello, Mr. Hoover," a low masculine voice responded. "I really appreciate you taking the time to talk to me."

"It's always my pleasure to hear from a concerned citizen," the Director said. "My secretary says you have information on some sort of plot against the President. That's very serious business, Mr. Wagner. Are you one hundred percent sure about this?"

"Well, at least ninety-five percent sure," the voice said. "I know that five Nazi agents are hiding out on a ranch near Leakey, Texas. I overheard them talking about assassinating Roosevelt. The owner of the ranch is mixed up in this thing, too."

"How were you able to learn all this, Mr. Wagner?"

"A young Mexican boy who worked for me was murdered last month. I got suspicious when I spotted these strange men on the ranch next to my farm. I just started nosing around."

"I understand you're calling from Uvalde, Texas," Hoover said. "Are you acquainted with Vice President Garner?"

"Not personally, sir. Naturally, I know who he is."

Hoover paused as he mentally reviewed his next sentence. "Surely, there's no connection between these men and anyone associated with Mr. Garner," he said.

The caller also hesitated briefly. "Well, come to think of it, this rancher I mentioned, Kurt Radke, *is* a big Garner supporter. I hear he contributed a bundle to Garner's campaign against Roosevelt for the '32 nomination."

"I see," Hoover said, leaning forward in his chair. "What else can you tell me about this Mr. Radke?"

All told, the conversation went on for about ten minutes. The longer it lasted, the more intrigued Hoover became. By the time it was over, he was as excited as he'd been in weeks. The part about the would-be assassins being Gestapo agents from Germany sounded utterly absurd, and even if there was a grain of truth to it, it would be disastrous if even a hint of it should reach the public. Communists or even pro-Soviet American liberals would be different, but Hoover had no desire to pick fights with the Nazis, either in Germany or the U.S. – at least not right now.

Even so, if a major Garner supporter was implicated in a plot to kill Roosevelt, that would be dynamite. Dear God, if only he'd gotten wind of this a few months ago, it could have changed everything. If he'd known, the Republicans might well be nominating *him* next week, instead of that insipid fool from Kansas. Yet there was still much that could be done with information like this. The Director would have to be very cautious with it, but the possibilities were virtually endless.

"You've done a great patriotic service, Mr. Wagner," he assured the man on the phone. "I can't thank you enough. Rest assured that the FBI will take it from here."

The moment he hung up, Hoover buzzed Helen Gandy on the intercom.

"Send Clyde Tolson in here immediately," he said. "And bring the recording of that call to me. I want to file it personally for safekeeping."

He'd decided to have an agent sent out from the San Antonio field office to do some discreet checking in this place called Reál County, Texas. The agent could talk with the local sheriff to find out more about rancher Radke and his ties to Garner. It would also be good to learn more about this Adam Wagner. At some point, it might become necessary to make sure Mr. Wagner never made any more phone calls.

As for as the so-called assassins, Hoover had no intention of trying to impede them, much less arrest them. If they should succeed in their plot against Roosevelt, it could only strengthen Hoover's position – especially if Garner could be linked to the crime.

The Director smiled. It was as if a veritable gold mine of material for political sabotage had just dropped into his lap out of the blue. Information like this meant power, pure and simple.

Under the circumstances, of course, the last thing on earth he planned to do was notify the Secret Service.

TWENTY-FIVE

Uvalde, Texas
June 5, 1936

Adam's chest was tight with eager tension as he knocked on Ellie's door shortly before 6:30 a.m.. The eastern sky was a brilliant pink above the green-and-red neon motel sign, and it was still pleasantly cool, but the hint of dampness in the air would burn away quickly once the sun was up.

He was five minutes early but too impatient to wait any longer. He'd already been awake for over an hour, and it was remarkable that he managed to sleep at all with Ellie so close, yet so far away.

When she opened the door and peered out at him, his throat went dry. She'd obviously just gotten out of bed. Her long hair was tangled, her eyes heavy-lidded, her face soft and childlike. The scent of her was sensual and sweet.

"I'm sorry," she mumbled. "I overslept. Can you give me about ten minutes?"

He stared at her silently for a moment, unable to speak for fear of blurting out what was racing through his brain. *Ten minutes wouldn't even get me started, lady. Maybe ten hours. Or ten days. Or . . .*

He shook himself. "Sure," he said, "I'll go down to the coffee shop and get us a couple of cups while you get ready."

She stifled a yawn. "Thanks. I'll hurry."

The day just past seemed both unreal and euphoric. They'd lunched without incident at the Elite Cafe, pored over a Texas roadmap, exercised Lobo, and taken target practice with the .30-30 in the countryside south of town. Then they'd stayed up late, reading about the Roosevelts, the New Deal, the Nazi Party, and the Texas Centennial in a pile of newspapers and magazines from the big newsstand on East Main Street.

"I think President Roosevelt's a very courageous man," Ellie remarked at one point, "but it's his wife I really idolize. She's influenced him to do more for equal rights than any President we ever had."

"Personally, I'm not that taken with his politics," Adam said. "But he makes a damn good speech, and I guess he's doing his best. The point is, he's the President, and he deserves some respect, whether you like him or not."

Ellie was intrigued by a long article in the *Dallas Morning News* on the wonders of the Centennial Exposition. "They have air-conditioned buildings where it stays seventy-two degrees all the time," she said. "And hundreds of shows and exhibits, and millions of lights, and every kind of new gadget you can imagine – like taking a trip into the future."

Adam glanced up from a *Collier's* article on the new German army. "They got a roller-coaster?" he asked.

"One of the biggest in the world," she said. "Fan dancers and strip-teasers, too. I'm sure you'd like that."

"I can hardly wait," he said.

Mostly, though, their conversations tended toward the serious, even when they weren't talking about FDR and the Nazis.

"I had job offers from three other school districts," Ellie confided, "but I felt like I had to come back to Leakey. Maybe not forever, but for a while. I wanted to do something for my people, but that wasn't the only reason. I had to prove something to myself, too."

"It was different for me," he said. "I never really wanted to come home after the war – not to stay, anyway. I wanted to see interesting places and do interesting things and be part of something bigger than Réal County."

"Wasn't the war big enough for you?"

"It was too big, and all it ever did for me was swing me back and forth between hysteria and boredom. I wanted a different kind of excitement, – the kind that revs you up without making you bleed. Then Pa got sick, and that was that. When you get right down to it, I guess most people end up doing what they're *supposed* to do, not what they want to do."

"I've always believed fate had something to do with things like that," she said.

Their eyes met for a second. "Maybe so. Anyway, I'm glad you came back."

She smiled and looked away.

❋

In the midst of all this, Adam began to grow uneasy again. As far as he could tell, the feeling was totally unrelated to his developing closeness with Ellie.

Something about his telephone conversation with J. Edgar Hoover gnawed at his mind and put him on edge. No patriotic citizen should be expected to do more than he'd already done, Adam thought. He'd given every shred of information he had to the top man in the whole FBI, and it was up to the feds now. Hell, they probably dealt with stuff like this every week at the FBI. So why was he still agonizing about it?

After talking to Hoover himself, Adam had been both awed and reassured. It was incredible to think that an ordinary sheep farmer from Réal County, Texas, could speak personally to one of the most famous, powerful men in America. But in the hours since, some troubling questions had eaten away at Adam's confidence.

What steps would the FBI take to protect Roosevelt? Would the presidential trip be summarily cancelled? Would federal agents – or even troops – swoop down on the Radke Ranch and arrest Kurt and his five visitors? What exactly had Hoover meant when he said the FBI would "take it from here"?

Insinuating little doubts gradually grew into larger ones. How could Adam be sure the situation was really under control? What if Hoover hadn't actually taken him seriously? What if Hoover's seeming receptiveness was only an act? What if he'd written the whole thing off as a crank call? On the surface, there was no reason to think so, but the more Adam replayed the conversation in his head, the more it seemed a little too easy. Too pat. In his experience, nothing in real life ever worked out that simply.

When he came back from the coffee shop carrying two soggy paper cups, Ellie was waiting on the steps outside her room. She had on a dark, full skirt and a low-necked red blouse. Her hair was braided in two long pigtails that made her look more girlish than usual. It reminded him of the way she'd looked that night long ago in the back seat of the fancy Cadillac when all the trouble had happened with Kurt.

"That was quick," he said, handing her one of the cups. "You ready?"

"Whenever you are," she said. He really liked the way that sounded.

❋

The newsstand wasn't open yet when they got there, but within a couple of minutes after Adam parked by the curb, a truck came by and dropped off a bundle of copies of the *San Antonio Express*.

Yesterday morning, they'd waited impatiently until 7 a.m. for the proprietor to show up and sell them a paper. Today they didn't bother with formalities. As soon as the bundle hit the sidewalk, Adam was out of the car. He cut the cord around the bundle with his pocket knife, left a dime on top of the stack, and he and Ellie each took a paper back to the car.

Yesterday, there'd been a maddening absence of news about FDR and not a word in the paper about his upcoming schedule. But today they had no trouble finding out exactly what the President was doing. Ironically, he was getting ready to go a funeral.

A bold headline across the top of the front page told of the sudden death of Speaker of the House Joseph W. Byrns, the Tennessee congressman who'd replaced John Nance Garner in the third most powerful position in Washington. Byrns had died yesterday morning a few hours after suffering a heart attack. His death was described as "wholly unexpected." Just below the main banner, a smaller headline noted:

President Will Attend
Speaker Byrns' Rites
In Nashville Saturday

"Maybe this means he isn't coming to Texas, after all," Ellie suggested. "Maybe he'll call the whole thing off because of this."

Adam read on silently for a minute. Then he shook his head.

"No such luck," he said. "The last paragraph says: 'Roosevelt will arrive back in Washington early Sunday morning, only about thirty hours before he is scheduled to leave again on a week-long, 4,000-mile train trip to Arkansas, Texas and Indiana.' He's still coming, all right."

"But why?" she demanded. "Even if he didn't want anybody to know he's in danger, this would be a perfect excuse to cancel the Texas trip. The FBI must have explained everything to him by now. Why doesn't he listen?"

Adam folded his paper and flopped his head back against the car seat. "All I know is that Mr. Hoover said the FBI would take care of it. Those G-men know a lot more about this kind of thing than we do. They're bound to know what they're doing."

Their eyes met over the edge of her newspaper. "Then why are you so worried about it?" she asked. "And why am I?"

As usual, the food at the Casita Blanca was cheap, plentiful and good, but Adam seemed to have lost his appetite. He barely finished half his enchiladas while drinking two bottles of Pearl beer – something he almost never did in the middle of the day. The beer did nothing to lighten his mood, but it gave him the resolve to do something he'd been thinking about ever since yesterday.

Ellie was still working on her flautas when he folded his napkin and pushed his chair back. She lowered her fork and looked at him.

"Is something wrong?"

"I'm going to call the Sheriff's Office in Leakey," he said. "If nothing's happening in Washington, maybe something's going on over there. I've got to find out."

She shook her head. "I don't think that's a good idea. It's just asking for trouble. Besides, why would the Sheriff tell you anything, anyway?"

"Streicher and I have known each other for a long time. If he's onto something and I catch him by surprise, maybe he'll let it slip." Adam leaned forward and lowered his voice. "Look, I can't see but two ways the FBI can deal with this thing. They can scratch the trip and keep Roosevelt out of harm's way – which they obviously aren't doing so far. Or they can remove the danger by going in and breaking up that rat's nest on the Radke Ranch. That seems a lot more logical when you stop to think about it."

She frowned. "Yes, I guess it does, but–"

"I don't think they'd make a move like that without letting the local Sheriff know. They'd probably do it as a courtesy, even if they didn't think they needed his help."

"But you can't trust Streicher," Ellie said. "He might run straight to Kurt and tip him off to the whole thing."

"It's a possibility," Adam said, "but somehow I just can't see Streicher ratting out to a screw worm like Kurt – not about something like this. Deep down, I think Sarge is a better man than that." He dug in his pants pocket and came up with a handful of change for the pay phone in the restaurant lobby. "Anyhow, I've got to make the call. There's no other way."

Ellie eyed him curiously. "What if the FBI does catch the Nazis? Does that mean we just go home and forget the whole mess? Does everything just suddenly go back like it was before all this started?"

For a long moment, he was too lost in his own thoughts to attempt an answer.

"Not a chance," he said finally. "No matter what happens from here on, I know I'll never be the same again."

TWENTY-SIX

Real County, Texas
June 5, 1936

Chief Deputy Luke Bodine had spent most of the morning trying to stay out of his boss's way. Luke had worked for Wilfred Streicher for nearly eight years, and ordinarily, they got along fine. But once in a blue moon, the Sheriff got some kind of burr under his saddle, and then look out! When it happened, Streicher tended to withdraw to the sanctity of his private office where he would first pace the floor, kicking at any object that got in his way, then sitting at his desk, glowering out the window and swearing audibly at frequent intervals.

The Sheriff was tough to deal with when he got that way. Saying anything to him while he was in this frame of mind – anything at all – could be like throwing gasoline on a brushfire. Sometimes the mood lasted a few minutes, sometimes all day, and once Luke remembered it stretching from a Monday morning to a Thursday afternoon. This time, though, he was afraid the Sheriff might be headed for a new record.

Streicher's mood had turned sour early in the week, right after Kurt Radke stormed in and raised hell because Adam Wagner hadn't been found and arrested yet. Kurt had sworn out a complaint against Wagner for criminal trespass and assaulting a Radke fence-rider, then warned the Sheriff and Luke to "catch the bastard or else."

So far, though, they hadn't found hide nor hair of Wagner, a fact that had already left the Sheriff as nettled as a pig in a cactus patch when the smart-aleck G-man in the pinstriped suit had shown up expectedly at the office yesterday afternoon.

"I'm Special Agent Pierce Larkin from the FBI field office in San Antonio." The man's accent branded him immediately as a damyankee. That was bad enough to start with, and it quickly got worse. "This isn't a courtesy call, Sheriff. I've been ordered by the Bureau's highest authority to carry out an official inquiry here. I want to ask you some questions, and I expect straight answers."

Larkin handed the Sheriff a small, white business card with well-manicured fingers, then parked his ample butt on a chair without being invited. Luke could tell the Sheriff didn't cotton much to the stranger's manners. The Sheriff liked to be the one asking the questions. He for sure didn't like being the one they were aimed at.

"It's a free country, I reckon." Streicher said. "At least it used to be. Ask whatever you want. Then we'll see if I feel like answering it."

Larkin took a pipe and tobacco pouch from his inside coat pocket, filled the pipe carefully, then struck a match and puffed vigorously, exhaling a cloud of Prince Albert fumes.

"You don't mind if I smoke, do you?"

"Not if you can ask your questions and smoke at the same time," the Sheriff said. "I don't have all day. What brings you to my county?"

"Are you acquainted with a man named Kurt Radke?"

"Sure I am. So's everybody in the county. Mr. Radke owns the biggest ranch in these parts. Not a finer man in the State of Texas in my opinion."

"And just how long have you known Mr. Radke, Sheriff?"

"I've known him all his life – thirty-some years – and his father before him. The Radkes helped settle this county. What's this all about, anyway?"

Larkin gazed calmly at the Sheriff. "Our headquarters in Washington got a report that some suspicious men are staying on Radke's ranch. Our informant says they're heavily armed and may be German aliens engaged in a clandestine espionage mission. I don't suppose you'd happen to know anything about this, would you?"

Luke had been watching and listening, and when he saw the expression on the Sheriff's face, he sensed that a thunderbolt was about to strike. He quickly found something to do in the next room, but he could still hear every word of the conversation.

"Well, your informant's full of shit," the Sheriff said. "Those men are wool buyers from Pennsylvania, and they've been guests on the Radke Ranch for the past couple of weeks. Mr. Radke's one of the biggest wool and mohair producers in the whole country, and they've been doing some business together. There's nothing secret about that."

"You're a hundred percent certain of this?"

"Hell, yes. I've met some of these men and talked to 'em. They're as American as you are – maybe more so. And I don't appreciate you federal men poking around my county and harassing innocent citizens, either. For your information, Kurt Radke's a close personal friend of John Nance Garner. And I don't think the Vice President would take too kindly to accusations like these."

Larkin puffed steadily on his pipe and returned Streicher's glare without blinking. "The FBI isn't intimidated by name-dropping, Sheriff. I have my instructions and I plan to follow them. Our information says these men are heavily armed with high-powered weapons. Do you know anything about that?"

"Everybody in this part of the country keeps a gun handy if they've got any sense, mister." Streicher paused and raked the agent with his eyes. "Around here, you never know when you'll run into a rattlesnake or a coyoté or some other varmint. Could be they've been doing a little deer hunting out at the ranch. Is there some federal law against that now?"

"No," said Larkin evenly, "but this is June, not November. Doesn't the State of Texas have something to say about shooting deer out of season?"

"I'm not a game warden," said Streicher, "but it's usually the landowner's prerogative if he wants to thin out an over-population of game during the off-season. It's shaping up as a dry summer. If there's a short acorn crop, a good many deer could starve to death on the hoof before fall."

"Well, so much for the wildlife outlook," Larkin said testily. "My main concern right now is Mr. Radke and his guests. Can you give me your word as a fellow law officer that these men aren't mixed up in any type of criminal activity?"

"Damned right I can – and I do. So why don't you just get out of my hair and go on back where you belong?"

Larkin stood up slowly. He tapped out his pipe in the large glass ashtray on Streicher's desk, then brushed at a fleck of ash on the sleeve of his coat.

"That's exactly what I plan to do, Sheriff." He turned toward the door, then looked back at Streicher. "But before I go, I want to make one thing crystal clear. If you're mistaken about these men – or if you aren't telling me the whole truth about them – I'll be back, and the next time I come, I'll bring plenty of company with me. If you haven't enjoyed my visit today, you'll really hate the next one. I guarantee it."

Streicher stood up, slowly balling and unballing his large fists. His right hand touched the .45 revolver at his hip. He didn't say anything, but his face was the shade of a ripe chili pepper.

In the adjoining room, Luke Bodine watched the FBI agent stride briskly past him and into the hallway, where his footfalls echoed for a moment, then faded away.

Seconds later, Luke heard the first loud crash from the Sheriff's office.

❋

It was about 1:30 on Friday afternoon when the phone on Luke's desk rang. He caught it quickly, halfway into the second ring, knowing how irritating the noise would be to his boss. The Sheriff had eaten a sack lunch in his inner office, and except for asking Luke to go across the street and get him a Dr. Pepper to drink with his sandwich, he hadn't said three words in the past two hours.

"Sheriff's Department, Deputy Bodine."

"I need to talk to Streicher." The male voice was audible enough, but it had a far-away sound that indicated the call was long-distance. "It's important."

"He's, uh, kinda tied up right now," Luke said, glancing at the frosted glass pane in the closed door of the inner office. "Can I do something for you?"

"Yeah, you can tell him this is Adam Wagner, and I want to talk to him . That means now, Luke."

Luke wished fervently that he'd gone into another line of work. "Hang on," he said heavily. "I'll see what I can do."

He tiptoed to the closed door and turned the knob. The door creaked slightly as he pushed it open. Streicher looked up and nailed him with his eyes.

"Sorry, Sheriff, but Adam Wagner's on the phone. I figured you'd want to talk to him." Luke shrank back and pulled the door shut as the Sheriff snatched the receiver off the hook.

"This is Streicher," he said. "Where are you, Adam?"

Luke made it back to his own desk in time to hear most of the reply.

" . . . better not tell you that, Sarge. Has the FBI been around to see you yet?"

There was dead silence for a second or two. "Just what the hell do you know about the feds nosing around in Reál County?" Streicher demanded.

"I called 'em," Adam said. "I told 'em they ought to check out Kurt Radke and the five goose-steppers he's got staying on his ranch."

"Damn it, Adam, they're wool buyers. That's what Kurt said, and that's what I told the FBI."

"In a pig's eye," Adam said. "They're Nazi assassins."

When the Sheriff spoke again, he seemed to have done an amazing job of getting himself under control. "That's crazy talk, Adam. You and I fought the Germans in France eighteen years ago, and if I thought what you're saying was true, I'd be ready to fight them again. I hate to say it, old buddy, but you're starting to sound like a man full of loco weed. Now why don't you just come to my office, and let's sit down and talk this thing over."

Adam laughed. "At this point, Sarge, I'd about as soon cuddle up with a mountain lion."

"You got no cause to feel that way, Adam. Can't you at least tell me where you're calling from? Your Pa said you were fishing over on the Guadalupe, but there's no phones down there on the river."

"You leave Pa out of this. What the hell are you bothering him for?"

"You're fixing to get yourself into deeper trouble than you already are, my friend," Streicher warned. "You can't go around making false charges against people. It's just going to make things worse for you if you don't cut it out."

"I don't know what you mean," Adam said. "What kind of trouble are you talking about?"

"Come on, Adam," the Sheriff said. "Everybody knows you tried to kill one of Kurt Radke's fence-riders when he caught you trespassing the other night. I've got an arrest warrant right here on my desk for you on that. And frankly, I'm wondering if we don't need to do some serious talking, friend to friend, about that Mexican boy that got killed last month, too. As weird as you've been acting, maybe you shot the kid yourself in a fit of rage. Maybe that fence-rider saw you do it, huh?"

"Damn you, Sarge," Adam said, "you're either in this mess with Kurt right up to your eyeballs, or you're the dumbest son of a bitch that ever lived."

The Sheriff kept his voice even, although obviously with great effort. "Why don't you just turn yourself in, and be done with it, old buddy? Maybe your Pa can get you one of those high-powered psychiatrists over in San Antonio. He might have a good chance of getting you off on a temporary insanity plea."

Luke waited expectantly for Adam's response, but after a second or two of silence, the line went dead.

TWENTY-SEVEN

The White House, Washington
June 5, 1936

The White House staff had grown somewhat under FDR, but it was still a close-knit group of just over a dozen people. Virtually every member of it had direct access to the President, and most dealt with him on a regular, often-daily basis. But except for Missy LeHand and Roosevelt's other personal secretary, Grace Tully, Stephen Early probably spent more private time with the Chief than the rest of the staff put together.

The President was fascinated with the power of the press – hostile though it often was. He knew the importance of cultivating it to his own ends, and because of Early's background as an Associated Press correspondent, he'd been highly successful in helping FDR accomplish this. Recently, however, Roosevelt had begun confiding in Early and seeking his advice on a wide range of issues. Early's title hadn't changed, but his responsibilities and influence now went far beyond those of a mere press secretary.

Steve's emergence as confidant and advisor had been sharply accelerated by the death of Louis Howe two months ago. Howe had been the President's friend and mentor since Roosevelt's earliest days in politics, and he'd served – in fact, if not in title – as FDR's chief of operations. Since no single individual could take Howe's place, Roosevelt had filled the void with a small cadre of associates, one of whom was Early. Except for such old friends as Harry Hopkins and Henry Morgenthau, Steve was now as close to FDR as anyone in Washington.

Even so, he'd never been the type to abuse authority or try to strong-arm people. He was basically a live-and-let-live kind of guy, and he didn't like being at odds with other members of the White House "family" – especially someone like Ed Starling of the Secret Service.

Ed was one of those people who never really loosened up. His mouth smiled easily enough, but his eyes never did. Part of him was always on alert, ready to serve as a human shield between the President and danger. That, of course, was his job, and no one took the responsibility more seriously than Ed. Steve respected him for that, and they'd always gotten along fine – until the past few days. It was a shame that so much friction had developed between them over something that seemed so insignificant.

It had started the minute Ed got back from making advance security arrangements for FDR's trip through Arkansas and Texas. If anything, it had only worsened since then, and there was still no resolution in sight. The courtly Colonel had been in a dangerous mood when he stormed into the press office that afternoon – and he left no doubt that 99 percent of his rancor was directed at Steve.

❁

Starling had taken a taxi straight from the airport to the White House. He was tired, rumpled, in need of a shave, and looked as if he could bite a nail in two.

"I want you to understand one thing, Steve," he said hoarsely. "If somebody's plotting against the President, you've managed to increase their chances of success by at least a hundred percent. What the hell's so important about that Cardenas press release that it had to go out yesterday?"

"I explained the whole thing to Nat Grayson this morning," Early said. "The Mexican ambassador's been giving us a lot of heat. Cardenas himself is supposedly put out about it. It's just a simple denial that there's going to be a meeting between the Chief and Cardenas on this upcoming trip. So let me ask you: What's so important about it that it *shouldn't* have gone out yesterday?"

Starling lowered his lanky frame into a straight-back chair beside Early's desk and fumbled in his pocket until he found a crumpled pack of Luckies and his lighter. "For one thing," he said, "the threat we were told about mentioned Mexico specifically. If somebody's waiting for Roosevelt on the border with a gun, you've given him several days' notice that Roosevelt's not coming. The more notice he has, the longer he has to set up an attempt somewhere else. For another thing, you promised not to issue the denial about the Cardenas meeting until we were ready to leave next week."

"If it was up to me, Colonel, I wouldn't have," Steve said, "but priorities change. Besides, the State Department thinks this whole plot business is a lot of bunk. Our intelligence people don't trust the British on this one."

"Then our intelligence people aren't very damned intelligent." Ed stabbed the air with the glowing tip of his cigarette. "One of my agents had a phone call from Texas the other day. The caller talked about a plot, too, but the call was lost before we could get anything concrete. If people are out to kill Roosevelt, I think we ought to make it as hard for them as possible – don't you?"

"Sure I do, but you know the Chief. He's not going to slow down for anything, much less go into hiding."

"If there was any way to get him to cancel the trip, I would," Starling said. "I've had bad feelings about it from the start, and they just keep getting worse. Now why don't you stop thinking about press coverage and diplomacy for a while and start thinking about keeping your boss alive."

Steve frowned. "Look, if I'd waited any longer, the Chief would've been on my neck himself. He's got very strong feelings about international protocol, and he hates to look disrespectful to a foreign government."

Starling slammed the corner of Early's desk with the heel of his hand. "Sometimes this fellow Roosevelt has to be protected from himself whether he likes it or not, Steve," he said. "If you couldn't kill the release altogether, you could at least have sat on it until we were on the train headed south Monday night. Damn it all, man, which is worse – breaking protocol or burying a President?"

Early sighed. "I'm sorry, Ed. There was nothing else I could do."

Starling stood silently for a moment, shifting his weight from one foot to the other and looking as if he wanted to pick up something and throw it. His face was like a slab of granite as he fired another complaint at the press secretary.

"I understand we've got a couple of newspaper guys who can't make up their minds if they want to go to Texas or not," Starling said. "It'll take us at least twenty-four hours to check these people out, so they'll have to decide by five o'clock today at the latest. Otherwise, you can tell them they won't be on the train."

"Well, okay, Ed," Steve said, trying to treat the matter as lightly as possible. "But what's there to check out? I've known both these guys for years, and they're perfectly all right. It's just that their editors won't give them a definite answer. What do you want to do, fingerprint 'em?"

Starling's expression didn't change. "I would if I could, and we *do* intend to run a thorough background check on every civilian on the train. No exceptions."

Steve shrugged. "I'll make that clear to the reporters. Is this going to apply to future trips as well?"

"Who knows?" Starling said. "Thanks to you and the damned press, Roosevelt may not be *making* any more trips after this one."

That Friday would mark the beginning of one of the most frantic periods ever experienced by members of the FDR White House staff. The rush to wind up essential business before the Texas trip would've been hectic enough even if the Chief hadn't decided to attend the funeral for House Speaker Byrns. Now, in the midst of preparations for the longer junket, the President was setting out this very evening on a 1,500-mile round trip to Nashville.

In the rush of the moment, the ill-timed press release was largely forgotten – by everyone but Ed Starling. Switchboard operator Helen Lance was blissfully unaware of the furor over the press release when, shortly before 4 p.m., she received a call from Starling, who told her that he and Nat Grayson were about to leave Washington for the weekend. At that moment, Roosevelt himself had just departed by car for the Capitol rotunda, where Byrns' body was lying in state.

"Oh, okay," Helen said. "Are you going to Tennessee with the President?"

"We don't have much choice," Ed said. "My wife's not happy about it, especially since I've already been gone for several days, and I'll barely get back before we have to leave again Monday for a full week. But we can't afford to let this fellow out of our sight right now."

"Well, have a safe trip, Colonel. Are you on your way out right now?"

"Yes. We're going straight to the depot to check everything over while the President's at the Capitol paying his respects to the Speaker. If anyone calls for Nat or me, be sure to take a message. We'll get back to them first thing Monday."

No more than two or three minutes had passed when a call came through on an outside line, and Helen heard an impatient, unnecessarily loud male voice:

"This is Adam Wagner in Uvalde, Texas. Can you tell me who's in charge of the Secret Service agents that work there at the White House?"

"That would be Colonel Edmund Starling, sir, but – "

"I need to talk to him right away. Can you connect me?"

"I'm afraid he's left for the weekend, sir. Would you care to leave a message?"

"Well, who's the second in command then? Let me talk to him."

"That would be Agent Nathaniel Grayson, but he's not here, either. He and Colonel Starling are both out of town on official business, but I'm sure one of them would be glad to return your call on Monday if you – "

"Oh, to hell with it," the voice snapped "I don't know why I keep trying to do this anyway. I give up."

"I'm truly sorry, sir," Helen began, "but I – "

She stopped when she heard a click, followed by the unmistakable hum of the dial tone in her ear.

For a second, Helen considered ringing the Secret Service office and reporting the call to whoever was on duty, but since there was no indication of what the man in Texas was upset about, it hardly seemed worth the effort. Still, she seemed to recollect another distraught caller from Texas a few weeks ago. Fleetingly, she wondered if both calls were somehow related.

A few moments later, however, a sudden flood of activity lit up her switchboard, and for the next forty-five minutes, Helen was totally absorbed in making connections and taking messages. By the time the impatient caller from Texas crossed her mind again, she was on a bus on her way home to Arlington, Virginia.

TWENTY-EIGHT

Uvalde, Texas
June 6, 1936

Early on Saturday afternoon, Adam made one final check through the interior of his old Model A for any small items he might have overlooked. Then he handed over the title to the rumble-seat roadster he'd owned since 1928, along with $225 in cash, to the salesman at South Texas Auto Sales. At that moment, he officially became the new owner of a gray 1934 three-window Ford coupe with red wheels.

"She's a hot number," the salesman said. "A genuine 'Bonnie and Clyde Special.' She'll do eighty in second gear. You're gonna love her."

The Ford coupe was, indeed, a handsome machine, Adam thought. It had a near-flawless body, virtually new whitewall tires, spotless upholstery, a great radio and heater, and only 14,000 miles on the odometer. It also had vacuum windshield wipers that worked all by themselves and even a fancy spotlight mounted on the driver's side door.

Ordinarily, Adam would've been thrilled to own such a sharp vehicle, yet he felt no particular sense of pride or elation as he drove it off the car lot. On the contrary, his mood was bleak. One reason, he supposed, was that he'd just said goodbye to one of the last physical links between himself and a simpler, less stressful time. But a bigger reason was that the new car somehow symbolized the ordeal that he foresaw ahead. It had been obvious that the aging Model A wasn't fit to cope with the crisis that he and Ellie now faced – and, in all honesty, Adam wasn't sure if he was, either.

Ellie touched his arm lightly as he stopped for a traffic light on Uvalde's downtown square. "Don't look so sad," she said. "It's a beautiful car. You should be happy."

"Yeah, I guess so," he said. "It's just that I keep thinking about where we have to go in it and everything we've got to do."

The new car's first mission would be to get them back into Reál County without being instantly recognized. Most county residents – including the Sheriff and his chief deputy – knew the Model A on sight, and an unfamiliar vehicle would offer a measure of anonymity. Adam had no desire to land in Sarge Streicher's jail, so keeping a low profile was now a top priortiy. If he succeeded, the car would also be critical to any hope they had of thwarting the plot against FDR.

From tomorrow on, the going would be tough. Maybe tougher than anything he or Ellie had yet experienced. Even with the newer, faster, more reliable car, the odds against them were incredibly high. That much was easy to figure out. The rest was considerably harder. Last night the two of them had finally faced up to what had to be done. Then they'd explored their options until the early hours of this morning.

Eventually a plan of sorts had taken shape. It wasn't the best plan in the world, but at the moment it was all they had.

❋

It had been long past midnight, and they were sitting on the floor in Ellie's cottage with a Texas roadmap, a scratch pad, and a jumble of other papers spread out on the carpet between them. Ellie's eyes kept blurring as she tried to concentrate on what Adam was saying. She glanced at

Lobo, who slept soundly in a corner, oblivious to their dilemma. She envied the old collie. She was dog-tired herself but too tense to sleep, even if there weren't so much to think about.

"Sometimes I could kick myself for not forgetting this whole mess while I still could," Adam was saying. "I could've just looked the other way like everybody else. If I'd had a lick of sense, that's what I would've done."

"Don't talk like that," she chided. "You did the right thing, and it took a lot of courage." She paused and looked at him. "A lot of caring, too."

"But I didn't have to drag you into it."

She eyed him steadily. "Would you rather I weren't here right now?"

"No, I'm glad you're here. I'd be lost if you weren't. Maybe dead, too."

"Then hush." Her tone was like a mother reassuring a child. "If we think about it long enough, we'll work something out."

"Well, it's too late to backtrack now," he said. "We've passed the point where we could just go home and drop the whole thing. If we did that now, neither of us would ever be safe in Reál County again."

"Then let's forget about it," she said. "It's not what either of us wants anyway. Isn't there somebody else in Washington that might be able to help?"

He made a sour face. "I think we can forget that, too. I don't know what's wrong with those people up there. They act like they're listening, but they don't seem to hear. I was so sure the FBI would do something. But all they did was send an agent to talk to the Sheriff, and when the Sheriff told the agent everything was just fine, that was the end of it."

Ellie sighed. "I still can't believe the Secret Service wouldn't be interested in what we know."

"Me neither, but it's been a total dead-end. First I get a run-around. Then I get some jerk who can't understand plain English. Then everybody's gone for the weekend. Monday's the last chance I'd have to get through to them before they leave for Texas, and I don't think we can wait around that long. It's even too late to send them a letter now. Not that it would've done any good anyway, but–"

"What if you sent a telegram to the President himself?" she asked suddenly. "There's still plenty of time for that."

He brightened for a second, then frowned. "Oh, he probably gets five hundred telegrams a day. Chances are, it'd just sit around in a stack someplace while he's out of town, and we'd never know if he saw it or not."

"That's true," she said. "But there must be *something* we can do."

She watched as Adam studied the map on the floor. She hated to see him look so defeated. For weeks, she'd felt a growing warmth toward him. It had started as the faintest spark, dampened by the past, and in the beginning it was easy to overlook, but within the past few days, it had glowed increasingly brighter.

She was struck by the emptiness she felt each evening when he said goodnight and went alone to his room. More than once on recent nights she'd awakened from dreams of him with a fire burning inside her. Even when she realized she was alone in the bed, the fire had smoldered on.

At the same time, she sensed Adam's guardedness toward her. Part of it might have been his preoccupation with the crisis engulfing them, but he always seemed wary and a little withdrawn. There'd been no repeat of the brief episode on his bed that morning at the motel, but it was bound to happen again. She wondered what she'd do when it did.

"Well," he said finally, "my grandpa always said, 'If you want something done right, you'd best do it yourself.' I reckon that's what we're going to have to do now. We can't depend on the government to stop this thing. If it gets stopped at all, looks like its up to you and me to stop it."

"But how? What can the two of us possibly do by ourselves?"

He looked at her and smiled vaguely. As soon as he started talking, it was obvious that he'd given her questions many hours of thought.

"There's a ridge on the Shuster Ranch that overlooks Kurt Radke's front gate," he began. "And there's an old wagon trail that runs along it, then winds down and comes into the main road to town about a quarter-mile away. Charlie Shuster and I drove up there dozens of times when we were kids, and I know the trail's still there. There's a gap in the fence where the trail hits the road. If we can get the car up on that ridge tomorrow night and hide it and ourselves real good, we'll be able to see everything that goes in or out of the Radke Ranch."

Ellie could feel the darkness of his mood lightening as he talked. "Keep going," she said. "I'm listening."

"According to the schedule in the papers, Roosevelt leaves Washington this coming Monday night, heading this way, but his train won't be in Texas till late Wednesday. He stops in Houston Thursday and doesn't get into San Antonio till early that evening. Then he heads on to Dallas and gets there Friday morning. Sometime between now and then, those friends of Kurt's have to make their move. They've got to get to wherever they have to be when they go for the kill."

"The papers mentioned San Antonio and Dallas both," she said, "and they could've even picked somewhere else by now."

"Doesn't matter," he said. "I figure the only way they can leave the ranch is by car. That plane of Kurt's is too small to carry all of them, and it'd draw too much attention, anyway, so they have to be driving. If we can get into position on the ridge and keep a constant watch with binoculars on the main entrance to the ranch, we'll be able to see them when they head out."

"But there must be all kinds of vehicles passing through that gate," she said. "How can we possibly know which one they'll be in?"

He chewed at his mustache for a moment. "Ninety-five percent of the traffic going through there is Radke Ranch trucks, and I guarantee you they won't use one of them. I can spot Kurt and Karla's personal cars, and it won't be one of those, either."

"No," she agreed, "Kurt's not stupid enough to let them use a fancy custom-built car that could be traced to him if something goes wrong."

"Right, so that narrows it down some – although I *do* figure the Nazis will be traveling in pretty high style. What we'll have to watch for is the first unfamiliar late-model car that comes out of there. If it's daylight, we might be able to see who's inside. If it's dark, then we'll just have to take an educated guess and hope for the best."

Ellie studied his face for several seconds. The frustration and disgust that had dulled his voice and clouded his expression for most of the day were gone now, replaced by a determined urgency. The change relieved her. On the phone that afternoon, Adam had said he was giving up, but she'd known it wasn't true – and as long as he didn't give up, she wouldn't, either.

She thought about the hours they'd spend alone together on the isolated ridge above the entrance to the Radke Ranch. In all likelihood, they'd be there for several days. She could feel the warmth inside her growing again.

"Assuming we *do* see them leave, what happens then?" She already knew the answer, but she wanted to hear him say it.

"Then we follow them to San Antonio or Dallas or wherever they're going," he said. "We stay as close to them as we can and look for opportunities. We also cross our fingers and say a prayer that they don't catch us and kill us both."

TWENTY-NINE

Leakey, Texas
June 7, 1936

It was early Sunday afternoon and the Mercado Velasco was closed for the Lord's day. After morning worship services at the Iglesia de Jesús, Ramon and Rachel Velasco had had a modest lunch and retired to their bedroom behind the store for a nap. Rachel was almost asleep when she heard someone pounding on the side door.

"Papa, wake up," she whispered, shaking him. "*Esta la puerta.*"

Ramon sat up slowly and listened as the pounding started again, angry and insistent. "*Quien es?*" he muttered. "Who could it be?"

He pulled on his trousers and stepped into his shoes, trying to imagine who could be making such a terrible racket. All his customers knew the store was closed on Sundays, and he doubted if any of them would be out there pounding like that anyway.

"I'm coming," he yelled. "Hold your horses!"

He made his way down the hall and through the living room, buttoning his shirt as he went. As he passed the front window, he saw a black sedan parked beside the house. It was unlike any car he'd ever seen before. Then he peered through the small glass pane in the door and saw something else that made his heart skip a beat.

In all the years since the death of his eldest daughter and the shame of her younger sister, Ramon Velasco had never once come face to face with Kurt Radke, the man to blame for both tragedies. But at this very moment, Radke himself stood on the porch just outside the door. With him was another man, a tall, fair-haired stranger whom Ramon didn't recognize.

Ramon's hand trembled as he slowly turned the knob and pushed the door open, but his voice was soft and steady when he spoke.

"Is there something I can do for you, Señors?"

Radke didn't bother with pleasantries. "For a start, you can tell Elena I want to see her," he said, looking past Ramon into the house. "Tell her to come out here and be quick about it."

Ramon could feel his pulse racing. Once he'd vowed to kill this man for what he'd done to his two children. He thought of the pistol under the counter in the store and the 12-gauge shotgun in the back corner of his clothes closet. He tried not to think about what he might do if either weapon were in his hands at this moment.

"She isn't here," he said.

Kurt's eyes bored into him. "Don't lie to me, old man. If you do, we'll just have to come inside and find her for ourselves."

"You're not welcome here, Señor Radke," Ramon said evenly. "Not on my porch, much less in my house. But I give you my word Elena isn't here. There's no one here but my wife and me."

The other man on the porch moved closer to the door. He looked at Ramon and smiled. "Perhaps we should talk to his wife then," he said to Kurt. "Perhaps she would show us a little more respect. I'm sure we could persuade her to be more truthful, too."

Kurt suddenly reached out and thrust the door wide open, sending Ramon stumbling backward a few steps. Then the two uninvited visitors shoved their way inside. Kurt sat down on one arm of the sofa. The other man pulled a semi-automatic pistol from under his belt and pointed it at Ramon.

"We're not going to diddle around with you all day, old man," Kurt said. "I want to know where Elena is, and I want to know now. Otherwise, I'll have my friend Ernst here discuss the matter privately with Señora Velasco. *Comprende?*"

Ramon's tongue darted over his lips as he glanced from one of them to the other. After everything else Kurt had done, Ramon knew he wouldn't hesitate to hurt Mama to get what he wanted. Kurt and the other man might even kill him and Mama both. And if either of them told where Elena was before they died, they would kill her, too.

For the first time, Ramon understood why Elena had seemed so nervous before she went away. He could also guess what had happened to Adam Wagner the day Elena had brought him to the house injured and looking more dead than alive. It was clear now why Elena and Adam had run away to Uvalde. Kurt Radke was the villain again.

"Elena doesn't want to see you, Señor," he said. "Surely you know that."

"I don't give a damn what she wants," Kurt said. "Where is she?"

Ramon had never been good at lying. In the first place, he'd never had much experience at it. It had been thirty years or more since he'd intentionally lied to anyone, and even then it only been to protect Mama and himself from *bandidos*. In the second place, he hated lies and liars, and he was sure that God did, too. But if there was ever a time to lie – and lie well – it was now. When the lives of his whole family might depend on it, lying was a forgivable sin.

Suddenly, something Elena had said once months before flashed through his mind. It was only a casual passing remark, and by now Elena may have forgotten she ever said it. But to Ramon, remembering it was like a gift from God, and he seized at it in blind desperation. It was his only hope.

Before he realized it, words were pouring from his mouth. He scarcely recognized them as his own, but they kept coming in a steady stream. As they did, they formed the most ingenious and convincing lie Ramon Velasco had ever told.

"Elena is in San Marcos," he heard himself saying. "She left last week to enroll in summer school at the teacher's college there. She's working on her master's degree. It's something she's wanted to do for a long time, and she decided not to wait any longer."

Kurt scowled at Ramon for several seconds. "And just how long is she supposed to be gone?" he demanded.

Ramon's knees felt weak, but he could tell by Kurt's reaction that the lie was working, at least for the moment. Kurt was still suspicious, but he was no longer so cocksure about everything.

"About six weeks," Ramon said. "That's how long the first summer session lasts."

"Well, how did she get there? Did she get a ride from somebody?"

"I drove her to Uvalde to catch the bus," Ramon said smoothly. The lies were getting easier. Maybe he wasn't such a bad liar, after all.

But Radke's next question shook his confidence all over again: "Did Adam Wagner go with her?"

Ramon tried to look puzzled, but it was hard. It was even harder to swallow the sticky dryness in his throat. "No," he said, "she went alone."

"Maybe Adam met her there later then. Is that it?"

"I don't know what you're talking about, Señor," Ramon said. "Elena's going to school. It has nothing to do with Adam Wagner."

"But she *does* know Wagner, doesn't she?"

"Si, of course. Everyone in Leakey knows him, just as everyone knows you. How could she *not* know him?"

"That's not what I mean, damn you." Kurt's face darkened and he took a menacing step forward. "She's been hanging around with the son of a bitch for the past few weeks. People have seen them together around town."

Ramon forced himself to meet Kurt's withering gaze. His heart was leaping like a bullfrog in his chest and he could feel the beads of sweat on his face. He struggled to keep his voice steady.

"I know nothing about that. Elena's a grown woman now, not a helpless child as she once was. She makes her own decisions and chooses her own friends, so what you say may be true. But if she should ask my opinion, I'd advise her to stay away from Señor Wagner and all other Anglos. She's better off among her own people."

Kurt seemed confused. He paced the length of the room several times. Then he stopped and glared at the man named Ernst.

"Damn it, I don't know what to believe. Put that stupid gun away."

"But what if he's lying?" Ernst said. "Maybe we should work on the old woman a little just to be sure. I can make her talk."

Kurt shook his head. "No," he said firmly. "You go on back to the car. I'll finish handling this."

Ernst shoved the pistol back under his belt, shrugged and moved to the door. "As you wish," he said.

When Ernst was gone, Kurt turned back to Ramon.

"Maybe I'll just drive to San Marcos right now and see if I can find Elena," he said. "I wonder what would happen if I did that. Maybe she's not there at all – and maybe you're just handing me a load of bullshit."

"If you go to the right room in the right dormitory, she'll be there, just as I said," Ramon insisted. "But she won't want to see you, Kurt Radke. She never wants to see you again, and with good reason. Now please go and leave us in peace."

Kurt stood motionless for a long moment with his hand on the door. Finally, he shook his head in something close to resignation.

"All right," he said heavily, "but you'd better get one thing straight, *Mister* Velasco. If I find out you're lying to me, I'll come back and burn this place to the ground with you and your damned squaw in it. That's a promise, you old bastard."

Ramon looked at him impassively. "What I tell you is the pure, unblemished truth, Señor," he said. "I swear by the Blessed Virgin."

As Kurt walked away, Ramon slammed the door and locked it. Quickly, he made the sign of the cross and muttered a prayer. First, he begged divine forgiveness for the falsehoods he'd just told. Then he asked a huge, hurtful favor of the Almighty.

"Please warn Elena," he whispered. Tell her never to come back to Reál County again."

THIRTY

Aboard FDR's Special Train
Near Lynchburg, Virginia
June 8, 1936

The President shifted uncomfortably in his wheelchair and looked up from the stack of papers that covered his lap and the small table beside him. His work day had continued unabated after he changed from his white linen suit into pajamas and a robe, but Missy LeHand could sense that he was about to call a halt. Finishing all the work before him tonight was out of the question anyway. It was just a matter of finding a stopping place.

Roosevelt swayed slightly with the rhythmic motion of the wheels meeting the rails beneath the Pullman coach as he removed his reading glasses and rubbed at the impressions they left across his cheekbones.

"Why don't you mix us a couple of nightcaps, Missy?" he suggested. "I think a good Manhattan might help me get to sleep."

Missy marked her place with an index card in the latest issue of *The Saturday Evening Post*, then went to the small glass-topped liquor cabinet in one corner of the compartment, where she removed a bottle of whiskey and another of sweet vermouth.

"I'll give it a try," she said, "but you know I'm not nearly as good at this sort of thing as you are."

He laughed and shook his head. He was proud of his drink-mixing skills – skills that he practiced virtually every day. "Maybe not," he said, "but right now I'm too thirsty to know the difference."

There were dark circles under Roosevelt's eyes, and the lines in his face seemed deeper than they were a few days ago. He'd spoken little since the train pulled out of Washington around 8:15 p.m. Even earlier, during the cocktail hour that was one of the daily rituals of the Roosevelt White House – a time when he normally cracked a few jokes and bantered with the staff – he'd been uncharacteristically quiet. Not a good sign, Missy thought.

Neither was the fact that he'd scarcely touched the dinner of quail in wine sauce with wild rice that he was served shortly before departure. He'd ordered the meal with much anticipation that morning, intending to take advantage of his wife's absence to enjoy one of the game dinners that he relished but Mrs. Roosevelt abhorred. Eleanor didn't approve of "fancy" food – or much of anything else that smacked of extravagance.

But the First Lady had chosen to stay behind in Tennessee following Speaker Byrns' funeral on Saturday. She'd wanted to meet with leaders of several women's groups and do some checking for the President on which way the political winds were blowing in the so-called "Solid South." Tomorrow morning in Memphis, she would board the train and resume the role of dedicated, dutiful wife. Meanwhile, Franklin was free to indulge his usually robust appetite for exotic food. He was also free to spend more time more openly with Missy. When he sent the quail away after only two or three bites, it was obvious that he wasn't feeling up to par. But Missy had no intention of letting him send her away as well.

Franklin didn't mind being tired. That was "something that goes with the job," as he often said. What he really hated, though, was *looking* tired. He placed great value on appearances. Sometimes Missy suspected they were even more important to him than substance. Tonight, he looked very tired, and what was worse, he knew it.

He'd spent four hours outdoors in stifling heat during and after the services in Nashville. The 1,500-mile train ride had been no picnic in itself, especially with the prospect of starting out immediately on another, even longer one. And if it had been hot in Nashville, what *would* it be like in places like Houston and San Antonio? Franklin always managed to look so jaunty and vigorous in his photographs, but Missy knew that pictures sometimes lie. His shoulders, arms and chest were muscular and well-developed from all the extra work they did, but his withered legs were pitifully frail despite his ongoing efforts to exercise them.

Missy was worried about him – and about the stresses of the next few days – but she'd have bitten off her tongue rather than let him know it.

"Here's your drink," she said, handing him a stemmed cocktail glass garnished with a cherry.

"Ah, that looks good." He transferred the unread papers from his lap to the table, folded his reading glasses, and took a long sip of the Manhattan. "Tastes good, too. Did you pour one for yourself?"

"Maybe I'll just have a sip of yours," she said. "Want me to light you a cigarette?"

"No, not now." He reached up and caught her by the hand, drawing her slowly toward him. "Right now I just want you to come here."

She laughed and allowed him to pull her onto his lap. There had been a time, years ago, when she feared her weight on his crippled legs would be harmful to them. But that was one thing she no longer felt any need to be concerned about. Because of the paralysis, his knees couldn't actually feel her presence, but they were quite capable of supporting her. They'd proved as much hundreds of times over the years.

She took a small drink from the glass in his hand, then kissed him lightly on the forehead. "You're really worn out, aren't you, darling?"

"Oh, I'll be good as new after a decent night's sleep," he said. "I have to confess I didn't rest well in Tennessee."

"Why? Because I wasn't there?"

"Well, that was certainly part of it," he said, hugging her. "But Ed Starling and his Secret Service boys didn't help matters, either. You know how Eleanor hates having them constantly underfoot, and sometimes they make me jumpy, too. Ed was exactly like an old mother hen with me as his errant chick. Every time I turned around, he was hovering there, looking as if he expected the world to end at any second."

"I noticed the extra security at the station today," she said. "The Colonel's people checked out everyone in the press corps before they let them on the train. Some of the reporters were griping about it. Is there a tangible reason for all these precautions?"

Franklin took another drink from his glass. "There've been some nebulous rumors about a plot of some sort. You always hear things like that, though. Ninety-nine point nine percent of the time they don't mean anything."

Missy looked at him closely. "You mustn't take any unnecessary risks," she said. "If anything should happen to you, I don't know what . . ."

His laugh sounded strangely hollow to her. "The President has to take some risks, my dear," he said. "Otherwise, he'd have to hide in a concrete room all the time and never venture out. I'm running for re-election, Missy. I have to let as many people see and hear me as I possibly can."

"Oh, but Franklin, you know you're going to win. Who could the Republicans possibly put up with any chance to beat you?"

His laugh was genuine this time. "If all the voters felt like you, that might be true, but I can't take anything for granted. Lots of experts in the press are saying I'm licked already because the Depression keeps hanging on. But things *are* looking up, and I've got to prove them wrong."

She took his glass and crossed the room to refill it. Then she deposited herself on his knee again. "I'm glad I'm with you this time," she said. "I don't want you to leave me behind anymore."

He smiled warmly at her. "Certainly not," he said. "If I did, I'd have to mix my own drinks. See how spoiled you've got me?"

She leaned back, snuggling into his powerful arms. "You know what I wish?"

"No, but I'll bet you're going to tell me."

"I wish we were back on the *Larooco* again." She referred to the weather-beaten forty-foot sloop where they'd whiled away so many months a decade ago. It was there that Franklin had finally come to terms with his disability and found the resolve to run for governor of New York. He'd discovered a great inner strength aboard that old boat. "I wish we could spend the whole summer there."

"So do I," he said softly, "but I'm afraid that time's gone for good, Missy. If we were on the *Larooco* now, Ed Starling and his men would be swarming all over it checking for leaks and searching the hold for secret agents."

She wished he hadn't brought up Starling again. It only made her worry more. "I guess you'll be parading around in an open car at every stop we make," she said.

He finished his second drink and reached around her to grope in his pocket for his cigarettes and holder.

"Only if it doesn't rain," he said.

THIRTY-ONE

Reál County, Texas
June 9, 1936

Ellie yawned again, feeling her eyes watering as she stared through the binoculars into the sea of darkness below. She'd yawned at least fifty times in the past two hours, but she wasn't the least bit sleepy. Her yawning reflex was related more to boredom and nervous tension than drowsiness. Despite the double thickness of the old quilt beneath her, her bottom ached from sitting on the rocky ground. It seemed as if they'd been camped on the ridge under the thick stand of cedars and liveoaks for a week instead of just under forty-eight hours.

She had Adam's pocket watch, but in the darkness she couldn't make out what time it was. By her estimate, the sun had been down for about two and a half hours, which meant it was half past ten or so. A few inches away, Adam was sleeping soundly on the other side of the bedroll. His breathing was soft and measured, but one hand rested lightly on the stock of his rifle. Millions of stars glittered in the clear, black sky. A southwesterly breeze moaned softly through the cedars. There was no moon.

She thought how pleasant it would be to lie down next to Adam and go to sleep. But he'd already stood two six-hour watches since midnight yesterday, and now it was her turn. Someone had to keep a constant eye on the main gate to the Radke Ranch some four hundred yards away and the stretch of driveway beyond that led toward the headquarters house. A lapse of even a minute or two could allow their quarry to slip past unnoticed.

Ellie was sure that hadn't happened since they'd started their surveillance Sunday night. A dozen or more trucks had passed in and out of the gate Monday and Tuesday but not a single car. She'd sworn to Adam that nothing would escape her attention during her watch, but as the tedious hours dragged by, a nagging doubt had first nibbled, then gnawed at her mind:

What if the assassins were already gone? What if they'd left before she and Adam had taken up their vigil? What if they were waiting right now in some secret hideaway in San Antonio or Dallas, their weapons primed and ready to strike?

She was certain that those same questions bothered Adam, but he insisted that such an early move was neither intelligent nor logical.

"They can't set up for the kill or be seen prowling around too early," he'd said earlier that evening. "Too many people might get suspicious, and they could get caught before they were able to do anything. Once their mission's complete, they'd probably kill themselves to keep from being captured, but that wouldn't accomplish anything beforehand."

His reasoning was sound, but the longer they waited, the more Ellie's doubts grew, especially in the dead of night when there was no one to talk to and it seemed ten times as hard to watch the gate. Ironically, while the darkness made it harder to see what was going on below, it made their hiding place more vulnerable to discovery than it was in daylight. She didn't dare strike a match or click on a flashlight without shrouding herself under a blanket first. The slightest glimmer or spark could give them away.

She lowered the binoculars and rubbed her smarting eyes, sorting back through the events of yesterday to try to ease the monotony.

❁

She'd felt a genuine sense of loss when they left the Leona Motor Courts behind and drove north out of Uvalde. It had been dusk on Sunday and it would be well after dark by the time they reached Leakey. Even in Adam's newly acquired car, they had no intention of being seen in Reál County in daylight. Their departure was the end of one of the strangest interludes of Ellie's life – and the start of another even stranger.

Their whirlwind visits to the Mercado Velasco and the Wagner Farm had been brief, tense and emotional. And when they were over, both sets of parents were probably more confused and upset than if Adam and Ellie hadn't come at all.

"Go!" Papa had whispered when he opened the door and saw her. "Get away from here, *hija*. Go quickly and far. Each moment you stay only increases the danger."

Mama had materialized in the doorway then, pushing past Papa and throwing her arms around Ellie with tears streaming down her broad face.

They blurted out the story about Kurt and the other man coming to the store that same afternoon. They repeated Kurt's questions and threats, and Mama proudly recounted the creative lies that Papa had told to protect his daughter.

"What if Kurt comes back later?" Ellie said. "What if he causes more trouble?"

"I think he'll only come back if he suspects you're here," Papa said. "For all our sakes, you must go quickly. Write and tell us where you are. We'll let you know when it's safe to come home. "

While Ellie snatched up a few clothes, Mama filled a pasteboard box with food. She packed black bread, corn tortillas, cheese, onions, tomatoes, canned beans, jerky, several links of the same dry sausage that had struck the fancy of the German named Otto, and other edibles that would keep well without refrigeration.

Adam declined Ramon's offer of the revolver he kept under the counter in the store. "Keep it," Adam told him. "You may need it worse than we do. I've got my rifle in the car, plus a pistol that might shoot in a pinch. We'll be okay."

They were in the house less than ten minutes in all. The goodbyes were wrenching, but they were over in seconds. Barely two blocks from the Mercado Velasco, they passed one of Sheriff Streicher's two patrol cars. The black Ford with the silver star on its side was parked on the south side of the courthouse square with its lights off and its motor idling. They passed close enough for Ellie to recognize the figure of Luke Bodine slouched behind the steering wheel.

She raised her hand to shield her face and held her breath. The Deputy never glanced their way as they drove slowly past, and he looked as if he might have been dozing, but Ellie didn't start to relax until they were a mile or two out of town.

If anything, their stop at the Wagner house had proved even more difficult. Adam's parents were much less aware than the Velascos of how dangerous the situation had become. Consequently, they were full of questions, and they were far less eager than the Velascos for Adam and Ellie to leave together again so soon.

"I don't understand what's come over you, Adam," his mother said. "You've always been so steady and responsible. Now you're acting so . . . so crazy."

"Look, Ma," he said," if I had two or three hours, I'd explain the whole thing to you, but I don't. I'll tell you all about it later, but right now we're in one helluva hurry, okay?"

George Wagner showed far more understanding. "You do what you think you have to do, son," he said. "But if I tell Kurt Radke you're still fishin' down on the Guadalupe, he's bound to know I'm lyin'. What do you want me to say if he comes around again?"

Adam thought about it for a moment. "Tell him I went to the Centennial Exposition in Dallas," he said.

His father studied Adam's face. "Is that really where you're a-goin'?"

Adam shrugged. "I'd say there's about a fifty-fifty chance."

It took about two minutes for Adam to grab the rest of the cash stashed in his closet and grab some extra shirts and socks. Then he pulled the car out back to the shed where the hunting and camping equipment was stored, selecting two of the least-worn bedrolls from a pile in one corner, unearthing an old tarpaulin, and digging through a box of gear until he found a canteen and an army-surplus mess kit.

While Ellie arranged everything in the car, he filled the canteen with water and got a handful of matches from the holder on the wall behind the kitchen stove. As he started to leave, he saw his father standing on the back porch holding a four-cell flashlight in one hand and a half-full bottle of bourbon in the other.

"Better take these," George Wagner said. "Just in case you get lost in the dark or get snakebit." The faint suggestion of a smile flickered on his pale lips.

Adam took the bottle and the flashlight wordlessly and put them through the car window into the seat. Then he turned back to his father. "Thanks, Pa," he said.

The old man hugged his son clumsily. "You be careful, son, you hear?"

"I will," Adam said. "We'll be back as soon as we can."

"Send your Ma a postcard from the Centennial. It'll make her feel better."

"Sure," Adam said, "if we get that far."

"You best get started then," George Wagner said. "Might not be a good idea to let anybody see you around here."

At that moment, Lobo came hobbling over to the car. The old dog had taken to travel like a duck to water, and he was eager to go again despite the trauma of his last excursion with Adam.

"Stay, Lobo," Adam said.

The collie sat down obediently on his haunches. But he pawed the air with his wounded leg and watched Adam expectantly, waiting to be invited along. Adam squatted down beside him and scratched his ears. "Sorry, boy, but you can't go this time," he said. "This trip's liable to be too long and hard for an old mutt like you."

Lobo whined as Adam moved away.

"He'll be fine, son," George Wagner said. "I'll take good care of him."

"I know you will, Pa," Adam said. "I want you to take good care of yourself, too. Stay out of the heat, and don't worry about us, hear?"

The older man grasped Adam's hand for a moment. Then, without another word, he turned and walked slowly toward the back porch.

I love you, Pa, Adam thought, slamming the car door and starting the engine. *Why is it so damned hard for me to tell you?*

As Adam switched on the headlights and circled around the house toward the road, Ellie glanced through the Ford coupe's small rear window. In the faint glow of the lights from the house, she saw Lobo still sitting forlornly in the yard, staring after them. It made her want to run back and get the old collie, but she knew he was a hundred times better off where he was.

About ten minutes later, when they were sure no other cars were in sight, Adam pulled off the road and killed the lights. Within seconds, he opened the gap in the barbed-wire fence and she eased the car through it onto the Shuster Ranch. This done, he walked in front of the car to guide her as she steered it along the narrow wagon trail. Inching their way in the darkness up to the ridge that Adam remembered, then getting the car turned around to face down the slope took a nerve-wracking three-quarters of an hour . Several times, the coupe came precariously close to going over the edge. They were both shaking and sweating by the time they got it in the right position.

Finally, Adam carefully covered the car with the tarpaulin and secured it. When morning broke, the olive-drab canvas would keep any sunlight from reflecting off the car. The dull green of the tarp would also blend closely enough with the trees and their shadows to make the vehicle virtually invisible from a distance.

After scrambling around in the dark to assemble the rest of their camp, Adam sank down on his bedroll and accepted the sandwich Ellie offered him. She watched him as he ate silently. He seemed strangely discouraged.

She put her hand on his shoulder. "What's the matter? After all, we *did* make it up here, didn't we?"

He sighed heavily. "Yeah, we made it, but now that we've gone to all this trouble, I'm not so sure it's really worth it."

"What are you talking about?"

"When the time comes, we're going to have to go down this trail a damned sight faster than we came up it," he said. "Otherwise, those

Jerries'll be fifty miles down the road by the time we get off this mountain."

She looked at the narrow ledge on which the car rested and at the steep slope that began just a few yards from its front wheels. Then she understood what Adam meant – especially if they were forced to make the descent at night.

The very idea made her shudder, but she shook it off and tried to smile. "Well, you told me you like roller-coasters," she said.

Ellie shifted on the hard ground and felt on the bedroll until she found the canteen in its leather case. She put the binoculars in her lap while she unscrewed the cap and took a long drink of the tepid water. Then she re-closed the canteen and picked up the binoculars again.

This whole process took less than a minute, but as she peered back through the glasses again into the darkness below, she felt her whole body tense. Two bright dots of light were visible in the distance beyond the Radke gate. There was no question that the dots were automobile headlights.

She let out one quick gasp, then threw herself across the bedroll toward Adam. Her hands found his inert form, and she shook him vigorously.

"Adam, wake up! Wake up quick and look."

He grunted and sat up, shaking his head and rubbing his eyes. "What is it? What's going on?"

"I see headlights down there. Somewhere between the ranch house and the front gate."

He crawled up beside her and took the binoculars. She could hear him breathing hard as he tried to focus the glasses with one hand and pull his boots on with the other.

"I can't tell yet if it's a car or a truck," he said. "All I can see are the lights, but it's lucky you spotted it when you did. We've only got a minute or two before it makes the gate."

"I'll get the gear together," she mumbled, grappling with the bedroll she'd been sitting on just a moment ago and tying it into a bundle. The flashlight fell to the ground with a clatter, and she stooped to pick it up.

A frenzy was boiling inside her, but as she ran for the car, her movements seemed to be in slow-motion. She jerked back the tarp and stuffed the bedroll into the floor of the trunk.

"I'm almost sure it's a car," Adam said. "Those lights are too bright for a truck."

His words threw her into a state of semi-shock. After all these endless hours, everything was suddenly happening too fast to digest. In the space of another minute or two, they could be hurtling down the twisting mountain trail on the wildest ride of their lives. She forgot what she'd intended to do next, but she knew the tarp had to come off the car before they could get underway. She tugged at the heavy canvas with both hands and felt it fall to the ground.

"They're slowing down for the cattle guard," Adam said. "Damn, they're almost to the road. I wish to God I could see better."

"Do you want me to start the car?" Ellie called. There was something else she was supposed to be doing, but she couldn't remember what.

"Yes . . . No! I don't know. I'm afraid they'll hear, but to hell with it. Go ahead."

She climbed in under the steering wheel and switched on the ignition key. For an instant, she thought detachedly how fortunate it was that the Ford had an electric starter and didn't have to be cranked by hand like the old car Papa used to have.

Then, before she could hit the starter, she saw Adam jump up and run toward her.

"Let's roll," he gasped as she slid over to let him in on the driver's side. "It's definitely a car. I could see the grille and part of the front end. It's a dark-colored sedan of some kind. Maybe a Buick or a Cadillac. Looks like a new one, too."

He found the starter with his foot and the engine sputtered, then roared.

"Maybe it's just Kurt or his sister," she said.

He shook his head. "It doesn't look like anything I've ever seen them driving before." The gears clashed slightly as he shifted into low. "As far as I can see, we've got no choice. We either follow 'em now or forget the whole thing. What's it going to be?"

She hesitated for only a split-second. "Follow them," she whispered.

The coupe lurched forward down the slope. The twin tracks of the trail ahead were only pale, indistinct streaks. She could barely make them out in the darkness.

"Aren't you going to turn on the lights?" she asked.

Adam peered intently through the windshield at the wall of blackness ahead. "Don't be silly," he said. "They'll see us if I do."

"Oh, my God," she said, closing her eyes as the car plunged downward.

THIRTY-TWO

Aboard FDR's Special Train
Memphis, Tennessee
June 9, 1936

It was almost midnight when Ed Starling felt the train lurch and start to move backward. He stretched and stepped out into the passageway between the President's coach and the one occupied by the Secret Service, watching the dim shapes of freight cars gliding past. There was a momentary pause as the engineer waited for the switchman to clear them onto the main westbound line. Then the train jerked forward. The locomotive belched white clouds of steam and steadily gathered speed as it left the railroad yards behind.

Ed had always liked trains. He'd spent several years as a railroad detective before joining the Secret Service, and he usually felt as comfortable in a Pullman berth as he did in his own bed at home. Now that they were finally under way, after spending the whole evening on a siding, maybe the swaying motion of the train and the soft rumble of the wheels would relax him enough to sleep. His shift had been over for nearly two hours, but he was still too edgy to think about turning in.

They'd stopped in Memphis early that afternoon, expressly to pick up Mrs. Roosevelt. Once the First Lady was aboard, she and the President had hosted a small group of local Democratic dignitaries for cocktails and dinner in the presidential coach, and the visitors hadn't left until after nine. There was no real hurry, though. Tomorrow's first official stop in Little Rock was less than three hours' travel time away.

So far, they were comfortably ahead of schedule, and there was no hint of any problem, but the first real opportunity for trouble was coming up. Until now, Roosevelt hadn't so much as set foot off the train, but tomorrow, he'd be surrounded by thousands of people at a major speech observing Arkansas' 100th anniversary as a state. He'd also be traveling many miles by automobile.

After his appearance at the State Capitol in Little Rock, another stop was scheduled at Hot Springs, where the President was to make a ceremonial visit to a hospital. After that, he'd spend most of the rest of the day in an open car, driving to the town of Couchwood for lunch, then to Rockport for a pageant, and finally to Malvern to re-board the train.

Knowing this fellow, Starling told himself, it would be a merry chase all the way.

Above the noise of the wind and rails, Ed heard the door of the Secret Service coach open and saw Nat Grayson's shadow silhouetted against the light.

"I thought you'd have called it a night by now," Nat said.

Ed lit what he hoped would be his last cigarette of the day. "Not just yet. Thought I'd have a smoke first and try to unwind a little."

"We'll be crossing the Mississippi River in a minute or two," Grayson said. "Think we can see anything from out here?"

"Not much. It's too blasted dark."

Ed felt the atmosphere changing as they approached the river, and the air seemed thicker and damper.. He peered out through the small window in the side of the passage and saw the passing outlines of steel girders against the sky.

"I guess we're on the bridge now," Nat said.

Ed nodded, wishing they were going the other way on it and heading back to D.C. He stared down toward the mile-wide expanse of muddy water passing beneath them. For the most part, the river was invisible, but here and there he could see a few ripples catching the light.

"All these trips are tough," he said, "but this is the toughest one yet for me. I keep thinking about all the things that could be hiding out there in the dark, waiting to jump us. Then I start remembering that phone call from the man in Texas."

"I've thought about him a lot, too," Nat said. "I'd give half my pension if I could talk to that guy face to face right now."

The forest of steel girders abruptly ended, and moments later, the train was rolling across swampy delta country and slicing through patches of ground fog. Apparently, they were now in Arkansas. But the clammy stickiness of the river still clung to Ed, and the thought brought him no comfort. At the moment, he would've given *all* his pension to know that Roosevelt would re-cross the Mississippi alive and well next week. But because of the phone caller who got away, there could be no such guarantee at any price. Right up to the last minute, Ed had tried to talk Chief Moran into sending a complement of twelve agents on the trip, but Moran wouldn't budge beyond seven.

"The military has thousands of personnel on standby at the President's major stops," Moran had said. "Five more men would only serve to get in the way."

Yes, maybe in the way of an assassin's bullet, Ed had thought. But he'd held his tongue. Moran didn't take kindly to backtalk.

Outside of the seven agents aboard, no one else on the train even carried weapons except Colonel E. M. Watson, FDR's rotund military aide, and Gus Gennerich, the President's personal bodyguard – unless you counted Mrs. Roosevelt, of course. And none of them would be worth much in a showdown. Ed stared into the muggy night and wondered where the telephone caller from Texas might be at this moment. What was he doing right now? What was he thinking? Had his call been nothing more than a vicious prank, or had it been an honest warning?

Somewhere in the infinity ahead lay the answer. Every passing mile brought them closer to it – and to potential disaster.

THIRTY-THREE

U.S. Highway 90
West of San Antonio, Texas
June 10, 1936

A three-quarter moon rose soon after midnight, but by then, Adam didn't care. They were almost to the town of Sabinal and only seventy-odd miles from San Antonio. The two-lane highway ran arrow-straight across the mesquite-studded barrens, and the little Ford V-8 was purring along a discreet quarter-mile behind the Nazis' sleek sedan.

A time or two as he followed it, Adam had observed the sedan through binoculars in fairly well-lighted areas. It wasn't a Cadillac or Buick, as he'd first guessed, but a black, four-door '36 LaSalle, a make and model he recognized from General Motors ads in several recent magazines. The LaSalle was a little smaller than its Cadillac cousin, but faster and more maneuverable, supposedly capable of speeds up to a hundred and ten miles an hour. Since this one was spanking new, it seemed likely that Kurt Radke had bought it especially for his guests. Adam wasn't concerned about the LaSalle's powerful V-12 engine and its vaunted top speed, however. As Texas outlaw Clyde Barrow had proved dozens of times, a '34 Ford V-8 could run away from virtually any other production-model vehicle on the American road, and this was especially true of the lightweight three-window coupe.

They'd passed only a half-dozen cars going in either direction since leaving Uvalde. But once they hit the outskirts of San Antonio, the traffic was bound to thicken up a little, even at this time of night. At that point, Adam would have to cut the gap between the coupe and the LaSalle to a few car-lengths or run the risk of losing their quarry. It was going to be tough staying that close without being spotted, but it was a problem that would have to be dealt with. The little Ford could more than hold its own in maneuverability and acceleration from zero to sixty. The only way the LaSalle might have a slight edge was if the driver took a notion to floorboard it on a straightaway. So far, however, the LaSalle was holding to a steady, law-abiding fifty-five miles an hour.

The first two hundred yards of the trip had been by far the toughest part so far. Adam had kept a death grip on the steering wheel as they careened down the mountain with no lights. Beside him, Ellie had clinched her eyes shut, whispered a prayer and held on for dear life. Adam felt as if he'd aged five years on the way down, and he still wasn't sure how they'd made it in one piece.

When they'd reached the gap in the barbed-wire fence, Adam could still make out the faint sparks of the LaSalle's taillights in the distance, and he knew then that the worst was over. The road to town was a good ten feet wide in most places, so following another car with the Ford's headlights off was a cinch compared to staying in the two twisting, twelve-inch-wide tracks of the trail.

Except for a few minor scratches on the fenders, the coupe had miraculously come through the descent unscathed. All told, everything had gone better than Adam had dared hope, but this was only the beginning.

Adam hadn't risked switching on his headlights until they were almost to the north city limits of Leakey. The LaSalle was nowhere in sight as they passed the courthouse, but Adam forced himself to proceed slowly and with utmost care until he was well south of town. The last thing he needed was to be pulled over by one of Sarge's patrol cars.

Within a mile or two, he managed to bring the taillights of the LaSalle back into view. This time he left the Ford's headlights on. It and the LaSalle had the Uvalde Road all to themselves at this hour, but Adam figured they were far enough from the Radke Ranch by now to show themselves without arousing the Nazis' suspicions.

Not long after they passed through Uvalde and turned left onto Highway 90, Ellie fell into an exhausted sleep in the seat beside him. Now her head rested lightly against his shoulder and the smell of her hair teased his nose. They'd been within a few feet of each other almost constantly for the past sixty hours – and under some of the grubbiest conditions imaginable. Yet the fact that they both were dirty, disheveled, and dog-tired did nothing to dull his desire for her.

He glanced down at her in the dim light from the dashboard, wanting to touch her but knowing it would only distract him from the task at hand and magnify his longing. One of these days, though, their time would come. A time free of urgency and crisis. A time unencumbered by standing watch. A time when there was no need to be at maximum alert.

He had to keep telling himself that – and somehow he had to make himself believe it.

It was almost 2 a.m., and Adam had been fighting to keep his eyes open for nearly an hour. The center line of the road had a mildly hypnotic effect, and there was nothing to see on either side of it except indistinct clumps of scrub brush and cactus. The smell of blooming sage drifted in through the open car window. Occasionally, the headlights reflected in the glassy eyes of deer grazing on the shoulders, and there was always the danger of one of them wandering onto the highway.

Searching the radio dial for company, he'd picked up WOAI in San Antonio just as it was playing the *Star-Spangled Banner* and signing off for the night. After that, the only thing he could find was a tinny Mexican station that faded in and out through bursts of static. Finally he'd given up on the airwaves and tried singing off-key to himself.

"The eyes of Texas are up-on you. . .
All the live-long day . . .

This, too, was a lost cause. Every few seconds, his concentration lapsed, and the words kept dying in his throat. Twice, he came perilously close to dozing off behind the wheel. The second time he jerked back to consciousness just in time to keep from running into the ditch. He was about to wake up Ellie and ask her to talk to him when he passed a sign pointing to Kelly Field, the big Army Air Corps base that lay just north of the highway, and he realized he was almost to San Antonio. Moments later, he spotted the first in a string of motels, cafes and beer joints that lined the highway in the distance ahead.

"Thank God," he said aloud. "We're finally getting somewhere."

Before he could enjoy any sense of relief, however, a troublesome question popped into his mind. He'd assumed all along that the LaSalle would stop in San Antonio, at least for the rest of the night. But what if it didn't?

What if the men in the big sedan kept going straight through the city, then struck out north toward Dallas on U.S. 81? In his present state, Adam doubted if he could even keep track of the LaSalle in the maze of streets ahead, much less stay with it for another two hundred and eighty miles. If the Nazis drove on, Ellie would have to take over the driving somehow, but there'd be no time to stop to switch drivers. They'd either have to make a quick change at a red light or an even quicker one while the car was in motion.

He tried to shake himself fully awake, but everything around him seemed fuzzy and out of context.

"Ellie, wake up!" Adam's voice was hoarse, but louder than he intended. He reached down and shook her shoulder. "Come on, wake up. I've got to talk to you." Still there was no response.

He noticed groggily that the LaSalle was still only about three hundred yards ahead of him, but suddenly there were other vehicles around, too. Headlights were coming at him from the opposite lane, and a few cars were pulling onto the highway. He had to slam on the brakes to keep from plowing into a late-model Studebaker that peeled out of a closed-up filling station directly into his path. It was only the third time since the trip began that another vehicle had separated them from the LaSalle. And once the Studebaker was in front of them, its driver seemed perfectly content to poke along at forty miles an hour.

Adam looked desperately for an opening to pass, but there was still oncoming traffic. As he fell back behind the Studebaker, a sticky apprehension welled up in his throat. It grew more intense as another car turned onto the highway between him and the LaSalle. Worse yet, he couldn't even see the LaSalle anymore.

Meanwhile, the abrupt force of the brakes and the Ford's brief skid had sent Ellie tumbling forward into the dashboard. Adam was able to grab her before she hit the windshield head-first, and fortunately the shock propelled her back to consciousness.

"What's happening?" she mumbled. "Where are we?"

"Welcome to San Antonio," he said. "Don't look now, but I may have just let our Nazi friends give us the slip."

"What do you mean? Where'd they go?"

"They're up ahead of us somewhere, but I don't know how far. Some guy pulled out and got in between us. It was my own stupid fault. I was about half asleep."

She yawned and squeezed his arm. "Don't blame yourself," she said. "I should've been awake to help. We can find them again, can't we?"

"Maybe. If they stop at one of the motels along here, that big, new LaSalle should be fairly easy to spot. If not, they may be in Timbuktu before I get around this moron in front of us."

Seconds later, an opening materialized in the opposite lane and Adam was able to squeeze past the sluggish Studebaker. In the distance ahead he saw a line of four or five vehicles rounding a slight curve, but he couldn't tell if the LaSalle was among them.

Within the next quarter-mile, business buildings closed in on both sides of them, and the open highway turned into a city street. The speed limit abruptly dropped to thirty-five just as they passed a police car parked in front of a darkened restaurant. One of the two cops inside it seemed to give them the eye as they passed, but the squad car made no move to follow them.

A cluster of multi-colored neon signs was coming up. There were at least eight or ten tourist courts just ahead – close enough that he could read the names:

Lone Star Cottages . . . El Rancho-tel . . . Alamo Plaza . . . Blue Top Courts . . . Western Skies Lodge . . . Most of them had their "vacancy" signs turned on, too. If the Nazis were going to stop for the night, Adam thought, this strip was probably the likeliest spot they'd find on this side of the city. He slowed down, straining his eyes against the darkness.

"They could be anywhere along here," he said. "You watch the right side of the road and I'll watch the left. Just try not to look like you're staring."

They traveled a block in silence, then two blocks, then three. Ellie sat motionless, gazing intently out her window. Adam's eyes were smarting, and he had to keep blinking to clear his vision. Twice, he saw dark sedans that he thought were the LaSalle, and his heart leaped, but both times he was wrong. Now the last of the bright neon signs were rapidly approaching. Beyond was a long, dark expanse with only scattered street lamps and closed commercial buildings.

He cursed under his breath. Damn it, the LaSalle and its occupants were gone. Their only hope now was to pull out all the stops and try to catch them, even at the risk of a speeding ticket – or worse. He was about to hit the accelerator when he heard Ellie gasp.

"Wait! Slow down. I think I see them."

Adam took his foot off the gas and leaned over to look out Ellie's window. To the right of the roadway was an arched stucco facade. As the Ford drew abreast of it, he could read its flickering green sign.

"Mission Courts. Kitchenettes. Vacancy."

Then he spotted the LaSalle. It was stopped beside the motel office with its lights still on and its rear end facing the street. There was no mistaking those taillights – not after staring at them for a hundred and fifty miles.

Adam held his breath as they coasted past the Mission Courts. A second later, he eased the Ford off the road and turned into the motel directly across the street.

A pink-and-blue sign identified this one as La Siesta Lodge, but Adam scarcely noticed the name. He was more interested in the fact that only about half of the twelve cabins had cars parked in front of them, indicating that the others were unoccupied. He eased to a stop in front of the nearest vacant-looking cottage and cut the headlights. So far, so good. To a casual glance, they almost looked as if they belonged here.

Ellie was leaning over the back of her seat, staring through the rear window toward the other side of the road

"Can you see still see them?" he asked, turning and putting his head next to hers.

"Yes," she whispered. "One of them's knocking on the door of the motel office."

A moment later, the door opened, illuminating a bulky male figure on the stoop outside. As the figure stepped through the doorway, it half turned, and Ellie gasped as she saw the man's face.

"My God, it's one of the same ones who came to the store," she said. "The other one called him 'Otto.'"

"Oh, yeah, the sausage-lover," Adam rasped. "It's a good thing he's not a better shot. He's also the one who tried to blow my head off that day in the truck."

After two or three minutes inside the motel office, Otto reappeared. He opened the front door on the passenger side of the LaSalle and got in. The car moved forward, stopping again at the fourth unit in a row of sixteen cottages, where Otto got out, and a smaller man emerged on the driver's side. Adam waited for the car's rear doors to open and other passengers to appear, but nothing happened.

Otto unlocked the cottage door while the small man who'd been driving opened the LaSalle's trunk and removed two pieces of luggage. As Otto entered the cottage, a shaft of light from its open door illuminated the interior of the dark sedan. To Adam's dismay, the car was clearly empty.

"But . . . there's only two of them." Ellie's voice was stunned. "What happened to the other three? Where could they be?"

"God only knows," Adam said, feeling sick inside.

THIRTY-FOUR

Wilhelm Lutz threw his jacket over the back of a chair and flopped down on the nearest of the motel room's two single beds. After driving all the way from the Radke Ranch, he was tense, tired and in need of sleep. Hauptman's non-stop talking over the past three-plus hours had served to keep Lutz alert at the wheel, but it had done nothing to improve his mood. All he wanted now was for Otto to hush and go to bed, but Hauptman seemed as wide-awake and eager as a child on Christmas Eve.

"We're in a real city, Villy," Otto exulted. "We should go out and have a look around. *Trinken das schnapps, ja?*"

"Speak English, damn it," Lutz snapped. "You know the Major's orders. Besides, it's past curfew. They don't sell alcohol in Texas at this time of night, and we wouldn't be going out if they did. There'll be no more drinking from this point on in the mission, Otto. Not a drop. Is that clear?"

Otto frowned. "You're just a cold blanket, as the Americans say."

"It's a 'wet blanket,' you imbecile. Now shut up about it. I'm in command here."

Lutz kicked off his shoes and lit a cigarette. Occasionally, he wished he were more like Otto, but drinking and chasing girls were the last things on his mind right now. He was bone-tired from the long drive, besieged by loneliness for his family, and wondering what his little daughter, Heidi, was doing at this moment. It was half past 9 a.m. back in Stuttgart, so she was likely in school. He felt a tear push at his eyelid at the thought.

Lutz hadn't wanted to be stuck with Otto. Keeping the big lummox in line was supposed to be Becker's job. But when Major Dietrich had divided the members of the mission into two teams, one for Dallas and one for San Antonio, both logic and circumstances dictated that Lutz and Hauptman be given the latter assignment.

Lutz was the munitions expert of the group, and the San Antonio situation appeared to lend itself more to explosives. In Dietrich's opinion, it also entailed more potential risk of hand-to-hand encounters with American police or soldiers than the Dallas scenario. This could mean a greater need for Hauptman's physical strength and his ability to kill with cold, mechanical efficiency.

"I'm going to bed, and I strongly suggest you do the same," Lutz said. "It's almost 2:30 a.m. and we have much to do tomorrow."

"I'm not sleepy," Otto said peevishly. "As long as we're stuck in this squalid little room, I think I'll try on my uniform and see how it fits."

Otto opened one of the suitcases and removed two neatly folded U.S. Army uniforms. Each consisted of a khaki blouse, matching breeches, leggings and garrison cap, olive tie, well-polished boots and Sam Browne belt. The top uniform was that of a private first-class in the 2nd Infantry Division, stationed a few miles away at Fort Sam Houston. The second uniform was identical, except that it was several sizes smaller and bore the chevrons of a staff sergeant.

"Do as you wish, but be careful not to get it soiled or wrinkled." Lutz said. "Approximately forty hours from now, we'll be greeting the President of the United States in these uniforms. We'll want to look our best for the occasion."

Otto slipped on the private's blouse and slowly buttoned it from the bottom. It was slightly tight across his broad belly, but other than that, it was a good fit. The drugged soldier from which it had been removed in

Nuevo Laredo had been somewhat trimmer than Otto, but almost exactly the same height and weight.

"What of the bomb?" Otto asked casually. He pointed to a small leather case on the floor as he slipped the tie around his neck and knotted it. "It is all assembled and ready, yes?"

"All except for the detonator," Lutz said, "and that must be attached at the last moment. It will take only a few seconds to arm the device when the time comes."

Otto turned to look at his superior. "You seem very certain that we'll be using the bomb here."

"Yes," Lutz said. "If we plan and reconnoiter well, we'll find a way."

Otto laughed softly. "The Oberhaupt said we must be extremely careful and activate the bomb only if we're totally sure of success. But you're always careful, aren't you, Villy?"

"I know my business when it comes to these things." Lutz was still angry that Dietrich placed such priority on the Dallas portion of the mission, and he seethed at the restrictive orders under which they were being forced to operate. The Dallas team had no right to all the action and glory, Lutz thought. He and Hauptman weren't here merely to observe and take notes.

Lutz wanted the Fatherland and little Heidi to be proud of him. If an opportunity presented itself, he had every intention of striking the decisive blow right here in San Antonio. The bomb was small and compact. It weighed just over three pounds, complete with the timing device. It would fit easily beneath a chair cushion, inside a cabinet, or under a bed. Yet it contained enough TNT to blow Roosevelt's Pullman coach to splinters.

Otto straightened his tie and studied himself in the mirror above the maple-veneer dresser. He'd apparently forgotten all about the bomb.

"Ah, Villy, if the American *frauleins* could only see me now," he said, staring admiringly at his reflection. "They would love me, ja? I mean, yes?"

"Go to bed, you conceited ass," Lutz said.

Adam had been almost zombie-like with weariness and dejection as he got out of the car, and even after sleeping within inches of Ellie for two and a half straight nights, he'd seemed strangely shy about checking into the La Siesta Lodge with her.

"Should I get us separate rooms?" he asked as he started toward the office.

She shook her head. "No, I want to stay with you."

Adam squinted quizzically at her. "Are you sure?"

"Well, it seems silly to pay for two rooms, especially since only one of us can sleep at a time anyway. Remember?"

"Oh, yeah, I forgot." Disappointment mingled with the exhaustion in his voice.

By the time he finished registering, he was almost literally sleepwalking. If Ellie hadn't waited for him just outside the office and let him lean on her on the way to the car, he might never have made it to the cabin. She put her arm around him for support as they stumbled along together.

He made several bleary-eyed attempts to unlock the cabin door, but finally gave up and handed the key to her. He sagged heavily against the wall while she opened the door.

"I'm dead on my feet, and my knees are stiff as boards," he muttered. "It's been a long time since I felt this tired."

"Go ahead and lie down," she said. "I'll take the first watch."

His half-smile seemed to take his last ounce of strength. "I guess I ought to argue about it, but I don't have the strength. Just let me sleep a couple of hours. Then I'll take over."

"How did you sign the register?" she asked.

He frowned. "Why do you want to know?"

"Just curious. How did you?"

He shrugged. "Mr. and Mrs. Adam Smith. Is that all right?"

She nodded. "It's fine. Not very original, but it'll do."

Adam was unconscious before Ellie finished tugging his boots off and lifting his legs onto the bed. She turned off all the lights except for the overhead bulb in the bathroom, then opened the front curtain an inch or two and checked to make sure the LaSalle was still parked across the road. It was.

She sat down in a straight-back chair and tried to relax, but she immediately began to fidget. There was nothing to do in the room. Of course, there'd been nothing to do on the ridge overlooking the gate to the Radke Ranch, either, but somehow that had been different. In desperation, she reached for the Gideon Bible on the dresser, intending to read a few of her favorite scriptures.

As she turned away, she saw herself in the mirror and grimaced. After crawling in the dirt and sleeping on the ground since Sunday night, she was a total wreck. Since she was wide awake anyway, she thought, she might as well utilize the time to get herself cleaned up. If she hurried, she could take a shower, shampoo her hair and be back at the window in twenty minutes at the outside. The Nazis undoubtedly weren't going anywhere for the next few hours anyway.

She started for the bathroom but stopped in mid-stride and turned back to take one last look outside. The lights were still burning brightly in Cottage No. 4 across the road. It was 2:30 a.m., she thought. What could the Germans possibly be doing over there? As she watched, she caught a fleeting movement in one of the windows. The shade wasn't down all the way, and she could see somebody walking around inside.

She shut the curtain and tried to forget about it while she unpacked her toiletries and assembled them in the cramped little bathroom. She took fresh underwear and her robe from her suitcase, closed the bathroom door behind her and started to turn on the shower. Then she stopped.

Despite herself, Ellie went back to the window and peeked again around the curtain at the lighted cabin in the distance. A hint of movement was still visible below the partly drawn shade.

She knew in that instant that her shower and shampoo would have to wait.

❋

Through the three-inch gap between the windowsill and the bottom of the shade, Ellie stared at an incredible scene inside the motel room. If the big man named Otto had been two feet closer to the slightly open window, she could've reached out and touched him. The thought made her skin crawl.

It was all she could do to force herself to squat there in the darkness outside Cottage No. 4 of the Mission Courts. Her senses told her to get away from the window as fast as humanly possible. Her rational mind screamed at her to run back to the cabin across the road where Adam lay sleeping, blissfully unaware of Ellie's clandestine prowlings. Dear God, she hated to think what he'd do if he found out where she was right now. That in itself was reason enough to run, but it was as if she were frozen there outside the Nazis' window by the same compulsive force that had led her to take this monumental risk in the first place.

Ellie was dumbfounded at her own impulsive behavior – and more than a little frightened by it. Maybe her foolhardiness had something to do with the shock of discovering that she and Adam had been following just two men, not five. Maybe it grew out of knowing that the other three Nazis were going about their deadly business somewhere else at this moment, and that she and Adam were powerless to do anything about it. But regardless of her motivation, she was certain now that what she was witnessing was well worth the risk – if only she could get back to her own quarters without being seen or caught.

She'd tried desperately to ignore the lighted window and the partially drawn shade. Again and again, she'd vowed to go ahead with her plans for a shower and a shampoo. But each time she'd pulled back the curtain to steal another glance toward the Mission Courts, the lights and the shade were still there, drawing her irresistibly toward the cottage across the road – like a moth to a flame.

She recalled sitting down on the edge of the double bed and touching Adam lightly on the forehead. He'd been sound asleep, and she doubted that she could wake him if the room were on fire.

"Don't worry," she'd whispered to his unconscious form. "I'll be back before you even know I'm gone."

Now she crouched transfixed just outside the open window, holding her breath and watching the scene in the room beyond.

"Ah, Villy, if only the American *frauleins* could see me now . . . " she heard Otto saying.

What the hulking Gestapo agent didn't realize, Ellie thought, was that one American woman *could* see him now. She could see him, his cohort and their plan with horrifying clarity.

When President Roosevelt arrived in San Antonio tomorrow evening, the two Germans would be disguised as American soldiers. With hundreds of troops assigned to guard the President, who would ever suspect that two of them were actually Nazi assassins armed with a time bomb? If Ellie hadn't seen the uniforms with her own eyes, she would never have believed it herself.

"Go to bed, you conceited ass," she heard Willy's voice say from inside.

Two minutes later, the lights abruptly went off in the cottage. In the darkness that followed, Ellie felt herself freed of the magnetizing force that had brought her there.

Now, finally, she was able to run – and she did.

THIRTY-FIVE

Aboard FDR's Special Train
Little Rock, Arkansas
June 10, 1936

It was barely 7 a.m., but Eleanor Roosevelt had already been up for over an hour. She'd bathed quickly and efficiently, then put on the floral print dress in which she'd accompany her husband to the Arkansas Statehouse later in the morning. She wore virtually no makeup, so she paused only briefly at the dressing table. When it came to her physical appearance, Eleanor had no remaining vanity whatsoever. She viewed makeup as a childish affectation and primping as a waste of time. It was in other, less outwardly noticeable aspects of her total person that she took fierce pride.

Although she had little appetite for breakfast, she'd drunk a cup of tea and eaten a piece of toast while she read over the notes she'd compiled for Franklin on political trends in Tennessee and the climate among voters in general in the Deep South.

Now she was ready for the morning conference with her husband that was standard procedure after one of her solo trips. In her travels, she always kept her ear to the ground in Franklin's behalf. Among close confidants, he called her his "legs." It was a role and responsibility she gladly accepted.

In her opinion, Franklin had few weaknesses as a political leader. As a male of the species, however, he had all too many.

She knocked softly on the door of his bedroom. "Come on in," his booming voice responded. "It's open."

She stepped through the narrow doorway and smiled tightly at her husband. He was sitting against the headboard of the bed, his back propped with several pillows. In one hand, he held yesterday's final edition of the *Washington Star* opened to the editorial page; in the other, a half-empty china coffee cup. The omnipresent cigarette holder and a smoldering Camel lay in an ashtray on the night table. Copies of various other morning newspapers were scattered around him on the bed.

"Good morning, Franklin," Eleanor said. "Is there good news today?"

He set his cup down, folded the paper in his lap and reached for the cigarette holder. "Oh, yes indeed, Maw," he said, looking at her over his glasses. "There's wonderful news – but in most of these papers, it's all about the Republicans."

"Well, you needn't worry." She sat down gingerly on the edge of the bed, placing her black leather handbag beside her. "From what I've seen and heard in Tennessee in the past few days, the Democratic ticket will carry the South handily in November. So don't begrudge Governor Landon a few headlines in the meantime."

"Well, that's nice to know. Do I even need to bother to campaign then?"

"Would it matter if you *didn't* need to?" she jibed. "I suspect you'd go right on doing it anyhow. You love it too much to stop."

He grinned again with the cigarette holder jutting from his jaw. "You know me pretty well, don't you, darling?"

"Oh, yes, I know you *very* well, my dearest." Her eyes seemed to look past him. "I predict you'll be re-elected by a huge margin in the fall, because, as you know, you're a magnificent President."

"I do believe I'll blush if you don't stop," he bantered. "Now if I were only a magnificent husband, too, right? I can almost hear you thinking that."

Her lips stretched against her prominent teeth in another tight smile. "I'm sure you do the best you can, my dear," she said. "Would you like me to help you get dressed, or are you waiting for Miss LeHand to do it?"

"Oh, there's time enough for that," he said, ignoring her insinuation. "We don't leave for the Statehouse until nine, so let's talk a bit. What do you hear about Texas? How do you think we stand in the Lone Star State?"

She pondered the question for a moment. "I think we're all right there," she said finally, "but not as strong as we are in Tennessee or Arkansas. And I'm afraid much of our strength there derives from Mr. Garner, rather than you, my dear. He isn't one of my favorite people, but I think you need to make a point of saying some nice things about him in your Texas speeches."

"Oh, I intend to. In fact, I already have something written out for our brief stop in Austin. That's real Garner country down there, they tell me."

"It wouldn't hurt to cast some bouquets his way in your other talks, too," she said.

"I always value your advice, Maw," he said, "and I'm glad you're going to Texas with me. Mighty glad and right proud, as they say down along the Rio Grande."

"Well, I think the trip can be very beneficial for you," she said.

He leaned forward and gave her a kiss on the cheek. As he did, one of his lifeless legs slid against her purse and sent it tumbling off the bed before she could grab it. When it hit the floor, several items spilled out of it. One of them was the snub-nosed .25-caliber revolver that she always carried in her travels.

Franklin grinned broadly when he saw the pistol on the floor.

"Looks like you're all set for Texas," he said. "I see you brought along your trusty shooting iron."

"Oh, dear," Eleanor said, stooping to retrieve the weapon. "I totally forgot that was in my purse." She laughed nervously. "It's all Colonel Starling's fault, you know."

"I know, my darling, I know. But if that's the purse you're taking to the Statehouse this morning, I'd suggest you stash the gun somewhere else for now. I wouldn't want you to shoot any of our good Arkansas constituents."

Eleanor stood up, fumbling to stuff the little pearl-handled revolver back inside the handbag. Franklin could make a joke out of anything, and he'd always had an uncanny knack for making her feel foolish.

"Forgive my clumsiness," she said. "I'll take it to my room and put it in one of my suitcases." She turned hastily toward the door.

THIRTY-SIX

San Antonio, Texas
June 10, 1936

Something wasn't quite right.

Adam could sense it the instant he opened his eyes. Even before he was fully conscious, he could feel his muscles tensing. He was sprawled face-down across the bed, lying on top of the covers with a pillow wadded under his head. Except for his boots, he was fully clothed. He knew he was in some kind of tourist court, but he had only the vaguest recollection about how he'd gotten there.

Bright sunlight streamed in through the curtains on the cabin window. Adam had no idea what time it was, but it felt late. Ominously late.

He rolled over and squinted at his watch. It was 8:17 a.m. on Wednesday morning. He'd been out like a light for six hours.

Six hours? How could that be? He'd promised to relieve Ellie on watch after a two-hour nap. Where the hell *was* Ellie anyway?

He sat up, rubbing his eyes and ready to call her name. Then he saw her. She was slumped in a chair by the window, wearing a fluffy-white chenille robe and a bath towel wrapped around her head. Her chin was on her chest, and except for the gentle rise and fall of her breathing, she was totally motionless. She was sound asleep.

Adam tiptoed to the window, pulled back the curtain and looked out. The sun reflected brilliantly off the row of white stucco cottages across the road at the Mission Courts. There were only two cars still parked in front of the cottages. Neither one of them was a black '36 LaSalle. The door to Cottage No. 4 stood wide open, revealing only emptiness inside.

The Nazis were gone. While he and Ellie slept, they'd disappeared.

His heart sank inside him. Then he felt a surge of hopeless anger. In that moment, every pain, hardship and sacrifice they'd endured to follow the German agents this far seemed utterly pointless. The fifty-hour vigil on the mountain; the wild, careening drive down the narrow trail; the tortuous miles of driving with no lights; the nerve-wracking ordeal of keeping the LaSalle's taillights in view hour after hour – all of it had been in vain.

The Nazis were gone, and it was pretty obvious they weren't coming back. He wanted to bang his fists against the wall and scream. In the end, though, he only slumped on the floor beside Ellie's chair and laid his head against her knee.

He wasn't sure how long he stayed in that position without moving. But after a few minutes, he felt her stir. She finally opened her eyes, reached down absently to touch his head, then stiffened abruptly.

"Oh, Adam," she blurted. "I didn't mean to go to sleep."

He got up and pulled the other straight-back chair away from the small table. He sat down facing her. "You couldn't help it. You were exhausted. We both were."

"What time is it?" she asked.

"About eight-thirty."

She was out of the chair like a shot. She sprang to the window and looked out.

"Oh, no!" she gasped as the realization crashed down on her. "They . . . they're gone." As she turned toward him, sudden tears welled in her eyes, running down her cheeks and dripping onto the collar of the chenille robe.

It was the first time Adam had seen her really cry since that night on the Radke Ranch so long ago. The sight of her distress made him forget how upset he'd been a few moments earlier. Even in his first blind burst of anger, he'd never blamed her. The Nazis had undoubtedly left at a time when he, not Ellie, should've been on watch. If anyone was responsible for letting it happen, he was the culprit.

He reached out and grasped her hands, drawing her slowly toward him. "Everything's going to be all right," he said. "We'll figure something out."

She didn't seem to hear him. "After all the trouble we went to, they've gotten away," she said brokenly, "and it's all my fault."

"Don't say that. It's nobody's fault. It's just one of those things."

"I went to sleep at my post," she insisted. "They shoot soldiers for that, and I don't blame them. God, I feel like shooting myself!"

She was shaking violently against him as he pulled her into his arms. He unwound the towel from around her hair and used it to dry the tears on her face.

"Hush now," he whispered. "If you really want to know, I'm almost glad they're gone. If we tried to tail them everywhere they went for the next thirty-five hours, they'd be bound to spot us, anyway. And that would be a hundred times worse than this. If we go where Roosevelt's going to be tomorrow afternoon, I have a feeling we can find them again – unless they leave town for some reason."

She laid her head on his shoulder. "Don't worry, they won't leave," she sniffed. "They plan to be downtown at the railroad station tomorrow to meet the President. They'll be dressed in American Army uniforms."

He wasn't sure he'd heard her correctly. "What are you talking about?"

She kept her eyes averted as she spoke. "I went over there and looked in their window last night. I saw the uniforms and I heard them talking. They have a bomb of some kind with them."

Adam's heart skipped a beat. He held her back from him and stared into her face. "You did *what?*"

"I saw their light on and I sneaked over there. I knew I shouldn't do it, but somehow I just couldn't help myself."

His eyes caught hers and held them. "Holy hell," he said. "Don't you know I'd die if anything happened to you?"

She looked as if she might start crying again. "I'm sorry," she said. "It was like an obsession."

"Well, I know all about obsessions," he said and kissed her.

His words were the last intelligible sounds that either of them made for a long time. The first kiss lasted for two or three minutes, building steadily in intensity. No sooner was it over than another one started, more urgent and demanding than the first.

She melted against him as his lips moved down her neck. He unfastened the top of the robe and it slipped down over her shoulders and the swell of her breasts. He felt her arms close tightly around him, her fingertips on the back of his neck. His hands moved inside the robe, and he made a pulse-pounding discovery: Beneath the fluffy-white chenille, she was wearing nothing at all.

His hand cupped one of her bare breasts. He felt the nipple shrivel against his palm. Thank God she'd let the two Nazis slip away, he thought. If only he could tell her how grateful he was to her for that. As a result, there was no crisis to demand their immediate attention right now. No watches to stand or life-and-death errands to perform. No one to run from or chase after. No unavoidable schedules to keep. Beyond this room, the world could cease to exist and he wouldn't give a damn. He wanted to tell her all that, but he wasn't sure he could make her hear above his hammering heart.

Somehow, they were on the bed. He had no idea how they'd gotten there, and he didn't care. The room seemed to whirl wildly around him as his awed fingers explored the dark, damp mystery between her thighs. She clung tightly to him, her own fingers digging into the flesh of his shoulders. Her body writhing, thrusting, undulating. Opening itself to him like a flower.

Her voice was a moan low in her throat as he loosened the belt of the robe and pulled it aside. He eased himself between her legs, grappling with one hand at the metal buttons of his Levis.

Then her moan twisted itself into an anguished cry – like the sound of a wounded animal.

"Noooo! Oh, God, no – I can't!"

Before he knew what was happening, everything came unraveled at once. She shoved him away, and her hands became frantic little fists, flailing at him with the same urgency as they'd sought to pull him to her seconds before. Her voice gasped out the same word over and over:

"No! No! No! No!"

In shock, he tried to draw back from her, and as he did, one of her fists caught him squarely in the mouth. He grunted and sat up, seeing stars and watching her wrap the robe securely back around her and retreat to the far side of the bed.

He tasted blood on his lip. It was a struggle to keep his voice even, but he managed. "I'm sorry," he said. "I didn't mean to upset you."

She coiled herself into a ball and kept her face turned away. He stared at her for a moment, then shook his head and walked around the bed to the bathroom, closing the door quietly behind him. He blotted his lip with a piece of toilet tissue, then washed his face in the sink and dried it with one of the white motel towels.

He looked at his stunned image in the mirror and resisted the urge to punch the wall.

❋

Ellie was staring morosely at the bathroom door when Adam finally opened it and came out. She watched him sit down in a chair by the bed and pull his boots on. Finally, her fragile whisper broke the heavy silence.

"Are you mad at me?" she asked.

"I don't know," he said without looking at her. "Maybe a little. The only thing I really know is that I love you. I'm not sure how I know because I've never loved anybody before – but I do."

"Couldn't you just yell at me instead of saying something like that? Couldn't you call me a slut and a tease and maybe throw something at me? I could deal with that."

He shrugged. "I guess I could, but it wouldn't change anything."

"I didn't mean to hurt you," she said. "I . . . I just panicked, that's all."

It was true. She'd been swept up by a powerful current of passion, but when she'd felt Adam between her legs, the old terror had surged up inside her. The same blind panic that Kurt had sent flooding through her. Only twice since that terrible night had she reached the ultimate stage of intimacy with a man – and never with an Anglo. Both times the panic had first convulsed her, then turned her to cold, unfeeling stone.

Now it had happened again. At first, she'd thought it wouldn't this time, but then, at the last moment, the terror had come back with the force of an avalanche, and everything had gone wrong.

Ellie had been thirteen that clear, moonless summer night, and she'd still thought of herself as Elena. Elena the child. Elena the innocent.

She'd spent most of the day reading a copy of Black Beauty *from the library, and she was almost to the last chapter when she heard Kurt Radke's Cadillac pull up outside the store. Mama and Papa had driven away that morning on one of their two-day buying trips to Mexico, leaving Elena and Luz in charge of the store. But almost as soon as Papa's old Franklin sedan was out of sight, Kurt had come screeching into the driveway in the Cadillac. Luz had jumped into the car with him, and the two of them had disappeared, leaving Elena alone to wait on customers and close up the store at six o'clock.*

Now it was after dark, and Elena wished that Luz and Kurt had stayed away. Ever since the night in the car, she'd hated the thought of seeing him. Luz was giggling and talking loud when she staggered into the living quarters behind the store, and Elena knew that her sister was drunk again. The door to Luz's room slammed shut, and Elena heard bedsprings creaking. She tried not to listen, but the sounds she heard unnerved her. Kurt was drunk, too – not as drunk as Luz but drunk enough to be mean and violent.

There was no lock on Elena's bedroom door, so she propped a chair against it and wedged the back of it under the doorknob. She also opened the window in case she needed to exit the room in a hurry. If she heard Kurt coming, she could jump out the window and run.

A half-hour passed, and there was now only silence from across the hall. Elena was trying desperately to concentrate on her book when a sudden wrenching noise filled the room and the door burst open. The chair blocked it for a second, then crashed to the floor. She turned and saw Kurt framed in the doorway. He was wearing a broad grin and nothing else.

"Hello there, baby sister," he said. "I think you and me got a little unfinished business to settle tonight."

"Stop it, Kurt," she said. "Stay away."

"Go on and yell if you want to," he said. "There's nobody around to hear you but Luz, and she could sleep through a damn tornado in the shape she's in."

Elena dropped the book and lunged for the window, but he was on her before she was halfway there. She could smell the raw, stinging odors of whiskey on his breath and sweat on his body as he forced her mouth against his. She could feel the immense strength in his powerful frame.

"No," she said, twisting her head away. "You're Luz's boyfriend, and it's not right. I don't want it this way. I don't want it to be you."

"I don't give a damn what you want. You'll like it, just wait and see."

She tried to squirm away as he extinguished the lamp, but he was too quick and strong for her. As he pinioned her arms with one hand and pawed between her legs with the other, she made the mistake of trying to fight him. For a moment, she was able to jerk free and rake her fingernails hard down the side of his face.

He howled with rage and swiped at the blood on his cheek.

"Okay, bitch, you want to play rough, that's the way we'll play."

He slapped her twice, very hard. The blows jolted tears from her eyes and made her head feel as if it might explode. In a daze, she felt him ripping her skirt, clawing at her undergarments, prying her legs apart – just as it had happened in the car that other night. Only this time it didn't stop. It seemed to go on and on forever, and Adam Wagner wasn't there to intervene. Nobody was there to help her. In the dim light, she saw a smear of her blood on the sheet. She squeezed her eyes shut and prayed for it to end.

And that was when Luz burst through the doorway, naked and glistening with sweat, and holding the foot-long butcher knife that Mama used to dissect chickens and filet fish. Elena was dimly aware of Kurt jumping off the bed, struggling with Luz over the knife.

Then Elena ran. She hugged the sheet around her and ran as fast as she could go. Stumbling. Falling. Crashing into furniture. She ran to the front of the store and felt under the counter where Papa kept his pistol, but it wasn't there. Maybe Papa had taken it with him. She heard a series of thuds and shouts from the direction of her bedroom, then a resounding crash. Then nothing.

"Luz," she cried. "Are you all right?"

Elena darted back into the living quarters. She reached the back door in time to see the Cadillac touring car careen wildly down the narrow driveway, its wheels spewing caliche dust and its engine straining. She caught a fleeting glimpse of Luz hunched over the steering wheel. The car's tires squealed as it lurched onto the roadway on two wheels. For an instant, Elena was sure it would either crash into the ditch or overturn. Then it somehow righted itself and streaked away. Within seconds, it had disappeared.

What was left of Luz's body after the wreck was found the next day halfway down the side of the Frio Canyon. Fifty yards away and almost to the bottom of the gorge were the charred and twisted remains of the Cadillac.

Luz wasn't the only one who'd died that night, however. An innocent young girl named Elena had also died, and a cynical, embittered woman who called herself Ellie had taken her place.

Ellie drifted back to the present and heard Adam's voice. "Look, it's okay. Don't worry about it. What's a split lip between friends anyway?"

She kept her head lowered, avoiding his eyes, and wondering: Why couldn't he be like all the other gringo men she'd known? Why did he always have to be so patient? So decent? So . . . *nice*? For two months, she'd waited for him to turn into a bastard like Kurt, convinced that, sooner or later, he'd justify her distrust.

That he never had was unsettling. It ate away at the foundation of all she'd believed for twenty long years. It made her wonder about herself and her innermost fears and hatreds. It made her wonder if the scars on her soul would ever heal.

Although Kurt had violated her in the most vicious way imaginable, she'd remained, at least in one sense, a virgin until now. Never before in her life had she experienced the slightest pleasure from a man's possession of her body. Never before had she felt like anything more than a handy disposable object – something to be used, then tossed aside. But for a few fleeting moments, it had been different this time.

"Do you still want to be friends?" she asked. "I wouldn't blame you if you didn't."

He managed a small smile. "Yeah, I guess that'll have to do," he said, "until something better comes along."

THIRTY-SEVEN

Reál County, Texas
June 10, 1936

When the phone rang on Sheriff Streicher's desk early that Monday morning and he heard Kurt Radke's voice on the line demanding to know where Adam Wagner was, Streicher lost what little was left of his temper. He'd been seething all weekend about the "wool buyers" on Radke's ranch, the FBI agent who'd shown up to check on them, and Adam's heated accusations over the phone. Kurt's agitated call was the last straw.

"Hell, no, I don't know any more about Adam now than I did the last six times you asked me," Streicher said. "Likely as not, he's gone to Dallas, like his daddy says, but right now I've got more important things on my mind. I tell you what, you just hold on, and I'll be out to your place in a few minutes. There's a whole damn bunch of stuff we need to talk about, and we may as well do it now."

"It's really not necessary to drive out here," Kurt said, sounding slightly unnerved by the Sheriff's assertiveness. "I can hear you just fine over the phone."

"I don't want to go into this on the phone. We need to talk about it face to face, just you and me, with no telephone operators listening in."

"But this isn't a good time. I'm real busy right now."

"Busy with who? Your damn wool buyers from Pennsylvania?"

There was a long silence, and when Kurt spoke again, his voice was as brittle as breaking glass "What my guests and I do is none of your concern, Sheriff. I suggest you mind your own business."

"Anytime the FBI comes poking around in my county, it *is* my business," Streicher said. "They seem awful damn interested in you and those wool buyers, and maybe I'm starting to understand why."

"I don't know what you mean." Now Streicher could hear alarm mixed with the anger in Kurt's voice. "Nothing you're saying makes any sense."

"Yeah, well I'll explain it to you when I get there," the Sheriff said and hung up.

A half-hour later, Streicher turned into the front gate of the Radke Ranch and was amazed to meet a car carrying several of the "wool buyers" speeding toward him, heading for the main road. The Sheriff realized instantly that this was no mere coincidence, and seeing the mysterious strangers' hurried departure only magnified his previous suspicions.

Streicher swore softly under his breath. If only he hadn't lost his composure on the phone with Kurt – wasting valuable time in the process – he might have reached the ranch before the so-called wool buyers had a chance to leave. He'd yearned to confront Kurt's visitors in person one more time. Then again, in his present frame of mind, it was probably wiser – and safer – that he hadn't.

Under the circumstances, the Sheriff wasn't foolhardy enough to try to stop them now. But in the ten seconds or so that he had a close-up view of the front of their car, he memorized the combination of letters and numbers on its yellow-and-black Texas license plate and repeated them to himself until he was positive he could remember them.

NE-7691 . . . NE-7691 . . . NE-7691 . . .

The car was a dark-blue Buick four-door, shiny and new-looking. Streicher could see three men inside, two in the front seat and one in the rear, each of their faces plainly visible and recognizable. They undoubtedly recognized his officially marked Sheriff's Department Ford, too, but they drove on without slowing down or so much as glancing in his direction.

The men in the car were wearing business suits and ties today instead of their usual khakis and open-collared sport shirts. Streicher watched in the rearview mirror as the Buick bumped across the cattle guard and turned onto the main road toward Leakey. There was an air of finality about their departure, as if they were going home to Pennsylvania – or wherever they'd come from – and Streicher had the distinct feeling that they wouldn't be coming back.

On one level, the Sheriff didn't give a tinker's damn where the occupants of the Buick went, as long as it was away from Reál County. If he ever saw any of them again, it would be too soon. On the other hand, he'd already stuck his head in a noose because of them, and he thirsted to know more about them. As the blue sedan shrank into the distance, Streicher was especially curious about where the other two "wool buyers" might be. He knew there were five of them in all, but only three were in the Buick.

Damn them, he thought, who the hell *were* they, anyway?

Ever since Streicher's face-off with the FBI agent from San Antonio, Kurt Radke's guests had never been far from the Sheriff's mind. After the agent left, he'd picked up the phone a dozen times to call Kurt about what the G-man had said and demand some explanation. But each time, he'd hung up without dialing.

Kurt was already severely nettled about Streicher's failure to locate Adam Wagner, and if Radke learned that he hadn't been told immediately about the G-man's visit and Adam's connection with it, he'd be mad as hell. But the agent's insinuations and Adam's wild outburst over the phone had raised unsettling questions that Streicher could no longer ignore. The harder he'd tried, the more they gnawed at him.

Digging into this barrel of snakes was the last thing the Sheriff wanted to do. Pressing Kurt too hard for information about his guests could be the biggest mistake of Streicher's career, but it was too late to turn back now.

Sarge Streicher was hardly the reflective type, but on the rare occasions when he looked back over his life, it was amazingly easy to pinpoint the most climactic event of his thirty-eight years. His breakup with Maggie Dickinson, a UT freshman who'd been his steady girlfriend for six months, had occurred with lightning suddenness on a May evening in 1917. Two days after Maggie had told him she was going to marry someone else – and while he was still yearning to get even with her somehow – he'd allowed Adam Wagner to talk him into joining the Army.

If not for that, he might never have gone to France or served in the same company with Adam during the Allied offensive along the Marne or won a citation for valor. And without his war record, Streicher could never have been elected as Réal County's "Doughboy Sheriff" two years after the Armistice. He'd been barely twenty-two at the time, and the incumbent he defeated had been in office since before Streicher was born.

A month ago, Streicher had won the Democratic primary by a five-to-one margin over his only opponent, and since he was unopposed in the general election, he'd been certain of winning his fifth four-year term in November – until today. After the showdown he now faced with Radke, the Sheriff might never again be able to take his future for granted.

His image as a war hero had been enough to catapult him into office in 1920, but to hold onto the job for sixteen long years he'd had to learn to keep certain people happy – especially the Radkes. It had started with the young Sheriff's acceptance of a few seemingly harmless favors from Gus Radke, the old patriarch. It had progressed to receiving regular payments from Gus for helping to "patrol" the boundaries of the Radke Ranch – and for looking the other way when certain incidents took place there. Then, after Gus's death, the system of favors, payoffs, and "selective blindness" on Streicher's part had accelerated still further when Kurt and his cocaine-snorting sister, Karla, took over the Radke empire.

Streicher knew all about the mess Kurt had gotten into with the Velasco girls, and he thanked his stars that he wasn't sheriff at the time. As a teenage volunteer with Leakey's one-truck Fire Department,

Streicher had helped recover Luz Velasco's battered remains from the canyon where she'd died, and nothing he'd encountered in France a couple of years later had been more horrible. He'd never forgotten how much he ached to smash Kurt's smirking face at the grand jury hearing into the case a few weeks later.

Even so, Streicher had helped over the past dozen years – however unwillingly – to cover up other messes involving Kurt that were almost as bad, and he'd given his deputies standing orders to avoid crossing the Radkes in any way. They were instructed to drive Karla home whenever she was too hopped up for her own safety and to ignore the illicit drugs they found in her car. Likewise, when a poacher or a trespasser disappeared on the Radke Ranch, no embarrassing questions were ever directed at Kurt by the Sheriff's Department.

There were sound political reasons for such leniency. With Radke support, a county official could stay in office for life if he wanted to. But if Kurt and Karla decided to back someone else, they could most likely buy enough votes to guarantee victory – or defeat – in any countywide election. With this in mind, the death of some nameless wetback could be overlooked as easily as a Mexican schoolgirl's claims of sexual assault. But this business with Adam and the wool buyers was a whole different matter. It could bring an avalanche of federal wrath down on Reál County.

Besides, the whole affair smacked of high treason – and whatever else he might be, Sarge Streicher was no traitor, by God.

The Sheriff's mouth was dry. After this morning, Kurt would probably organize a write-in campaign against him. After today, Streicher might not be able to win a political race in Reál County even if he was running against a dead man.

Hell, after today, Streicher thought, he might *be* a dead man.

Kurt's hands were shaking slightly as he closed the ledger before him and took a cigar from the silver humidor on the desk, but his voice was firm, and his eyes were icy as he addressed the Sheriff.

"First I want to know what you meant when you said the FBI was 'poking around' in Reál County. Then I want to know why I'm just now hearing about it if it happened last week."

Streicher sat down stiffly on the edge of a chair. "I had a visit from one of their agents," he said. "He claimed they had information that the men who've been staying here were German aliens on some kind of spy mission."

"And what did you tell him?"

"I told him you were the leading citizen of the county and a personal friend of the Vice President. I told him his information was bullshit."

"Well, that's exactly what you should've told him," Kurt said. He shifted uncomfortably and lit his cigar. "It *is* bullshit, but why didn't you tell me about it when it happened? And why did you feel so compelled to come out here and tell me about it now?"

"Because I can't get it off my mind," Streicher said. "After the G-man left, I found out his information came from Adam Wagner. Adam called me later and told me so. He says your wool buyers are a bunch of Nazi agents and they're out to assassinate President Roosevelt."

Kurt coughed on a mouthful of cigar smoke. His face went pale, and his laugh sounded forced and unnatural. "Wagner must be totally insane. That's the only way to explain it. The son of a bitch is crazy."

"I thought the same thing at first," Streicher said. "I told him he needed a psychiatrist. Trouble is, he didn't *sound* crazy, just mad and disgusted."

"Where'd the call come from?"

"I don't know. I think it was long-distance."

"Damn it, you were a fool not to tell me about this before," Kurt said. "We've got a really dangerous situation here with Wagner running around spilling his guts to the FBI. God knows who else he's talked to about this."

"If it's not true, why is it so dangerous?"

"Well, hell, it's slander, that's why. It's criminal libel. It could ruin those men's reputation if it gets out, and it won't help my business any, either. Can't you see that?"

Under past verbal assaults by Radke, Sarge had usually backed down. This time he was determined to stand his ground. "Who are those five men, Kurt? I want you to look me straight in the eye and tell me who they *really* are."

Kurt stubbed out his cigar in a cut-glass ashtray. His hand was still shaking. "They're wool and mohair buyers from Pennsylvania," he said hoarsely. "You know that as well as I do."

The Sheriff shook his head. "I don't recall you having any wool buyers staying here before," he said. "Not any that hung around for four or five weeks at a stretch, anyway."

'What's the difference? They're gone now, and they won't be back."

"Yeah, I know. I passed three of them on their way out the gate a few minutes ago. Where are they headed, back to Pennsylvania?"

"Sure, where else would they go?"

"I don't know, but I noticed their car had Texas license plates."

"They bought the car while they were here. Why should you care about that?"

"I don't know," Streicher said again. "There were only three of them in the car this morning. What happened to the other two?"

"They left earlier. They, uh, had some stops to make."

"Maybe you can give me their phone numbers in Pennsylvania," the Sheriff said. "That way I could call 'em up and verify everything – just to be sure."

"It'll take them days to drive back. I think you ought to just forget about it."

Streicher stared at Radke for a long moment. "I'd really like to do that, Kurt," he said then. "Believe me, I'd like to forget I ever saw any of them."

"That would be the smart thing to do, Sheriff," Kurt said, "if you know what I mean."

Streicher bit his lip and nodded.

THIRTY-EIGHT

San Antonio, Texas
June 10, 1936

Tim Spurlock grinned at Adam Wagner over the rim of his beer glass and shook his head. He'd been grinning and shaking his head for most of the past quarter-hour. His expression made it obvious that he still couldn't believe what he was seeing.

"My God, man," he said, "you look just like Hoot Gibson or somebody. If I'd run into you on Congress Avenue in Austin, I'd never have recognized you in a million years."

To Adam, it seemed almost that long since he and Tim had last drunk beer together. It had been in a smoky speakeasy long before the repeal of Prohibition, and the drink of choice had been a cloudy, sour-tasting homebrew that came with a guaranteed headache. Now they sat in the lobby bar of the Crockett Hotel, just behind the Alamo, trying to catch up on the events of the intervening years.

As two of UT's more promising undergraduates, they'd once talked alike, thought alike – and some said looked alike. Not anymore, though. Tim wore a snap-brim straw hat, light blue seersucker suit, red bowtie and two-tone oxfords. Adam had left his sweat-stained Stetson back on the Wagner Farm, but he still wore faded Levis, an open-at-the-neck western shirt, and boots that needed polish. His deeply tanned face was at least two shades darker than Tim's, and his windblown hair and untrimmed moustache were in sharp contrast to Tim's neatly barbered look.

It was more than mere appearances that set them apart, though. After a dozen years with the *San Antonio Express*, Tim was a crackerjack $75-a-week courthouse reporter whose byline was familiar to tens of thousands of daily readers. He was on a first-name basis with Bexar County Judge Frost Woodhull, as well as dozens of other judges, prosecutors, defense attorneys and lawmen. He drove a late-model Chrysler and lived in a plush apartment overlooking the river. In short, he had everything that Adam had once dreamed of having for himself. Until a few weeks ago, Adam had felt a twinge of jealousy whenever he thought of Tim, but not anymore.

Adam smiled at Ellie and took a swig from his long-neck bottle of Pearl. "Times change," he said. "People, too, I reckon. While you've been chasing ambulances, I've been running after goats and catching stray lambs."

Tim looked at Ellie, who leaned quietly against Adam's shoulder, sipping a Pepsi-Cola and seeming slightly bemused as she listened to the banter between two old college chums.

"Yeah, well, it looks like stray lambs aren't all you've been catching, Mr. Good Shepherd." Tim turned his grin toward Ellie. "Tell me, Miss Velasco, how did an ugly galoot like this manage to latch onto a girl like you? And a school teacher yet – how could this be?"

"I just got lucky," Adam said. "Once in a while, even a goat-roper gets lucky."

Ellie winked playfully. "Maybe we both got lucky," she said.

Tim shook his head one more time. "Damned if I ever thought I'd say this, Wagner, but I think I envy you."

Adam smiled and signaled the bartender for another round. He felt good. More than a little nervous at what he was doing, but good nevertheless.

"So what brings you to the big city?" Tim said. "You sounded kind of mysterious on the phone."

"We just came to see *El Presidenté*," Adam said. "Since shearing season's over and school's out, we didn't have anything better to do. Mr. Roosevelt's a big favorite of Ellie's."

"Yeah, I kind of like him, too," Spurlock confided. "But for God's sake, don't let my editor find out I said so. He hates old F.D.'s guts. The President of the whole damned United States is making his first trip ever to San Antonio, but my editor's attitude is 'what the hell?' You can bet your boots F.D. won't get the top spot on *our* front page tomorrow morning. That's reserved for Alf Landon and the Republicans up in Cleveland."

"It should be a pretty wild scene when the President's train pulls in tomorrow night," Ellie said. "We hoped maybe you could tell us how to get a really close look at him."

"It'll be a zoo," Tim said, "and I'll be in the big middle of it. I'm one of three, four guys at the *Express* with all the credentials to stay with Roosevelt's party the whole time. Security'll be tight, with lots of soldiers from Fort Sam. But the deputies from the Sheriff's Office are the ones to watch out for. They're tough monkeys, always ready to bust somebody's head."

"We don't want any trouble," Adam said. "We're just looking for the best – and safest – place to see Roosevelt. What do you recommend?"

Tim frowned. "The main crowd's gonna be at Alamo Plaza, but there'll also be a lot of people down in Montana Street at the Southern Pacific crossing, where the caravan of cars is supposed to form up. Nobody's likely to get close to him at either of those places. But hey, F.D.'s changing railroads here, you know. After he leaves for the Alamo, they're going to move his train over to the MK&T station and hook it up to a new engine. Most folks won't know that, and I doubt if many people are around the Katy station when he comes back to the train."

"Then that's where we ought to go," Adam said. He wondered if the Nazis knew about the switch in railroads. If they did, the Katy station might well be their destination, too.

Tim nodded. "Sure, it'll be about sunset by then and maybe a little dark, but I still think that's your best bet."

Adam took another sip of his beer. "What's on the big man's official agenda?"

"He'll be met by Governor Allred and the Mayor and a bunch of other local VIPs," Tim said. "Then he goes to the Alamo to lay a wreath and make a speech. The route takes him down Commerce Street to Santa Rosa, then over to the Plaza. Afterward, he comes up South Alamo Street to Nueva, then to Flores and Durango and on to the Katy depot."

"What time's the train supposed to get here?" Ellie asked.

"About six o'clock, and it'll all be over by seven-thirty if everything goes off on schedule."

When Adam thought of the bomb the Nazis were carrying, Tim's casual remark took on an ominous new meaning. Despite the beer, his throat was suddenly dry.

THIRTY-NINE

San Antonio, Texas
June 11, 1936

Beneath his crossed arms, Ed Starling kept his sweating right hand pressed firmly against the butt of the .45 under his suitcoat. The sun was almost down, but it was stifling hot in the Alamo. The air was thick and oppressive, smelling of ancient dust, and the density of the crowd made it worse. Odd, Starling thought, that such a famous place – a shrine he'd always pictured as larger-than-life – could actually be so small and cramped.

The President, however, seemed totally unfazed by the heat, the hectic schedule, or the surrounding crush of humanity. When he was on center stage, Roosevelt could ignore almost any discomfort or distraction, and he was in his element here. He listened intently as a local woman told about the siege of the old mission by the Mexican army in 1836, stopping her several times to ask questions.

Roosevelt scarcely seemed aware of his own infirmity as he was helped forward from his wheelchair, held erect by the heavy braces on his legs. The crowd was hushed as he placed a wreath in honor of the 182 Texans who died defending the Alamo.

"The valor of these men lives on today," he said. "I can feel it within these walls."

As FDR stepped back, Mrs. Roosevelt came forward with a cluster of orchids and laid them beside the wreath. Then, as the brief ceremonies ended, the solemnity of the occasion dissolved into informality. Starling stood ten feet away, watching warily as two Secret Service agents helped Roosevelt back to his wheelchair.

Once seated, the President immediately struck up a conversation with San Antonio Mayor C. K. Quin. He seemed totally engrossed as the Mayor pointed out various plaques on the rough stone walls, but a subtle motion of Roosevelt's right hand told Ed that what FDR wanted more than anything else right now was a cigarette. Ed know from experience that Roosevelt wouldn't light up until after his speech, and this made Ed's hopes rise a little. If Roosevelt was desperate enough for a smoke, maybe he'd hurry and get this business over with. Ed fervently hoped so; he could use a jolt of nicotine himself.

"Hey, chief!" Nat Grayson's urgent whisper penetrated Starling's thoughts. Ed turned and saw the worried expression on his lieutenant's face. "It looks like Mrs. R's taken off on us again."

"Oh my God, where'd she go?"

"Down that way," Nat said, pointing. "Callahan asked her to stay with the official party, but I guess she wants her own private tour of the place."

Starling bit his lip. "Tell Callahan to stick to her like glue. Even if she goes to the ladies room, I don't want him to lose sight of her for a second. Meanwhile, keep everybody else as close to the President as you can."

Starling cursed under his breath as Grayson moved away. It was totally in character for the First Lady to pull a stunt like this, but why couldn't she just behave herself for once? Outside, soldiers and local cops were all over the place, and uniformed police were stationed at the entrances with orders to stop anyone without credentials. Yet within the confines of the Alamo itself, guarding the presidential party was the sole responsibility of the small Secret Service detail.

Starling had considered leaving a man on the train as a precaution, but quickly changed his mind. There looked to be plenty of railway dicks and sheriff's deputies to cover that end, and God knows, the deputies had been aggressive enough. They'd been shoving news photographers around and threatening to smash their cameras before the presidential party even got off the train. Secretary Roper himself had had a hard time getting past them. But right now, Starling and his six men were on their own, and the detail was stretched tissue-thin, even without Mrs. Roosevelt's latest escapade.

Although the elapsed time seemed more like an hour, less than ten minutes had actually passed. Both Roosevelts were back in the limo with a rifle squad of infantry standing at parade rest nearby. If anything, though, FDR appeared more vulnerable than before as he stood in the open car, leaning against the seat in front of him for support and speaking over a portable microphone. By Starling's estimate, at least five thousand people were listening in the plaza. His eyes scanned their faces, their hands. Any one of them could have a concealed weapon.

"I cannot help but feel that the brave men who died here saw on the distant horizon some forecast of the century beyond . . . " Roosevelt was saying.

A breeze stirred in the humid dusk, but Starling was still sweating profusely.

". . . I hope they know that the great majority of Americans in 1936 are once more meeting new problems with new courage . . . "

Starling's gaze jumped to an abrupt flurry of activity to his left, his hand starting instinctively for the .45. Then he saw two small, irreverent boys of about ten. They were laughing and pummeling each other, oblivious to the President's message.

The speech ended. The crowd applauded. Roosevelt waved and sat down. Within a few seconds, auto engines began springing to life all along the thirty-car caravan. Lonnie Crow, the San Antonio policeman assigned to drive the President, applied the gas and eased the old seven-passenger Marmon forward.

Starling threw himself into the front seat of the follow-up car just as Grayson jumped on the running board. It was 7:15 p.m. as the procession pulled away from the Alamo. The sun had dipped behind the buildings to the west, casting long shadows across the teeming plaza. It was less than a mile to the Missouri-Kansas-Texas Railway station and the waiting train, Starling calculated. Just a few more minutes. A few more turns. A few hundred more windows and doorways. Then everything would be all right for a while.

Ed heard the bells ringing in the tower of St. John's Lutheran Church as they passed slowly along Nueva Street.

He wiped his face on his coat sleeve and wished it were darker.

❋

Adam's new blue serge suit felt itchy and uncomfortable. The collar of his new white shirt was too stiff, and his new red tie was about to strangle him. The narrow brim of his new straw hat with the red feather in the band kept sliding down into his eyes, and his new wingtip shoes were killing his feet.

In fact, of everything Adam had bought to outfit himself for this mission, only the phony but official-looking badge he'd found at a downtown police-supply store seemed to be doing what it was supposed to do. The railroad switchman in the striped coveralls accepted its authority without question.

"I'm Deputy Adam Smith of the Bexar County Sheriff's Office," Adam told him, flashing the badge in its leather folder. "I have to check and make sure everything's okay. Is that the President's train over there?'

"That's her, all right," the switchman said. "You won't see much of anything else moving around here tonight. All the other traffic's at a standstill for at least thirty minutes after the President's special clears the yard. We've got her all hooked up to her new engine, and we're just about to put a new dining car on her for the trip north."

"Oh, yeah? Why's that?"

"Nothing's too good for the President," the man said. "Everybody knows the Katy has better food than the Southern Pacific. We aim to see he travels first class."

"Is anybody in the dining car right now?"

"Yes sir, there's a steward and a cook. They're getting everything ready for dinner. Train's due to pull out in another twenty minutes or so." He squinted at his pocket watch.

"Okay, thanks," Adam said. "I reckon I'll just have a look around."

"You're not expecting trouble, are you, Deputy?"

"Everything looks fine so far," Adam said, "but you can't be too careful when it's the President of the United States. If you see any suspicious characters hanging around, be sure and let us know."

Adam's patched-up knees felt weak, but he turned and trotted back across the railroad yard as if he owned the place. A hundred yards away in the gathering twilight, Ellie was waiting for him in the Ford.

As he trotted, the switchman's words kept repeating themselves in his head:

Train's due to pull out in another twenty minutes or so. Another twenty minutes. Another twenty minutes.

Hard as it was to believe, that meant Roosevelt had already been in the city for almost exactly an hour. Yet it seemed only a few frantic minutes ago that the presidential caravan had first pulled out into Montana Street.

Time was running out, Adam thought. The assassins had to do something soon, even if they did it wrong. Even if it was something desperate, something crazy, it damned sure had to be something fast.

Adam leaped across the last set of tracks and broke into a run.

FORTY

Over an hour earlier, Adam and Ellie had tried their best to explain the urgency of the situation to a hardheaded sheriff's deputy who wouldn't listen. The deputy was too busy threatening newsmen and yelling at bystanders – and too impressed with himself – to pay attention to anything else.

"I don't care who you are or what you want," he railed. "You get the hell away from these cars and these railroad tracks or you'll be watching tomorrow's sunrise through the bars at the county jail."

"Just listen for a minute," Adam pleaded. "We've got to talk to the Secret Service. The President may be in danger. Some people . . . "

"To hell with the Secret Service. I'm in charge here, and don't you forget it. Now you get out of here and take your girlfriend with you. I ain't gonna warn you again."

Adam was opening his mouth to say something he probably would've regretted when he heard a quiet voice beside him:

"You might as well forget it, Mac. That's Andy Barker, the meanest deputy in town. He wouldn't give Jesus himself the time of day, and he'd as soon throw you in a paddy wagon as look at you."

Adam looked down at a short man in a rumpled tan suit and a battered felt hat with a press card tucked in the band. He was lugging a heavy Speed Graphic camera and a bag filled with flashbulbs and film holders.

"Yeah, I got that feeling," Adam said. "Who're you?"

"Mitch Lozano. I take pictures for the *Express*.

"Then you must know Tim Spurlock," Adam said. "He's an old buddy of mine."

"Sure, I know him. He's one of the lucky ones – gets to ride in the press pool car so he doesn't have to put up with Barker. The Secret Service already told us we could stand up there by the cars to get our pictures. Then that asshole comes along throwing his weight around." Lozano nodded at Ellie. "Sorry, ma'am, but that's the only word I can think of to describe that asshole."

"Have you actually seen somebody with the Secret Service?" Adam asked.

"Yeah, a guy named Starling's the man in charge."

An instant bell rang in Adam's mind. "He's the one I need to talk to," he said.

"Well, he must of gotten back on the train. I guarantee you Barker wouldn't be popping off like that if Starling was still out here."

Adam started to move away, then stopped and turned back to the photographer. "Listen, if you see Starling again, would you tell him something for me?"

Lozano shrugged. "Sure, what do you want me to say?"

Adam took a deep breath while he tried to decide how to explain it. Then he decided the only thing to do was just spit it out. "Somewhere around here close, there's a couple of guys dressed like soldiers," he said. "They've got a bomb with them, and they're planning to blow Roosevelt up with it. Tell that to Starling if you get a chance."

Lozano stared at Adam as he might have stared at an inmate in a lunatic asylum who'd just told him the sky was falling. Then he laughed. "Okay," he said. "Absolutely. You can count on me."

Weighted with an increasingly familiar feeling of hopelessness, Adam and Ellie had watched from a distance as the President's caravan departed a few minutes later. Then they'd jumped back into the Ford coupe and wound through narrow downtown streets that more or less paralleled the parade route. It looked a little like Fiesta time in the plaza as they passed within a couple of blocks of the Alamo.

Hundreds of soldiers were stationed at ten-yard intervals along both sides of the route, and it gave Adam a sinking feeling to realize how hard it would be to pick out two disguised Gestapo agents from among them. After hours of speculation, he and Ellie had reached one basic conclusion: If the assassins hoped to kill Roosevelt with a bomb, it had to be planted in one of three places – in his limousine, somewhere in the Alamo, or on his railway coach. There'd been no explosion yet, which tended to rule out the first two options. Roosevelt had ridden all over downtown in the open car without incident, and apparently he'd already departed the Alamo intact. That left the train.

Adam was panting heavily by the time he reached the Ford. He jerked the door open and grabbed for Ellie's hand.

"Come on," he gasped. "Hurry."

"What's happening?" she asked. "Where are we going?"

"To hop a train," he said.

Deputy Sheriff Andy Barker stood in the shadow of a tanker car on the track adjacent to the presidential special and watched two khaki-uniformed Army troopers approaching. Their insignia identified them as members of the 2nd Infantry. One wore sergeant's stripes on his sleeve, and the other was a PFC, but Barker showed no interest at first. Several dozen soldiers were stationed at intervals across the crowded rail yards, where a half-dozen trains had been shunted onto sidetracks pending the special's departure. As far as Barker could tell, there was nothing noteworthy about these two.

It was only when both of them drew their .45 automatics and pointed them straight at him that Barker decided differently.

"No civilians allowed in this area," the sergeant snapped. "State your business and be quick about it."

"I'm a police officer assigned to presidential security," Barker said heatedly. "Just who the hell do you think you are?" Nobody pushed Andy Barker around, by God. If any pushing was to be done, he'd be the one to do it. He'd shown the smart-aleck newshounds up on Montana Street who was boss, and he'd show these guys, too. He'd never had much use for soldier-boys, anyway.

He reached inside his coat for his badge and ID, but he froze when the PFC leveled his pistol. Barker could see the trooper's finger tighten visibly on the trigger.

"Hands in the air," the PFC said. "Hands up or you're a dead man."

"I've got identification, damn you," Barker protested. "It's in my pocket."

"Don't move," the sergeant said. "Check his pocket, Private Hoffman."

Barker raised his hands and stood still as the PFC stepped close to him. Barker was big – close to six-foot-four and two hundred and fifty pounds – but the PFC was bigger. Besides, there was no need to get rough. As soon as these two yardbirds saw his credentials, everything would be fine.

That was what he thought, at least. Then the PFC clubbed him over the head with the barrel of his .45 and everything went black.

"I'm Agent Adam Smith of the U.S. Secret Service," Adam said in as authoritative a tone as he could muster.

His heart was pounding, but he seemed to be getting pretty adept at impersonating a law enforcement officer. His hand shook slightly as he showed his badge to the white-jacketed dining car steward, but the steward apparently didn't notice.

"At your service, Cap'n," the steward said. "What can I do for you?"

Adam shoved the badge back inside his coat and gestured toward Ellie. "This is Miss Velasco from the Health Department, and we need to inspect your dining car. We have to make sure everything's okay before the President arrives."

"Man, man," the steward exclaimed. "Anything special I can show you folks?"

"No, we'll just have a quick look around," Adam said. "No need for you to go with us. We can find our own way. Just go on about your duties."

"Yes, suh, Cap'n," the steward said, turning toward the kitchen. "If you need anything, just holler. I'll be right back here."

Adam felt a gentle lurch and the car eased forward a few feet. Then a slight shudder passed through it, apparently as it completed its coupling to the special train.

Adam looked at his watch. It was 7:18.

"What now?" Ellie whispered.

"Just go back into the kitchen and poke around a little," Adam told her. "Keep the steward and whoever else is in there occupied for a couple of minutes. Act like you're looking for germs or something. I'm going to try to get into the other part of the train and check the President's coach."

He could tell that she wanted to protest, but for once she didn't.

"Be careful," she said. "And remember, whatever we're looking for is small – small enough to fit inside an attaché case. It could be almost anywhere, and – "

Her voice broke and she looked away. Then she took a deep breath and squeezed his hand. "And if you're not back in five minutes, I'm coming after you."

There was a fierce pain in the back of Andy Barker's head, and he could feel blood in his hair when he rubbed it with his fingers. As his senses slowly returned, he realized that he was on the ground a few feet from the hissing MKT locomotive that had just joined the special presidential train. At first he remembered nothing about how he'd gotten there. Then it started coming back to him.

Two soldiers had ordered him away from the train, then one of them had clubbed him over the head without giving him a chance to identify himself. Why would two soldiers do that? It was all very strange. There was no sign of the soldiers now. In fact, except for the indistinct figure of the engineer up in the cab of the locomotive, Barker didn't see anyone.

He stumbled slowly alongside the train, feeling dizzy and disoriented. Just behind the engine and its tender was a baggage car. Beyond that was the diner, a parlor car, several Pullman coaches, and finally the observation car at the far end. In the gathering darkness, the lighted windows of the coaches stood out vividly against the dull red sky, and Barker saw a man's silhouette moving through the parlor car toward the next coach to the rear. He wondered for a moment if it was one of the soldiers, but the man was wearing civilian clothes.

Barker reached instinctively for his .38 Police Special. He half-expected it to be gone, but it was still there in his shoulder holster. Despite the throbbing in his head, he broke into a ragged trot and reached the open passageway between the parlor car and the first Pullman coach just as the man burst through the door.

Barker leveled the gun unsteadily, holding it with both hands. "Halt! Don't move or I'll shoot."

The figure stopped and raised his hands. His face was a featureless shadow, but Barker sensed something vaguely familiar about him.

"Come down from there," Barker ordered. "I want to take a look at you."

As he waited for the man to descend the metal steps, Barker felt himself swaying slightly. Blood was oozing from the wound in his scalp and trickling down the back of his neck. His knees were like rubber. The man didn't say a word, and his face was still a black void.

"Who are you and what the hell are you doing on this train?" Barker's tongue felt thick and heavy in his mouth.

"I'm Agent Adam Smith of the U.S. Secret Service," the man said. "The question is, who are you?"

Just then, the man turned toward the light from the windows of the Pullman car and Barker saw his face distinctly for the first time. "Hey, I remember you," he exclaimed. "You're no damned Secret Service agent. You were down in Montana Street trying to cause trouble." He raised the .38. "By God, I'll give you more trouble than you bargained for."

Without warning, the man charged. He crashed into Barker with the force of a bull, knocking the gun from his hand. An instant later, both of them hit the ground hard. The man, whoever he was, was big and strong.

They threshed savagely, gasping for breath and pummeling one another. After a minute or two, Barker could tell he was losing the fight, but he refused to give up.

Ellie didn't wait the full five minutes as promised. As soon as Adam was out of sight, she was seized with a premonition of disaster. She tried to act interested in the veal cutlets and roast beef and gravy simmering in the dining car kitchen, but after a few seconds, she couldn't concentrate on anything except the warning that her mind was screaming at her:

Something's wrong. Something's wrong.

She had no idea what it was, but the premonition convulsed her with fear. Adam was in trouble. The Nazis were somewhere close by. The President was coming. She had to do something – but what?

"What time is it?" she asked the steward.

He pulled his gold railroad watch out of his pocket and squinted at it. "Twenty-two minutes past seven, ma'am. Almost time to feed the great Mister Roosevelt."

"Well, everything seems fine here," she said. "Thank you very much for your cooperation. I'm going to go join Agent Smith now."

She ran blindly toward the rear of the train. Immediately behind the dining car was a parlor car with formations of green upholstered chairs and couches, interspersed with tables. Beyond that was a Pullman coach filled with empty staterooms, then another and another.

"Adam!" she called. "Adam, where are you?" The only response was a deep, empty silence. She ran on.

It took her several seconds to realize that she'd entered the President's coach. At first, it seemed like just another Pullman car, but then she could sense the difference. There was a *feel* about it that coaches occupied by ordinary people didn't have.

She peered inside two small compartments, which apparently housed some of the President's personal aides. When she was sure both were empty, she pulled the doors shut again and moved on. She'd just come abreast of two more compartment doors when she heard low male voices.

"Are you ready, Villy?" one of the voices asked.

"Just another moment," another voice replied. "The detonator's in place, and I'm setting the timer now."

Ellie felt icy panic explode in her chest as she recognized the voices.

It was the Nazis. They were rigging the bomb at this very instant, and she'd blundered right into them!

Desperate for a place to hide, she turned the knob on the door of the stateroom on her left. Then she gasped in fright and anguish as the knob made a loud, echoing, metallic click.

"What was that noise?" she heard one of the Nazis say.

"I don't know," the other one said. "You'd better have a look."

Ellie threw herself into the compartment and pressed the door shut behind her. Her heart was racing a thousand miles an hour. She heard heavy footsteps in the corridor outside.

Holy Mary, mother of God . . .

In another few seconds, one of the Nazis was going to throw the door open and find her. There was no place to turn. There was only a couch that made out into a bed. Only a tiny closet containing a half–dozen frocks in bright floral prints. Only a large brocade handbag standing open on the floor beside the couch.

Vaguely, she realized that she was standing in the middle of Eleanor Roosevelt's private stateroom. Not that it really mattered. It wouldn't be private much longer.

In sheer panic, she grabbed the brocade bag. Maybe inside it was something she could use to defend herself. If not, maybe the bag itself could be flung as a missile. Adam was lost to her. She had no idea where he was. An instant from now, she'd have to fight for her life with anything she could lay her hands on.

When she opened the bag, her heart leaped. She couldn't believe her eyes. The first object she saw was a gun – a small, snub-nosed silver pistol with pearl grips. She seized it in her trembling hands, remembering the pistol that Papa kept behind the counter in the store. She had always known she could shoot somebody with it if she had to.

The door burst open with a crash. It reminded her of the sound that her bedroom door had made the night Kurt Radke came in and attacked her. She saw Otto, the sausage lover, standing there. His massive form filled the doorway. His broad face was wet with sweat. She saw the surprise in his eyes, and she knew he recognized her. She also saw the .45 automatic in his hand.

He lowered the .45 and smiled. "So nice to see you again, *liebchen*," he said. "Pity there's so little time for us to get to know each other better."

He was still smiling as he reached for her. But the smile froze on his face when he spotted the pistol in her hand.

Then she shot him. She kept on shooting him until the little silver pistol was empty. He sprawled in the doorway, his blood spreading into a widening pool on the floor.

FORTY-ONE

The War Office, London
June 12, 1936

Light rain had been falling intermittently for hours, and now, early on a Friday morning, the city was shrouded in fog. Innocent objects took on sinister shapes in the headlights of each passing automobile. To Lieutenant Commander Niles Sherwood of U.S. Naval Intelligence, the scene brought to mind stories of Jack the Ripper.

Sherwood had spent the early part of the evening at a pub called the Coach & Four, where he'd had dinner with two other officers from the American Embassy and enjoyed several pints of brown ale. But he'd been asleep at his flat for almost three hours when the phone rang. Through the crackling interference on the line, he recognized the caller as Sir Francis Hawthorne, a deputy minister at the War Office.

"Awfully sorry to disturb you at this hour, Commander," Hawthorne had said. "But I rather think you should come down here right away.

Security prohibits my discussing it over the phone, but it's a matter of utmost importance."

Sir Francis was a typically dry-stick British bureaucrat. Under normal circumstances, he was reserved to the point of downright dullness, but since he happened to be the man in charge of the labyrinthine British spy network in Germany, people generally came in a hurry when Hawthorne called.

Less than half an hour later, Sherwood was still brushing the drops of moisture off his white uniform when Hawthorne opened the door to his inner office and motioned Sherwood inside.

"Hate to be a bloody bother," Hawthorne said, "but we've had a new contact from the same operative who alerted us concerning a threat against President Roosevelt. Given the urgent nature of the matter, I thought it best to pass it on to you directly tonight, rather than go through normal channels in the morning."

Sherwood frowned. "How urgent is it?"

"The message specifically mentioned yesterday's date and today's – Friday's, that is," Hawthorne said quietly, lighting his pipe. "It indicated that something important was due to happen on one day or the other."

"But I thought you'd lost contact with the agent who sent the original message," Sherwood said. "How can you be sure it's the same person? If the Gestapo caught him they could be sending out phony messages just to confuse us."

Hawthorne smiled. "We have certain safeguards against that, Commander. The coded call-letters used by our operatives have proved impervious to the Nazis so far. I think it's safe to say our chap just had to lie low for a while."

"Even courageous men can yield to torture," Sherwood said. "As we both know, the SS is very adept at such things."

"I'm confident that no amount of torture could break this chap," Hawthorne said. "Heckstall's his name, and he's tough as nails. He's been in Germany so long that he barely speaks the mother tongue anymore. He got his information from one of Himmler's own aides. The man was a fierce supporter of the former Weimar government, and he despises the Nazis. Heckstall's been cultivating him for three years."

Sherwood nodded. He rather liked Sir Francis. In his own stodgy way, Hawthorne seemed to be an all right guy, but the experts at the State

Department had been suspicious of this whole scenario from the start, and to some extent, Sherwood shared their suspicions. If he'd learned anything during his ten months in London, it was how desperate many high-ranking Brits were to swing U.S. sentiments over to their side in the looming conflict with Germany. They wanted to seize any available opportunity to influence the feelings in Washington, fearing that Britain couldn't count on France for meaningful support in a showdown. In the long run, they believed, America was their only hope against Hitler.

On the other hand, the British intelligence network on the Continent had no peer. Its spies in Germany were among the world's most daring and efficient. Some of its "moles" had lived there since before the World War. They taught in German schools, held jobs in German industry. A few even worked for the German government. Consequently, Hawthorne's information had to be taken seriously.

"So what does the new message say?" Sherwood asked.

"I had the decoder write it out for you," Hawthorne withdrew a small sheet of notepaper from a drawer and handed it across the desk.

Sherwood frowned as he read the words on the paper: "Re FDR plot . . . Texas not Mexico . . . Pegasus . . . 11 or 12 June . . . "

"Is that all?" he asked.

"Unfortunately, yes. At that point, the transmission ended abruptly and the wireless went dead."

A few minutes ago, Sherwood had heard Big Ben striking the hour. He glanced at his wristwatch and made a quick calculation. In London, it was 2:09 a.m. on June 12. But with the seven-hour time difference, it was just after 7 p.m. on June 11 in Texas.

The U.S. Embassy had received a copy of the President's itinerary by cable a few days earlier so Sherwood had already known that Roosevelt was traveling through Texas this week. He couldn't recall exactly where FDR was supposed to be at this moment, but he was pretty sure it was either Houston or San Antonio.

"It's still yesterday in the States," he mused. "But it's after office hours. There's no way to get through to anybody."

"That's true." Hawthorne's voice had an apologetic tone. "Pity. Under the circumstances, perhaps I should have spared you the trouble of coming down so late."

"No, you did the right thing, Sir Francis." Sherwood stared at the sheet of notepaper again. "What do you make of that word – Pegasus? What's a winged horse got to do with this? Any idea what it means?"

Hawthorne pursed his lips in thought, then shrugged. "Could be a code name of some sort. Otherwise, as you Americans say, I'm afraid it's all Greek to me."

FORTY-TWO

San Antonio, Texas
June 11, 1936

For an electrifying instant, Ellie stared in horror at what she'd done. Her heart was a melon-size boulder pounding in her chest. Her head was spinning, and her knees were like jelly, but semi-rational thoughts were somehow forming in her mind.

There was no doubt whatever that the burly German was dead. Otto lay as he'd fallen, his arms reaching out, his head turned slightly to one side, his mouth agape, his eyes open and staring. The sight of him was terrible, but she knew she had nothing further to fear from him or from the .45 automatic a few inches from his fingertips.

The pressing question now shifted to the other Nazi: Where was he, and what was he doing? Otto had called him "Villy," and he was almost certainly somewhere on the train. Probably somewhere very close. Perhaps moving stealthily toward her at this very moment.

She barely kept from gagging as she stepped over Otto's body and into the passageway, but she forgot her churning stomach instantly when she heard a muffled crash. She couldn't tell which direction the sound came from, but instinct told her to retrace her path toward the front of the train instead of venturing farther toward the unexplored observation car. It also sent an urgent message:

Run! Run!

She dashed down the passageway, still holding the little silver pistol. Although the gun was empty now and next to worthless as protection, the mere sight of it might slow down an attacker for a second. But her principal reason for still clutching it was that she lacked the presence of mind to throw it away.

Just as she was moving into another Pullman car, a shadow sprang from one of the compartments and grabbed her. She slashed at it with the pistol, but the shadow caught her arm and held it. She tried to scream, but a hand covered her mouth.

"Be quiet!" Adam's voice hissed in her ear. "It's me, for God's sake."

Ellie sagged against him as tears flooded her cheeks.

"I . . . I killed someone," she gasped.

"I heard the shots," he said. "Who was it?"

"The big German. He's in there." She pointed. "In Mrs. Roosevelt's bedroom."

"Where'd you get the gun?"

"Out of Mrs. Roosevelt's purse."

He stared, first at her, then down at the little silver pistol. "Eleanor Roosevelt had a *gun* in her purse?"

"I wouldn't be here now if she hadn't," Ellie said.

"Does that thing have any bullets left in it?"

She shook her head. "No, I . . . I used them all."

"Where's the other German?"

"I don't know. I didn't see anything of him." As she looked into Adam's face, she noticed a bleeding laceration on his forehead. "What happened to you?"

"I had a run-in with a deputy. I had to bust his head." He reached inside his coat and pulled out a large blue-steel revolver. "I took his gun, too, mainly so he wouldn't be chasing me with it when he wakes up – which he probably has already."

Ellie felt her terror accelerating into panic. "God, Adam, what're we going to *do*?"

He raised his watch and they both looked at it. The hands pointed to 7:27.

"FDR's due back here any minute," he said. "And if the Secret Service catches us prowling around on this train, we may spend the rest of our lives in a federal pen – especially after what I did to that deputy."

"Not to mention what I did to Otto," she said, wiping her eyes. "Let's get going."

He caught her arm and squeezed it. "You did the world a favor when you shot that ape, but we can't leave yet. We've got to go back and search Roosevelt's coach. We've got no choice."

She started to ask why, but then his meaning dawned on her. It seemed like hours, instead of only a few minutes, since they'd boarded the train. In the wild rush of events, she'd almost forgotten why they were there in the first place.

The bomb. At best, they had maybe three or four minutes to find it. Otherwise . . .

"Come on!" Adam yelled. "This way! It's quicker."

By the time she could react, he was already bolting toward the rear of the train. She stuffed the little pistol under the waistband of her skirt and stumbled after him.

FORTY-THREE

Aboard FDR's Special Train
Near New Braunfels, Texas
June 11, 1936

They were eighteen minutes north of San Antonio and mounting a full head of steam to try to make up part of the half-hour they'd lost when Ed Starling first noticed the blood on the floor.

There was a sizable smear of it along the baseboard just outside Mrs. Roosevelt's bedroom. Ordinarily, it might have been overlooked indefinitely in the dimly lit corridor. As it was, it was already drying and turning brown in the heat, but Ed realized immediately what it was. He also knew that it hadn't been there long.

Unless he missed his guess, the blood had some tenuous connection with the dazed deputy sheriff who'd been crawling on the ground near the train when the presidential party returned. The deputy, though not fully coherent, had talked of seeing two civilians – a man and a woman – aboard the train. A dining car steward had also seen the couple and given a sketchy description. Agents had already gone through the train from front to back looking for extra passengers. That was what had caused the delay getting away from the station. And now this.

Starling's knees ached slightly as he stood up, but the ache in his head was far worse. He touched the .45 in his shoulder holster and instinctively reached for a cigarette, then stopped himself with his hand halfway to his shirt pocket. He didn't have time to smoke. He had to think. What the hell was going on?

He sprinted down the corridor to the next car forward, stopped outside Nat Grayson's compartment and pounded on the door. The door opened a crack and Grayson's head appeared in the opening.

"What's up, Colonel?"

"We've got big trouble," Ed said. "I'm not sure just what we're dealing with, but we've got to search every inch of this train. Bring Callahan and Morgan to help us, and have the rest of the men stay with the Roosevelts, but I don't want them alarmed. Don't let anyone in the presidential party get wind of this till we know more ourselves."

"The President's in the dining car having dinner," Grayson said. "Most of the others are up there with him."

"Good. Have our people keep them there till we can go through the President's coach with a fine-tooth comb. It'll be a lot simpler without them underfoot."

"Just what is it we're searching for?"

"I don't know yet. I found some blood in the passageway outside Mrs. Roosevelt's room. It looks like somebody tried to clean it up and missed part of it."

"Damn," Grayson said. "We may be looking for a dead body then."

"That's a distinct possibility," Ed said. "We could also be looking for an armed killer."

Seven or eight minutes later, Grayson found two bloody bath towels stuffed into a laundry hamper in the President's bathroom. Approximately thirty seconds after that, he jerked back the shower curtain and saw the disarmed explosive device floating in six inches of water in the bathtub.

The time bomb was small and compact, consisting of about three pounds of TNT, a detonator cap and an ordinary mechanical clock. When Grayson was sure the wires from the clock to the detonator were disconnected, he glanced at his wristwatch. It was exactly 8:33 p.m. The bomb had been set to explode at 8 o'clock. Even with the delay in San Antonio, the Roosevelts would surely have been back in their quarters by then.

Nat shuddered as he showed the package to Starling. "I'm no expert on explosives, but I can tell there's enough stuff here to make the whole back half of this coach disappear. If it had gone off, there's no way the President could've survived."

Starling pulled a Lucky out of his pack and lit it. "Any idea where it was before it ended up in the bathtub?"

Nat shook his head. "Could've been hidden in any of a dozen different places – under the President's favorite chair, in the cabinet beside it, behind the couch, under the bed. It's small enough to slide into almost any small space."

Starling took a fierce drag from his cigarette. "This gets stranger by the minute. Somebody's bleeding and somebody else is wiping up the blood, then somebody's planting a bomb and somebody else is disarming it. There's two sides battling each other right under our noses, yet there's no trace of any of them, except for a bomb and some bloodstains."

"Yeah, we've got multiple players involved here for sure," Grayson said, "and they obviously aren't all on the same team. But how the hell did they get on this train in the first place?"

"An even bigger question," said Starling grimly, "is how many of them are still somewhere on the train right now."

Nat studied his watch and made a quick calculation. "We're about twenty-five minutes from our next stop in Austin. We're also moving at sixty miles an hour, so until we get there, I don't think anybody's going to be getting off the train alive."

Starling stubbed out his cigarette and drew his .45. Out of force of habit, he checked the cylinder to be sure it was fully loaded.

"Send Callahan and Morgan up to the diner with the others," he said. "Tell them to keep everybody there till further notice. Then you and I are going to start at the observation car and work our way forward all the way to the engine if necessary. If there's any stowaways aboard, we've got to find them."

❁

Wilhelm Lutz' senses had gradually adjusted somewhat to the situation, but he was still dizzy from the contant lashing of the wind and disoriented by the rushing darkness around him. His eyes burned from the smoke and cinders that billowed back from the smokestack of the locomotive fifty feet ahead. It was particularly bad whenever the train went through a tunnel. He'd almost suffocated once or twice.

Lutz had no idea how long he'd been clinging to the roof of the tender, but it seemed like hours. He was near enough to the lighted cabin of the engine to see the engineer's arm on the window ledge, but he was also trapped in a hostile, punishing environment. Climbing on top of the train had seemed his best hope of escape at first, and it might yet prove to be, if only the infernal train would stop. When it did, he'd be on the ground and gone in seconds.

It didn't matter anymore that his and Otto's efforts had failed, that the bomb had been discovered and Hauptman had been caught and perhaps killed by the Secret Service. Lutz no longer cared if he made it to Dallas to join the others or not. The only thing he cared about now was getting off this *verdammit* train. To keep from screaming, he thought of his daughter, Heidi. He closed his eyes and pictured her playing in the garden behind the white house overlooking the Aller River, but her image kept slipping away. If he ever saw her again it would be a miracle.

The mission had gone totally awry. Lutz had sensed it the instant he heard the volley of shots from the presidential coach. He'd just finished positioning the bomb beneath an overstuffed chair in the part of the coach set aside as Roosevelt's study, and he was on his way off the train through the observation car when the shots came.

Seconds earlier, Hauptman had been close on Lutz' heels. But Hauptman had heard a noise somewhere behind them and paused to listen.

"I better take a look, Villy," Otto had whispered, turning back.

"No! There's no time!" But then Otto was gone.

In the maddening silence following the gunfire, Lutz had listened intently but heard no other sound. His mind had told him to flee, to get off the train as fast as possible – run to the rear platform of the observation car, leap to the ground, and walk very deliberately away, like a good soldier following orders. But as he was trying to do exactly that, urgent voices rang out in the corridor close behind him.

"Come on!" someone shouted. "This way!"

He'd pictured armed Secret Service agents charging toward him and in a moment of panic, he'd climbed onto the railing around the observation platform, then hoisted himself to the roof.

For a long time after that, the train had remained motionless, but there were too many people moving about for Lutz to leave. He was certain to be seen if he climbed back down, so he'd stayed still, thinking about the bomb. If the Americans hadn't found it and it was still operational, the bomb might explode before the train was under way. It would blast the coach just ahead of Lutz to splinters, and unless he moved, he'd be blown up with it.

With that in mind, Lutz had slowly made his way along the length of the train from the observation car to the tender, hoping for a chance to jump when the train began to move. Unfortunately, by the time he could feel his way down the ladder in the darkness, the train was going too fast.

He'd been a captive there ever since, hanging on for dear life whenever the train rounded a curve, hugging the roof each time it passed under a low bridge, breathing its acrid smoke, feeling its greasy soot blackening his face, and wishing he'd taken his chances on the ground.

Now – to make matters worse – there were sudden noises on the platform below. Somebody was down there. He heard a metallic thud as a foot struck the ladder. *Herr Gott*, were they coming up?

"Good night, little Heidi," Lutz whispered. Desperately, he groped for the .45 automatic at his belt.

FORTY-FOUR

By the time Starling reached the tender at the rear of the engine, he was thoroughly winded and sweating profusely. He paused on the platform at the forward end of the baggage car and leaned against the wall, stifling a cough and fighting to catch his breath. At times like these, Ed could feel the advancing years taking their toll. His increased cigarette consumption wasn't helping matters, either. He'd already gone through nearly two packs today, and it was shaping up as another long night. Somehow, he was going to have to cut down.

He remembered the doctor frowning over the x-rays during his last physical. *Your lungs look like a coal cellar, Ed, and all that nicotine's got them where they can't filter properly or fight off infection. You're asking for a good case of pneumonia – and maybe congestive heart failure – if you don't get rid of those damned coffin nails.*

He listened intently for some sound that might blot out the warning echoing in his mind. But all he heard were his own gasping breaths and the whine of the wind whipping through the open platform. They were only about fifteen minutes from the outskirts of Austin, but the horizon was an unbroken sea of darkness against the pale night sky. The only visible illumination came from the cab of the engine ahead.

Starling felt infinitely alone. The sense of impending disaster that had haunted him for days was stronger than ever. Apprehension and frustration were like twin drums pounding in his head, and he was as puzzled as he was exhausted. He and Grayson had covered the interior of each passenger coach on the train, but they'd found nothing. Nothing but the bomb and the bloodstain. It was maddening.

Grayson had stopped off in the diner to give an update on the situation to Gus Gennerich, the President's bodyguard. Gennerich had downed a few whiskies during his stay in the diner. Now he was irritated at being "held prisoner and kept in the dark" when he wanted to go to bed.

Ed remembered the day President Hoover had vacated the White House and Roosevelt had moved in. He vividly recalled the new President's confidence and self-assurance at their first face-to-face meeting.

"Happy to see you, Ed," FDR had said. "I hope you'll stay on as long as I'm here."

"I'll be honored to, sir," Ed had heard himself reply as he shook the new President's hand. Now he wondered fleetingly if his answer would be the same today if he had it to do over.

Undeniably, Starling and the rest of the detail were at a dead end in their search of the train. As of this moment, there were no unauthorized persons inside any of the passenger coaches. He was satisfied of that. Based on the fruitlessness of their search, he was tempted to believe that whoever had been aboard had somehow gotten off before the train left San Antonio.

But if an intruder *were* still on the train, he'd have only a couple of conceivable places left to hide. If a man was desperate enough, it was possible to ride the rods underneath the coaches. More than a few hobos had done it over the years, and some had lived to brag about it, but there was no way to reach the rods while the train was moving without being chewed to pieces by the wheels. And if an intruder had had time to crawl onto the rods while the train was sitting still, he would also have had time to leave it completely – which would have been a far more intelligent choice.

That left the roof. In Ed's opinion, this was a much more viable option for someone seeking a hiding place. Still plenty risky, but not impossible.

Suppose, for instance, an intruder found himself in Starling's own current situation – unable to go any farther toward the engine unless he wanted to climb to the top of the tender and make his way across its roof to the locomotive. This was dangerous business, as Ed knew from his days as a railroad cop. It was tricky enough on a slow-moving boxcar in broad daylight, but on the curved tops of passenger coaches ripping through the night at sixty miles an hour, it could be suicide.

A feeling of dread passed through him. He wished he'd never noticed the rungs of the metal ladder ascending the rear end of the tender. The ladder was well within his reach. He stared at it for a long moment, then glanced queasily upward into the impenetrable blackness above.

You're too damned old for this, an inner voice warned. But in the same instant, he knew he had to try.

He grasped the handrail of the ladder firmly with both hands and pulled himself slowly upward until he could plant his feet against the lower rungs. His body felt heavier than it should have, and there was a slight dizziness in his head, but he forced himself to keep climbing.

One rung. Then another. And another. Two or three more and he'd be able to see over the edge of the tender onto the roof. He could already feel the velocity of the wind up there, and he wasn't yet even in its direct path. Coupled with the wind, the train's swaying motion gave him a touch of vertigo, especially when he made the mistake of looking down once. But he was almost to the top now. He could see the glowing cinders from the smokestack streaking overhead. Just one more rung . . .

Then, above the wind, he heard a faint sound. A scraping, scuffling noise that was almost – but not quite – obscured by the hissing roar of the engine. A grunting, gasping noise with overtones of alarm laced through it.

Ed pulled himself upward the last few inches and peered over the edge of the tender's roofline. For an instant, he saw the jet-black outline of a human head and shoulders framed against the starlit sky. The figure below the head was crouched in a kneeling position. It appeared to be scrambling on all fours in the opposite direction.

"Stop where you are!" Starling yelled. "Federal officer! You're under arrest!"

While his left hand kept a death-grip on one of the ladder rungs, his right hand clawed for the .45 in his shoulder holster. But as he opened his coat, the rushing wind filled it like a balloon, destroying his balance and threatening to sweep him away. His hat was suddenly gone and his hair was flapping in his eyes.

The figure seemed to freeze for a second. The groping fingers of Starling's gun hand were tangled in the blowing coat. He jerked at the pistol, but it refused to come free.

Cr-rack!

He recognized the sound of the first shot instantly – flat, muted, and half swallowed by the wind – and he felt the bullet strike the top of the tender just inches from his face. He ducked although it was much too late to do any good. Then his foot slipped and he started falling.

In his distress, Ed abandoned his struggle with the .45 and grabbed at the ladder with both hands. Once he managed to steady himself, he retreated a step or two until he was out of both the wind and the line of fire. Finally he was able to get the pistol drawn. Cautiously, he started back up.

Cr-rack!

The second bullet slammed against the tender's metal roof and sent Starling ducking again. But this time, he rebounded quickly – and this time he came up shooting.

The .45 bucked twice in his outstretched hand. He saw the fire leap from the barrel, but the sound was lost in a piercing blast from the whistle of the locomotive.

Starling shrank back, deafened by the whistle's scream. When he stole another glance over the edge of the roof, the figure of his faceless adversary was right on top of him. Somehow the man had risen to his feet. It was too dark to tell for sure, but he appeared to be wearing a military uniform of some sort. He was swaying there in a crouch, his feet planted on either side of the slight ridge that ran down the center of the tender's roof, his hair billowing around his head like a halo.

The barrel of the pistol the man was holding was no more than five feet from Starling's face. It looked as big as a cannon.

"I kill you now!" he heard the man cry.

But in that instant, Starling also caught a glimpse of the approaching overpass. On the distant horizon, he could see the lights of some small town whose name escaped him. Outlined against the lights was the dark form of a concrete highway bridge. It was streaking toward them at sixty miles an hour. The bottom of the bridge would clear the top of the train by no more than three feet.

"Look out!" Starling shouted. "The bridge – "

Then the hurtling overpass exploded the man's skull. His last spasmodic reflex caused the pistol to discharge, but the shot went wild.

Starling felt a shower of blood and brain tissue spatter his face as the headless corpse plunged past him into the gap between the tender and the baggage car. For a split-second, the body bounced against the platform between the two cars. Then it slid out of sight under the grinding, relentless wheels of the train.

FORTY-FIVE

U.S. Highway 81
Near San Marcos, Texas
June 11, 1936

For the first few minutes after their wild flight from the railroad yards, Ellie could only huddle low in the car seat and try not to think about anything. Next to her, Adam hunched over the steering wheel, his mouth set in a hard, silent line. Between furtive glances at the rearview mirror, he kept his eyes fixed on the road ahead. Ellie envied his ability to concentrate. At this moment, she thought, she couldn't have driven the Ford coupe a hundred feet without wrecking it.

They were approaching the northeastern edge of San Antonio by the time she managed to relax a little. Traffic had been light and no one seemed in any hurry to get where they were going. To the people they passed, she thought, it was just a normal Thursday evening. She wondered if she'd ever feel normal again.

Night had closed in around the car when the headlights glared on a small, shield-shaped sign that said "U.S. 81." She didn't know how they'd gotten there, but at least they were on the right road. They were heading north toward Austin and beyond, to Dallas and other places she'd never been. But what else were they headed for? What really awaited them beyond the curtain of darkness ahead?

At that point, the main line of the MKT Railroad still paralleled the highway a short distance to the west. And although Ellie couldn't see the tracks, she knew they were well ahead of the President's train. As dulled as her senses were, she still would've noticed if the train had passed them. Maybe, she thought, the train was still at the depot. Maybe the rest of the President's trip had been cancelled. Maybe there was no need to go to Dallas after all.

Maybe, but in her heart she knew it was too much to hope for.

Thinking about what might be happening aboard the train only increased the tightness in her chest until she felt as if she were about to burst into a million fragments. Then her whole body started shaking uncontrollably. She wished that Adam could hold her for a few minutes, but there was no time for that now. Maybe there'd never be time for it again. She tried not to cry, but she cried anyway.

"It's okay," he said, reaching out to touch her knee. "We're going to make it."

She bit her lip. "I just can't get used to the idea of being a murderer."

"Killing a coyoté like Otto isn't murder. It's more like garbage disposal. You think he'd have hesitated to kill *you*? Hell, you ought to be proud of what you did."

"I could never be proud of something like that." There was a quaver in her voice. "Not even if it was Kurt Radke. I might not be sorry, but I wouldn't be proud."

"Well, then, I'll be proud for you," Adam said. "You showed more guts back there than any two men I've ever known."

He half-turned and smiled at her. His face was only an indistinct shadow in the dim light of the dashboard, but she knew exactly how he looked when he smiled. She knew how his mouth curled up at the corners, how his moustache drooped down over his upper lip and how small, improbable dimples formed in his cheeks.

"What did you . . . do with him?" she asked hesitantly. "After you dragged him off the train, I mean."

"There were a bunch of freight cars on the next track over," he said. "I found an empty one with the doors open and threw him inside. Maybe he'll be in Kansas City by the time they find him."

"I . . . I tried to wipe up the blood," she said. "But there was so much of it. I hardly knew what I was doing."

She lifted the hem of her skirt and wiped her eyes with it. It was something she would never have done in Adam's presence a week ago, but now she didn't care if he saw her bare legs. In fact, she almost wanted him to see them. She wanted him to stop the car and take her in his arms. She wanted to tell him she was sorry for the way she'd acted in the motel room yesterday.

She sat silently as they entered the city limits of San Marcos, where she'd spent four years of her life. The street that led to the campus of Southwest Texas State Teachers College looked no different from the last time she'd seen it years ago. In fact, everything about the town looked just as it had then. It was amazing, she thought, that San Marcos had stayed exactly the same – while everything about Elena Velasco had changed.

"What about the other Nazi?" she asked as the town's lights faded in the distance behind them. "You think he's still on the train somewhere?"

"I don't know," Adam said. "If I was in his shoes, I'd be gone like a shot. But you never can tell about some goose-stepper like that. If he's aching to die for the good old Reich, there's no telling what he might do."

"He's not likely to do too much without his bomb. Are you sure you fixed it so it couldn't go off?"

He shrugged. "Well, I yanked all the wires loose. Then I put it in some water just to be on the safe side. Bad thing is, though, they're bound to find it pretty quick."

"Where'd you leave it?"

"In Roosevelt's bathtub. It was the only place I could think of."

She smiled in spite of herself. "Can't you just see the President's face when he goes in to draw his bath?"

Adam managed a laugh. "Oh, I doubt if he draws it himself. Some servant probably does it for him. What worries me is that Secret Service guy Starling. What's *he* going to do when he sees that bomb?"

Ellie leaned heavily against him. She didn't want to think about any of it anymore, yet it was impossible to think of anything else. "He's at least going to know somebody's serious about killing the President," she said. "I mean, that *is* what we've been trying to get across to him, isn't it?"

"Yeah, but just put yourself in his position for a minute and think about it. He's sure to have talked to that deputy I slugged – and the steward on the diner. And God knows how many people saw us running back to the car. Somebody's sure to have told him about us, but maybe nobody even noticed the two Nazis dressed up like soldiers. I mean, why should they, with soldiers all over the railroad yards? Anyway, let's say the dead one's in a boxcar right now headed for god-knows-where, and the other one got away somehow. Starling may not know either one of them exists. So when he finds this bomb all of a sudden, what's he gonna think?"

At first, Ellie had a hard time following his scenario. Then the realization struck her with the force of a slap in the face.

"You mean he's going to think it's *us* trying to blow up the President? My God, that *is* what he's going to think, isn't it? That we're the ones who planted the bomb in the first place."

"I can't see why not," he said. "Especially if we're the only suspects he knows anything about."

Suspects. The word had an ugly, ominous ring to it, and it repeated itself over and over in Ellie's mind. *Suspects. Suspects. Suspects.*

"But surely the Secret Service could tell the bomb was somewhere else before it ended up in the tub," she insisted. "If we'd have planted it, why would we move and disarm it?"

He shrugged. "Maybe we panicked. Maybe we changed our minds. Maybe . . . Hell, I don't know. All I know is we need to keep our eyes open and stay alert. Every cop between here and Dallas could be looking for us by now."

For a moment, Ellie caught herself hoping the police *would* catch them. Even sitting in jail might be better than these endless games of cat-and-mouse. At least if they were in jail, their chances of being shot or blown to bits would be vastly reduced.

"What do we do when we get to Dallas?" she asked. "*If* we get there, I mean? We'll be totally lost in a strange city. We won't have any idea where to look for the other Nazis. Oh, Adam, what good is it going to do? What chance do we really have?"

"Look, we stopped them once, and we didn't know what we were doing then, either. We can stop them in Dallas, too. Besides, I found something in Otto's pocket that might help. I'm not sure what it means, but it's bound to be a clue of some kind. Here, I'll show you."

She watched as he steered with one hand and dug in a pocket of his suitcoat with the other. Then he held his hand out and she saw a half-empty book of paper matches in his palm. The name on its cover was one she was never likely to forget: *Mission Courts*.

"But it's only a matchbook," she said.

"Open it."

When she did, she saw something scrawled in pencil on the inside of the cover. She squinted in the glow of the dashboard until she was finally able to make it out:

Commerce & Akard. Pegasus.

She shook her head, puzzled by the odd assortment of words. "What does it mean?"

"I don't have the faintest idea," he said. "That's what we're going to Dallas to find out."

FORTY-SIX

Aboard FDR's Special Train
Near Round Rock, Texas
June 11, 1936

The President looked tired, uncomfortable, and on-edge. Nat Grayson could sympathize. He felt the same way.

"All right, you've succeeded in making me a little nervous," Roosevelt admitted. Nat noticed a slight tremor in the President's hand as FDR fitted a cigarette into his holder. "Vague plots and nebulous threats don't normally bother me, but this one seems to be getting a bit too specific."

"Forgive my saying so, sir, but it's about time you got nervous," Ed Starling said. "We've been trying to alert you to the gravity of this situation for several weeks now."

There were five of them crowded into the President's study for what FDR lightly referred to as a "council of war." Ed had brought Nat along as his second-in-command, and Roosevelt had asked Steve Early and Gus Gennerich to sit in. Starling wasn't too pleased to see Early and Gennerich there, but there was nothing he could do about it. The President had agreed not to include Mrs. Roosevelt in the discussion for the time being, only because he saw no need in upsetting her.

"Yes, yes, I know," Roosevelt said, allowing Early to light his cigarette for him. "But we can't be governed by fear, Ed. Taking risks is part of a President's job. You remember what I told the American people when I was inaugurated: 'The only thing we have to fear is fear itself . . .'"

"I understand, sir, but sometimes a little fear can also be a healthy thing."

Thank God the last scheduled event of the day was finally behind them, Nat thought, as the train bore steadily north. The stop in Austin had lasted less than twenty minutes, and with everybody so agitated, it was little more than a blur.

Starling had sweated blood the whole time the President was speaking from the rear platform. Fortunately the speech had been unusually brief, consisting mostly of praise for Vice President Garner. Now they had a few hours to assess the situation and plan some strategy. By the time Roosevelt made his next public appearance at 9:30 tomorrow morning in Dallas, maybe they'd know more about what was going on – and how to deal with it.

Before they reached Austin, the agents had given FDR a cursory update on the man who'd fallen from the train. By then, Roosevelt already knew about the explosive device found and disarmed in his coach, and even he was willing to concede that it was no joking matter.

"How soon do you think you can identify the man who was hiding on the tender?" Early asked.

Starling shook his head. "I asked the railway police to check around the tracks in the vicinity of the highway overpass and wire me a confidential report, but we may never have any meaningful ID. Except for the locomotive and the tender, every car on the train passed over the body. I doubt there's enough left to pick up with a sponge."

"What about the other suspects in this alleged plot?" Gennerich demanded. "What's being done about them?"

"We've issued an all-points bulletin with as complete a description as we could get," Starling said. "I also telephoned the San Antonio and Dallas police from Austin and passed the description along to them. It's an approach-with-caution situation. From what we know about them, these subjects are armed and dangerous."

"I heard about the guy who jumped the deputy sheriff and got on the train in San Antonio," Gennerich said. "But what makes you think there's two of them?"

"There was a woman with the guy," Nat said. "The deputy remembered seeing them both earlier down around Montana Street where the train first stopped. A dining car steward also saw both of them on the train. A white male, late thirties, and a Latin-looking woman, late twenties to early thirties. The steward said the guy had some kind of badge and claimed to be one of our agents."

"Impersonating a federal officer," Early said. "That's a serious crime."

"So is trying to assassinate a President," Starling said. "I'm urging you to cancel the rest of this trip and return to Washington immediately, Mr. President."

Roosevelt's eyes moved slowly around the small circle of faces. Then he shook his head. "I appreciate your concern, Ed, but I'm not going to over-react to this thing. As far as I can see, the threat may very well be past history as of now. The bomb that was placed in this coach has been discovered and rendered harmless. Now it's up to our fingerprint people and other experts to see what they can learn from it. Meanwhile, you've assured me the train is secure. I don't know what more I could ask."

"But, sir," Starling interrupted, "once you leave the train tomorrow, we can't guarantee your safety."

"I don't ask for guarantees, Ed," Roosevelt said, "only reasonable assurances. I see no reason to stir up the public or sound international alarm bells by calling off the trip at this stage. I'd much prefer to keep the whole affair under wraps until we can investigate thoroughly and find out more about what we're dealing with."

Nat's thoughts jumped back to the radio message out of Germany picked up by British intelligence. "Suppose it turns out that Germany's involved in this thing somehow," he heard himself saying. "What happens then, Mr . President?"

Roosevelt closed his eyes for a moment without replying. He seemed troubled and perplexed by the question.

"Then in the interests of our own national security, we'd have to be very, very careful that no hint of that involvement ever went beyond this room." Roosevelt turned and looked meaningfully at Steve Early. "Neither the press nor the public could be allowed to find out – not under any circumstances."

Early frowned. "You mean we'd keep the whole mess a secret?"

"We'd have no choice," Roosevelt said. "Regardless of how much justification we may have, we're in no position to fight a war right now."

Shortly after ten that evening, as the train rolled smoothly across the prairie north of Waco, Eleanor Roosevelt finished another chapter in the book she'd been reading for several days. She marked her place, carefully removed her reading glasses and reflected briefly on the progress of the trip. She was quite pleased with the effect of Franklin's public appearances thus far in Texas and Arkansas. The lusty cheers of the crowd at the station in Austin had been especially gratifying. From all indications, the Democrats could expect to carry the state by a wide margin in November.

There was one more brief unofficial stop scheduled at Corsicana, some fifty miles south of Dallas, before the train reached the siding near the town of Lancaster, where it would remain until after sunup. The Corsicana stop was only for five minutes, just long enough to pick up a packet of messages and memoranda that needed the President's attention before the ceremonies started in Dallas in the morning.

Franklin had said he was too tired to put in even a token appearance on the rear platform when the train reached Corsicana. But as First Lady, Eleanor felt a responsibility at least to step outside for a moment and wave to the people at the station. It might not be a large crowd, but she knew from experience that some curious onlookers would be there. They always were.

She started toward the bathroom to freshen up in preparation, but paused halfway there and decided to go ahead and pack her book in the large floral-print handbag on the opposite side of the small room. There would be no time for reading during tomorrow's crowded schedule, but once they reached the home of their son, Elliott, in Fort Worth tomorrow evening, it would be different. Packing the book now would mean just one less item to pick up when they left the train in the morning.

When she reached down to pick up the bag, she noticed that it was standing open, although she distinctly remembered snapping it shut the last time she'd used it. She recalled doing so with unusual clarity because she'd been so aggravated at the time about letting her pistol fall out of her small purse while Franklin was watching. She'd put the little weapon in the larger handbag for safekeeping and . . .

And now where was it? Not only was the bag open and its contents in disarray, but the little pistol was nowhere to be seen. Eleanor leaned down to look on the floor, but it wasn't there either. Over the next few minutes, she checked in every corner and under every piece of furniture, but the little silver pistol had simply vanished.

She remembered there being a commotion earlier in the evening, Something about prowlers aboard the train, and the Secret Service had searched this room, but it was beyond belief that any of the agents would have tampered with her personal possessions.

"How odd," she mused aloud. "I could have sworn I put that gun in this bag. I wonder if the maid could have . . . "

FORTY-SEVEN

***U.S. Highway 77,
Near Lancaster, Texas
June 12, 1936***

It was almost 2 a.m. when Adam pulled into the small roadside park and surveyed the surroundings. The park was dark and deserted. Its facilities consisted of three stone-and-concrete picnic tables, a couple of stone fireplaces and a garbage can. A narrow gravel drive curved back toward a creek bank and a thick grove of trees.

According to the newspaper he'd bought at an all-night cafe in Hillsboro, Roosevelt's first official appearance today was seven and a half hours away – enough time for a respite from the endless highway. Before they faced whatever lay ahead, he and Ellie desperately needed a break.

"What do you think?" he said quietly. "Do we stop for a while or drive on to Dallas and look for a tourist court?"

Ellie's head was against his shoulder. He could feel her hair touching his cheek. For the past hour or two, only his desire for her had kept exhaustion from overcoming him. To do what had to be done, they both had to have rest. But at this moment, he doubted that he could sleep. The urges inside him were fierce, almost painful.

This time, though, he wasn't starting something he couldn't finish. The last thing he wanted was to find himself in the same position as he had the other morning in San Antonio. If it happened again, he wasn't sure he could control himself.

To guard against any repeat of that scene, he'd slept on the floor during their last night at the motel. After the lights were out, they'd lain awake in the darkness for a long time, talking. But she hadn't invited him to join her on the bed, and he hadn't pushed it. Until she was sure – if she ever was – he'd sworn not to venture across the invisible line between them. If he went too far and couldn't stop, it would mean she'd been right about him all along. In a way, he would be no different from Kurt Radke, after all. He couldn't have stood that.

"You think it's safe?" she asked softly.

For the hundredth time since accidentally leaving it behind on the Shuster Ranch, Adam sorely missed the .30-30, and he mentally kicked himself for throwing down the pistol he'd taken from the deputy in the railroad yards. With either gun, he would've felt no hesitation to stay in the park. As it was, the only weapons they had were the little empty pistol from Mrs. Roosevelt's purse and the waterlogged Luger from the bottom of the stock pond. Neither offered any security, and the idea of sleeping unarmed in the open worried him.

On the other hand, he also doubted the wisdom of trying to slip into Dallas at this ungodly hour. The police could be looking for them by now. They could have a description of the Ford, possibly even a license plate number. In the light of morning, when the streets were crowded with rush-hour traffic, they'd face significantly less risk of being spotted than cruising the predawn streets of a strange city, where they'd stand out like a sore thumb. The park wasn't especially inviting, but all in all, it seemed a better option.

"If we go back as far as we can from the road and pull in behind those trees, the car'll be pretty much out of sight of any passing traffic," Adam said. "I think we'll be okay."

"You must be exhausted," she said. "I couldn't possibly have driven all this way."

He eased the Ford onto the grass under the trees, then doused the lights. It felt good just to be sitting still. He closed his eyes and stretched, clenching his fists to keep from reaching out for her.

"Adam . . . "

He tensed, feeling her mouth close to his. "Hmm?"

"I've been thinking about making love with you." She touched his face. "I've been thinking about it for at least a hundred miles."

He laughed softly. "Seems like I've been thinking about it for at least a hundred *years*."

"I . . . I won't disappoint you this time," she whispered as her mouth met his.

The moment he kissed her, he knew she was telling the truth. For whatever reason, her terrible inner struggle was finally over, and the kiss was like a solemn vow. It was also like a drug. He couldn't get enough of it – or of her.

Giddy and groping, he unbuttoned her blouse and touched her breasts. He bent to kiss them, and the taste of her flesh inflamed his senses. He heard her sigh above the short, hard gasps of his own breathing.

His hands went under her heavy skirt and moved slowly upward. The insides of her thighs were moist and warm where they came together. She whimpered as he touched her, and he felt as if the bomb from the train were ticking inside him. The scent of her was powerful, spellbinding. He was about to explode into a million ecstatic fragments. But not yet.

"I thought I'd never be ready," she said huskily, "but I was wrong. I was wrong about a lot of things."

He felt blindly for the bedroll wadded behind the seat of the car. "I'll have to spread this on the ground," he muttered. "Is that okay?"

"It's fine, if . . . if you're sure you still want to."

"More than I ever wanted anything," he whispered.

Adam returned to consciousness slowly, unaware at first of where he was. Then he felt Ellie stir slightly in his arms and he remembered. They were in the bedroll beside the car with their clothes piled haphazardly on the ground beside them. He cringed at how vulnerable they'd been while they slept. Fortunately, though, they hadn't been disturbed or molested, except for a few bloodthirsty mosquitoes.

It was too dark to see his watch, but the bedroll was damp with dew, and pale light was beginning to seep into the sky to the east. The morning was on its way, and there was no way he could stop it. He would've frozen the sun forever below the horizon if he'd had the power.

He propped himself on one elbow and stared at Ellie's face. He ran his hand down her back and pulled her tighter against him, marveling at the silky smoothness of her skin. It still seemed unbelievable that they were here together this way.

She murmured in her sleep and hugged him closer. He could've spend a solid week without moving from this spot. Of course, they'd get pretty conspicuous after a while. Somebody would most likely be selling tickets up on the highway by then.

Within seconds, he was inflamed with desire all over again. He needed her the way he needed oxygen in his lungs, but he knew they'd stolen as much time as they could afford for now. Somewhere not far away at this moment, President Roosevelt was also awakening – to what might be the last day of his life.

He kissed her tranquil sleeping face and sat up reluctantly. The light seemed to grow perceptibly brighter as he dug through the pile of clothes. A car passed on the highway, making him acutely aware of his nakedness and his glaringly obvious state of arousal. But the car was gone in an instant without slowing down.

Finally, he located his undershorts and stepped into them. The suit he'd worn in San Antonio was wrinkled, smudged and hardly fit to wear again, but he was as disheveled as the suit. Changing into fresher clothes in his condition would be ridiculous, and it would take too long to find something else anyway. So he pulled the rumpled trousers back on and re-buttoned his soiled white shirt.

It was light enough to see his watch now. It was almost six o'clock already – just over three and a half hours until the welcoming ceremonies for Roosevelt at Union Terminal in downtown Dallas. He could feel the time racing by. They had a hundred things to do between now and then, and they were still about fifteen miles from Dallas.

He knelt and shook Ellie gently. "Sorry, darlin', but it's time to get up." The term of endearment slipped off his tongue before he realized it.

He'd never called her anything like that before. He felt himself flush in the pale light.

She opened her eyes for a second, then shut them again. "Oh, God, I wish it wasn't. Can't we just stay here?"

"I was thinking the same thing," he said. He started to kiss her, then stopped, knowing where it would lead. Instead, he scratched at a mosquito bite on his shoulder, shoved his feet into his shoes and tried to concentrate on something else. He would've given a ten-dollar bill for a cup of coffee and a place to wash his face.

She hugged the bedroll around her as she tried to reassemble her clothes. Adam politely looked the other way while he picked up her skirt and handed it to her. As he did, Eleanor Roosevelt's silver pistol tumbled out of its folds and bounced on the grass.

"Maybe I should throw that thing in the garbage can," Ellie said. "I'd just as soon not carry it around anymore. I don't like what it reminds me of."

"No, don't do that," he said. "We can pick up some ammunition for it, and it might come in handy later, but you can't just keep it stuck in your waistband. You need someplace to stash it so it's safe and out of sight. You got anything you could use for a holster?"

She frowned in thought as she buttoned the skirt and brushed at the dry grass clinging to it. "I've got a coin purse it might fit in," she said, "but then what? I can't just carry it around in my hand."

"You've got a needle and thread, don't you?"

She smiled wanly. "I never leave home without one."

"You could sew the purse up in the hem of your skirt. Over to one side, so you don't bump it when you walk, and about so high." He squeezed her leg just above the knee. "As full as this skirt is, nobody'll ever know the gun's there, and I'll feel better knowing you've got it. It's always good to have an ace in the hole."

"But you don't even have a gun anymore yourself," she said. "At least not one that can shoot."

He grinned. "So this way I can borrow yours."

He put his arms around her and drew her to him. In a way, the interlude in the roadside park reminded him of his "bushwhacking" nights with Teresa when he was a pup. But in other ways, there was no resemblance – especially in how he felt looking back on it.

"I really love you, Ellie." His throat was tight with emotion.

She touched his lips with her fingertips, then kissed him lightly. "You don't have to say that. I wanted what happened as much as you did. You don't ever have to say anything to me that you don't mean."

His gaze didn't waver as his eyes locked with hers. "I do mean it. That's why I want you to be careful. If we ever get out of this mess we're in, I aim to ask you to marry me."

She shook her head. "People like you don't marry people like me. It could give your father another heart attack. Your mother would have a cat."

"Not so," he said. "Pa likes you, I can tell, and he's smart enough to know how I feel. And Ma'll get used to the idea. Everything will be fine. You'll see."

"What about the rest of the county?"

"To hell with the rest of the county. The rest of the world, too."

She arched her eyebrows at him. "You're serious, aren't you?"

"Yeah," he said. "I don't get any more serious than this."

Her smile was half-teasing, but there was something grim in her eyes. "Then don't wait till later. Ask me now – just in case. I want to have a chance to hear it."

He frowned. "Okay then, will you?"

"Will I *what?* Come on now, you have to say it right."

"Doggone it, will you marry me?"

His heart skipped as her smile faded. For a second, she seemed lost in thought. Then the smile returned. "Yes," she said, "on two conditions."

"All you have to do is name them."

"First, you still have to want me when the time comes – the way you did when we stopped here. Just as strong. Just as much. If you don't, it's no good."

"You don't need to worry about that," he said. "What's the other one?"

She looked away. "Both of us still have to be alive."

FORTY-EIGHT

Dallas, Texas
June 12, 1936

No one paid any attention to the three strangers who mingled with the crowds along Commerce and Akard Streets this Friday morning. In their stylish pinstriped suits, silk neckties and wide-brimmed hats, they looked no different from the scores of bankers, brokers, accountants, insurance executives, and oilmen on their way to work in downtown Dallas. Nothing about them suggested that their expensive cowhide briefcases contained the dismantled components of two high-powered rifles and several dozen rounds of ammunition.

S.S. Major Ernst Dietrich smiled and nodded as people hurried past him toward the elevators in the lobby of the Magnolia Building. It was a minute or two until eight o'clock, and all the secretaries, clerks, and other underlings in Dallas' tallest office tower were rushing to be at their desks on time. Dietrich paused to check the building directory and wait for Rudolf Becker and Wolf Reinhardt to catch up with him. Unlike the scurrying employees, he and his two comrades had plenty of time.

It was amazing how American they looked and sounded, how inconspicuously they blended in. After so many days of practice, Dietrich could think of them by their American names almost as easily as by their German ones. Wolf was William Runnels. Rudy was Randolph Biggers. Dietrich himself was Earnest Dickerson. And they were all from Pennsylvania, of course.

"Are we going up now?" asked Becker, the mission's second in command.

"In a minute," said Dietrich. "Let the elevators clear out a little first. Then we'll ride up and introduce ourselves to – " he took a notecard from his pocket and glanced at a name written on it " – to Paul Hadley, who's supposedly expecting us."

Reinhardt leaned over to look at the directory. "What floor is he on? Ah, good – six. That's about right. Do you suppose he'll find a place for us on that same floor?"

"Probably," Dietrich said, then added in a lower tone: "Try to relax a little, okay?"

"Don't worry, I'll be fine," Reinhardt assured him.

Dietrich nodded. He couldn't blame Reinhardt for being a little edgy. As the mission's designated shooter, Wolf bore a singularly heavy responsibility. But Dietrich had come to know Reinhardt's personality traits as intimately as his skills as a marksman. The closer the moment came to pull the trigger, the more focused and collected Reinhardt would be. In about three and a half hours, when he fired the bullets that killed Franklin Roosevelt, Wolf would be the calmest one among them.

Paul Hadley was expecting the three men when they stepped off the elevator.

"It's a pleasure to meet you, Mr. Hadley," one of them said, extending his hand. "I'm Earnie Dickerson. Sure hope we're not putting you out."

"Not at all," Hadley said. "Glad I could help. I found a place for you in a room down the hall. Come on, I'll show you."

During his undergraduate days as a business major at Southwestern University, Hadley had rarely envisioned himself working for an oil company. But he'd spent the past seventeen years becoming as familiar with geology as he was with personnel management. As one of three assistant managers in the Exploration and Development Division of Magnolia Petroleum Company, he spent most of his time dealing with leases and expense vouchers. It was an unexciting job, but it paid reasonably well. He and his wife, Lucille, were able to own a new Buick and a nice three-bedroom brick house on Monticello Avenue. They could afford music lessons for their daughter, a country club membership, and vacations in Florida.

At a time when many other salaried professionals were hurting financially, raises had come to Paul with comforting regularity. The money had been especially good since the oil boom in East Texas had made Dallas a major hub of the petroleum industry. "Bored but comfortable" was how Paul usually thought of himself, and there were much worse ways to be.

Paul had been mildly surprised by Kurt Radke's phone call. Kurt had been a big man on campus when they were classmates at Southwestern, and it was flattering to be asked a favor by someone so rich and well connected. Paul didn't mind doing favors for people like that. You never knew when or how they might pay off.

❋

"Some business associates of mine from Pennsylvania are planning to be in Dallas for the Centennial Exposition in a couple of weeks," Kurt had said. "As it turns out, they'll be there at the same time as the President. Isn't Roosevelt's cavalcade supposed to pass right by your building?"

"That's right," Paul had said. "He'll be going out Main Street to the Exposition grounds that morning. Main's half a block from here. But later on, he's to come back downtown for lunch at the Adolphus Hotel. That's right next door to us."

"These fellows are big Roosevelt fans," Kurt had said. "They were hoping maybe they could get a good look at him when he passes by. Think you could find someplace where they can watch from a window and not be in the way?"

"Sure, there's a file storage room on my floor that's right at the southwest corner of the building. They ought to be able to get a good look at old Rosie from there."

"Great. I suppose there's a lot of security precautions for Roosevelt's visit. Your place will probably be swarming with cops that day, right?"

"Not as far as I know," Hadley had said. "Some detectives and a Secret Service guy came around a while back to look the building over. Said they'd be posting a couple of guards on the skybridge on the nineteenth floor and one or two in the lobby, but that's about it."

"I guess there'll be a big demand for window space on your floor around noon."

"Oh, I don't think it'll be a problem. I've told my people there'll be no lollygagging out the windows. If anybody's on their lunch hour when Rosie shows up, they can go down and watch from the sidewalk. Otherwise, it's business as usual."

"Then having some outsiders on the premises won't cause you any trouble?"

"Nah, nobody'll even notice them in that file storage room."

"It's swell of you to do this, Paul," Kurt had said. "I owe you one, hear?"

Hadley had smiled as he hung up the phone. Having a person like Radke indebted to you was a pleasant feeling. It was a lot like having money in the bank.

*

Dietrich stood at the only window in the small, drab room and looked down into the intersection six stories below. Just across Akard Street to the west was the main entrance to the Adolphus Hotel, where the open limousine carrying Roosevelt was scheduled to pull up at 11:55 a.m. Dietrich could almost envision the scene as it would look from the window: The crippled President being helped from the car by Secret Service agents, then making his way slowly through cordons of police to the hotel entrance; the sun blazing in a cloudless sky directly overhead.

He closed his eyes, imagining the sound of Reinhardt's shots. Then he glanced at Reinhardt, and he could sense the same imagery flashing through the shooter's mind.

"A wonderful view," Wolf said softly.

Dietrich smiled at Hadley, who was watching them expectantly. "This is perfect," Dietrich said, "absolutely ideal for our purposes."

Hadley looked relieved. "Anything for friends of Kurt Radke's," he said. "Listen, I'm sure you don't want to sit in here waiting all morning. I'll just leave the door unlocked, so you can come and go as you please."

"That's very kind of you," Dietrich said. "We may go out for a bit of sightseeing. This is our first trip to Dallas." He almost bowed, but caught himself in time. He stuck out his right hand instead, and Hadley shook it vigorously.

"Have you been to the Centennial yet?" Hadley asked.

"The Exposition? No, we plan on going later. It's quite fabulous, I hear."

"It's a big deal in Dallas." Hadley winked. "Personally, I'd just like to see that stripteaser called Lady Godiva. They say she's naked as a jaybird behind those fans."

For a moment, Dietrich thought of giving Becker the signal to kill Hadley now while it could be done neatly and conveniently. It would take only seconds to force the poison down his throat. As the only person who could link Radke to the mission, Hadley couldn't be allowed to live. Dietrich had promised to dispose of him, regardless of the mission's outcome. Now was a golden opportunity.

Yet logic told him it was much too early. They might need Hadley again before the climactic moment arrived. Besides, if they killed him now, his absence would surely be noted by his co-workers. It could lead to all sorts of complications. Better to wait.

"That sounds very interesting," Dietrich said. "We'll have to take a look at this Lady Godiva when we visit the Exposition."

"Wish I could take off and go with you," Hadley said. "I'll be in my office if you need anything,"

"Thanks," said Dietrich. "We'll be in touch."

FORTY-NINE

Nat Grayson tiptoed warily toward the dining car table where Ed Starling sat staring at today's early edition of the *Dallas Morning News*. The Colonel had been awake all night. His eyes were red, and his face was pale and unshaven. A half-empty coffee cup and an ashtray with a smoldering cigarette occupied the table in front of him. There were ashes and spots of spilled coffee on the white tablecloth.

"We'll be pulling into the Dallas station in about ten minutes," Grayson said. "Chief Jones is standing by to meet with us as soon we get there."

Ed's tone matched his spent, sour expression. "I want to be extremely careful what we tell the local police about this. There'll be no mention of bombs or bodies. We have unconfirmed reports of a threat against the President, and we want every possible security measure taken. That's all we're saying. Understood?"

"Yes, sir. I've made that clear to all the men."

Starling flipped the newspaper he'd been reading across the table to Nat.

"If all Will Rogers knew was what he read in the papers, he didn't know much," he said. "Look at this." He jabbed a forefinger at a block of headlines and subheads at the top of the front page of one section:

RAILROAD MEN SPEND NIGHT GUARDING ROOSEVELT ROUTE

—

Katy Track Walkers Inspect Every Foot of Rail Between Dallas, San Antonio for Trip

—

Hundreds Involved in "Unusual Precautions"

"I don't know how the press got hold of this story," Starling said. "As usual, they got the facts totally screwed up, but I'm just glad they didn't find out the real reason we had all those people tramping around out there."

Nat nodded as he scanned the story below the headline. The report made it sound as if all the "inspecting" took place before the special train's arrival. Actually, of course, the most frantic searching had come after the train passed.

The train had been a half-hour north of Austin when the remains of the man who'd fallen from the top of the tender were located a few dozen yards from the highway overpass. The head and torso were mangled beyond any human resemblance, and a pack of wild dogs was already fighting over what was left. But one severed lower leg and part of a right forearm with the hand still attached were recovered pretty much intact. So were a .45 automatic and some shredded fragments of a military uniform.

By 11 p.m. the night before, a Secret Service agent and three military policemen had escorted the remains to a laboratory at Fort Sam Houston for examination. Considering the Colonel's frame of mind, Nat hated even to ask about them, but his curiosity got the better of him.

"Have they come up with any kind of ID on the dead man yet?"

Starling shook his head. "No, and I'm not holding my breath about it. All they know so far is the subject was a white male in his late twenties or early thirties. Blood type A. He was wearing a uniform from the Second Infantry, stationed at Fort Sam Houston. No dogtags or papers were found, and the base commander reports nobody missing or on leave. My guess is it was a stolen uniform, and there's probably no hope of tracing the guy through the Army."

"What happens next?"

"We've still got people combing the scene for clues. They may find something yet. Meanwhile, all we can do is beef up security and try not to be too predictable."

"But we *are* predictable," Nat said, leafing through the newspaper. "Everything that's going to happen today's all spelled out right here in black and white. They've practically got a minute-by-minute schedule."

"I know, but the President's agreed to juggle the schedule today wherever possible. We've got to do everything we can to throw off their timing."

"You think it's a sniper we're looking for this time?"

"Almost has to be," Starling said. "We won't give a bomber another chance to get anywhere close. We're going to move this fellow at a fast clip on the way to the Exposition and back. No ten-mile-an-hour stuff or playing to the crowd. I want to speed everything up, get him where he's going up to a half-hour early. We'll need plenty of help from the local cops."

The train stopped with a slight shudder. "It's a quarter of nine," Nat said. "Forty-five minutes till the welcoming ceremony. Want me to go and meet Chief Jones?"

Starling yawned and finished his coffee. "I guess you'll have to. I've got to shave and shower and try to pull myself together. Tell him what we're trying to do with the schedule. If he's holding any men in reserve that can possibly be put on presidential security, ask him to do it. Tell him I'll see him in about twenty minutes."

"Anything else?"

The lines in Starling's face deepened as he frowned. Nat had never seen him look so worn and untidy, so old. "Yeah, see that every local officer in the depot gets descriptions of that couple who boarded the train in San Antonio. I've got a really strange feeling about those two."

"You think they'll show up again today?"

Starling raised his bloodshot eyes as he fumbled for another cigarette. "I can't tell you why," he said hoarsely, "but I'd damned near guarantee it."

FIFTY

Looking down from the ninth-floor window of the Jefferson Hotel gave Ellie a funny feeling in the pit of her stomach. From this height, the passing cars looked like toys. Only a few times in her life had she ever been this high off the ground – and never in a building so elegant.

The hotel faced due south, toward the long concrete viaduct they'd crossed a short time earlier. Curving from south to west, the Trinity River formed a muddy ribbon between dirt-brown levees and marshy green lowlands on either side of it. To the east, she could see most of the city's major skyscrapers, but her gaze was drawn to the tallest of them – the one with the revolving "Flying Red Horse" on top of it.

Something about the building and the symbol bothered her. It nagged at her mind, but she couldn't quite put a finger on it. She tried to concentrate, but her thoughts kept sliding away in all directions. She was too dazzled and dazed by the events of the past half-hour to think clearly.

The hotel had been the second thing she saw after Adam drove into downtown Dallas on Houston Street. The first thing to catch her eye was the magnificent Union Terminal, where the President was due to arrive in less than two hours. They passed within a few feet of the line of cars and police motorcycles already forming in front of the terminal.

He's going to be right here – the most famous man in the world. . .

Then she'd turned to the right, and there, directly across the street from the terminal, was the hotel. It was a massive structure of brown brick and concrete that faced Wood Street and a small park just beyond with a fountain in its center. "Welcome Mr. President," said the marquee sign above the main entrance, then added: "Sky Terrace Now Open. Dance Nitely With Henry Halstead & His Orchestra." A ludicrous image of Roosevelt dancing on the rooftops of Dallas had flashed through her mind just as Adam hit the brakes.

"We couldn't hope to get any closer to the action than this," he'd said, making a quick right turn and pulling up directly in front of the hotel's broad veranda. "Let's see if they've got any rooms."

"It looks awfully expensive," she'd said uneasily. "Besides, look at us. How could we possibly go into a place like that looking like this?"

Adam had eyed his rumpled suit and shrugged. "You deserve to stay in a high-class place for a change. Wait here while I go in and talk to the desk clerk. The worst thing they can do is throw me out."

When he'd re-emerged ten minutes later, his expression told her instantly that they were the newest registered guests at the Jefferson Hotel.

"It cost me eleven bucks – six for the room and five more to get the desk clerk to remember that he *did* have one vacancy left for tonight, after all. But at least we got it."

They'd parked the Ford coupe on a lot adjacent to the hotel and hauled out their disreputable luggage. Ellie felt painfully self-conscious as they followed the bellhop across the lobby to the elevators. Except for the crowd in the coffee shop, there were only a few people around, but she felt as if all of them were staring at her.

"Thank God that's over," she said when the bellhop had accepted Adam's quarter tip and left. "I don't think I've ever been so uncomfortable."

"Relax," he said. "Go take a shower. It'll make you feel better. You can have the bathroom first, but don't spend all day in there. I've got to get cleaned up, too."

"But I haven't got anything but dirty clothes to change into."

"The desk clerk says there's a department store called Sanger Brothers just a few blocks from here. We'll have time to run over there and grab some fresh clothes before Roosevelt shows up." He took her face between his hands and kissed her. "If you don't hurry up, I'm liable to get in the shower with you. What do you think about that?"

Her stomach fluttered. "We'll never make it to see the President if you do."

Tomorrow, she thought. *Tomorrow will be different – if it ever comes.*

After sorting through her clothes to find the least smelly among them, Ellie selected a reasonably clean pink blouse and decided to wear the same full skirt she'd had on for the last two days. The skirt wasn't the cleanest thing she had, but it didn't show dirt as much as her other garments. As of the past hour, the skirt also held the coin purse containing the little silver pistol securely stitched to the underside of it. She'd spent much of the trip into the city with the skirt folded back in her lap while she worked to attach the purse to it with her needle and thread.

After she emerged from the shower, her gaze ventured back to the Flying Red Horse slowly rotating on top of the building five or six blocks away. Why did the symbol seem so disturbing? Why was her attention drawn to it again and again?

She'd watched the sign's glowing outline grow larger and larger on the horizon as they drove the last few miles from Lancaster to Dallas. It was hard to take her eyes off it as they crossed the river. And she'd glanced at it from the hotel window at least fifty times.

The Flying Red Horse was the trademark of Magnolia Petroleum. She knew that much. They'd passed at least a hundred Magnolia service stations on this trip, and each of them displayed a Flying Red Horse. But whatever was tugging at the back of her mind had nothing to do with advertising gasoline. It was about something else entirely.

Suddenly, it dawned on her: *Pegasus*.

Could this red neon sign be related somehow to the word Adam had found scrawled inside a matchbook cover?

She turned as the bathroom door opened and he came out. His hair was wet, and steam was still rising from his skin. He was wearing only a faded pair of Levis. He smiled and she almost forgot what she wanted to ask him.

"Come here," she said. "I want to show you something."

He came to the open window, and his eyes followed her pointing finger.

"That building," she said. "The big one there . . . "

"It's the Magnolia Building," he said. "Tallest skyscraper in Dallas, according to something I read. What about it?"

"Look at the Flying Red Horse. Doesn't it remind you of something?"

"I don't know. Should it?"

"Remember the matchbook in Otto's pocket? Remember what was written on it?"

His blank look made her wonder how he could possibly forget. The words on the matchbook cover were indelibly engraved on Ellie's brain:

Commerce & Akard. Pegasus.

For the time it took the red horse to turn halfway around, Adam stared in silence at it. Then he re-crossed the room, picked up his discarded trousers from the bed and retrieved the matchbook from one of the pockets. He opened it and read the scribbled message again.

"Damn," he said, looking back at Ellie. "Do you really think that red horse is the Pegasus Otto mentioned?"

"It's a little far-fetched, I guess," she said. "Maybe just a coincidence."

He pounded his fist abruptly against his forehead, and his voice rose with excitement and irritation "Don't kid yourself. It's too big and obvious to be a coincidence. That's where it's gonna happen. I'd bet my last nickel on it. God, why I didn't think of this before?"

"But I didn't think of it, either," she said. "Not until just now. Why should you?"

He grabbed a wrinkled shirt, thrusting his arms into it and groping on the floor for his boots at the same time. "Because it's not just the horse. I remember the address of the Magnolia Building, too. For some reason, it stuck in my mind. It should've rung a bell the minute I saw it in the matchbook."

"You mean it's – "

"Exactly. It's at the corner of Commerce and Akard Streets. Come on, let's go!"

FIFTY-ONE

Police Sergeant Thomas McCafferty knew he was no spring chicken anymore. He was a few months past his forty-sixth birthday, and he'd added thirty pounds to his weight and three inches to his waist since he was a rookie patrolman. But if he'd lost some of his youthful vigor in his twenty-three years as a Dallas cop, McCafferty liked to think he'd gained more than enough savvy and experience to make up for it.

No officer on the force was more adept at staying out of trouble and keeping on the good side of his superiors. McCafferty believed in following orders to the letter and being punctual, and he insisted that the men serving under him do the same. So he and the five officers assigned to him today were already at their designated posts in the Union Terminal's main waiting room. The Mayor and the rest of the welcoming committee weren't due to show up for another half-hour, but it never hurt to be early.

"This is your last call for the Fort Worth & Denver Silver Zephyr, now boarding on Track Number Four for Wichita Falls, Amarillo, Raton, New

Mexico, and Pueblo, Colorado," the voice on the loudspeaker announced. "All aboard please!"

The Western Union clock on the wall showed 8:24 a.m., and the Zephyr would be the last train to arrive or depart from the terminal until the Presidential Special was securely berthed and its famous passengers were on the ground. From now until the President and his party detrained at 9:15, all rail traffic would be at a standstill.

When the Roosevelts, Governor James Allred, Senator Morris Sheppard and all the other bigwigs came through the waiting room, McCafferty and his men would become part of a solid human shield of police on either side of the official party. Until then, there was nothing to do but stand around and look alert.

As he glanced toward the "To Trains" sign and the sloping ramp leading down to the main passenger tunnel, McCafferty was surprised to see Police Chief Robert Jones coming briskly up the ramp toward him. He was wearing his ceremonial uniform and fancy white cap with the gold braid, and he was flanked by two captains, also in their spit-and-polish best.

Jones was still a good two dozen steps away when McCafferty called his men to attention and snapped off a crisp salute. "Top o' the morning to you, sir," he said. "Can we be of service?"

"Morning, Mac," Jones said. 'We just had a meeting with an agent from the White House Secret Service Detail. He asked us to alert all our officers to watch out for two subjects that may pose a threat to the President when he gets off the train."

"Aye, sir," McCafferty said. "Can you give us a description?"

"It was dispatched earlier," Jones said. "One's a white male in his late thirties, tall with a husky build, longish blonde hair and a moustache. The other's a young, attractive Latin-looking woman. Black hair, olive complexion, around thirty years old. They're armed and dangerous. Attacked an officer in San Antonio last night."

"We'll keep our eyes peeled," McCafferty assured the chief. "You can bet they'll not get past us if they come this way."

"If you spot these two, use extreme care. They may be part of a large-scale plot. The Secret Service wants them in custody, but they have to be able to answer questions. No rough stuff unless they start it. No shooting unless they shoot first. Clear?"

"Very good, sir." McCafferty saluted again as Jones and his aides hurried toward the terminal's main entrance and the motorcycle squads gathering outside. Then he shook his head. That was the feds for you, he thought, always wanting what they couldn't deliver themselves. But Tom McCafferty would follow his orders to the letter. He hadn't gotten where he was today by rocking the boat, and he wasn't about to start now.

It was less than ten minutes later when the Sergeant spotted the young couple. The man was big and sunburned with a mustache and a mane of unruly blonde hair. The woman's hair was shoulder-length and black, but McCafferty couldn't see her face. They were half-walking, half-running as they crossed the waiting room. Their clothes looked mussed, as if they'd been slept in, and both of them seemed nervous, uncertain and confused. They paused for a few seconds, talking urgently to each other, and McCafferty saw the woman point to the "To Trains" sign. Then they rushed on.

McCafferty signaled to Patrolman J. C. Turner, the nearest other officer to him, and they started cautiously toward the couple. The subjects were only about thirty feet from the down-ramp when the woman stopped and looked behind her. McCafferty saw her face then for the first time and his heart leaped. It was a pretty face, dark and striking and almost surely Mexican. It fit Chief Jones"s description to a tee.

McCafferty made an instant decision. As it turned out, it was a bad one. He sprang forward, resisting the impulse to draw his service revolver. As he broke into a trot, he yelled:

"You there, stop! I want to talk to you!"

If he'd waited until the subjects were descending the ramp itself, his quarry would have been trapped. But the woman was quick as a cat. The man was fast on his feet, too. They were off like a shot before the echo of McCafferty's outcry died. And to his chagrin, they bolted in different directions instead of staying together.

"Stop those people!" McCafferty shouted, lumbering after them. But the bystanders only shrank away as the subjects raced past.

The woman was through one of the outside doors and gone before McCafferty knew it. Meanwhile, the man was clear on the other side of the waiting room, and McCafferty was losing ground on him with every step. He finally stopped in the middle of the huge room, staring after the fleeing figure and panting.

Turner paused beside him, reaching for his revolver.

"Don't do that," McCafferty wheezed. "The feds don't want any shooting."

"If we can find them outside, maybe we can run them down," Turner said. "One of them anyway."

McCafferty shook his head. "No," he said, still struggling to catch his breath. "Our orders are to stay in the terminal and provide security for the President. We can't go chasing off down the street. If those two were the ones the feds are looking for, I don't think they're likely to come back, anyway."

"Maybe I could get the motorcycle jockeys to help," Turner persisted.

"That's not their job," McCafferty said. "They've got their orders, too. Now get back to your post and forget it. I'll tell the Captain about it later."

Turner shrugged and moved away, plainly upset that he couldn't continue the pursuit. McCafferty understood the younger cop's feelings, but Turner was barely twenty-five. Someday he'd learn.

❋

Ellie leaned against a building, gasping for air. A second later, Adam sagged beside her.

"Maybe we should just give ourselves up," she puffed. "That way we'd at least get to talk to the Secret Service eventually. We're not accomplishing anything like this."

"No, damn it, we can't give up yet. Judging from the way they've handled things so far, the feds could screw up a mud fight. Who's to say they'd even listen to us at this point? We've got to stay on the loose. We may be Roosevelt's only hope."

After taking a wide detour and making certain they weren't being chased, they circled back to the Jefferson Hotel, approaching it warily from the side opposite the terminal. The crowd of curious civilians along Houston Street was steadily growing, but everything else looked normal as they slipped into the lot where the Ford was parked. The only police in sight were the motorcycle officers still lounging in front of the terminal.

"Every cop in Dallas must know what we look like by now," Adam said, slumping behind the steering wheel. "We've got to find a way to disguise ourselves or we're dead ducks. We'll either be in the slammer or too busy running for our lives to warn Roosevelt or anything else. If we could get to this Colonel Starling, we might be able to do some good, but we've got to keep the local cops from grabbing us first."

"What do you mean, disguise ourselves? What kind of disguise?"

"I don't know. Different clothes. Dark glasses. Maybe a veil for you or something to lighten your skin. If I could find a barber, I could get rid of this moustache and get my hair cut short. It's worth a try. What else can we do?"

"What about the car? You think they've got a description of it?"

"I don't know, but we've got to risk driving it. The town's too spread out to go on foot, and we don't know it well enough to take a bus or a taxi."

"Let's try to find that department store," she said.

❋

Adam held his breath as he pulled slowly around to the front of the hotel and tried to organize his racing thoughts.

It was two minutes after nine. They had about forty minutes at best before Roosevelt's fifty-car caravan left the terminal and headed for the Exposition grounds some two miles away. From then on, the assassins could strike at any time.

According to yesterday's newspaper, the parade would follow Main Street to the State Fair Park, then return downtown via Commerce Street. Main Street was a block north of Commerce – and a block north of the Pegasus building. This meant the outbound trip to the Exposition was relatively safe. It would be hard to shoot Roosevelt on Main Street from the Pegasus building – and stupid, too. It was going to be a lot easier a couple of hours later.

The end of the trip back downtown, when the caravan reached the corner of Commerce and Akard, would be the time of ultimate risk. There was no other possible meaning for the words inside the matchbook. It had been a long time since he'd been at Commerce and Akard, but Adam remembered this particular intersection with crystal clarity. The Baker Hotel on one corner. The Adolphus Hotel on another. The

Magnolia Building on another. All of them clustered there together at the busiest intersection in Dallas. How convenient.

The open car would be easing into the hotel. It would be stopping, maybe even fully stopped. Roosevelt would be preparing to drag himself out of the car. He'd be surrounded by police and federal agents, all of them intent on what was happening at ground level. They wouldn't see the gun barrel in the open window. Even when they heard the shots, they wouldn't realize what was happening. Not until too late.

The man with the rifle would be a handpicked sharpshooter. The best marksman the Nazis could find. How could he possibly miss?

"Just go north on Houston Street," the bell captain was saying. "Better hurry, though. I think they're going to stop traffic along here pretty soon. After a block or two, you'll see the new Dealey Plaza and the Triple Underpass on your left. Main Street runs through the middle of the plaza. Take a right on Main and go three blocks to Lamar. Sanger Brothers is on your left. You can't miss it."

Can't miss. Can't miss.

Don't say that, Adam thought. Don't even think it.

The son of a bitch has to miss. We've got to make him miss – somehow.

FIFTY-TWO

A small group of colored redcaps stood at worshipful attention beside the line of Pullman coaches, awaiting the appearance of their President. Their soft laughter was as warm and languid as the morning itself.

But a few yards away, where Nat Grayson stood, the humid air crackled with tension. It filled the cavernous boarding area and hung heavily over the uniformed police and military personnel standing guard beside the special train, and it radiated from Ed Starling like heat waves from hot concrete. Starling was newly shaved and showered, but his face still had a grayish cast.

In about five minutes, Roosevelt would be helped from the train and wheeled to the welcoming ceremonies. Every member of the Dallas Police Department was on duty at this moment, half of them working double shifts, and eight hundred Army troops – three hundred more than originally planned – were bivouacked at the Exposition grounds. Yet no amount of security seemed enough to Starling as he listened to Nat run through a checklist of last-minute concerns.

"We've gone over the car from stem to stern, and it's clean as a whistle," Nat said. "It's been under constant guard in the City Hall basement. The driver's a detective named Jack Archer. We've checked his background all the way to Noah. No problems."

The attempt at levity brought only a curt nod from Starling. "Okay, but I still want an agent on each running board enroute to the Exposition grounds and back, and I want you to be one of them. Tell Archer and the two lead car drivers to keep their speed at twenty to thirty miles an hour on the straightaways. Who's driving the car with our other agents?"

"A homicide detective named Will Fritz. He's a top-notch officer and outstanding driver by all accounts. Again, no problems, unless you count past membership in the Ku Klux Klan. If you do, it'd rule out two-thirds of the veteran cops in Dallas."

Starling's face was like stone. "I'll be next to Detective Fritz in the front seat to make sure he keeps pace. If the rest of the cavalcade falls behind, it's not that critical. But I want to keep plenty of firepower around the President. Every agent's to have a machine rifle. Neither driver's to stop for any reason, clear?"

"Aye, sir, but does the President know? He sure likes to stop and press the flesh."

"He knows," Starling said, "and he's promised not to cause any delays. Are all our dignitaries here and accounted for?"

"Yeah, Congressman Rayburn boarded the train a few minutes ago. Mayor Sergeant and the rest of the welcoming committee are ready and standing by."

"Anything else I should know?"

Nat bit his lip. "There was a minor disturbance in the waiting room a few minutes ago. A police sergeant thought he spotted our two suspects from San Antonio. He chased them briefly, but they got away."

"Description?"

"Big, thirtyish white guy. Young, Latin-looking woman. That's about it."

Starling sighed. "Just one more headache to add to the list. If my hair looks grayer than usual, it's because the Dallas FBI field office had two messages waiting for me when we got here this morning. I wish I'd never seen either one."

"What did they say?"

"The first was a cable from London relayed through Washington. Basically, it repeated the warning picked up by British intelligence several weeks ago. Only this time it said the danger was in Texas, not Mexico. This is our last official stop in Texas, Nat. The President's final public appearances in the state are in Dallas and Fort Worth today. You can figure out what that means."

Despite the muggy warmth of the morning, Nat felt a cold surge of apprehension. "Does the President know about this?"

"Of course, but he thinks the warning refers to what happened last night."

"And you obviously don't."

"I might," Starling said, "if it hadn't been for the second message this morning. This one's from Army intelligence at Fort Sam. It seems railroad police found the body of a uniformed soldier early this morning in a boxcar at Durant, Oklahoma."

Nat shook his head. "I don't get it. What's that got to do with us?"

"The boxcar had just come from San Antonio, and the dead man was wearing a uniform from the Second Infantry, but no dogtags or other ID – just like the guy who got knocked off the train last night."

Grayson whistled. "And we already know nobody's missing or on leave from the Second Infantry. So we've got two dead soldiers who aren't really soldiers at all."

"At least not in *our* Army," Starling said, "but that's not all. This guy was shot four times in the chest and abdomen with a small-caliber pistol, but there was almost no blood in the boxcar. What does that tell you?"

"He was already dead when somebody dumped him there – which means he had to have been shot somewhere else."

"Yeah," Starling said, "like the corridor outside Mrs. Roosevelt's bedroom."

❋

Rudolf Becker strolled slowly east along Elm Street past a series of theatre marquees. He paused now and then to read the garish posters on display in front of the Rialto, Capitol and Palace Theatres:

"Grace Moore and Franchot Tone in 'The King Steps Out' . . . "

"'Murder by an Aristocrat' starring Lyle Talbot and Marguerite Churchill . . ."

"Jean Arthur is 'The Ex-Mrs. Bradford,' co-starring William Powell . . . "

The names on the posters meant little to Becker, but by feigning an interest in them, he hoped he'd look less nervous than he felt. He kept having the urge to look over his shoulder to be sure no one was following him.

There was no word from San Antonio, and that made Rudi uneasy. Hauptman and Lutz had been told to follow one of three courses of action. First, if they were unable to mount any sort of strike against Roosevelt, they were to proceed immediately to Dallas and join the others. Second, if their attempt failed but they escaped cleanly, they were to apprise the others by phone and receive instructions. Third, if they were in danger, they were to head for one of the safe houses in Laredo and wait for transport across the Mexican border.

Clearly, since Roosevelt was here in Dallas and very much alive, Hauptman and Lutz hadn't succeeded in their mission. Beyond that, Becker and the others knew nothing of what had happened in San Antonio or where Hauptman and Lutz might be. It had worried Rudi all morning, but the Oberhaupt seemed unconcerned.

"We can assume that both men are either safe in Mexico by now or soon will be," Dietrich had said as they left their hotel rooms this morning. "On the other hand, if they should show up here, they know where to rendezvous with us."

"But there's been no news of any incident yesterday involving Roosevelt," Becker said. "If Willy and Otto made an attempt that put them in enough danger to use the Mexico option, surely it would've been reported."

Dietrich had only smiled. "Maybe the Americans have learned what we've known in the Reich for a long time – that a free, well-informed press is government's worst enemy. Maybe Roosevelt and his henchmen are keeping it a secret."

Becker didn't want to doubt the Oberhaupt. A good soldier of the Reich never questioned the judgment of his superiors, and Becker was a good soldier. He always put duty above all else, like his father before him.

Young Rudi had been only twelve that spring of 1915 when scores of German units hurled themselves at the British lines before Ypres. He knew that the battalion of Prussian Guards commanded by his father, Major Felix Becker, was one of them, but it never occurred to him that his father would die. Rudi had always thought of his father as invincible. He remembered how pale his mother's face had been the day the telegram arrived from the Western Front. He could still see the tears on her cheeks and feel her arms trembling around him as she whispered the shattering news.

Becker had hated the English and all their cousins and allies ever since. He hadn't been old enough to avenge his father in the Great War, but now he was. He'd joined the new Wehrmacht as soon as there was one and devoted his life to being a good soldier in his father's image. Disobeying orders or disputing a decision by his commander was unthinkable. That was one reason he'd been designated second in command of the mission.

Still, he didn't share Dietrich's confidence. If the impetuous Hauptman had been on his own, it might've been a different story. But Lutz was as dedicated to the mission as Becker himself, possibly even more so. Barring a total disaster, Lutz would've found a way to contact them. Something was wrong. Becker could feel it in his bones.

What if Hauptman or Lutz had somehow been captured alive? As Becker well knew from his weeks of playing nursemaid to him, Otto was capable of a stupid mistake that might play into the enemy's hands. If the Americans had used torture or drugs to learn about the other members of Operation Pegasus, U.S. counterintelligence agents could be stalking the rest of them at this very minute.

Even as worried as he was, Becker had been able to hold his misgivings in check as long as he was with Reinhardt and the Oberhaupt. He'd only gotten jumpy when Dietrich insisted they leave the Magnolia Building and separate for the time being. From then on, Rudi's anxiety had steadily grown.

"If we stay in this building constantly for the next two and a half hours, we're sure to attract attention," Dietrich had said. "Some casual observer might give our description to the authorities and hamper our escape. It's best to scatter out and avoid being seen together. We'll each familiarize ourselves with the surroundings and watch the caravan when it passes the first time. Then we'll meet back in the sixth-floor room no later than eleven-fifteen to complete our mission."

Dietrich's reasoning was sound, and Rudi had no argument with it. But he'd been on edge from the moment Dietrich ordered him to go north of Main Street and mingle with the crowds while Dietrich and Reinhardt stayed in the area south of Main. They'd been out of sight for over twenty minutes, and the longer Rudi was alone, the more vulnerable he felt.

His sense of isolation intensified when police blocked Main Street to traffic and ordered pedestrians not to cross it until after the parade. This left him totally cut off from the others. To fight his nervousness, he'd ventured a block further north to Elm Street, remembering Dietrich's warning:

"Keep moving. Look purposeful. No loitering."

Becker did his best, pausing only briefly, then moving on again. Past the closed theatres, an amusement arcade and a clothing store with a sign in the window that said "Sale – Ladies Dresses From $2.98." Past a jewelry shop with a Jewish-looking clerk who eyed him suspiciously. Past an Orange Julius stand and a barbecue emporium with sawdust on the floor.

He looked warily at the faces of the people he passed, but he saw no recognition there. At the end of the block, he crossed the street, then started down the opposite side in the direction he'd come.

He looked at his watch. It was 9:32. The caravan would be coming soon.

Rudi tried to steel himself. He was determined to see the mission through to its conclusion – just as his father would have done.

FIFTY-THREE

The traffic light at Pacific Avenue and Field Street turned yellow just as the Ford coupe reached the intersection. Adam resisted the urge to try to beat the light and jerked to a stop. There was no use tempting fate. If a traffic cop pulled them over, it could mean real trouble. He knew now how Clyde Barrow and Bonnie Parker must have felt with every lawman in the Southwest breathing down their necks. You couldn't let your guard down for a second.

He barely recognized his own image in the rearview mirror. With his clean-shaven upper lip, short haircut, new white Palm Beach suit, and dark-green sunglasses, he bore no resemblance to the person he'd been slightly more than thirty minutes ago.

Neither did Ellie. She still wore her full skirt – although the pistol beneath it was now fully loaded with .25-caliber bullets – but nothing else about her was the same. Her long hair was coiled in a tight bun and hidden under a black hat with a net veil that half covered her face. Layers of pale makeup from her neck to her hairline made her look more Anglo than he'd ever thought possible. A lacy red blouse and red patent-leather shoes completed the ensemble. Even with all the distractions, it was hard to keep his eyes off her.

Luckily, they'd found everything they needed at the huge Sanger Brothers store. Adam hadn't wanted to park in the path of the parade, so he'd found a space a half-block north of Main Street. As it turned out, that was the luckiest part of all. By the time they came out of the store, police had stopped traffic on Main and blocked the intersections so that no cars could cross. Elm, the next parallel street to the north, had been heavily congested with delivery trucks, streetcars and automobiles, so they'd continued north to Pacific Avenue, then turned east in search of Akard Street.

Finally, the light changed. Adam hit the gas, and the coupe lunged ahead.

"What time is it?" Ellie asked, glancing uneasily through the rear window. "Are you sure the caravan hasn't passed already?"

"No, it should be leaving the depot any minute now. My watch says nine forty-three. Hey, there's Akard Street dead ahead."

At the intersection, Ellie peered around the corner. "I'd stay on Pacific if I were you. It's too crowded down there. Just take the first parking place you see and we'll walk to Main."

"But it'll take so long – damn, I just remembered something."

"What is it?"

"The Magnolia Building's on the other side of Main. There's no way we can get across till the parade's gone by."

"We'll just have to get as close as we can," she said.

FIFTY-FOUR

"Here he comes! Here he comes!"

The crowd at Main and Akard surged to the curbs of both streets as the open car approached. From the edge of the sidewalk where Adam stood with Ellie, he got a clear look at the white-suited figure in the rear seat. For an instant, he saw Roosevelt smile and raise his arm to wave. Then a forest of bodies blocked the view as a cheer rose from the crowd.

"Wave, Betty Jean!" a woman yelled as she held a toddler high in the air. "Wave at the President!"

Almost before it was possible to grasp the moment, it was over. The limousine passed, and the wave of cheers rolled on down the street along with it, leaving the crowd strangely quiet and subdued in its wake.

"I seen him," mumbled a black man in awe. "I seen him jist like me an' you!"

As the limo shrank into the distance, Adam's relief was like a breath of pure oxygen to a suffocating man. Roosevelt had made it safely past the Pegasus building unscathed – at least this once. But it was too early to celebrate, and there was too much still to do. Roosevelt would be back in a couple of hours, unless there was some way to divert him, and the danger would be incalculably greater then.

As the crowds dispersed, it was obvious that only a fool would've attempted a shot into Main Street from the Magnolia Building. Not only was the building too far away, but the angle of a shot from any of the upper stories was too acute to be practical. The odds against success would've been a thousand to one at best, even for the best marksman with the most accurate telescopic sight.

Sensing Ellie close beside him, Adam reached out for her. Just as he did, a familiar face flashed by, almost near enough to touch. It vanished quickly into the crowd, but in the fraction of an instant it had been there, the face was eerily familiar. It was out of context but Adam knew he'd seen the face before – not once but numerous times. In the time it would take to click a camera shutter, it was lost in a choppy sea of other faces. Yet the familiarity of it was seared into his mind.

Adam turned abruptly, dragging Ellie after him. His gaze swept north along Akard Street in the direction from which they'd just come. The human kaleidoscope before him kept shifting. And shifting. Then the shutter snapped again.

Click-click.

For a split-second, the face popped up again in the sea of bodies. It looked back from twenty feet away, wide-eyed with startled recognition and alarm. Like a white-tail deer bursting from the brush on the first day of hunting season.

The thing was, the eyes weren't actually looking at Adam at all. Instead, they were fixed on . . . Ellie. It was Ellie they recognized.

Click-click.

In the twitch of an eyelid, the face was gone again. This time, it disappeared in a flurry of pumping legs and flailing arms as someone struggled frantically to get through the mob of onlookers.

"Wait!" Adam yelled. "Who was that?"

Ellie stared at him. "Who was what?"

"I saw somebody in the crowd. He saw us, too – saw you. He was right there." Adam pointed down the street. The very closeness of the face was what had thrown him. Always before, he'd seen it from a considerable distance – and through binoculars – but now he knew for sure who it was.

"My God," he said. "It was one of *them*! Right here under our noses."

Then Ellie recognized the fleeing man, too. "It's the other one from the store," she said. "The one named Rudi."

Down the block, the body attached to the face broke into a dead run, shoving bystanders aside. A woman cried out as she was flung violently to the sidewalk. The man darted into Akard Street against the light just as a line of traffic delayed by the parade surged forward. One car bumped the man slightly, but he managed to make it to the opposite sidewalk. He glanced back once, then ducked into an alley.

"We've got to catch him," Adam said, plunging into the street in pursuit. "We can't let him get away."

"Look out!" Ellie yelled. "There's a car – "

A honking Olds sedan missed Adam by inches. The brakes squalled, and the driver cursed. On the opposite sidewalk, most of the pedestrians dodged and shrank back, clearing a path and casting puzzled looks as Adam charged past. He heard Ellie pounding along at his heels.

But, damn it, where was the Nazi? Adam stared down the alley, but the man was nowhere in sight.

Ellie ran up beside him. "Where'd he go?"

"He's got to be down there somewhere," he said. "Come on!"

After fifty yards, the alley crossed a narrow sidestreet. Adam tripped over a pile of pasteboard boxes and almost fell. As he stumbled into the street, he caught a glimpse of the German disappearing around a corner a half-block away. His legs were a good six inches shorter than Adam's, but they undoubtedly had no eighteen-year-old metal fragments embedded in them, and the German moved with enviable speed. He'd more than tripled the distance between himself and his pursuers since the chase started, and if he could slip out of sight for even a few seconds, there were countless places to hide. Adam was testing his damaged knees as they'd never been tested before, and he knew the odds of running his quarry down were stacked against him. If he lost any more ground, the fugitive would get away, and their best opportunity yet would be lost.

Ellie was lagging twenty or thirty paces behind Adam now, hopelessly hobbled by her new shoes, her voluminous skirt and an ankle still affected by the sprain she'd suffered on the Radke Ranch. Much as he wanted to, there was no way Adam could wait for her if he wanted to keep pace with the German. He sprinted west down Elm Street, scanning the sidewalks on both sides. In a few more seconds, Ellie was swallowed up in the distance behind him.

When he saw Lamar Street and the Sanger Brothers store just ahead, he heard an inner voice shouting a warning:

Don't let him get inside that store. If he does, you'll never find him!

At the intersection, the light was red in Adam's direction, but he didn't break stride. He lunged off the curb, waving his arms at the skidding oncoming cars. Miraculously, he made it unscathed to the other side.

At the main entrance to the department store, he hesitated. By all logic, the German should have ducked inside. If their situations had been reversed, Adam would've done precisely that. Among the six floors of endless aisles and counters, he'd be next to impossible to find. Yet something told Adam to stay on the street, so he slogged on, his lungs burning, his knees wracked by shooting pains, and his legs leaden with fatigue. He didn't know how many more steps he could take before his lower body gave out completely.

Just then, he spotted the German again – less than a half-block ahead on the opposite side of Elm . The sight gave Adam a fresh burst of adrenaline, a second wind, and new determination. Somehow he ran harder, increasing his speed until he was almost parallel with the German, but by now, the pain in the bones and muscles of his legs was like a series of explosions.

Even at this point, if Adam's quarry had ducked into one of the buildings he was passing, he might easily have vanished before Adam could cross the street through the traffic, but instead the German simply kept running. He was clearly rubber-legged and exhausted himself, but his only remaining strategy seemed to be blind flight. If he realized that Adam was now almost beside him sixty feet away on the opposite side of the street, he gave no sign of it.

They crossed Austin Street, then Market, then Record. Just ahead was Houston Street, which formed the western boundary of Dallas's central business district. By now, the chase had covered seven or eight blocks, and the downtown buildings and sidewalks were rapidly running out. At Houston Street, they simply ended.

Beyond lay a grassy, park-like area that the Jefferson Hotel bell captain had called Dealey Plaza, a new feature that hadn't existed the last time Adam was in Dallas. Until recently, the Trinity River had flowed just west of the plaza site, about where a triple underpass now stood. Downtown's three main east-west streets – Commerce, Main and Elm – now ran through the fan–shaped plaza, converging just past the underpass and becoming the main highway to Fort Worth. Beyond the underpass was only a mile-wide expanse of levees and bottomlands with the river in its center.

Just south of the plaza was Union Terminal and the railroad yards. But north of the plaza was nothing but an empty, overgrown floodplain stretching toward the levees on the east side of the river. Except for some railroad tracks that bisected it, it was one vast sea of high weeds, Johnson grass and scrubby willows – a virtual wilderness just a stone's throw from one of the busiest commercial districts in the Southwest.

The German crossed Dealey Plaza without slowing down, then scrambled up the embankment beside the triple underpass and slid down the other side. Adam was no more than a dozen steps behind him as they crossed the railroad tracks and plunged into the tangled weeds and undergrowth of the flood plain.

Beneath the thick carpet of vegetation, concealed patches of mud sucked at Adam's shoes. He tripped once and almost fell, leaving a muddy grass stain on one knee of his white trousers. He felt as if his lungs would burst, but the agony in his legs had largely turned to numbness, and he refused to give up. The fact that he was totally unarmed was the furthest thing from his mind.

"Stop, you bastard!" he rasped. "You can't get away from me."

The German offered no response. He just kept running.

They were almost to the earthen levee on the east side of the river when Adam fell for real. He felt his feet slipping out from under him, and he grabbed for a willow sprout to steady himself, but it was too late. He went down on all fours in a patch of Johnson grass. His right hand sank to the wrist in thick, oozy mud. Before he could regain his footing, the German was standing over him with a drawn pistol.

Rudi was breathing hard and his face was flushed beet-red. But the hand that held the .45 automatic was steady and unwavering. There was a smile of bitter satisfaction on his lips.

"I must salute you . . . my friend," he panted. "Radke was right. You're a . . . very tenacious man. Also a very lucky one. Otherwise, we would . . . have killed you a week ago. But now I think . . . your luck has run out."

He leveled the gun at Adam's head as his finger tightened on the trigger.

FIFTY-FIVE

From the front seat of the Secret Service car just behind the President's limo, Ed Starling watched the last of the high-rise downtown buildings slip past. He felt a muted sense of relief at being out of the central city, but the tension in his muscles and the knots in his stomach refused to go away. Before today was over, the presidential party still had two more trips to make through these shadowy brick-and-concrete canyons. Two more trips beneath these thousands of blankly staring windows.

Still, they'd made the first hurdle without incident. The rest of the trip to Fair Park and the Cotton Bowl should be a breeze. No structure along the rest of the route was taller than two or three stories. At the speed they were traveling, the danger would be minimal – as minimal as it ever got.

As the caravan passed Pearl Street, the motorcycles just ahead of the car sped up with a roar. The car's driver, Detective Fritz, accelerated smoothly after them, and the speedometer needle settled at 30. Starling sighed, looking straight ahead at Roosevelt.

The President and First Lady sat next to one another in the rear seat of the open limousine. The President was grinning and talking animatedly to Mayor George Sergeant, who was across from him on the jump seat. Governor James Allred and Elliott Roosevelt were in the next seat forward. FDR appeared relaxed and jaunty in his white suit and dark tie. In a few minutes, his voice would be heard by millions of Americans from coast to coast via two nationwide radio networks. He was in his element. If he had a worry in the world, it was invisible.

Starling shook his head and turned for a final look at the downtown skyline now jutting up behind them against the western sky. The Magnolia Building stood head and shoulders above every other structure in Dallas. It looked especially imposing right now with its eastern walls and the bright red trademark atop its roof catching the full brilliance of the morning sun.

For a long moment, Ed stared intently at the Flying Red Horse symbol, and as its revolving shape glittered briefly in the sunlight, a small door opened somewhere deep in Starling's mind. He found himself remembering the wire he'd received this morning, repeating a warning that had found its way from Berlin to London to Washington to Dallas. He tried to reconstruct the warning's exact wording in his mind, but it wouldn't come together. What the hell *had* it said, anyway? And why should this building with the red horse remind him so strongly of it?

Starling was confounded by his own tangled thought patterns. He reached inside his jacket and found the crumpled telegram in an inner pocket. Carefully, he unfolded it and read it over slowly to himself:

"Message received in London reads as follows: 'Re FDR plot . . . Texas not Mexico . . . Pegasus . . . 11 or 12 June.'"

The revolving red horse turned its full profile toward Starling again. His eyes riveted themselves to its winged shape, and he was unable to tear them away. It was 10:02 a.m. on the twelfth of June, and what must surely be the largest Pegasus in all of Texas towered before him at this very moment. Was it merely an odd coincidence or an apocalyptic omen of disaster?

Ed's head was swimming as he turned to Detective Fritz. "How much longer till we get into the stadium?"

"We're just a couple of minutes from Fair Park," Fritz said, without taking his eyes from the road. "But the crowd's sure to slow us down when we get inside. We estimate up to two hundred and fifty thousand people on the grounds and another fifty thousand in the bowl. I'd say fifteen to twenty minutes all told."

"Do the best you can," Starling said. "I'm going to have to get one of your units to take me back downtown as soon as we get the President to the speaker's stand."

Fritz threw him a questioning glance. "What's the problem?"

"It's . . . just something I need to check out before the President goes back for lunch," Starling said. "Kind of a hunch, you might say."

As they made the turn onto Exposition Avenue, he looked again toward downtown. The red horse was still there, its neon outline vivid against the sky.

"God," he muttered, "could it actually be that ridiculously simple?"

FIFTY-SIX

Ellie had come about three-quarters of the way across the overgrown flood plain when she suddenly heard the voice. She was picking her way through a thick stand of sunflowers when the sound reached her. At first, it was barely audible above the wind rustling in the grass and the faint hum of distant traffic.

Then she heard it more distinctly, although she still couldn't make out any of the words. It came from somewhere in front of her, and for a moment, panic froze her in her tracks. The silence had been ominous enough in the midst of this no–man's land, but the sound of a human voice was somehow even more unnerving – especially when she could tell it wasn't Adam's.

Thoroughly winded, Ellie had reached Houston Street just in time to see Adam and the German clamor up the bank beside the triple underpass and vanish into the wilds beyond. At that point, it had seemed impossible to catch up with them. The new shoes had made a painful blister on her heel. Every step was misery, but she forced herself to keep trying.

The knowledge that Adam had no gun – and that the Nazi named Rudi almost surely did – was enough to spur her on.

As the pursuer, Adam might not realize the danger. But if the German decided to turn and fight, their roles could change in the flick of an eyelash. The prey could abruptly become an armed and deadly predator.

The echo of her hurtful footsteps repeated an urgent message in Ellie's ear as she ran across Dealey Plaza:

Adam, watch out. Adam, watch out.

Now she crouched in the tall grass, picking her way around the mud-holes – not that it mattered where her shoes were concerned. The shoes were already ruined. You could scarcely see them for the mud. And – dear God! – they were killing her feet.

Impulsively, she pulled off the two most expensive pieces of footwear she'd ever owned and tossed them away. She'd gone barefoot half her life, and there was no reason she couldn't do it now. Years of treading on rocky ground had given the soles of her feet a permanent toughness. The mud was soft between her toes, and at least there were no prickly pears lurking in these marshy wastes.

As she eased forward, she heard the voice again. It spoke haltingly, its words interspersed with labored breaths.

". . . Otherwise, we would . . . have killed you a week ago . . . "

Just then, Ellie caught a glimpse of Adam through the weeds. He was a dozen yards to her right, standing up slowly, shaking mud from his fingers. She could tell at a glance that he'd fallen, and he looked more disgusted with himself than afraid. But even in the fix he was in, he still had enough presence of mind to invent a convenient lie. She'd never understand how he managed it at a time like this.

"I don't know what you're talking about, Mister," he said, raising his hands in protest. "I'm a store detective from Neiman-Marcus, and I was chasing a shoplifter when I saw you running down the street. I can see now you're not my man. Just a case of mistaken identity. I apologize."

Ellie saw Rudi now, too. The German was a yard or two beyond Adam, standing on a slight rise at the edge of the levee. He held a large pistol aimed squarely at Adam's head. She crouched lower, snaking her way through the undergrowth. If she could somehow maneuver her way behind the German, maybe . . .

"You can spare the stupid charades, Herr Wagner," Rudi said. "I know exactly who you are – "

Ellie grappled with her full skirt, searching desperately for the tiny handgun hidden somewhere within its heavy, voluminous folds. In a matter of seconds, the German was going to stop talking and start shooting. She could sense it.

Sweet Mother of God, help me. I've got to stop him – but how?

". . . somehow guessed our mission here," Rudi was saying. "There's only one way to end this – "

She wanted to scream. The skirt was impossible – dripping with muddy water, covered with burrs, and tangled in the damp, sticky weeds. It was hopeless. By the time she could extricate the pistol and get it into firing position – if it wasn't too wet to fire at all – it would be too late.

It's no good, no good. Got to find something else.

Inches from her bare left foot, she spotted a sizeable piece of wood on the ground. It was three or four feet long and over an inch thick. It looked like part of the trunk of a small sapling.

She scrambled forward and grabbed it. Her heart sank when she found it was rotten and pulpy at one end, but fortunately it was solid enough at the other. Not a perfect club, but it would have to do.

"*Auf wiedersehn,* my stubborn friend," Rudi said. "This is for my father."

Ellie could sense the pressure of the German's finger on the trigger as she raised the stick with both hands and sprang forward. Adam spotted her when she was still six feet behind Rudi, and he cringed, either in anticipation of Rudi's shot or Ellie's blow – or maybe both.

She was off-balance when she swung the stick, but she knew she'd hit the German solidly because she heard a sharp, satisfying *crack.* A half-second later, the gun discharged.

The shot was strangely muted, scarcely louder than the sound the stick had made against Rudi's skull. Adam lurched to one side, and for a second she was afraid he was wounded. But he straightened up almost immediately – just as she struck Rudi a second telling blow.

The Nazi groaned and stumbled, blood oozing from his scalp. The pistol fell from his hand, and Adam snatched it up almost before it hit the ground. He whirled toward Rudi with it as Ellie raised the stick again.

But by now the fight was clearly over. The German turned dazedly away and staggered up the embankment to the top of the levee. He swayed there with blood streaming down his face while Adam and Ellie followed at a cautious distance.

"Put your hands up and come on down," Adam told him. "The Secret Service is gonna want to talk to you."

Then as they watched, Rudi pulled a small white packet from his coat pocket. "*Heil Hitler*," he gasped. "*Deutschland über alles!*"

Before either of them could move, Rudi popped the white packet into his mouth and bit into it. A terrible choking sound came from his throat, and he fell backward from the top of the levee. His body was only inches from the edge of the muddy river when he finally stopped rolling.

By the time they reached him, he was obviously dead.

"My God," Ellie said. "He killed himself."

"Better him than me," Adam said grimly. He put his arms around Ellie and hugged her fiercely to him. "I don't know how you got here or where you came from, but I've never been so glad to see anybody in my life."

Tears of relief flooded her face. "It was poison, wasn't it?" she said. "He had poison in that little package."

"Yeah, cyanide probably. And the only way to stop him from swallowing it was to shoot him. I don't guess it really matters. You can't die but once, anyway."

After a minute, Adam bent down and turned the body over. He went quickly through the man's pockets and removed a handkerchief, a pocket comb, a few coins and a wallet. Inside the wallet were a small roll of bills, a few cards and receipts, and a Pennsylvania driver's license with the name "Randolph Biggers" typed on it.

Adam shoved the wallet into one pocket of his mud-smeared white jacket and slipped the .45 automatic into another. Then he rolled the body into the river and watched it float slowly downstream on the slight current.

"Will anyone ever know who he really was?" Ellie wondered, staring after the body.

"Maybe the Secret Service can figure it out." Adam said, stooping at the water's edge to wash some of the mud off his pants. "If we ever get a chance to talk to them, that is."

Ellie thrust her bare feet into the water and shuddered. "What time is it?"

He looked at his watch. "Twenty-six past ten."

"We're running out of time, aren't we?"

"Yeah. Let's go back to the car and drive out to the Exposition. If only we could get somebody to listen to us, we might still have a chance to keep Roosevelt away from that damned Pegasus building."

Ellie nodded, but she didn't want to go. Not to the Exposition or anywhere else. Not now. Not like this. She wanted to close her eyes and lie down on the riverbank with Adam and stay there from now on.

"Sometimes it all seems so hopeless," she said. "We've gotten rid of two of these animals all by ourselves. We've found their bomb and disarmed it. We've saved the President's life at least once. We've taken all kinds of risks. But no matter what we do, it's never enough."

She looked up and saw Adam holding his hand out to her.

"We can't give up now," he said. "We've still got at least two more Nazis running around here someplace and a couple of hours – maybe less – to stop them. After that, it'll probably be too late."

FIFTY-SEVEN

Reál County, Texas
June 12, 1936

Kurt Radke paced the length of his luxurious office. He stared at the silent telephone on his desk, trying through sheer concentration to make it ring. When it failed to comply for the hundredth time, he aimed a futile kick at the base of the massive credenza against the wall.

"Damn you, Dietrich," he said. "How dare you ignore me!"

Kurt's temper had hovered near the boiling point all morning. He'd been agitated from the moment he opened his eyes, and his mood had grown steadily uglier as the minutes dragged by. By now, his nerves were as raw as saddle sores. It was after 10:30 a.m., and by noon or shortly after, the history of the nation – perhaps the whole world – could be changed forever. If the outcome was right, Kurt would have a glorious future. If it was wrong, he'd most likely have no future at all.

He lit a cigarette and stared moodily into the dregs in the bottom of his coffee cup. His mood wasn't helped when he buzzed for the Mexican valet to order fresh coffee and got no answer. He picked up the cup and stormed down the hall toward the kitchen.

When he got there, he found his sister Karla sitting at the breakfast bar. She was wearing only a halter top and slacks, and her long, uncombed platinum hair was spilling over her bare shoulders. Her eyes were red, but she seemed relatively sober for once. She was smoking one of those damned Fatima cigarettes that he hated, and the glass of orange juice at her elbow looked suspiciously pale, no doubt because it was liberally laced with gin.

Karla's slim but shapely figure and finely chisled facial features always made Kurt think of their mother. At Karla's age, Henrietta Radke had looked enough like her daughter to be her twin. There were still a few old photographs of his mother around that confirmed the uncanny resemblance. They were alike in more than looks, too. Karla had the same flighty personality, the same affected mannerisms. This was why the mere sight of Karla sometimes made him want to punch her.

He strode past her directly to the coffee urn, but he knew it wasn't going to be that easy. He was right. Karla delighted in needling him.

"Well, if it isn't the conquering hero." She smiled crookedly at him, then struck a coquettish pose that she thought made her look like Jean Harlow. "What's the matter, brother dear? You look like you just shot your best friend."

He ignored the jibe. "What're you doing up so early? It's not even noon yet."

Her face turned suddenly pouty. "Who'd know the difference out here in the middle of oblivion? I may go to New York tomorrow. I don't think I can stand this smelly goat farm another day. I've been bored to death ever since Ernst left."

He stopped pouring his coffee and looked at her.

Ernst? Ernst? The name sent up red warning flares in his mind.

Karla had started cozying up to Dietrich the first day he arrived. Kurt knew they'd slept together more than once over the past few weeks. He didn't like the idea, but he'd learned to be philosophical where Karla was concerned. It wasn't as if it were anything new, after all. She'd bedded down with countless men in her thirty-nine years. Better Dietrich than another half-breed fence-rider or Negro musician.

But as far as Karla was concerned, SS Major Ernst Dietrich wasn't supposed to exist. The man she'd been playing around with at the ranch was Earnest Dickerson of Reading, Pennsylvania. Once Kurt saw what was happening, he'd warned Dietrich in the strongest possible terms not to let Karla know his true identity – much less why he was in Texas. She could never be trusted. Hell, after she had a snort or two, she might blurt out the whole thing to anyone from the Governor on down.

"Ernst?" he said heavily. "I think you mean Earnest, don't you? That *is* Mr. Dickerson's first name."

She laughed. "Oh, come on, Siegfried, cut the crap." The nickname was one she'd used to tease him since they were teenagers. "I know exactly who Ernst is and where he's from. He told me all about himself. In fact, Major Dietrich's invited me to come and visit him in Berlin later this summer."

Kurt's mouth opened involuntarily as he stared at her in disbelief. "Exactly *what* did he tell you?"

The coquettish look was back. "That he's an officer in the SS, of course – *and* a close personal friend of Hitler's." She smiled and sipped her drink. "I knew he was no wool buyer the minute I saw him. You should've made up a better story than that. He said you're afraid it'll hurt you politically if people find out you're friends with a Nazi."

Kurt wanted to slap the silly smile off her face. He wanted to slap her so hard she'd never smile again. "Why do you have to be such a prying fool?" he demanded. "Why do you enjoy it so goddamn much?"

"Why not?" she said lightly. "It's no crime to be German. Men are the same, no matter where they're from. I can make any man tell me his secrets – especially when he wants me as much as Ernst did."

Kurt took two slow steps toward her, and her smile faded as she recognized the look in his eyes. She'd seen it before when he was enraged enough to commit murder – or when he already had. He could've strangled her, and she knew it.

"Stay away from me, Kurt. Don't you dare touch me."

"You stupid, troublemaking slut!"

He stopped in his tracks and threw his coffee at her, cup and all. He threw it so hard it might have maimed her if it had been on target. As it was, only an ounce or so of the coffee actually hit her. The rest splashed darkly across the floor. The cup crashed against the stone wall of the kitchen, and the pieces flew in all directions.

"If you weren't my sister, I would've killed you a long time ago," he said quietly when the echoes had died. "If you ever mention Ernst Dietrich's name to anyone else, I won't let that stop me."

Back in his office, Kurt removed his favorite rifle – a long-barreled .30-40 with an elaborately hand-carved stock – from the gun cabinet and loaded it with seven rounds of ammunition. As he slipped the shells into the clip, he thought of what he would do if Dietrich were standing there before him at this very moment.

It was a good thing for Dietrich that he had no plans to come back this way. Kurt had once thought the two of them were true *kameraden*, but no more. He could never remain a friend to someone he couldn't trust. It had been that way with Adam Wagner after the scene at the cabin that long-ago night. Now it was the same with Dietrich. Even Adam had never lied to him, Kurt thought. Never broken a promise or gone back on his word. But Dietrich had done all those things.

Barring complications, all survivors of the mission would go straight to Laredo. If they made it that far, they could easily slip into Mexico undetected. If Dietrich escaped cleanly, the odds were that Kurt would never see him again unless he made a point of looking him up on his next trip to Germany. It would be next to impossible to settle accounts with Dietrich there, where he was surrounded and protected by his fellow stormtroopers. But if the lying bastard were to walk in the door right now . . .

Dietrich had given his solemn oath as an officer of the Reich never to reveal his real identity to Karla. He'd also promised to stay in close touch by phone. He knew how much Kurt had at stake in Operation Pegasus. He knew how much Kurt stood to lose if the mission went wrong. In both cases, he'd broken his vow. Kurt had heard nothing from Dietrich or any of the others in more than thirty hours.

This is how he repays me for all the risks I'm taking, all the money I've spent. Damn his soul!

The San Antonio operation must have failed– or perhaps been cancelled. Kurt's own contacts in San Antonio said FDR's visit had gone off with no apparent hitch. If Hauptman and Lutz had had to flee to Mexico, Kurt would've been informed, but there was no information on either man's whereabouts. Since Becker had called yesterday in Dietrich's place with a routine status report, there'd been only a maddening silence.

Shortly after eight this morning, Kurt had called the hotel in Dallas, but there'd been no answer in any of the three rooms. About an hour later, he'd fought off his misgivings and phoned Paul Hadley at Magnolia Petroleum . For all Kurt knew, Hadley could have been dead by then, but he was very much alive and disgustingly cheerful.

"Your friends got here just fine, Kurt, and I've got them all fixed up," Hadley had said. "They went out to do a little sightseeing while they wait for the President."

"Well, thanks a lot, Paul," Kurt had replied helplessly. "If you happen to see Mr. Dickerson in the next little while – he's the tall, blond guy, remember? – ask him to give me a call, okay?"

"Sure, Kurt. And if I don't see him beforehand, he said something about us getting together for lunch, so I'll be sure he gets the message."

"I appreciate it, Paul. More than you know."

Kurt's palms had been sweating as he hung up the phone. Before lunchtime today, Paul Hadley was supposed to meet with a fatal accident. To Kurt, nothing was more important than knowing if the accident took place on schedule. Hadley's mouth had to be shut forever before he could tell the authorities about Kurt's "three friends from Pennsylvania." One of those "friends" had already talked far too much. And if Hadley wasn't dead by lunchtime, Kurt suspected he'd be as good as dead himself.

What was happening in Dallas right now? If he only knew, he could feel some reassurance – something to sustain him for the next little while. In an hour and a quarter, the die would be cast, one way or another.

He sat by the office window with the cocked rifle, staring across the rocky ridges and verdant valleys of the Radke domain, and waiting.

FIFTY-EIGHT

Dallas, Texas
June 12, 1936

It was an idyllic political scene. A brilliant sun shone in a cloudless blue sky above the emerald-green floor of the Cotton Bowl. Hundreds of uniformed troops stood at attention while a rifle company offered a twenty-one-gun salute. Military aircraft roared overhead. Flags and bunting were everywhere.

A slight breeze stirred Franklin Roosevelt's hair as he stood at the podium. People from coast to coast could hear his resonant voice as it rolled through the overflowing stadium:

"Today we have restored democracy in government. We are in the process of restoring democracy in opportunity . . . "

The huge oval was six years old, but it still held the lingering smell of fresh concrete and the pungent earth into which it had been carved. Rising around it was what amounted to a modernistic city of exhibit halls, theatres, pavilions, fountains, lagoons and statuary, all coordinated in the new style called "art deco."

Every seat in the stadium was filled, and the aisles were jammed with standing onlookers. According to Dallas police, it was the largest crowd in the Cotton Bowl's history. Outside, hundreds of thousands of others swarmed the Exposition grounds, most of them listening to the President over a system of loudspeakers:

"In our national life, public and private, the very nature of free government demands that there must be a line of defense . . . "

Even in this picture-perfect atmosphere, Nat Grayson was wary. This was the first time in his Secret Service career that he'd been in full charge of the White House Detail. So far, everything had gone like clockwork, but that didn't mean it would stay that way.

With the intense security in the stadium, only the most suicidal fanatic would try anything here, but any situation involving such massive crowds was a giant responsibility for the detail. And Starling's final instructions before heading back downtown only added to Grayson's nervousness.

Nat had still been trying to shake the effects of the long ride on the running board of the President's limo when Starling came running up. It was obvious at a glance that the Colonel's expression meant only one thing – trouble.

"I've got to go someplace in a hurry, and I'm getting a police captain to drive me," Starling said. "You'll be in charge of the caravan when I leave."

"Now? In the middle of all this? I hope you're kidding, Colonel."

"I'm sure as hell *not* kidding, and there's no time for long explanations. I'm certain there's going to be another assassination attempt today, and I think I know where. I've got to get there fast, and you've got a big job to do here."

Nat frowned. He wondered if the tensions of the past few days had finally pushed Starling over the edge. Was the Colonel cracking under the strain? Was he in full control of his faculties, or was he irrational?

"I don't understand, sir. Where – "

"Never mind, just listen. The President knows we've got to speed up our schedule, and he says he'll cooperate. I want to cut twenty-five to thirty minutes off his time here at the Exposition. I want him at the Adolphus Hotel by 11:30, not 11:55 as originally planned. If anybody's going to try anything, that may throw off their timing."

Nat's mouth felt dry and sticky inside. "I'll do my best, sir."

"That's not good enough, Nat. Give me your word you'll get it done."

"Okay, you've got it. But how – "

"He's trimming three or four minutes off the speech. That's a start. He's got a meeting with some Indians that can be speeded up, too. You can steal the rest of the time from his tour of the Exposition. At 11:10, if not earlier, he's off for the hotel, clear?"

"Yes sir," Nat said. "Come hell or high water, we'll be there by 11:30."

He knew it was the only answer Starling would accept. What he didn't know was how he was going to make it happen.

The President's speech was winding down.

"We seek to banish war in this hemisphere . . . to extend good will . . . "

It was 10:49. Nat turned to Callahan and whispered: "The minute he finishes, get him back in the car. We've got to roll."

In just over twenty minutes, they had to be driving out of Fair Park on their way downtown. It always took at least five minutes to get everybody loaded into the limo. How in God's name were they going to make it?

"I salute the empire of Texas!" Roosevelt said.

The speech was over. The stadium erupted in thunderous applause.

Nat raised his eyes to heaven, praying for a miracle.

FIFTY-NINE

It looked to Ellie as if everyone in the world had come to the Texas Centennial Exposition. The only available parking place was in a residential area five blocks from the main entrance. By the time they got inside the gates, she felt as if she'd run a mile, and it was still a long hike to the stadium.

The scenes en route were only a blur before her eyes: Giant painted murals depicting scenes from Texas history; two seventy-foot-long dinosaurs rearing lifelike against the sky; buildings shaped like a huge cash register and a steamship; German castles and Oriental palaces; a medieval English theatre and an Alpine village; freak shows and bigger-than-life pictures of women with no clothes on; ferris wheels and a roller-coaster. The sharp-voiced sideshow barkers seemed to be urging them on:

"Alive! Alive!"

"Hurry, hurry, hurry!"

She held tightly to Adam's hand as they fought their way through the swarming people. If they got separated, they might never find each other again. The crowds were even bigger near the stadium. It was inconceivable that so many people could be in the same place at once. It seemed possible that there were more people within her field of vision right now than she'd seen in all the rest of her life put together.

"We'll never get through this melee," Adam yelled over his shoulder. "We may as well forget it."

Fifty feet from the stadium's nearest gate, their path was blocked by a solid wall of humanity. Above the crowd noise, they could catch only snatches of the President's speech over the blaring loudspeakers. Then a huge ovation went up inside the stadium. Adam stopped, listening intently as Ellie pressed close to him.

"What is it? What did he say?"

"The speech is over," he said heavily. "We got here too late."

Within seconds, a tidal wave of people started flowing out of the stadium. For a while Adam and Ellie were swept along with the tide, but they finally managed to edge their way through the gate. The narrow passages leading down to the seating areas were still clogged, but once they reached an area of empty bleachers, they could see down onto the floor of the stadium.

The raised speaker's platform was virtually empty now. The President himself was hidden by clusters of people around his limo. Hundreds of soldiers stood in formation flanking the caravan. Some members of the official party were already back in their automobiles.

Ellie shook her head. "You're right, it's useless. Even if we could get down there before he leaves, the soldiers wouldn't let us get anywhere near the cars."

"He's supposed to tour the Exposition before he heads to the hotel for lunch," Adam said.

"How long will that take?" Ellie asked.

"I don't know, but not long enough. We've got to get out of here. We never should've come. It's nothing but a water haul."

He sounded as weary and worn-out as Ellie felt. She wanted to collapse. She wanted to stretch out on the bleachers and go to sleep in the sun. The thought of having to run all the way back to the car was almost more than she could bear.

"Maybe we could get close enough to talk to the Secret Service while he's riding around the grounds," she suggested.

He shook his head. "We can't afford to waste time on any more 'maybes.' Besides, there's too many soldiers around, too many things that could go wrong. Both of us know where the real danger is."

"You mean the building with the big red horse on top?"

"Yeah, we may not have enough time left to search the whole damned place, but we've got to try. It's our only hope now."

SIXTY

Ed Starling stared at the ruined right rear tire of the police car and fought down the urge to beat his fists against the steel roof of the vehicle. Instead, he shoved both hands into his pockets and turned to Police Captain J. W. Grisham, who'd been driving when the blowout sent them lurching to the curb.

"Sorry, sir, I know you're in a rush." Grisham opened the trunk and checked the spare. "There's a service station about a block away. To be perfectly honest, they could probably change this thing faster than I could."

"But can't you radio for another car?" Starling asked tightly. "Wouldn't that be quicker than trying to change the tire right now?"

"I'll try," Grisham said, "but all available radio units east of the river are under orders to maintain specific positions along the caravan route. Maybe I can get the dispatcher to contact an uninvolved unit in Oak Cliff and send it to pick you up."

"How long will that take?"

"On a code three, we can probably have one here in ten or twelve minutes."

Ed looked at his watch. It was 10:43. "Where the hell are we, anyway? How far's the Adolphus from here?"

"We're at Main and Oakland, sir, and it's right at a mile to the hotel."

"Okay, go ahead and have a unit dispatched, but meanwhile I'm going to start walking, just in case there's some kind of delay." Starling forced a smile. "I used to be able to do a twelve-minute mile before I got so old and frazzled."

"I hate for you to have to go it on foot, sir."

"Believe me, Captain, you don't hate it nearly as much as I do."

"There should be a streetcar along in five or ten minutes," Grisham protested. "Or maybe I can flag down a civilian and commandeer his car."

Starling didn't reply. He was already striding west on Main Street – and trying hard to keep from swearing under his breath. He was going to need every bit of wind he had left for walking.

After half a block, he could see the top of the Magnolia Building in the distance. Bumping up the schedule had seemed like an excellent idea when he'd given the order. Now he wasn't so sure.

It was 10:46. In less than forty-five minutes, Roosevelt would be riding, literally, into the shadow of Pegasus.

The worrisome question had been gnawing at Dietrich's mind since soon after the caravan had passed, and he and Reinhardt had started looking north of Main Street for their missing comrade. By now, the question had repeated itself so often in his head that it formed a monotonous tattoo:

Where could . . . Becker be? Where could . . . Becker be?

Initially, Dietrich had merely been puzzled by the disappearance of his second-in-command. Of all the mission's members, Becker was the most devoted to punctuality, organization, and detail. Such an unexplained absence was totally out of character for someone so dependable and so steeped in Prussian military tradition. In all previous situations, Becker had proved to be the kind of man you never had to worry about.

Perhaps Becker had sensed a problem and simply taken a detour to avoid it, Dietrich thought. But surely, as soon as the problem passed, he'd be along.

By 10:55, however, it had been a full hour since the scheduled rendezvous with Becker on the southeast corner of Main and Akard. Now the original question gave way to an urgent, drumming warning in Dietrich's brain:

Something's gone wrong. Something's gone wrong.

For at least the tenth time, Dietrich and Reinhardt were standing at the spot where they'd last seen Becker, still with no sign of him. Most of the spectators had left, although some would undoubtedly reappear as the time neared for Roosevelt's return. At the moment, only scattered pedestrians were moving along the sidewalks. It would be impossible not to see Becker if he were anywhere nearby.

Ernst hadn't worried when Lutz and Hauptman failed to show up or call. He'd monitored the radio news broadcasts and scanned the newspaper for any hint of trouble, but there was nothing. He could make himself believe that Lutz and Hauptman were safe in Mexico by now. But with Becker, it was another story. It was as if the earth had opened and swallowed him up.

Dietrich stepped out of the heat of the sun and into the lobby of an office building. His face was grim as he turned to Reinhardt. "It's almost eleven. We can't wait any longer. We have to take our positions."

"But it makes no sense," Reinhardt said. "How could Rudi vanish without a trace?"

"I don't know, but I think he'd be back by now if he were coming. Our only course is to carry on without him. When the time comes, I'll go down to the street and act as lookout. I'll give you the signal, just as we planned. The difference is, you'll have to handle the other part alone, without a backup. Can you do it, Wolf?"

Reinhardt's eyes were steady as they met his commander's gaze. "Absolutely," he said.

Dietrich glanced around to make sure no one was within earshot. "There's also the matter of this man Hadley to be dealt with. With just the two of us, it won't be as easy to force the packet into his mouth. There's greater risk involved. What do you think?"

"I'm a soldier of the Reich, Oberhaupt. I'll do whatever I'm ordered to do."

"I know, Wolf," Dietrich said, "but the situation has changed, and I want us to be in full accord on how to proceed. The success of our mission may depend on it. That must be our foremost concern."

Reinhardt thought it over for a few seconds. "If Hadley should interfere with us in any way," he said finally, "he should, of course, be eliminated. But as I see it, once we complete our mission and escape from the immediate area, he poses little risk to us or the Fatherland. The long-term threat is mainly to our American host, correct?"

Dietrich nodded. "If he were questioned by the American authorities, Hadley's the only one who could connect our presence here with Kurt Radke, and . . . "

Dietrich's words drifted off, but his thoughts raced on. The little man named Hadley was now in a position of key importance. If Hadley told the FBI or the Secret Service about Radke, the guilt-by-association thread would be unlikely to stop with him. Federal agents would be certain to discover the ties between Radke and Vice President Garner, and if no member of the Pegasus mission were captured alive, a finger of suspicion would point squarely at the man who stood to become President within the next hour.

Dietrich's mind was drawn back to Heinrich Himmler's closing remarks at their meeting in Berlin:

"Since Garner is from Texas, what are the chances of making it appear that he and his supporters are somehow involved? If this should happen, it could only add to the chaos and confusion in America – and to the glory of our ultimate triumph."

Despite his rising concern about Becker, Dietrich felt a surge of fresh resolve. Himmler's words were another omen that the mission would ultimately succeed, that National Socialism would prevail.

"I agree with your reasoning, Wolf," he said. "We'll make every effort to avoid Hadley when we go back to the sixth floor. If he stays out of our way, we'll let him live."

As they walked south on Akard Street, the Flying Red Horse symbol towered above them, blood-red against the sky.

SIXTY-ONE

Adam paused in the alley just off Commerce Street and glanced back toward the sidewalk to make sure no one was watching. Ellie huddled close to him as he pulled the dead Nazi's .45 automatic from his coat pocket and checked the clip. There were six rounds left. It wasn't a lot of firepower, especially if it came down to a shootout, but it was a damned sight better than nothing.

Finding a metered parking place on a sidestreet south of Commerce and less than two blocks from the Magnolia Building had been a surprising stroke of good fortune. He'd expected to have to walk a lot farther, and after re-crossing Fair Park, he felt as if they'd already covered at least five miles on foot this morning.

He thanked God for the .45. Hunting heavily armed assassins in an unfamiliar skyscraper would be tough enough at best, and with only the little.pistol stashed under Ellie's skirt, it would be courting disaster. The .45 at least evened the odds a little.

"You'd better get your gun out, too," he whispered. "It's too hard to reach where it is. I wish I'd had time to get you an ankle holster."

"Just what I always wanted. Never mind, I'll just stuff it in my purse."

He shielded her as well as he could while she pulled up her skirt and grappled unselfconsciously beneath it for the gun. The skirt came up almost to her waist at one point, and he caught a tantalizing flash of white panties. Even amid the biggest crisis of his life, her movements aroused him, but he knew better than to touch her right now.

As they stepped back onto the sidewalk, the sun was still slightly to the east. Soon, though, it would be directly overhead. It was three minutes until eleven o'clock.

"Oh, Adam, how will we ever do this?" she said, looking up at the tallest structure in Dallas. "The building's so big, and there's so little time."

His gaze followed hers, and the full magnitude of their task hit him for the first time. Above the ground floor were twenty-six stories encompassing hundreds of offices. Probably only the executive suites and penthouse on the top two floors would be inaccessible to the assassins.

The problem had seemed insurmountable at first, but the longer he thought about it, the more it simplified itself. For a successful downward shot with any legitimate hope of escape afterwards, a shooter would probably need to be at least four stories above the street. Any lower and signs, utility poles, and power lines would be in the way, and above the eighth floor, the angle and distance would severely hamper a shooter. Only the fourth through eighth floors were well-suited for an assassin's purpose – and searching five floors was a lot more doable than searching twenty-four.

As they neared the building's Commerce Street entrance, Adam saw the Adolphus Hotel directly in front of them across Akard Street. Above the drive-up entrance to the hotel was a marquee advertising the Century Room , where Roosevelt was to have lunch – if he lived that long. Adam could see two uniformed patrolmen on the Magnolia Building's sky bridge on the nineteenth floor, and he knew instinctively that they were too high to be any help.

"It gets harder and harder to shoot accurately above seven or eight floors," he said, "and anything above eleven or twelve is almost out of the question. The likeliest spots are between floors four and eight on the south or west side of the building. That's where we've got to look first."

Ellie brightened a little. "Okay, maybe it's not so impossible, after all."

Two more uniformed cops stood in the main elevator lobby, one near the Akard Street entrance and the other near the Commerce Street entrance. Both looked bored, as if they'd been there far too long.

"We can go twice as fast if we split up," she suggested, lowering her voice as they passed the nearest cop.

"Forget it," he said. "It's too dangerous."

"But we're talking about the President. What if we get there too late?"

He caught her by the shoulders and stared into her eyes. "Look, if I have to choose between saving him and keeping something from happening to you, there's only one choice. If it comes to that, I'm sorry, but Roosevelt won't stand a chance."

He pressed the button for the elevator, and they waited. It was exactly 11:02.

SIXTY-TWO

Ed Starling was at Commerce and Preston Streets when he heard the siren approaching behind him. He was only five or six blocks from his destination, but he'd never heard a more welcome sound. He was dripping with sweat, as breathless as a beached whale, and he felt as if someone were kicking him in the lungs. There was no use kidding himself. He might not have made it another five or six blocks.

He turned and coughed just as the black Ford sedan pulled up to the curb. The car door popped open, and Captain Grisham jumped out.

"Sorry it took so long, sir. Get in and we'll have you to the hotel in a minute or less."

Ed was too spent to reply. He sagged into the front seat of the squad car and let Grisham slam the door after him. A second later, the cop behind the steering wheel hit the gas and the car shot forward, its sudden motion pressing Starling back against the upholstery. He mopped his face with his sweat-soaked handkerchief and closed his eyes. He almost reached for a cigarette, then caught himself.

"Actually, it's not the hotel I want," he croaked. "Take me next door, to the Magnolia Building."

"Coming up, sir," the driver said, accelerating through a red light.

In the heart of downtown Dallas, other police units were already in the process of clearing Commerce of vehicular traffic. This allowed the patrol car to cover the few blocks in seconds, but it only added to Ed's unease. He was almost out of time.

He heard Grisham's voice from the back seat. "We just got a radio report that the President's motorcade left Fair Park a minute or two ago,. It's on schedule and headed this way. We're doing all we can to be ready."

Ed winced and looked at his watch. It was 11:13.

The tires squawked on the hot pavement as the squadcar lurched to a stop.

Starling pushed the door open, dragged himself out of the seat, and shoved through the building's revolving doors with Grisham and the driver close behind. The two other uniformed cops on duty in the lobby rushed over when they saw Grisham.

"Trouble, Captain?" one of them asked.

"This is Agent Starling of the Secret Service," Grisham said. "I guess you'd better ask him."

"I don't have time to explain it all right now," Ed said, "but I need some help for the next few minutes. I want as strong a police presence as possible here in the lobby. Nobody enters the building unless he can prove he's got legitimate business here, and keep a sharp eye on anybody who leaves. If they look or act suspicious, hold them for questioning. Captain, can you scare up some extra men to go upstairs with me?"

"It'll take a while. We're spread awfully thin right now."

"Forget it then. There's no time. Just stay here and help the other officers."

Starling turned and sprinted toward the elevators.

Above a dozen stories, a rifleman's chances of hitting his target would be next to nil, he thought, so he'd start at the twelfth floor and work his way down. That way he could use the stairs if the elevators were too slow or crowded. He might still have enough wind to run *down* a stairway, but running up was out of the question.

As the operator closed the doors and the elevator started up, Ed realized he'd left the police with no description of who they were looking for.

In reality, he had no clue himself. Was it a tall, blond man and a dark-skinned woman with a knack for being everywhere at once? Bogus soldiers in stolen uniforms with no dogtags or other identification? German espionage agents? Men from Mars? What?

Starling patted the pearl-handled .45 under his jacket and touched the single-shot .38 "squeezer" in his watch pocket.

It was 11:17.

SIXTY-THREE

The rifle was a Mauser, and in Reinhardt's skilled hands, it took less than two minutes to assemble. To Dietrich, the angle from the corner window looked perfect –like a cat-bird seat overlooking the passenger-unloading area in front of the Adolphus. For a marksman like Wolf, it was virtually point-blank range. Roosevelt's car would either be in the process of stopping or already at a standstill.

Duck soup, as the Americans said.

The only drawback was that the window afforded no view of the street on which the car would approach. From here, it was impossible to see more than a few yards of Commerce Street east of its intersection with Akard. Still, Dietrich couldn't have felt more confident, and, in fact, he wouldn't have wanted it otherwise. Because of the restricted view, Ernst would play as vital a role as Wolf himself by standing watch on the street corner and giving the critical signal a second before the limousine pulled into the kill zone.

Dietrich's excitement was like an electrical current coursing through his body, but Reinhardt was the picture of composure as he checked the

Mauser's telescopic sight. Judging from Wolf's demeanor, they might as well have been in church.

"I have to leave you now, my friend," Ernst said, extending his hand. "It's time to take my position on the street. The early bird gets the worm, and I learned long ago never to trust a politician's schedule. Herr Roosevelt may be impatient for his lunch."

"Too bad," Reinhardt said. "He's already had his last meal."

Wolf stood up, and they shook hands solemnly.

"We're experiencing one of the climactic moments in history," Dietrich said. "We're both instruments of fate, Wolf – especially you. I know you're equal to the task."

"It's a great honor to be chosen, Oberhaupt."

"All Germany will one day hail you as a hero. If we meet again when this is over, we'll celebrate as never before. If not, we'll rest in the knowledge that we've done an unparalleled service for our country."

"That thought will sustain me, regardless of the outcome."

"When I reach the designated area on the street, keep your eyes on me constantly," Dietrich cautioned. "When I raise my right hand and put it on top of my head, it means Roosevelt is about to come into your rifle sights. Aim well and shoot straight, my friend."

"I won't fail." Reinhardt clicked his heels, and his right hand shot out in the Nazi salute. "Sieg heil! Long live the Fatherland!"

Dietrich returned the salute and picked up the briefcase containing the other rifle and extra rounds of ammunition. The backup weapon was useless here now that Becker was gone, and there was no point leaving it behind for the authorities to find, although it was unlikely they could trace it to the mission.

As Ernst walked down the corridor toward the elevators, he glanced into the large office where Paul Hadley worked, but Hadley was nowhere in sight.

When the elevator doors opened on the first floor, Dietrich tensed as he saw four uniformed police in the lobby. Two of them stood near the Commerce Street entrance, obviously watching him.

He nodded and smiled. "Morning, officers," he said cheerfully. "Everything under control?"

They seemed to relax a little. One of them smiled back.

"No problems, sir," he said. "Just a little added security for the President's visit. You have business in this building, Mr. – ?"

"Dickerson. Earnest Dickerson. Yeah, I was visiting Mr. Hadley up in the Explorations Department. I'm just heading out for an early lunch now, before everything gets crowded."

The officer stepped back. "Okay, thanks, Mr. Dickerson. Go right ahead."

Dietrich took a deep breath as he went through the revolving doors. His amazing record since entering the U.S. was still intact. No one in authority had yet asked to see his identification.

It was 11:21.

SIXTY-FOUR

The receptionist outside the large seventh-floor office was young, friendly and so talkative that she was hard to get away from.

"No, I don't remember seeing a single soul this morning that I didn't recognize," she said. "Only people who work on this floor, as far as I remember. But if you'll tell me what these folks look like, I'll sure keep an eye out for them."

"Well, thanks," Adam said, "but I guess we're on the wrong floor. We'll just go down to six and look around there. That may be where they are."

"You're sure you don't want to describe them for me?" she persisted.

"No, that's okay," he said. "We may check back with you later."

The receptionist kept talking as Adam grabbed Ellie's hand and edged away.

"Lots of people will be leaving for lunch in the next few minutes to try and see President Roosevelt," she said. "He's going to be right across the street at the Adolphus, you know. I heard somebody say he was already on his way back downtown."

Adam paused in spite of himself. "I didn't think he was due back till noon."

"According to the radio, he's coming early," the receptionist said. "He'll be here in just a few minutes. Isn't it exciting?"

Adam turned and sprinted down the hall, pulling Ellie after him, while the receptionist's voice still droned behind them. They'd covered barely half the territory they had to cover, and now, if what the receptionist said was true, there was almost no time left. Yet there was no way to go faster.

At the elevators, they found a cluster of people waiting to go down. Adam whirled toward the stairwell, then stopped abruptly. Something clicked in his mind – an idea of sorts. It filled him with instant misgivings, but it was all he had to work with right now.

"You've got to get on that elevator," he told Ellie. "Shove somebody out of the way if you have to, but get on it. Go down on Commerce Street and watch for the caravan while I keep looking. If Roosevelt shows up before I find those bastards, you've got to try to warn him."

"But how?"

"Yell at him. Wave your arms. Throw something. Do anything you can think of, but do it before he gets to the corner. And for Christ's sake, stay out of the line of fire."

Her face was stricken. "I can't leave you here," she said. "If you find those men, they'll kill you. You won't have a chance alone. Come with me."

He forced a smile. "Don't you know that one Texan's worth a dozen goose-steppers any day? I'll be okay." He pulled her close to him for an instant.

"Oh God, don't make me go," she breathed. Adam had never heard such a beseeching, hopeless tone in her voice before.

He squeezed her arms, his fingers digging into her flesh. "Listen, you've got to do this, Ellie. We've both got to do it. There's too much at stake, and we've come too far to quit now."

The elevator bell dinged. The doors slid open. The operator stepped out. "Going down please?"

Ellie kissed him quickly. The crowd in the hallway pressed forward.

"I love you," she said. "Remember it."

Then she was gone. He felt dead and empty inside as he ran for the stairs.

It was 11:27.

SIXTY-FIVE

Ed Starling flashed his badge at the young receptionist outside the office on the seventh floor. "Secret Service," he said. "You noticed any strangers around in the last little while?"

She looked from the badge to Starling's flushed face. "Matter of fact, I have. A young couple was here just a few minutes ago, and it's odd but they asked me the very same thing – had I seen anybody this morning I didn't recognize. I said, 'No, I sure haven't,' but now I guess I can't say that anymore. I mean, since I did see this young couple and all – "

Ed tensed instantly at her words. Everywhere he'd been for the past eighteen hours, a mysterious young couple had been turning up. Could this be the same young couple spotted on the presidential train in San Antonio? The same one seen earlier this morning at Union Terminal?

"What did they look like?"

"Well, the guy was kind of tall. Real nice-looking, too, except his white suit was all wrinkled and dirty. I couldn't tell much about the lady's face. She was wearing a hat with a veil. She was about my size, I guess, only with black hair."

"Where'd they go?"

"Said they were going to the sixth floor to look for somebody."

Starling ran for the stairs as hard as he could go. It was 11:29. If Roosevelt was on schedule, he was exactly one minute away.

SIXTY-SIX

Adam peered cautiously into the large office on the south side of the sixth floor. The sign outside the door said "Exploration & Development Division." At least thirty people were at work in the room, but he saw at a glance that none of them was preparing to fire a rifle from any of the windows overlooking Commerce Street.

Another dry run, he thought. Another in an endless series of blank walls. By his watch, it was almost exactly 11:30. His head hurt and his legs felt dead, but he pushed on.

At the southwest corner of the building he started north along another long corridor, then he noticed a closed door to his left. There was no lettering on the door's frosted-glass pane, but a shadowy hint of movement behind it caught his eye. Adam hesitated.

If there was a window in the room, he thought, it would look down directly onto the Commerce-Akard intersection.

He was at the door in one swift stride. He half expected it to be locked, but the knob turned easily in his hand. His other hand fumbled for the .45 under his jacket, and he felt its trigger guard snag against the lining of the inside pocket. His heart was a bass drum pounding in his ears.

Adam flung the door open and saw a man's dark silhouette framed in the open window against a square of glaring sunlight.

The silhouette clutched a rifle in its hands. Tense and ready to fire.

As a cheer rose from ten thousand throats on the street below, Adam hurled himself at the silhouette in blind desperation..

SIXTY-SEVEN

Somewhere in the crush of the crowd, the hat with the veil had been swept from Ellie's head and trampled under the feet of a flailing sea of humanity. Not that she really cared. Right now, all her attention was focused on getting past the two large Anglo men blocking the view in front of her.

"Please let me by," she implored the man closest to her. "I have to get closer to the street. It's very important."

"Tough luck, Sis," the man said. "Everybody here wants closer to the street. What makes you so special?

"I've got to tell the President something."

"Oh, sure, so do I. Hey, Mister FDR, how about sending me some of that Social Security? If I join the CCC, can I have a job with the WPA? I want an answer PDQ, you hear?" The man nudged his companion and laughed.

"You could let me stand in front of you," Ellie persisted. "You're plenty tall enough to see over me."

"Look, we got here first, *Señorita*. Just beat it, okay?"

Ellie gave up and moved away, hugging her purse tightly against her to keep from losing it, too. She'd almost panicked when she saw uniformed police questioning people in the Magnolia Building lobby. They'd apparently assumed she was an employee and let her pass with the rest of the group from the elevator. But if she'd had to open the purse for any reason, the police would've seen Mrs. Roosevelt's little pistol for sure.

Along with the fear of dropping the purse or having it ripped from her hands, this had prompted her to duck into a phone booth long enough to take the weapon out of the purse and tuck it back into its makeshift holster under her skirt.

She picked her way east along Commerce Street, trying to separate herself from the masses of people packing the sidewalks in front of the Adolphus and Baker Hotels. After half a block, the crush eased slightly, but onlookers still stood three and four deep along the curb.

Just then, a ripple of cheering, whistling and applause rolled down the street toward her. By standing on tiptoe and craning her neck, she could make out a V-shaped formation of police motorcycles rapidly approaching with their red lights flashing.

Oh, no, he's here, she thought. *What am I going to do?*

She lowered her head and burrowed her way toward the street. Several people yelled at her as she pushed past, and one swore at her, but she ignored them all and plowed on until she managed to reach the curb.

Ellie saw the lead car in the caravan, now only a block away, but there were only police or G-men inside. Her eyes moved farther along the procession as she was shoved and jostled from behind. The President's car was the third one in line. She could make out the President's figure, still smiling and waving as he'd been two hours earlier.

Could it really have been only two hours since Roosevelt had left for the Exposition grounds? It seemed a lifetime ago. She wondered if he'd still be smiling when the bullets struck him?

She stepped off the curb as the limo drew abreast of her. One of the motorcycle cops swerved at her and motioned her back. She stumbled but managed to keep her feet. She waved her arms and screamed as loud as she could.

"Stop, Mr. President! For God's sake, stop! They're going to kill you!"

She screamed until she was lightheaded, but as she did, hundreds of other onlookers also shouted out a greeting, and Ellie's frantic, flailing hand motions were obscured by hundreds of other waving arms.

In the deafening blast of sound, it was as if she'd turned mute, and her cries were totally swallowed up in the roar of the crowd. Still shouting, she whirled and tried to run into the street after the limousine. A Secret Service agent in the trailing car pointed a machine rifle at her.

Dear Mother Mary, is he going to shoot me?

She stopped and steeled herself, but the Secret Service car moved on. Her eyes followed the President's head. She saw him turning. Nodding. Smiling. Then he disappeared in a blur of futile tears.

She waited for the shots.

SIXTY-EIGHT

Dietrich was in the very act of raising his right arm to give Reinhardt the signal when the woman ran into the street. At first, the SS Major had only a peripheral awareness of her. He was too totally focused on what was about to happen to think of anything else, and the woman seemed as insignificant as a snowflake in a blizzard. Then, as it dawned on him what she was doing, he stared at her, and his jaw dropped.

Varten. Vas ist?

He saw the woman's mouth moving, shouting something at Roosevelt. Above the crowd noise, Dietrich couldn't hear a single syllable of what she said, but as she ran toward him, he could actually read her lips.

"Stop! Stop! They're going to kill you!"

His brain recorded the words but didn't instantly process their meaning. It filed them for a second in a mental "in" basket while he finished the all-important task before him. He placed his left hand squarely on top of his head, then lowered his right hand smoothly to his side.

The signal to Reinhardt had been delivered, and the marksman was taking aim. The car was entering the kill zone. Ernst had done everything he could conceivably do. In a second or two, he thought, it would all be over. Now . . .

Now he could absorb the meaning of the woman's words.

Stop! Stop! They're going to kill you!

He turned, frowning. The woman was much closer to him than before. Dark-skinned, pretty and voluptuous – like Veronica, the call girl in Nuevo Laredo, and the gypsy woman of his youth. Her wide eyes bored directly into his, and . . .

Herr Gott, she recognized him!

Along with the words she'd shouted, her eyes were a dead give-away. They revealed her thoughts as clearly as if she'd held a sign saying, "I know who you are and I know what you're doing." Then, to emphasize the point, she jabbed her finger at Dietrich and screamed again.

"Killer! Assassin!"

Why didn't Reinhardt shoot?

SIXTY-NINE

Ed Starling burst out of the stairwell in time to see a man in a white suit leap through a doorway at the far end of the corridor and disappear.

"You! Halt!" Starling tried to yell the words, but the only sound that came out was a weak, breathless squeak that died as it left his lips. He was too spent to try it again.

Through the open door where the man had gone, Starling detected rapid, violent movement in the room beyond. He drew the .45 and lumbered down the hall, holding the pistol out in front of him with both hands as he ran.

Reinhardt was calm inside, but his body was already tensed and set to fire when he saw Dietrich's right hand go up. Seconds later, the target car moved into the circle of his telescopic sight. The small figure in its rear seat was sharp and clear.

The car was barely moving, coasting to a halt The back of Roosevelt's head was squarely in the center of the crosshairs. The sun was incandescent on the American President's white suit. There was no way to miss.

The exuberant noise of the crowd rose in Reinhardt's ears. His finger tightened on the trigger.

He detected a faint, indefinable sound behind him, but he blocked his mind to it, refusing to let anything break his concentration now. The moment of ultimate triumph was firmly within his grasp. He thought of what pretty Katrina would say when he got back home to Saxony. He could see the smile on her full lips, the sparkle in her blue eyes. He could almost hear her voice.

Wolf, my hero! I love you so!

An involuntary reflex caused the gun barrel to waver a fraction of a centimeter. For a micro-second, Reinhardt lost the target. But he found it again almost instantly. The car was nearly stopped. A solid wall of police was closing around it, holding the crowds at bay. Roosevelt half-turned in his seat, preparing to get up.

Now it was perfect.

SEVENTY

Oh, God, I'm too late! Too late! Too late!

The thought was an aching pulse in Adam's brain. He gave up on freeing the .45 from the inside pocket of his jacket and threw himself bodily at the sniper. In that frenzied instant, he wasn't sure if the Nazi had fired the rifle yet or not.

Adam hadn't heard a shot, but that didn't mean much. Even without the noise from the crowd below, the sound of his own blood pounding in his ears could easily have drowned out the crack of the assassin's weapon.

He launched himself like a human cannonball, hitting the sniper hard in the small of the back. His weight drove the man into the windowsill with crushing force. Adam locked his arms around the man, slapping and grabbing at the rifle.

"Drop it, damn you!"

They wrestled for the gun, clawing at each other, but the German never had a chance. It had been eighteen years since Adam's last hand-to-hand struggle against an armed enemy, but – inexplicably – he knew beyond doubt that he was going to win this fight. Moments before, he'd been ready to drop from fatigue. Yet now he was energized by the most consuming fury he could remember – fury fueled as much by the tragedies of Earl Garrett, Cisco Lemos, and Julio Hernandez as by the one about to engulf Franklin Roosevelt.

You can do it, Sergeant Wagner, a chorus of dead voices seemed to be assuring him. *Trust us – You can do it!*

Adam ripped the rifle out of the sniper's hands, flung it crashing against the wall, and pounded the man savagely with his fists. The German's nose dissolved in a shower of blood. He crashed face-first into the side of a file cabinet and slid slowly to a sitting position on the floor. Then he lay there dazed and not moving.

Adam ran past the sniper to the window and looked down. He saw two men helping Roosevelt out of the limo in front of the hotel. Lines of police formed twin barriers all the way from the car to the hotel entrance.

Adam felt himself go limp with relief. Roosevelt was safe. The plot had failed.

But as he turned back to the prostrate Nazi, he heard a sharp sound from the open doorway behind him and whirled to find himself staring into the most terrible face he'd ever seen. It was livid, angry and covered with sweat, its eyes burning with unspeakable anguish. Its mouth was wide open, gulping air in shuddering gasps. The whole body below the face seemed wracked with agonizing pain.

By far the most unnerving thing about the figure confronting Adam, however, was the massive six-shooter clutched in its outstretched hands. The hole in the pistol barrel was no more than two feet from Adam's face and aimed squarely between his eyes. It loomed as large as the mouth of a cave.

❊

"Secret Service!" Ed Starling wheezed. "Get your damn hands up! If either of you moves, you're dead! You're both under arrest."

His voice was hollow, like steel pipe being dragged over rough concrete, but that was okay with Ed. He was surprised to be able to talk at all.

"You don't understand," protested the young guy in the soiled white suit. "I've been trying to warn you people for two weeks." He pointed toward the other man, who slumped dazed on the floor, his face a mask of blood. "This son of a bitch is a Nazi assassin, and he's got at least one accomplice somewhere close by."

Starling's expression remained impassive. "If you've got a pistol under your coat, you'd better pull it out slow and drop it on the floor," he panted. "Right now."

A disgusted look crossed the young guy's face, but he removed a blue-steel .45 automatic from inside his soiled jacket and tossed it away. It skittered across the floor and hit the wall with a thud.

Ed lowered his own pistol slightly. He looked down at the second man, still sprawled semi-conscious beside the file cabinet, then to the open window and the rifle on the floor. One of these men had tried to shoot the President with that rifle, but the other one had stopped him. As the realization sank in, Starling's mind jumped back to the night before aboard FDR's train. He remembered the bloodstained floor outside the presidential quarters, the disarmed bomb – and the explanation offered by Agent Nat Grayson:

No question we've got multiple players involved here, and it's pretty clear they aren't all on the same team.

Starling studied the young man in the soiled suit. "Maybe you mean there's another accomplice besides yourself. Is that what you're trying to say?"

"Don't be stupid," the man said. "If I'd gotten here two seconds later, you'd have yourself a dead President right now. I'm Adam Wagner, a sheep farmer from South Texas, and I wouldn't be here if I had any choice. I called the Secret Service. I called the FBI. Hell, I might as well of been howling at the moon."

A bell rang dimly in Starling's head. There had been a phone call several weeks ago from somewhere in Texas. The caller had claimed the President was in danger, but he'd been disconnected before anybody could get his name.

"You wouldn't happen to have a Mexican girlfriend, would you?" Ed asked.

Wagner started to nod, but then a startled look flashed across his face. He leaped to the window and leaned out over the street.

"In all the confusion, I forgot she was down there," he muttered. "My God, I've got to find her. That other Nazi – "

Without the slightest hint of warning, the man on the floor picked this moment to make his move. He'd seemed too dazed and defeated to cause trouble, but he was obviously faking. Before Starling realized what was happening, the man was on his feet and almost to the door.

"Stop or I'll shoot!" Ed yelled.

But the German agent – if that's what he was – was incredibly fleet and nimble. By the time Ed could raise his revolver, the man was out the door and running down the corridor like a scalded cat.

Starling swore and bolted after him, mentally kicking himself for not staying on his toes. After a dozen yards, he realized that Adam Wagner was running beside him, but he had neither the strength nor the time to figure out why or what Wagner's stake was in all this.

Ed still had the .45 in his hand, but the last thing he wanted was to shoot the fleeing man. Right now, the Secret Service needed some answers, not another unidentified corpse. If there was any possible way to do it, he *had* to take this guy alive.

But an instant later, Ed realized how incredibly difficult this was going to be when the fugitive whipped a pistol from under his coat, threw back his arm and fired an off-balance shot over his shoulder. Ed ducked out of instinct, but the shot was wild.

"Oh, no," he heard Wagner grunt beside him. "Not again!"

SEVENTY-ONE

Ellie never would've noticed Dietrich if he hadn't raised his hand. In fact, all she could see of him at first was his arm thrust high in the air, rigid and motionless above his head, and it had seemed odd that he wasn't waving like everyone else.

Getting a clear view of him among the throngs jamming the intersection was utterly impossible, but as she ran after the President's car, a brief opening materialized in the crowd, and suddenly there he was, his hand still raised. He wore a dark-blue suit and wide-brimmed white hat, and he stood well back from the curb, not seeming to care if he actually saw Roosevelt or not, yet intent on the approach of the limousine.

Then, as he lowered his arm and placed his hand on top of his head, she recognized him immediately. She'd seen him that first day he arrived on the Radke Ranch and several times later through binoculars. He was the one Adam called the Oberhaupt – the chief Nazi.

And he was giving the signal to fire. The realization struck her like a whiplash.

She yelled and pointed at him, but no one seemed to notice – no one but him, that is. She saw him glaring back at her from fifty feet away, her look of recognition mirrored in his own eyes. Then he was gone.

She struggled forward and caught sight of the man again as he darted across Commerce Street and ran south on Akard. Instinctively, she started to follow, then hesitated. After chasing the other Nazi, she knew that going after this one alone was risky business. But Adam was still somewhere in the labyrinthine corridors of the Magnolia Building. If she waited for him, the Oberhaupt would get away. It was that simple.

She glanced around quickly, searching among the unfamiliar faces for one that looked friendly and trustworthy. Two teenage girls ran past her, giggling. A young father tried to reason with his squalling three-year-old son. A businessman avoided her eyes as he hurried by.

Then she noticed a frail, elderly black man standing alone on the rear fringes of the crowd. He leaned on a cane near the wall of the Magnolia Building, trying to stay out of other people's way. He was smiling slightly, as if he saw something in the scene that nobody else could see. He obviously was in no big hurry to get anyplace.

She leaned close to him. "Excuse me, sir, would you do me a big favor?"

His eyes were puzzled behind his gold-rimmed spectacles. "Yes'm, I sho' try."

"In a few minutes, you're going to see a tall white man come running along here. He's got big shoulders and yellow hair, and he's wearing a dirty white suit. He'll be looking for somebody and acting very upset."

The old man's smile broadened. "I bet he be lookin' fo' you, missy," he said.

"That's right. So just tell him I went that way, okay?" She pointed south down Akard Street, the direction the Nazi had gone.

The old man nodded, and she raced away.

Panic gripped her momentarily as she scanned the crowds on the far side of Commerce Street. The Oberhaupt was no longer in sight, but he couldn't have gone far. The light was already yellow when she stepped off the curb and ran across the street. A policeman blew his whistle at her, but she kept going.

SEVENTY-TWO

At the end of the sixth floor corridor, there was no place left for the would-be assassin to run. When the fugitive found himself cornered, he whirled toward his pursuers and raised the automatic, but this time Starling shot first. The roar of his revolver echoed like thunder in the hallway as the bullet ripped into the Nazi's gun hand and his weapon clattered to the floor. He grabbed with his other hand at the bleeding wound in his right palm.

"Hands in the air," Starling said hoarsely. "It's over."

Ed was almost as winded as before. The chase had seemed to last a mile, finally ending in an unpopulated stretch of hallway on the building's east side. Now, as the fugitive faced Starling and Adam Wagner, his back was literally to the wall – a wall with a lone exterior window. Beyond the window was a six-story drop to the concrete floor of an alley. Unless the man chose to run straight at both of them, Ed thought, this was the end of the line.

The chase had led away from the elevators, and they hadn't encountered a single bystander along the way. Most of the employees on the sixth floor had left for lunch by now. There was no indication that anyone had heard the shot fired by Starling, and the corridor was now eerily quiet. The fugitive clasped his hands above his head in a gesture of submission and sagged against the wall.

"I pray you never learn the truth, Katrina," Ed heard the man say softly in perfect English. "I pray you never find out how miserably I failed."

He turned then, very slowly and deliberately, with his hands still raised. For a second or two, he gazed almost wistfully out the window. Then, without warning, he hurled himself headlong at the glass.

Starling realized too late what was happening. He and Wagner both yelled at once, but by then there was nothing they could do.

The man slammed his two locked fists into the windowpane with incredible force. Blood sprayed in a crimson cloud from his hands and wrists as the glass exploded into a thousand fragments around him. Before Starling could take a half step toward him, the Nazi plunged head-first through the jagged opening. As far as Ed could tell, the man made no sound of any kind from the moment he leaped from the window until his body landed sixty feet below. Starling re-holstered his pistol, moved unsteadily to the window ledge, and stared down at what was left of the fugitive smeared on the concrete floor of the narrow alley.

"My God," he said softly, shaking his head.

Along with a heavy sense of defeat, Ed felt anger – mostly at himself. If he'd been more careful and alert, they'd have a live suspect in custody right now. Instead, all they had was another mess to clean up – and a growing string of questions that might never be answered. But he was angry at the dead German, too.

"Damn you," he groaned. "It's not fair."

A moment later, his feelings of failure and frustration only deepened. When he turned around, the corridor behind him was empty. Adam Wagner had disappeared.

SEVENTY-THREE

Above the sound of her own rushing footsteps, Ellie heard two drunks taunting her from the front steps of a dingy rooming house.

"Hey, what's your hurry, *chiquita?*"

"Come on back, baby. I'll trade you some wine for a little sugar."

She ran on without looking at them, her eyes sweeping the sidewalks in front of her for the Oberhaupt. She'd caught sight of him several times as she chased him south on Akard Street. But no matter how hard she pushed herself, he always seemed to stay a half-block ahead of her. Then she totally lost track of him again.

Not nearly as many people were around now, and Ellie had a clear view of the street for more than a block, but the Oberhaupt had vanished, and she wasn't sure she even cared anymore. She could barely stand the thought of venturing any deeper into this no man's land.

A short distance south of Commerce Street, the surroundings had changed abruptly for the worse. One minute she was passing the stately facade of the Dallas Federal Reserve Bank. The next minute she was in a seedy area of rundown two-story houses, beer joints, walk-up hotels and greasy-spoon cafes. The farther she went, the more unsavory the neighborhood became. Prostitutes openly hawked their wares on the street corners. Derelicts slept in littered doorways. Mangy dogs prowled the garbage-strewn alleys, watching her with hostile yellow eyes.

Many of the people she encountered along the street worried her almost as much as the Oberhaupt himself. She wanted to turn around and get out of this hellish place. She wanted to find Adam and make sure he was all right. She wanted to go back to the Jefferson Hotel with him and forget everything else. She wished that the little pistol were in her purse and not under her skirt, but there was no way to transfer it without showing her underpants to anyone within a block. In this area, if a man saw her make such a move, he'd probably interpret it as advertising.

Ellie ran on, stepping around broken beer bottles and old newspapers in her path. She ignored the obscene gesture of a Mexican boy of about twelve. She tried not to react to a big-breasted whore with orange hair, who scowled at her from a second–floor window and shrilled:

"Get outta here, pepperbelly. This here's my territory."

One more block, a voice in her head whispered. *I'll go one more block, and if I still don't see him, I'll give up.*

She was only about twenty steps from the next corner when another alley opened off to her right between two flophouses. Despite her fear of what might be lurking in it, she jerked her head around to look as she passed. She saw nothing but the usual jumble of trash and overturned garbage cans. She heard no sound at all.

But then she *felt* something – a presence behind her. The back of her neck tingled in warning. She gasped and tried to run faster, but it was too late.

A hand clamped itself firmly over her mouth. In the same precise instant, she felt the cold barrel of a gun pressed hard against her skull, just behind her right ear.

"I'd much rather have you alive than dead, but the choice is yours." The voice in her ear was harsh but surprisingly calm and even. "Make so much as one small sound, and I promise I'll blow your head off."

Ellie could see the pistol distinctly now in the corner of her eye. The hand that held it was steady and sure. So was the hand that covered her mouth. It had a grip like steel. Hard. Relentless. Unfeeling.

It convinced her not to struggle or try to scream as the Oberhaupt dragged her back into the shadows of the alley.

SEVENTY-FOUR

As he bolted out the Commerce Street entrance of the Magnolia Building, Adam had a childishly simple plan of action. It was the focal point of his entire existence, and it consisted of three parts: (1) Find Ellie, (2) locate the parked Ford coupe, and (3) get the hell out of Dallas as fast as they could go.

That was all he wanted now – all he could think about. He didn't give a hoot in hell about anything else. Not the Nazi who'd jumped out the window or the one still on the loose somewhere. Not dead Otto in the boxcar or dead Rudi floating down the Trinity. Not Colonel Starling or the Secret Service or the stupid cops. Not Roosevelt or Hitler or J. Edgar Hoover or the man in the moon.

If he and Ellie ever got back to Réal County, he'd deal with Kurt Radke in his own way, but at the moment, even that didn't matter. He didn't care if they went home or not. He didn't care where they went as long as it was away from here and Ellie was with him.

He glanced quickly in all directions as he reached the intersection. Everyone in Roosevelt's entourage was inside one hotel or the other by now, and except for the line of cars in front of the Adolphus, traffic was pretty much back to normal. A lot of people were still milling around, but Ellie wasn't one of them.

He wondered if she'd gone back inside the building looking for him and decided it was a definite possibility. A good six or seven minutes had passed since he'd wrested the rifle away from the assassin. Once Ellie had known Roosevelt was safe, there was no reason for her to stay on the street. She would've been anxious to find out what was going on in the building, eager to help if she could.

For a second, he considered retracing his steps, but he knew that wasn't a good idea. He might run into Starling again, and that could wreck his plan of action once and for all. Still, what if Ellie *was* poking around somewhere inside? It was an unsettling thought, but he couldn't imagine where else she could be.

"'Scuse me, Cap'n," said a sudden low voice at Adam's elbow.

He tensed at the sound, then looked down and saw a wizened old black man standing there.

"If you done lost a young lady, Cap'n," the old man said, "I knows where you might find her."

"You do?" Adam said. "Where?"

"She say tell you she went thataway." He pointed a bony forefinger down Akard Street to the south.

❋

Four or five minutes later, Adam found himself walking through the middle of the city's most notorious red-light district. Block after block of once-palatial homes had fallen into disrepute and disrepair. Homeowners had moved away, and a transient subculture had taken over, gradually transforming the area into a wasteland of tenements, flophouses and bordellos.

Eyes peered furtively at him through filmy stained-glass windows and from behind dingy Greek-revival columns with peeling paint. Ragged children played among rusty car parts in weedy front yards. Winos, beggars, chippies, and thieves lounged on sagging porches once reserved for gentlefolk.

"Looking for a good time, big boy?"

"Hey, buddy, can you shpare a dime?"

"Just a dollah, sugah. Thass all it takes."

With each step, Adam's uneasiness grew. There had to be some mistake. What could Ellie be doing in a place like this?

Then he looked up the street, and his mouth fell open in shock.

As impossible as it seemed, Ellie was driving toward him in a shiny, black Buick sedan. He saw her through the windshield as plain as day. She was gripping the steering wheel with both hands and staring straight ahead. A man in a dark business suit was sitting beside her.

At first, Adam thought he was hallucinating. His exhaustion and his fierce yearning to find Ellie were making him see things that weren't there. Then, just as the Buick drew even with him, she tapped the horn, and he knew it was really her.

"Ellie!" he yelled. "What the hell are you doing?"

She waved frantically at him as the car passed. For a second, her face in the Buick's open window was no more than ten feet from him, and he could see every detail of her anguished expression. Her eyes were wide with fear, and her mouth was suppressing a scream.

The man beside her shouted something, grabbed angrily at her waving hand, and brandished a pistol in Ellie's face. The instant Adam saw the gun, he realized who the man was. It was the Oberhaupt himself. The rest was obvious.

"Damn you!" Adam howled. "You hurt her and you're a dead man!"

The Buick was already past him before he found the presence of mind to reach in his jacket for the .45 he'd been carrying. Then he remembered it wasn't there anymore. Starling had made him throw it down. He was unarmed, alone, powerless, and utterly out of luck. He was on foot, too. The Ford coupe was seven or eight blocks away, at least.

He ran on blindly, hoping Ellie could still hear him. "Stop! Hit the brakes!"

But the Buick never slowed down. In seconds, it was a full block away. Then two blocks. Then several other vehicles pulled into the street and Adam lost sight of the Buick completely.

He slogged north on Akard Street, half blinded by tears and feeling all hope draining out of him. The Buick would have at least a twenty-minute head start by the time he reached the Ford. Even then, he could only guess at the Oberhaupt's intended destination.

Hollow despair filled Adam's chest. He'd never see Ellie alive again. He knew it with terrible certainty. His guts felt dead inside him. Something made him keep going, but he knew it wasn't reason or logic. What good did it do to run when you didn't know which way to go? What was the sense in fighting when the war was already lost?

By the time he dragged himself into the coupe and wiped his sweating face on his coat sleeve, he knew the answer to his own bleak questions.

Kurt Radke was the answer. Kurt had created this monster in the first place. He'd crafted and nurtured it, bought and paid for it. He'd pulled the strings and made the arrangements. It was all Kurt's doing.

If the Nazi bastard killed Ellie and escaped, that would be Kurt's doing, too. The difference was, when the Oberhaupt was safely back in Berlin and beyond Adam's reach, Kurt would still be around. There was no place he could go that Adam couldn't hunt him down.

It was 12:26 p.m. by Adam's watch. In the time it took Franklin Roosevelt to eat his lunch, Adam Wagner's world had come to an end. The Buick could be almost to Lancaster by now. Or halfway to Fort Worth. It could be heading for Shreveport or Oklahoma or . . .

He started the engine and drove west as fast as he dared toward the viaduct to Oak Cliff. There were many roads out of Dallas, and the Buick might be on any one of them. But there was only one route for Adam to take: South toward San Antonio, Uvalde, and the Radke Ranch.

Whatever else happened, he'd have his moment of reckoning, by God.

And it wouldn't be over until he killed Kurt Radke.

SEVENTY-FIVE

Benbrook, Texas
June 12, 1936

"I want your frank, unvarnished assessment of the situation, gentlemen," the President said as Nat Grayson watched him fit a cigarette into his holder. "Don't spare me any of the gruesome details, either. Tell me in all candor where we stand."

FDR sat facing Nat, Ed Starling, Steve Early and Gus Gennerich. The President's military aide, Colonel E. M. Watson, nervously paced the length of the small room. Nat was nervous, too. The enormity of the situation was staggering.

"As far as the direct threat to your life, I think the worst is over," Starling said. "But to be blunt, you came awfully damn close to buying the farm today, sir, and we're not out of the woods yet." Starling coughed and lit a cigarette of his own. Nat's boss looked to have aged ten years in the past two days.

"That's especially true for the political ramifications," Early said. "If this *is* a German plot, it could touch off the biggest international crisis in modern history."

"That's why our discussion can never leave this room," FDR said. "We'll have to involve other Secret Service and military personnel in the investigation, of course, but whatever we say here has to remain absolutely confidential. Once we've examined all the possibilities, then we'll decide what to do."

The strain of the day was clearly etched on Roosevelt's features. Being constantly "on stage" for hours in front of tens of thousands of citizens was wearing enough in itself. In addition, the Chief fully realized what a close call he'd had. With his "game face" off, he looked drawn and shaken.

The presidential party had reached the large, secluded house owned by FDR's son, Elliott, shortly before 4 p.m. In its suburban setting fifteen miles northwest of Fort Worth, the house seemed a world away from the noisy crowds, and there were no more public appearances until the day after tomorrow in Indiana. Normally, this kind of quiet family atmosphere quickly restored the President's vitality and sense of humor. On an ordinary day, he'd be ready to mix a big pitcher of cocktails, relax and make small talk with the staff.

This, however, had been the least ordinary day of his presidency.

"I think we're dealing with a well-organized plot by a crack team of Nazi espionage agents," Starling said. "I don't know how many there are, but I think they're all trained professional assassins – and I think they're working under direct orders from Berlin."

"But why?" Colonel Watson demanded. "Our relations with Germany are normal in every respect. The Neutrality Act prohibits us from aiding those who oppose Hitler's ambitions. Wrongheaded as it is, isolationism is our prevailing national sentiment, so why should the Nazis take such a massive risk?"

"Don't be naive, Wat," FDR said. "High-risk adventurism is Hitler's whole strategy. He gave us a clear demonstration of that three months ago in the Rhineland, and we can expect more of the same in months to come." He smiled bitterly. "Besides, maybe the Nazis have figured out how I feel about them. I know we've got to stop them sooner or later, regardless of the cost."

"The three bodies we recovered are almost surely foreign nationals," Nat interjected. "The latest guy, the sniper in the building in Dallas, had papers identifying him as William Runnels of Reading, Pennsylvania. We checked with the Reading PD, and there's apparently no such person."

Starling nodded. "We've got phony IDs, stolen Army uniforms, a German-made rifle, a sophisticated explosive device. This is no bunch of hayseeds we're dealing with. It all points to a precision military operation."

"What happened to the body of the sniper?" Roosevelt asked.

"We commandeered a city-owned ambulance and took it to Love Field," Starling said. "It was taken by Army plane to Fort Sam Houston in San Antonio, since that's where the other remains are. It should be there by now."

"Who else knows that besides us?" Gennerich asked.

"A Dallas police captain and a patrolman helped us get the ambulance and load the body," Starling said. "Luckily, the sniper landed in an alley, and there were no witnesses around. The two cops are the only ones who saw the sniper, and they don't know what he was doing or where he was taken. I told them it was a federal matter and they should forget the whole thing."

"Do the police in Dallas or Pennsylvania have any inkling that the dead sniper may be a German national?" Early asked.

"No, there was no mention of any foreign connection," Starling said. "They know absolutely nothing about the man."

"If there's any doubt about what they know – or may have guessed – better have someone talk to them again," FDR said. "We can't allow the slightest hint of Nazi involvement to reach the press or the general public. This is a national security matter of the most urgent kind, gentlemen."

"What're the odds that other assassins from this same group are still running around loose out there?" Gennerich asked.

"Pretty high," Nat said. "I can't believe we got them all, but the ones that are left may not be in any shape to try – "

"Let's get one thing straight," Starling interrupted. "The Secret Service can't take any credit for stopping these people. Except for the man on top of the train, they were all kept from succeeding by somebody else." He turned to Roosevelt. "Truth is, if it'd been left up to me and my detail, you'd most likely be dead right now, sir."

The President raised an eyebrow. "You're much too hard on yourself, Ed, but I'm not sure I follow you. Just who is this 'somebody else' you mentioned?"

"His name's Adam Wagner, and he says he's a farmer from South Texas. He and a young Mexican woman were involved in this from the beginning – on our side, fortunately. It was Wagner who stopped the sniper from firing. He'd already subdued the suspect and separated him from his rifle when I got there."

"We also think it was Wagner and the woman who found and disarmed the bomb on the train," Nat added.

FDR frowned. "Then I owe these people a huge debt of gratitude, and I'd like to thank them personally. Where are they now?"

Starling stared at the floor and shook his head. "That's the problem, sir. We don't have the faintest idea."

SEVENTY-SIX

U.S. Highway 90
Near Castroville, Texas
June 12, 1936

Dietrich didn't begin to breathe easily until he was past San Antonio and on the first long expanse of open highway west of the city. After that, he grew more confident with each passing mile. By now, he'd been on the road almost six hours, and it was increasingly obvious that the American authorities weren't in hot pursuit. It was doubtful if they even had a description of him or the car.

The mission had failed, but he was going to get away. That was the important thing. Against all odds, he was going to escape and live to fight another day. He was convinced of that now.

Before turning west on Route 90 toward Uvalde, he'd considered staying on Route 81 all the way to the Mexican border, which conformed with the overall plan for the mission. Once he reached one of the safe houses in Laredo, he would've been driven to a remote spot on the Rio Grande and spirited back into Mexico.

But he'd ruled out this course of action for two reasons. For one, he feared the possibility of roadblocks north of Laredo. The news broadcasts on the car radio made no mention of an assassination attempt at Dallas, but that wasn't surprising. Dietrich smelled a Yankee trick. The fact that Reinhardt had never fired his rifle proved something had gone awry. If the Americans had surprised him at the crucial moment, he could've been taken alive. Under torture, Reinhardt might talk. The safe houses in Laredo might not be so safe anymore.

The other factor, of course, was the woman. The woman with the rich olive skin and the eyes of a startled doe. The woman whose seductive lips and ripe breasts bore a haunting resemblance to those of the gypsy wench who'd scarred him so long ago.

At the moment, she was locked in the trunk of the Buick awaiting Dietrich's pleasure, but his Mexican contacts wouldn't like it if he brought her to Laredo. They'd consider her presence a threat to their security. They might even view Dietrich himself as a threat.

The only alternative was to take her back to the Radke Ranch. Dietrich and the others had stayed there for weeks in perfect safety in the isolated little stone house. He'd be safe there again for a day or two. Perhaps a little longer. Just until he finished with the woman. Then he'd go.

The woman had been his instrument of deliverance from Dallas. She was like a gift dropped into his lap by the gods of war. And because of her, he could still salvage something from this long, ill-fated journey. After she satisfied his lust, she'd also provide him with a priceless memento of his escape – a trophy to treasure forever. He didn't know yet what it would be, only that it would be very special. He'd be remembering the gypsy bitch when he took it from her.

❋

Except for a brief gasoline stop, Dietrich had been driving most of the afternoon without pause. Now it was after 6 p.m., and he was growing increasingly uncomfortable. The heat of the day was beginning to ebb slightly as the sun dipped lower, but the highway ran due west, and the setting sun was a painful, blinding glare in Dietrich's eyes. It was time to stop for some rest and relaxation – and perhaps even a few minutes of diversion with the woman.

Some twenty miles south of Dallas, he'd ordered the woman to turn off Highway 77 onto a lonely byway and stop the car. She'd been so sure he was going to kill her that she actually seemed relieved when he only taped her mouth shut, tied her hands and feet, and dumped her into the trunk. Once she was bound and gagged, he considered taking her once right there, but he decided he was still too close to Dallas to risk it.

A few miles past the town of Castroville, he started looking for a place to stop and wait for the sun to slip below the western horizon. He was about to pull onto the shoulder of the highway when he spotted a gravel road leading off to the left. On an impulse, he turned down it.

He drove slowly for a quarter-mile and didn't see a house, another car, or any sign of human presence, so he stopped and switched off the engine. He stretched out across the seat and closed his eyes, wishing he had some beer. A pint or two of beer – even the watered-down American kind – would taste *wunderbar* right now.

Then he thought again of the woman. If he told her he was merely letting her out of the trunk for some air and a drink of water, she'd be too grateful to scream when he took the tape from her mouth. And after he got her into the back seat it wouldn't matter if she screamed or not. There was no one to hear her, anyway, and she'd still be bound and helpless. He'd put the gun to her head and warn her not to resist. Then . . .

Dietrich opened his eyes and sat up as he heard a vehicle approaching. He turned to see a battered pickup jerk to a halt beside him.

In the cloud of dust kicked up by the truck's wheels, he could see two figures in the cab, their grizzled features and worn Stetsons outlined against the fading sun. The nearest one stuck his head out the window and grinned.

"You okay, mister? We seen you layin' there with your head on th' seat and we thought maybe you was sick or somethin'."

Dietrich's fingertips touched the .45 automatic under his coat. "Thanks, but I'm fine. I just pulled off the highway to rest my eyes for a minute."

"That sun's pure hell if you're headin' west this time of day," the cowboy said.

"You're telling me," Ernst said. "I'm headed for Uvalde, but I figured I could make better time after sunset."

"Well, be careful, podnuh." The cowboy waved, and the truck's engine roared. Then it bounced on down the road, leaving the Buick in a pall of dust.

Ernst didn't move until the pickup was out of sight. He couldn't get his mind off the woman in the trunk, but he knew he couldn't do anything now, not even here in the middle of nowhere. He was only glad she hadn't started kicking at the trunk lid while the two cowboys were there – damn them.

No matter. His time would come later. He envisioned his captive spread-eagled on a bunk in the remote little house at the Radke Ranch. He could almost feel her warm flesh and hear her low cries.

The gypsy slut would pay dearly for the trouble and pain she'd caused him – and this time there'd be no one to interfere.

SEVENTY-SEVEN

Georgetown, Texas
June 12, 1936

The radiator was boiling like mad when Adam pulled the Ford coupe into the big Sinclair station in the center of town. The mechanic shook his head. "Could be a thermostat," he said. "Could be a fanbelt. Could be a hose. Could be she's clogged up with rust. I'll get her cooled down and we'll have a look."

He sprayed the radiator until the spewing and gurgling from its innards gradually subsided. Then he filled it with fresh water and crawled underneath. After a maddening wait, he emerged from beneath the front end of the car and wiped his hands on a greasy rag.

"Shoot, I thought at first it was just a leaky hose," the mechanic said cheerfully, "but you got yourself a little hole spang in the bottom of the radiator."

"Oh, great," Adam said. "How long will it take to fix it?"

The mechanic glanced up at the clock on the wall. "I doubt I can get her out today. I'll have to drain the radiator, then pull it off and solder it and put it back on. That's gonna take a good hour, maybe two, and it's after five o'clock now."

Adam kicked at one of the front tires as he weighed his options. As he'd driven south from Dallas, pushing the coupe as fast as dared between towns, his gloomy mood had lightened a little. Maybe the situation wasn't totally hopeless, after all. With some luck, he still might have a chance to catch the Oberhaupt and get Ellie back alive.

While the head Nazi could be going in any direction, logic almost dictated that he was bound for one of two destinations. Either he was making a beeline for the Mexican border, where he'd come from in the first place, or he was heading back to the Radke Ranch to hide out. Nothing else made any sense.

Before the overheating problem started just south of Salado, Adam had been wracking his brain for a way to cover both eventualities. But once the little Ford started steaming, he hadn't been able to think of anything else. He'd already lost a lot of time searching for water and sitting beside the highway waiting for the car to cool down.

Now what was he going to do? Driving on with a bad radiator – even with a gallon can or two of water – meant stopping every few miles to give the coupe a drink. Covering the two hundred-plus miles he still had to go would take forever that way. But even if he could sweet talk the mechanic into staying late to fix the radiator, he couldn't afford to sit here twiddling his thumbs for another two hours, unless . . .

"You got a phone I can use?" he asked.

"There's a pay phone out by the front counter," the mechanic said.

"Look, I'll make you a deal. I'll pay you an extra five bucks over whatever the charges are if you'll hang around and fix this thing. And I'll give you five bucks more if you get it done in an hour and a half or less. What do you say?"

The mechanic grinned. "Are you kiddin'? I'd work all night for ten bucks. Just pull her up in that second bay over there, and I'll get started."

"There's one other thing," Adam said.

"What's that?"

"I need five dollars in change for the pay phone."

"Man alive! Where you figuring to call? Mars?"

Adam thought uneasily about his past experiences with long-distance calling. "It may be even harder than that," he said, "but I've gotta give it a try."

SEVENTY-EIGHT

Leakey, Texas
June 12, 1936

If this had been a typical Friday night, Sheriff Streicher wouldn't have seen the dark Buick cruise slowly north along Main Street shortly before 8 p.m. He wouldn't have been in a position to notice the rear license plate as the Buick passed Streicher's parked patrol car in front of the courthouse – much less follow it to the edge of town to make sure he'd read the license number correctly.

At first, he hoped he was wrong about the Buick. It wasn't nearly as clean and shiny as he remembered, and there was only one person visible inside, so maybe it was actually a different car. But after following it at a discreet distance well beyond the north edge of town, he knew for sure that its license number was the same one he'd memorized two days ago.

NE-7691.

As Streicher made a U-turn back toward the square, there was also no doubt that the Buick was headed for the Radke Ranch. At least one of the "wool buyers" hadn't gone back to Pennsylvania, after all.

By the time Streicher's car screeched to a halt at the courthouse steps, a furious tension was building inside him. His fingers shook as he unlocked his office door, and his palms were damp with sweat as he picked up the phone and dialed.

He was damn sick and tired of being lied to. Whatever the consequences, it was time for a showdown with Kurt Radke.

On most Fridays, the Sheriff turned things over to Luke Bodine a little after five and went home to an early supper, usually pan-broiled beefsteak and fried potatoes. Afterward, he liked to pour himself a bourbon-and-branch, settle down on the living room sofa and see what he could pick up through the inevitable static on the radio. Sometimes he was there early enough to tune in *The Fred Waring Show*, and he almost never missed *The March of Time* or *Amos 'n' Andy*.

But Streicher's usual routine had been altered abruptly this afternoon. Charlie Shuster had seen to that. Next to Kurt Radke, Charlie was probably the biggest rancher in the county and not somebody the Sheriff could afford to take lightly. So when Charlie walked into the office about three o'clock carrying a well-worn .30-30, he'd gotten Streicher's immediate attention.

"I hear you've been lookin' for Adam Wagner," Shuster said. "That's why I figured you might be interested in this." He slid the weapon gently across the Sheriff's desk.

The rifle was an old lever-action Winchester, the kind of saddle gun any of a hundred men in Réal County might own. The difference was, this one had the initials "A.W." carved into the stock.

There was a thin film of rust on the blued-steel barrel, as if the gun had been left out in the rain recently. Like maybe in the thunderstorm night before last. Streicher pulled back the lever and looked into the chamber. It was fully loaded.

"That's Adam's carbine." Charlie's wind-burned face was grim as he spoke. "I'd know it anywhere. I also know he'd as soon throw his mother in a nest of rattlesnakes as go off and leave this gun where one of my fence-riders found it this morning."

"Where *did* he find it?" Streicher asked.

"Come on out to my ranch, and I'll show you," Shuster said.

"Can't you just tell me, Charlie?"

"I could, but you really need to see this."

There were definite remains of a recent campsite on the old wagon trace that curved up the side of the mountain. That much was obvious, although there was no evidence of a campfire. The odd thing was that the campers had left so much of their gear behind. In addition to the .30-30, there was a perfectly good olive-green tarp still on the ground. Nearby was a half-full canteen of water and a pair of binoculars.

"I don't get it," Streicher said.

Shuster walked to the edge of the narrow trail and pointed down. "Take a look here with those binoculars and tell me what you see."

Streicher squinted through the glasses for a moment, then lowered them and looked at Charlie. "That's the main gate to the Radke Ranch."

"That's right," Shuster said. "Adam's one of the few people outside my own family that knows how well you can see it from up here. Looks like he was watching for somethin' to come through that gate, but I'm damned if I know what. Also looks like he left in one helluva hurry, but I'm damned if I know why."

SEVENTY-NINE

It was after six o'clock when the Sheriff got back to town from the Shuster Ranch, and his mind had been strangely troubled ever since. For a long time, he'd sat at his desk, wondering what to do. Then he'd gone out to the car, but instead of driving home, he'd sat there to think some more. Gradually, he lost his appetite. Eventually, he forgot all about his supper.

He remembered Kurt's fury over Streicher's failure to find and arrest Adam. He remembered Adam's crazy phone call and his wild claims that the men on the Radke Ranch were Nazi assassins. He remembered the visit from the smart-aleck G-man and the murdered Mexican kid found in a Wagner stock pond about the same time the first two "wool buyers" showed up.

Then there was Adam's own mysterious disappearance. If he was really in Dallas like his daddy said, why had he left his rifle and other belongings behind at the spot where he'd apparently been spying on Radke's main gate? Was he really living it up at the Centennial, or were the coyotés making a meal of him somewhere right now?

The most disturbing questions of all revolved around the car that had driven out that same gate two days ago with three of Kurt's wool buyers inside – the dark, shiny Buick with the license number NE-7691.

Streicher remembered how upset Kurt had been when the Sheriff confronted him about the three men. He remembered Kurt's veiled threats and pointed suggestions to forget about them. Streicher had tried to convince himself he'd never see the men or the car again, but deep down he'd never really believed it.

Now he knew why.

At the other end of the line, he heard Kurt's voice. It sounded strained and brittle. "Hello. Who is this?"

"It's Streicher," he said. "Looks like one of your wool buyers decided not to go back to Pennsylvania. I just saw him drive through town heading for your ranch."

"That's impossible. What the hell are you talking about?"

"You heard me, Kurt," Streicher said. "He ought to be there in about twenty minutes, and I'm wondering what business he's got with you this time. I think I'd better come out there and have a talk with both of you."

"No!" Kurt shouted, then added in a milder tone: "There's no need for that, Sheriff. I don't really understand why you're so concerned, but I know there's a perfectly logical explanation for why he came back. Drive out tomorrow if it's still bothering you, and we can all discuss it calmly."

The Sheriff bit his lip. "Oh, sure. Maybe in the meantime I'll call up the FBI and have 'em send a few G-men out there with me. I've got a feeling they'd be damned interested in talking to you and your wool buyer."

Radke was silent for a moment. When he spoke again, there was almost a pleading tone in his voice. "Come on, Sarge, be sensible. You don't want to do that. You'll only end up embarrassing yourself. In the morning the three of us can sit down and have some coffee and talk the whole thing out. I'll explain everything to you. I promise!"

Against his better judgment, the Sheriff felt himself wavering. Kurt made it all sound so innocent, so reasonable. Radke's nervousness was obvious, even over the phone, and something peculiar was definitely going on, but still . . .

"If I hold off till morning, I want your word that you won't let this man out of your sight – much less off your ranch – till I get there," Streicher said. "Otherwise, I'm hanging up right now and heading for my car."

"You've got it, Sarge. You've got my solemn word of honor. I swear on a stack of Bibles!"

The Sheriff took a deep breath and exhaled slowly before he replied. "Okay, Kurt," he said finally. "But I'm making you a promise, too. I'll be knocking at your front door no later than eight o'clock tomorrow – and before I leave your ranch, I'm gonna get to the bottom of this. You can bet your life on it."

And this time, Streicher thought as he hung up the phone, *I'm not listening to any more fairy tales or bullshit. This time I'm gonna know the truth – or else!*

Three minutes after the Sheriff broke the connection with Kurt, Slater Tillman and Paco Ortiz were standing in front of Radke's desk. They'd been eating in the mess hall when Kurt called on the intercom and told them to report to his office on the double. It seemed to take them forever to get there.

Kurt could never remember being this unstrung, this close to losing control. He knew the mission was a washout. The news would've been all over the radio by now if it had succeeded – or even come anywhere near succeeding. All his planning and sacrifice had been for nothing. Roosevelt was alive and well – damn his soul!

And now one of the fools who'd botched the mission dared to come back here? Today of all days? After ignoring Kurt and leaving him totally in the dark, how could any of them have the nerve to drive blithely back into Réal County as if nothing had happened? For all Kurt knew, the whole U.S. Army could be chasing the Buick by now. What the hell could its driver be thinking to run the risk of leading them here?

Whoever he was, the driver would be better off if the Army *did* catch him before he got here. Otherwise, he'd find a very unpleasant surprise waiting for him – especially if he happened to be Kurt's loose-tongued former friend, Major Ernst Dietrich.

"We got trouble of some kind, Bossman?" asked Paco Ortiz.

Paco was a cold-blooded half-breed who admitted to killing half a dozen men in his life and might well have killed twice that number. He relished violence the way some men relish sex or whiskey. He was a crack shot with either pistol or rifle and equally adept with knives, clubs, or fists. These qualities had won him a foreman's job on the ranch during Gus Radke's heyday, and nobody had ever been man enough to take the job away from him in the thirteen years since.

Paco wasn't smart or energetic. He wasn't responsible or resourceful, and he wasn't worth a damn with animals. But he hadn't been hired to herd goats or shear sheep or mend fence. Paco was the most efficient troubleshooter Kurt had ever known. Slater Tillman wasn't as good with a gun or knife, but he was a match for Ortiz in sheer ruthlessness and disregard for human life. Together, they were capable of handling any dirty job Kurt threw their way. That was why he'd sent for them.

"Yeah, big trouble," Kurt said, "and we've got to move fast to take care of it. There'll be a dark blue Buick pulling up to the main gate in a few minutes. The word is, there's only one person inside. Round up a couple of other men you can trust and get down there in a hurry. Pull that car over and disarm whoever's inside. Then bring them straight to me, understand?"

"What about the car?" Paco asked. "What you want us to do with it?"

"Put it in one of the garages," Kurt said. "Get it out of sight as quick as you can."

"This hombre in the Buick," Tillman said. "Is it somebody we're supposed to know, Mister Kurt?"

"It's one of the men who stayed here on the ranch for the past few weeks," Kurt said. "I just found out he's a liar and a cheat. He's trying to wreck my business and ruin my reputation. He's out to stab me in the back."

Paco wiped his mouth on his shirtsleeve and grinned. "Mebbe I should stab him a few times instead, huh?"

"Not just yet," Kurt said. "I want to talk to him first. But once I find out how much trouble he's already caused, I won't care what you do. As far as I'm concerned, you can deal with him like you'd deal with any other poacher."

"Maybe we'll have ourselves a little deer hunt," Tillman said.

Paco laughed low in his throat. "Yeah, we ain't had a deer hunt with a poacher in a long time."

"Go get him first," Kurt told them. "Then we'll see."

EIGHTY

Fort Worth, Texas
June 12, 1936

It was barely dusk outside, but Ed Starling was already half asleep when the phone rang in his room at the Texas Hotel. He'd checked in just over an hour ago, and after a lukewarm shower, a room service dinner and a glass of dry sherry, he felt more relaxed than he had in days. But he was bone-tired. The greatest restorative of all would be ten hours of deep, uninterrupted sleep.

While he waited for the room service waiter, he'd put in a call to Flora. It was his first opportunity to talk to her in three days, and although he couldn't tell her anything about what had happened in the last seventy-two hours, it was good just hearing her voice. It soothed him in a way, but it filled him with pangs of loneliness, too.

"God willing, I'll be back in D.C. by Monday night," he said. "I can hardly wait to see you."

"I miss you so," she said. "It seems like you've been gone forever."

"I know, sweetheart, but after this trip, I'll be home every night for almost two weeks – until we have to leave for the national convention."

"I'm worried about you," she said. "You sound so hoarse – and tired."

"I'll be okay. If I made it through today, I can make it through anything." But even as he'd reassured Flora, Ed wondered if he ought to make an appointment with the doctor before the convention trip. There was a dull, persistent burning in his chest, and he could hear a faint wheeze when he breathed. Maybe the doctor could give him some pills or something.

When the bedside phone rang, he stared at it with distaste. He wasn't expecting any other calls. He'd left Nat Grayson in charge of a three-man contingent at Elliott Roosevelt's home, along with explicit instructions not to disturb him unless something really urgent came up.

He grunted into the receiver and heard Nat's voice.

"I hate to bother you, Colonel, but there's something you need to know about."

"Oh, God," Ed said, "what is it?"

"Fort Worth PD got a strange phone call a few minutes ago. The lieutenant who relayed the message said it was an emergency person-to-person call from a pay phone in Georgetown, Texas. The caller identified himself as Adam Wagner."

Starling's grip tightened on the receiver. "Did he leave a call-back number?"

"Yeah, Operator Four in Austin. The calling number's three-one-seven Georgetown."

Ed was already dialing "O" as he pushed himself into a sitting position against the headboard of the bed. He wasn't the least bit sleepy anymore.

EIGHTY-ONE

Réal County, Texas
June 12, 1936

Ellie hovered in an airless, pitch-black void somewhere on the edge of unconsciousness. She'd lost all concept of time, location, or her own relationship to anything. For the first half-hour or so after being cast into her small prison, she was afraid of suffocating from lack of oxygen, and later she fully expected to die from the stifling heat inside the trunk of the Nazi's car. Apparently, though, she was still alive. Sometimes it was hard to be certain, but she doubted that she'd feel such pain in her head or discomfort in her limbs if she were already dead.

At some point, the car had left the smooth highway on which it had traveled for countless hours. Then it had bounced and lurched for another eternity over a jarring surface of bumps and potholes. Finally, it had stopped.

In the stillness, Ellie came slowly to full consciousness. She listened intently and seemed to hear another automobile engine somewhere nearby, followed by the sound of doors opening and closing.

The sound of voices drifted to her for a moment. Low, urgent voices mingled with angry, strident voices. She heard footsteps on both sides of the car, accompanied by grunts and the sounds of scuffling. Then all four of the car doors were jerked open almost simultaneously, and several people jumped inside. She could feel the car shifting under their weight until, one by one, the doors slammed shut again.

"You're making a big mistake, my friends," she heard the Oberhaupt say. "When Kurt Radke finds out about this you'll be very sorry."

"Shut up, asshole," another voice said.

The car started and moved forward. In a few minutes, it stopped again and everyone got out. They all seemed to be walking away at once.

The Oberhaupt's spoke again, but Ellie couldn't make out the words.

"Shut up," somebody repeated.

Receding footsteps grew fainter and fainter. Then there was silence. Ellie was alone.

She felt around in the darkness. Her hands were still tied behind her, but the cords didn't feel quite as tight as they once had. And now that the constant motion had stopped, she could at least explore a little without fear of injury.

Besides Ellie herself, the largest object in the trunk was the wheel holding the spare tire. Fastened across it was a jack. The base of the jack had edges that might be sharp enough to saw into the cords binding her hands if she could figure out a way to get to them. Protruding from the hub of the wheel were also several clips designed to hold a hubcap in place when the wheel was in use. These clips were also reasonably sharp and offered some possibilities.

She twisted around until she could bring her bonds into contact with the base of the jack and the clips on the wheel. She dragged the cords methodically against them, alternating back and forth between the jack and the clips. It was slow work, and sometimes it felt as if she were doing more damage to her hands than the cords. But at least it helped keep her mind off how hungry and thirsty she was.

The last thing she'd eaten was a hamburger at an all-night diner in Hillsboro, where she and Adam had stopped on their way to Dallas. It seemed a week ago, but it had been less than a day, actually. Thinking of the hamburger made her mouth water. That was good because it made her less thirsty.

But thinking of Adam made Ellie cry, and that was bad. It made her nose run and she had no way to wipe it. She wondered where Adam was right now and what he was doing. She wondered if she'd ever see him again. Occasionally, she drifted off for a few minutes. Then she awakened and resumed the tedious sawing motions.

Sooner or later, she knew someone would come and open the trunk. The idea filled her with dread, and she tried to put it out of her mind. As terrible as it was to be entombed this way, what awaited her outside could be infinitely worse.

She kept sawing at the cords.

EIGHTY-TWO

Benbrook, Texas
June 12, 1936

In a small bedroom at the rear of Elliott Roosevelt's sprawling ranch-style house, Missy LeHand lay reading by the light of a single small lamp. As darkness descended, the faint noise of crickets and other insects intensified beyond the screen on the slightly open window. But except for their muted symphony, the only sound in the room was the gentle hum of the oscillating electric fan on the nightstand beside the bed.

For the past few days, ever since Mrs. Roosevelt had boarded the special train, Missy had had little else to do with her evenings but read. She'd been well prepared in advance, however, for a period of enforced loneliness on this trip. Before leaving Washington, she'd picked up a copy of *Gone With the Wind*, the new bestseller by Margaret Mitchell, and she was still only about halfway through it.

An unspoken understanding had existed for years between FDR's wife and his personal secretary. When the First Lady accompanied the presidential party outside the friendly confines of the Executive Mansion, Missy kept a discreet distance between herself and Franklin after business hours. The rest of the time, it was Eleanor who busied herself elsewhere in the evenings and looked the other way. The two women would never be friends, but they adhered to this long-standing arrangement because they shared the same overriding motivation: To spare the President any potential public embarrassment.

The knock at the bedroom door was so soft at first that Missy didn't hear it above the drone of the fan and the insects. Then it came again, and she lowered her book and looked questioningly toward the door.

"Who is it?" she called softly.

When nobody answered, she pushed the sheet back and reached for her pale blue robe at the foot of the bed. She slipped it on quickly over her high–necked satin gown and tied the sash at her waist. Her bare feet found her slippers on the thick wool carpet just as the knocking started again, a little louder this time.

She opened the door a few inches to find herself face to face with Mrs. Roosevelt. The First Lady's expression revealed no emotion whatsoever, but Missy felt her heart jump into her throat. She knew about the threat on the President's life. There hadn't been an opportunity to discuss it with him directly, but she'd overheard Gus Gennerich and some of the Secret Service agents talking about it.

"Mrs. Roosevelt," she said in a voice barely above a whisper.

Her first thought was: *My God, something's happened to Franklin. She wouldn't have come here otherwise.*

If her visitor's first words did nothing else, they instantly eased Missy's fears. In an actual emergency, even Mrs. Roosevelt couldn't keep such a cool, dispassionate tone.

"I do hope you'll forgive the disturbance, Miss LeHand. I need to speak with you, but not here in the hallway. May I come inside for a moment?"

Missy tried to cover her puzzled frown with a smile. "Certainly," she said, stepping back. "Please do."

Eleanor paused in the center of the small room and kept her eyes averted as Missy shut the door behind her. For an instant, it was so quiet that Missy could still hear the faint buzzing and chirping of the insects outside.

"Is . . . there something I can do for you?" she asked

Eleanor looked awkward and ill at ease. When she spoke, her high-pitched voice cracked slightly. "I don't know how aware you are of what's taken place in the past few hours, but this has been, without question, the most difficult day of Franklin's presidency – possibly of his whole life. I'm deeply concerned about him."

Missy's frown deepened. "I heard earlier there were some threats of some kind, but I never dreamed . . . "

"They were a great deal more than mere threats," Eleanor said. "The truth is, Franklin was very nearly shot by a sniper at noon today as we arrived at the hotel. From what I know of it, it's a miracle he wasn't killed."

"Good Lord." Missy's hand sprang to her throat. "Do you think he's still in danger?"

"Apparently not from an assassin, at least that's what the Secret Service says." Eleanor's eyes focused directly on hers; it seemed to require great effort. "But he's been terribly upset by all this. He doesn't show it outwardly – we Roosevelts never do – but he's full of tension, anger and anxiety. He was already under tremendous stress, and Dr. Burke says his blood pressure's quite high. He tried to give Franklin a sedative, but Franklin refused. He said he has too much thinking to do to be all fuzzy-headed from some pill. But if he doesn't calm down, I'm afraid he could have a heart attack or a stroke."

Missy felt a sudden stab of fear. She remembered how worn Franklin had looked the last evening they spent together. "Is there something I can do?"

For a long, silent moment, the two women's eyes met. Then Eleanor nodded and looked away. "Yes, you can go to his room and stay with him. Try to make him stop thinking about what happened today and all the complications that may come tomorrow. Try to help him relax."

It took Missy a few seconds to comprehend the full meaning of what she was hearing. When she did, a wave of conflicting emotions swept through her – embarrassment, excitement, confusion. She wanted to charge past Eleanor and run down the hall to Franklin's room as fast as she could go. Yet she also felt a surge of sympathy for the woman standing before her.

"But shouldn't you be the one who . . .?"

Eleanor shook her head. "He needs the kind of comfort tonight that I can't give him anymore. The kind I haven't been able to give him in a long time. And even if I *could* give it to him now, he wouldn't accept it."

Missy hugged her robe tightly around her. Unaccountably, she felt a chill in the warm room. "I don't want to cause trouble – not for any of us. Someone might – "

"Don't worry," Eleanor said. "Agent Callahan's standing watch outside Franklin's bedroom door. I told him to go somewhere and take a ten-minute break. I also told him that when he came back, the President wasn't to be disturbed for any reason until morning. You'd better hurry."

Missy went back to the bed and picked up the copy of *Gone With the Wind*. She folded down the corner of the page she'd been reading and closed the book. Then she took her purse off the dresser and turned toward the door. She paused with her hand on the knob.

"Why are you doing this, ma'am?" she asked.

For the first time since entering the room, Eleanor smiled. Despite her receding chin, protruding teeth and craggy features, Missy thought, the First Lady's face possessed a certain beauty when she smiled.

"As you're well aware, my husband and I have a most unusual relationship," she said. "I do care about him, and I do worry about his health and welfare. But in a situation like this, my concern is more for the people of the United States and their President than for the man I married so long ago."

Missy nodded. "He's a truly great President."

"History will be the judge of that," Eleanor said quietly. "But at the moment, I'm not sure the country could survive without him – and I don't want us to have to find out the hard way."

As Eleanor slipped through the open door, Missy pulled it shut behind them and watched the First Lady move slowly down the hall. Then she turned and hurried in the opposite direction.

EIGHTY-THREE

Uvalde, Texas
June 12, 1936

The neon sign in front of the Elite Cafe had been turned off, but the interior lights were still burning as the Ford coupe rumbled past on Main Street. It was approaching ten o'clock on a Friday night, and except for the marquee of the Palace Theatre, most of the rest of downtown Uvalde was dark.

Only an occasional car was moving on the streets, but Adam resisted the urge to speed. The extra minute or two he could save by breaking the thirty-mile-an-hour limit wasn't worth the risk of losing ten minutes while a cop hauled him over and wrote him a ticket. Besides, as far as Adam knew, he was still a wanted man in this neck of the woods. The Uvalde County Jail was the last place he wanted to spend this night.

Bittersweet memories flooded his mind as he glanced into the Elite's main dining room, where a handful of patrons were finishing their dessert and coffee. Incredibly, it had been just a week since he and Ellie had sat together at a corner table in that same dining room. Even then, their lives had been filled with chaos and uncertainty, but nothing compared to the crisis engulfing them now.

Adam could only wonder if Ellie was still alive at this moment. He had no real assurance of it, only the fragile hope that her captor would find her more valuable alive than dead. It seemed logical that a live hostage would give the Oberhaupt a negotiating ploy if the authorities should run him to earth. Of course, the Nazi also might have other ideas about what to do with Ellie before he killed her. But that was something Adam tried to lock out of his mind.

Based on past experience, he didn't dare rely on the feds for any significant help, but at least he'd tried. The radiator problem with the car had wiped out any hope he had of overtaking the Oberhaupt's Buick on his own. His call to the Fort Worth cops with a message for Starling had been his last shot. Miraculously, though, it had hit the mark.

Some three hours earlier, as Adam paced the floor of the service station in Georgetown, he'd stared at the darkening sky and seen his life passing before his eyes. It was already after seven o'clock, and a taunting, two-word admonition kept repeating itself in his brain.

Too late. Too late.

He'd watched the mechanic tighten the last hose clamp and prepare to refill the radiator. If the phone didn't ring by the time he was done, he'd told himself, his only alternative was to hit the road again and keep pushing south as fast as the little coupe would roll, knowing with dread certainty how futile it all was.

Too late. Too late.

Yet it would be equally pointless to wait here by the phone any longer. If Starling hadn't called back by now, he probably never would. Head down, Adam turned listlessly back toward the work area and the open hood of the coupe, the sound of his footsteps on the concrete floor forming a repetitive dirge:

Too late. Too late. Too la–

He jumped as the pay phone beside the front counter rang sharply.

The doors to the service bays had been pulled down and latched. The gasoline pumps had been turned off and locked. As far as the rest of the world was concerned, the service station was closed for the night. The mechanic had already called his wife and told her he'd be late.

Only one person in the world could be dialing this number right now, Adam thought. His heart went wild in his chest as he snatched up the receiver.

"Hello."

"Is that you, Wagner?" The voice was hoarse and far-away. "This is Starling."

"You sure took your sweet time calling."

"I just got your message two minutes ago. Come on, talk to me."

Adam's head was spinning. With Starling now actually on the line, there was so damned much to tell – all of it crazy and complex – and there was so little time. When he opened his mouth, the words all tried to spill out at once.

"At least one Nazi's still on the loose. He's the guy in charge of the mission, and he's got my girlfriend Ellie with him. They left Dallas just after noon in a dark, new Buick sedan with Texas plates. I think I know where he's headed, and he may already be there. I tried to follow him, but my car broke down. Damn it, he's got the only woman I ever cared about, and I know he's going to kill her – if he hasn't already. You people have airplanes. You could get there in a few minutes. Oh, God, if only – "

"Hold on," Starling interrupted. "Try to slow down a little. Exactly where do you think this guy's going?"

"He could've lit out straight for Mexico, but I don't think so. He's likely headed back to the Radke Ranch instead. That's where he and his men were holed up for the past few weeks. Kurt Radke's in this thing with them. He owns the ranch, and he – "

"Easy now, easy! Where is this ranch? I never heard of it. How do I get there?"

"It's in Réal County west of San Antonio. About twelve miles north of Leakey – that's L-e-a-k-e-y – and forty miles north of Uvalde."

"This girlfriend of yours, what's her name again?"

"Elena Velasco. Her parents run a store in Leakey called the Mercado Velasco. Listen, you've got to get there. If that son of a bitch hurts Ellie, I swear I'll kill him if I have to chase him all the way to Berlin."

"I'll do everything I can," Starling said, "but that's rugged country down there. Even if we can get a plane, is there any place to land?"

Adam frowned. "There's only one landing strip closer than Uvalde. It's on the Radke Ranch itself, and that's not a real safe place to go flying into. Kurt's got a bunch of mean hombres working for him. They don't know Secret Service from Santa Claus, but they don't like trespassers. They'd soon shoot you as look at you."

"I'll try to figure something out. Where'll you be in the next hour or so?"

"Driving south," Adam said. "As fast as I can."

"What kind of car you got?"

"Thirty-four Ford coupe," Adam said, without thinking. "Gray with red wheels." He wondered almost instantly if he'd made a mistake, but if he had, it was too late to unmake it. Besides, he had to trust Starling. At this point, he had no choice.

The line went silent briefly, and Adam almost panicked, thinking he'd been cut off. Then he heard Starling's voice again, above the sound of rustling papers. "I'm looking at a Texas map here. Christ, if you're in Georgetown, you're still a long way from Réal County."

Adam laughed bitterly. "Yeah, tell me about it."

"You'll be driving half the night. If I can run down a military plane, we could pick you up someplace. I'd like to have you with us. You could be a big help. Hell, man, you already have been."

"No," Adam said. "Don't waste time with me. Just go. All that matters to me is getting Ellie back alive. If you get there too late, like you did at the Magnolia Building . . . "

"I can't guarantee anything, but we'll do our best," Starling said "Be careful, Wagner – and thanks."

Adam heard a click, then a high-pitched tone in his ear. The line was dead.

EIGHTY-FOUR

Réal County, Texas
June 12, 1936

Even with both barrels of Paco Ortiz's sawed-off shotgun jammed hard between his shoulder blades, Ernst Dietrich appeared poised, self-assured, almost arrogant as his eyes met Kurt Radke's icy stare. His voice was calm, and he wore a tight smile.

"Your men made a terrible mistake," he told Kurt, "but I'll overlook it this once if you'll just send these imbeciles away. I have to talk to you in private. It's very urgent."

Kurt's face was as pale and hard as limestone. His eyes moved slowly from Dietrich to Ortiz and the others. Slater Tillman stood just to Ortiz's right, also holding a double-barreled shotgun. It was aimed at Dietrich's waist and loaded with enough buckshot to cut a man in half. Behind Tillman and Ortiz stood two other armed men.

From the desk in front of him, Kurt picked up a long–barreled .41 Colt revolver once owned by his grandfather. According to Gus Radke's accounts, old Karl Radke had used the pistol to kill two marauding Indians who threatened his family when the Radke Ranch was only a trackless wilderness. Now, if necessary, Kurt was prepared to use the same weapon against another threatening marauder.

"Shut up, Ernst, or so help me, I'll kill you where you stand," Kurt said, then turned to Ortiz. "Did you shake him down good?"

The half-breed nodded. "We took a .45 automatic off him."

"All right, you men can go," Kurt said. "But I want you to wait right outside. When I buzz for you, get back in here in a hurry."

"You sure you don't want one of us to stay, Mister Kurt?" Tillman asked.

Kurt shook his head. "No, just be alert. I'll take care of this."

He watched uneasily as the four men filed through the door into the adjacent room. He felt much more secure with them present, but there was far too much that he couldn't afford for them to hear – not even longtime troubleshooters like Ortiz and Tillman. Kurt could trust them to kill for him, but not to keep quiet about this thing with Roosevelt. It was too big. Too bizarre.

In an amazing stroke of good luck, Kurt had persuaded his sister Karla to leave today for San Antonio so she could get a morning flight to New York tomorrow. She'd offered no argument when he suggested it. In fact, she could hardly wait for the driver to load the car, and for Kurt, the timing had been perfect. Karla could've caused all kinds of trouble if she'd been around tonight, but now she'd never know about the dashing Major Dietrich's farewell visit to the Radke Ranch.

As the door closed, Kurt leveled the Colt revolver at Dietrich. "You fool. How dare you come back here and put me at such risk? How dare you stand there smirking at me after what you've done? I ought to blow your brains out right now – if you had any."

Dietrich's smile faded. Uneasiness flickered in his eyes, but his voice was still steady. "I'd hate to see you compound your men's mistake by making an even bigger one yourself, my friend. After all, we are *kameraden*, yes?"

Kurt bit his lip. "We were comrades once, but not anymore. You not only failed miserably in your mission; you disobeyed orders, too. You may have led the G-men straight to me. Don't you know what this could mean?"

"You're worrying for nothing," Dietrich said. "I assure you no one followed me. I was very careful."

"Careful, my ass. The Sheriff spotted you when you came through Leakey and followed you for close to a mile. That's how I knew in advance you were coming. How could you be such an idiot?"

Dietrich paled noticeably. "But he's only a backwoods Sheriff. What does he know? What does he matter?"

Kurt's finger tightened on the trigger of the Colt. He lined up the sights squarely on Dietrich's breastbone. But he stopped himself.

"Where are the others?" he demanded. "What happened to them?"

"I . . . I don't know. We never heard from Lutz or Hauptman. I assume they're in Mexico by now. Becker vanished without a trace in Dallas, and Reinhardt failed to fire when I gave the signal. I can only believe someone stopped him, but – "

"Damn it, you can't be stupid enough to think the feds don't know something," Kurt said. "Why haven't there been any news reports of any kind? Why are they covering it up?"

"There's nothing unusual about government concealing information," Dietrich said quietly. "It doesn't mean they know anything. There's no reason for alarm."

"Like hell there's not. From where I sit, there's a huge reason for alarm."

Dietrich seemed genuinely puzzled. "I don't understand."

Kurt kept staring at him. "Paul Hadley," he said without blinking.

"What . . . about him?" The uneasiness in Dietrich's eyes turned slowly to hopeless despair.

"He called me about four this afternoon," Kurt said. "Said he was disappointed that you and the others didn't stop by after the parade like you said you would. He was going to take you to lunch at the Petroleum Club."

When he'd first gotten the call from Hadley, Kurt was seized with unspeakable fury. If Dietrich had been there when he hung up the phone, he would've killed him for sure. Later, though, the fury had given way to other emotions. Hadley apparently knew nothing about any assassination attempt, but Kurt was scared, and his fear steadily grew. What Dietrich had done – or, more precisely, *not* done – filled him with pain, too. It hurt to be stabbed in the back by someone he'd considered a trusted friend.

"Why didn't you kill Hadley, Ernst?" he asked softly "You promised me you would. You knew it was the only way to protect me – the only way to make sure nobody could connect the Vice President with our mission. Why didn't you keep your word?"

For the first time since he'd been led into the room, Dietrich looked truly frightened. "I *wanted* to kill him. I swear I did. But after Becker disappeared, everything got confused. They speeded up Roosevelt's schedule, and we didn't know. We were running low on time. I thought when it was over . . . I thought . . . "

"You betrayed me." Kurt touched the buzzer on his desk. The door opened immediately, and Paco Ortiz came into the office with his shotgun.

"As soon you can round up enough men," Kurt said, "I want you to take this poacher out for a deer hunt, Paco. Use at least five or six riflemen to make sure it's a successful hunt, and don't leave the area till you're certain of your kill."

"You mean a night hunt, Bossman, or do you want to wait for sunup?"

Kurt shook his head. "Go ahead with it now. It'll be more sporting that way."

❖

Dietrich's eyes darted from Kurt's face to Paco's and back again. He couldn't believe what was happening. "I don't understand," he heard himself say in a strange, strangling voice. "What are you going to do?"

Paco laughed. "Have ourselves a deer hunt. You gonna be the deer."

Dietrich turned pleadingly to Kurt. "I appeal to you, my friend. You can't be serious about this. It's . . . inhuman."

"Get him out of here," Kurt said. "I'm sick of looking at him."

Dietrich felt himself slipping toward the brink of hysteria. "Please, I'll . . . I'll give you something if you'll let me go." He moved a step or two toward Kurt with his hands raised in supplication. "A special gift. Something you'll really like."

"What're you talking about?" Kurt said. "What kind of gift?"

Sweat was running down Dietrich's cheeks and dripping on the floor. "Will you let me live if I tell you?"

"I'll think about it. What is it?"

"It's a woman," Dietrich said. "A beautiful woman. I brought her all the way from Dallas for you. She . . . she's in the trunk of my car."

Before he closed his mouth, Dietrich knew he'd committed a fatal blunder. The expression on Kurt's face made his heart sink. He'd played his hole card, and it wasn't high enough. He had no more chips with which to bargain. The game was over.

"Go check the trunk of the Buick, Tillman," Kurt said. Then he turned to the others. "Proceed with the hunt."

"But you promised," said Dietrich. "You promised to think about it."

Kurt turned away. "I *did* think about it. Proceed with the hunt."

Dietrich stared in anguish as Kurt opened the door and several other men filed into the room. His eyes darted over their merciless faces, and he wanted to scream.

Of them all, only the one called Paco and one other were swarthy and dark-skinned. But to Dietrich they all looked like gypsies.

EIGHTY-FIVE

About nine o'clock, Sheriff Streicher finally went home. He nibbled at the food the housekeeper had left on the back of the kitchen stove and sipped a little bourbon, hoping it would relax him. It didn't. He tried again to put Kurt and the wool buyers out of his mind until morning. He failed. At ten, he switched on the cathedral-model Westinghouse radio in the living room and tuned in the news on WOAI.

"President Roosevelt is spending a quiet evening with family members near Fort Worth tonight after a busy day in Dallas," the announcer said. "Earlier, the President addressed a nationwide radio audience from the Cotton Bowl, toured the Texas Centennial Exposition, attended a luncheon at the Hotel Adolphus and dedicated a statue in Dallas' Lee Park . . . "

The announcer droned on for another thirty seconds about FDR's Texas trip, but didn't mention any disruption in the day's activities or hint of trouble. Maybe Radke had been telling the truth, after all. Maybe Adam Wagner *was* crazy. Maybe Streicher was worrying for no good reason.

The newscast ended with a rundown of the day's major league baseball scores. The Yankees' sensational rookie, Joe DiMaggio, had gone two-for-two to boost his batting average to .363 and propel New York to a 9-6 victory over the Detroit Tigers.

The Sheriff switched off the radio and went to the bedroom. He turned back the covers and stared at the bed. He sat down on the mattress and started to take his boots off. But by the time the first boot hit the floor, he knew it was no use. He was too wound up to sleep.

Instead, he retrieved the bottle of bourbon from the kitchen pantry, poured a couple of ounces into a water glass, added a splash of tap water and sat down with his drink at the kitchen table. For several minutes, he tried to bring the faces of the five so-called wool buyers into focus in his mind, but he couldn't remember any of them distinctly. They'd all looked so *ordinary*. One was big and burly, another tall and rather handsome. But all the other images blurred and ran together.

For some odd reason, he also found himself remembering the night of Luz Velasco's death. Streicher had been an eighteen-year-old volunteer fireman at the time, and the terrible images of that night were still burned irrevocably into his mind: He could still see Luz's battered body as it looked when they'd recovered it halfway down the mountainside. The swollen eyes of Luz's little sister, Elena, as she accused Kurt Radke of raping her. Gus Radke's table-pounding denunciation of "those two wetback tramps." Kurt's own guileless expression as he denied everything.

That night, for the first time, Streicher had realized that Kurt was a liar, but he'd had the realization driven home to him on a regular basis in the years since. Kurt was lying about the wool buyers, too. Even at this late date, the Sheriff had no court-worthy evidence of that fact, but he knew it as well as he knew his own name.

He'd finished the drink and was considering another when the phone rang in the parlor. Two longs and one short. It was his ring on the party line, all right. He wanted to ignore it, but he knew he didn't dare. Grudgingly, he went into the next room. The phone was on its third sequence of rings when he lifted the receiver.

"This is Streicher," he grunted.

"Sheriff, I'm real sorry to bother you at home so late," said a voice he recognized immediately as JoNell Joiner, the local switchboard operator, "but as I was about to close down for the night, a man called from someplace near Dallas. He says he's with the U.S. Secret Service, and it's very urgent. He's already called three times tonight, but always before he had me ring your office. This time he insisted that I try you at home. I'll tell him you're not there if you want me to."

Streicher frowned, debating what to do. He didn't like dealing with any kind of federal officers, but he already couldn't sleep for worrying about what was going on at the Radke Ranch, and it was a pretty safe bet that the man on the phone knew something about it. The Sheriff also had a strong hunch that everything wasn't nearly as routine in Dallas as the radio made it sound.

He took a deep breath, like a swimmer about to dive into deep, uncharted waters. "Okay, put him through, but you'd better get one thing straight, JoNell." He paused for emphasis. "Don't you even *think* about listening in, you hear?"

"Why Sheriff," she protested, "you know I'd *never* do anything like that."

"That's good," he said, "because if Kurt Radke ever gets wind of this call, I'll put you so far back in my jail they'll have to pipe in daylight to you!"

Ellie's wrists were raw from the constant friction, but the cords that bound them were frayed and weak. She thought she'd be able to break them soon, if she could stand the pain. And once she was free, it would take only a second to get at the little silver pistol under her skirt. Then, when the Nazi and his friends came to get her, she'd give them the surprise of their lives.

She assumed it was long past dark – probably the middle of the night by now – but the occasional sounds that penetrated her cell made her wonder. At one point, she heard a large group of horsemen go pounding past the car. Some of them were yelling and boisterous.

After the shouts of the riders and the hoofbeats of their mounts faded away, she went to work on the cords again, but before long she heard someone else approaching on foot. Hands fumbled with the trunk lid, trying to insert a key in the lock.

She squirmed away from the spare wheel and jack she'd been using to saw at her bonds and tucked her red, lacerated hands under her to keep them out of sight. Then she closed her eyes and lay very still as someone turned the handle of the trunk and raised the lid. The bright beam of a flashlight moved slowly over the length of her.

"Well, looky what we got here," said a low masculine voice. "Ain't you and me met someplace before, sugar?"

In the glare, she couldn't see the man with the flashlight, but his voice sounded oddly familiar. Then she remembered. It was the fence-rider who'd fought with Adam at the Wagner-Radke property line on a night that now seemed strangely long ago. How could she ever forget?

She shrank back as he reached for her, but there was no place to go.

"Come on now, honey, don't be shy." He grabbed the collar of her blouse and pulled her roughly toward him. She could hear the fabric tear as she tumbled forward.

Behind her, she jerked her sore wrists against the cords binding her hands. She jerked as hard as she could, but the cords held. The man lifted her effortlessly from the floor of the trunk and set her on the ground. She tottered there, her legs weak and numb from disuse.

The man studied her for a moment. "Sure, I know you, honey," he said. "The difference is, you ain't got that damn dog with you tonight, have you?"

EIGHTY-SIX

Hensley Field, Grand Prairie, Texas
June 12, 1936

It was 10:05 p.m. when Starling heard the drone of approaching aircraft engines. He dropped his cigarette butt on the edge of the tarmac and ground it out under the toe of his shoe. His throat and lungs felt as if he'd smoked half the cigarettes in Texas today. The rest of him felt as if he hadn't slept in a week.

"Jeez, it's about time," Nat Grayson said from a few feet away. "If this is as fast as the Army can move in a national emergency, I'd hate like hell to see us get in a war."

As of three hours ago, Starling and Grayson had been personally assigned by the President to lead a team of G-men in an ultra-secret raid on the Radke Ranch. But it had taken a frustrating series of phone calls between Fort Worth, Benbrook, Washington, Fort Sam Houston and Kelly Field at San Antonio to spur the Army into providing transportation.

As Starling had quickly learned when he began looking for a plane, the only military aircraft based in the Dallas-Fort Worth area were three two-seater T-33 trainers hangared at Hensley. A squadron of five visiting P-35 Buffaloes had remained at Love Field following their ceremonial fly-over of the Cotton Bowl this morning. But a larger craft was needed – one capable of carrying six heavily armed federal agents in addition to its crew. The nearest plane that filled the bill was at Kelly, at least an hour and a half's flying time away.

The roar of the plane grew louder as its blinking wingtip lights descended rapidly out of the starlit sky to the south. The tires screeched as they touched down on the main north-south runway. A minute later, the plane taxied to a halt thirty yards from where Grayson and Starling stood. In the floodlights from the field, they could see that it was a brand-new, twin-engine DC-3 with the red, white and blue ball-and-star insignia of the Army Air Corps emblazoned on its silver fuselage.

Grayson whistled. "First time I ever saw one of these," he said. "It ought to get us there in style."

"Yeah, it's supposed to cruise at a hundred and ninety miles an hour," Starling said. "But it's what happens after we get there that worries me." He slung his Thompson sub-machinegun over his shoulder, picked up a duffle bag filled with emergency gear and extra ammunition, and started for the plane.

Just then, the side door of the transport opened. A figure in a flight jacket and leather helmet scrambled down the folding ladder and trotted toward them.

"Evening, gentlemen," he said, saluting. "I'm Lieutenant Scott, the navigator. Is one of you Colonel Starling?"

"That's me," Starling said. "What's up?"

"We'll be ready to take off in ten minutes, sir. But frankly we've got a problem. I've discussed the situation with Captain Wentworth, the pilot, and . . . Well, we know you're in a rush, sir, but we strongly recommend waiting till first light to try a landing in Réal County."

"But why?" Nat demanded. "Christ, as fast as this plane flies, we can be there by a little after midnight. Every minute counts."

"I understand, but according to my charts, the only landing strip in the area consists of about four hundred feet of runway wedged in between two mountains. It's supposed to be a lighted field, but if this is unfriendly territory, we may not have any lights, and it'd be suicide to try to land there in the dark."

Starling sighed, thinking of Adam Wagner driving alone through the night. It was barely possible Wagner was already at the ranch, maybe in a peck of trouble at this very minute.

"This is a matter of life and death," he said. "We can't wait for daylight. If we have to put down in Uvalde and go the rest of the way by car, we'll do it. But I finally managed to reach the Sheriff in Leakey a few minutes ago. He said he'd try to get to the landing strip and get the lights on. The field may be heavily guarded, but he said he'd try. If that doesn't work, maybe the Highway Patrol can help. Maybe we can find an open stretch of highway. Or a big meadow – or something."

The Lieutenant shrugged. "The Captain won't be happy, sir, but I'll tell him."

"We've got to have some help on the ground," Nat said as Lieutenant Scott jogged back toward the plane. "What're the chances the Sheriff can get the lights turned on?"

"No better than fifty-fifty at best," Starling said. "From what he and Wagner both say, that ranch is fortified like a military outpost. But I also talked to Highway Patrol headquarters in Uvalde and got their radio frequency. They could send up to four units in a pinch. We might be able to land by their car lights, but I hate like hell to get a state police agency mixed up in this."

Grayson's tone was puzzled. "Don't we need all the help we can get?"

"Sure, I'd like to have the whole state militia with us, but this mission's top-secret by executive order of the President. Once it's over, it's to be forgotten by all concerned and never discussed again under any circumstances. The fewer outsiders we have to deal with, the better."

"But it's impossible to cover up something this big," Grayson said. "This time yesterday, we might've pulled it off. But by now, two dozen people already know the Nazis are involved. And that's not even counting the crewmembers on this plane or the Sheriff down in Leakey or whoever else we might have to bring in. The word's bound to leak out."

Starling shook his head with more firmness than he felt. Earlier tonight, Roosevelt had saddled him with the weightiest responsibility of his life. It had been part of the price for approving the clandestine strike on the Radke Ranch.

"It's up to you and me to see that it doesn't happen, Nat," he said. "It'll cost us our jobs if it does. At my age, it wouldn't matter much, but you've got your whole career in front of you."

Nat stared at his boss in disbelief. "You mean we're supposed to keep this thing secret forever – regardless of what happens in the next few hours?"

"That's exactly what I mean," Starling said. "No matter what happens, it never happened – none of it. That's how it's got to be."

EIGHTY-SEVEN

Réal County, Texas
June 12, 1936

"It really *is* a small world, isn't it, little sister?" Kurt took a slow, appreciative sip of his brandy and laughed. "Too small and intimate for comfort sometimes, right?"

Ellie sprawled helplessly on the horsehide sofa where Slater Tillman had deposited her. When he'd dragged her out of the trunk, she'd half hoped the fence-rider would untie her feet and make her walk wherever they were going. But he'd carried her all the way to Kurt Radke's office, leaving her ankles securely bound. Behind her, meanwhile, one of the cords around her wrists was now down to a single frayed strand, but she didn't quite have the strength to snap it.

She watched Kurt swirl the rest of the brandy in his glass, then toss it down. It was the third drink she'd seen him finish, but he still seemed distressingly sober. He set the glass down carefully and picked up a hunting knife from his desk.

"You know, I really cared for you once." He spoke thoughtfully as he toyed with the knife. "There was a time when I would've spent as much money as it took to make you care for me the same way. Now I don't give a damn. Tonight you aren't going to cost me a red cent, but you're going to provide a very satisfying ending to an extremely bad day."

He came slowly around the desk and stood there, studying her intently. His eyes prowled over her like claws, and the hot, hungry glow in their depths was all too familiar. She turned her head as Kurt leaned toward her, slowly running his finger from the ruined collar of her gapped-open blouse to the deep crease between her breasts. She tried to squirm away from him, but it was impossible.

"Just think about it, *chiquita*," he said. "Just think about us being together again after all these years. Doesn't it excite you to imagine what's going to happen?"

Slowly, one at a time, he lifted the straps of her brassiere and sliced them in half with the razor-sharp tip of the knife. When the severed straps fell away, the cups of the bra were left clinging tenuously in place, until Kurt pulled them roughly down. Ellie shut her eyes as his mouth moved greedily over her bare flesh. She felt his fingers squeezing, bruising her.

Only the tape covering her mouth kept her from spitting in his face. Even if she could have screamed, it would be pointless. Kurt had quickly sent Tillman away, telling him to "go join the others" – whatever that meant – and there was no one left to hear her, much less help her. Beyond the office, the cavernous house was dark and deserted.

As far as she could tell, she and Kurt were the only ones there.

Adam switched off the headlights and ignition, letting the coupe coast to a halt a few feet from the entrance to the Radke Ranch. A thick, heavy silence descended around him as the car stopped. He could never remember feeling so alone.

He'd wanted desperately to stop off at the Wagner farm long enough to pick up Lobo. The old collie would've been a priceless ally tonight, but Adam was afraid to lose even an extra minute or two. He was also afraid of waking his father. If George Wagner found out what was happening, he'd have another heart attack for sure.

In the recess beneath the car seat, Adam found the dirty towel with the waterlogged German Luger inside. As he unwrapped the gun, a hundred unanswerable questions raced through his mind. Was there any remote chance of the pistol firing after all these weeks? How long would it take for someone to spot him as he headed up the long drive toward the main house? Would there be guards or fence-riders posted along his path? What unpleasant surprises might lie in wait around the big house itself, assuming he got that far? How would he get inside?

He wondered if he should drive the car closer to the house or try to cover the whole distance on foot? The car would be much faster but also much noisier. It would offer a measure of protection if someone took a shot at him, but on foot he'd have a better chance of ducking for cover or melting into the darkness. The questions had perplexed him for the past fifty miles, but there was no time left to grasp for answers.

Was the Oberhaupt actually here at the ranch, or was he already safe in Mexico? If he was here, had he warned Kurt that trouble might be following him? Where was Kurt at this very moment, and what was he doing? How many armed men did he have with him? Where were the feds? Were they actually coming, or was it all a pipe dream?

Was Ellie alive – or dead?

By comparison, every other question paled into insignificance as Adam closed the car door softly behind him. He threw the towel back through the open window and shoved the Luger under his belt. The time for plotting elaborate strategies was over. Unless he got Ellie back alive, nothing else mattered anyway. He took one last look back at the Ford coupe, then crossed the cattle guard and ran at a crouch up the long driveway.

He'd covered about half the three-quarter-mile distance from the front gate to the house when he heard the sound of gunfire. First a single, distinct shot, then another. Then a volley of a dozen or more high-powered rifle rounds, sharp and clear in the night. The sounds tied knots in Adam's insides. He tried to make his weary legs move faster, and he seemed to hear an infantry officer's phantom voice bellowing from the distant past:

Forward, men! Stay low and keep moving! Cha-a-arge!

At first, the shots had seemed to come from the direction of the ranch house. But a moment later, he realized they were actually much farther away – somewhere to the southwest.

EIGHTY-EIGHT

Ellie also heard the shots. She didn't know what they meant or where they came from, but they made her think instantly of Adam. It seemed years since she'd driven helplessly away from him on Akard Street in Dallas. But behind her closed eyes, she could still see his expression of horror reflected in her rearview mirror as he ran after the car. Impossible as it seemed, she thought she could sense his presence near her. She could almost feel him moving toward her, surrounded by danger.

None of the vileness directed at her by Kurt had yet made her cry. But now her own terrifying thoughts brought tears to her eyelids:

What if it's Adam they're shooting at? Are they killing him at this very instant?

Kurt laughed when he heard the shots, but he was too aroused to lose his concentration for long. Except for a few tattered remains of her blouse, Ellie was naked from the waist up, and now his attention was focused on her long, heavy skirt.

He pushed her back on the couch, grappling with the bulky mass of fabric. She felt a button pop, then another as he yanked and tugged at the skirt. Instinctively, she twisted her body in an effort to squirm away from him, and as she did, she caught sight of the hunting knife on the floor where Kurt had dropped it in his eagerness. Then, even as her pounding heart seemed ready to explode in her chest, a strange, calm logic took control of her mind, and the germ of a plan began to take shape there.

If he expects to rape me, he'll have to cut the cords around my ankles sooner or later, she thought. *Otherwise, it's physically impossible to do what he wants to do. Once my feet and legs are free, I'll kick him so hard he'll never forget it – and then, if I can somehow manage to get my hands on that knife . . .*

The headquarters house of the Radke Ranch stood majestically on a slight rise, its dark shape outlined against the night sky like a giant, grounded ship. At first, Adam thought there were no lights on at all. Although it was close to midnight, this struck him as strange. Maybe there was nobody home.

Then he noticed a faint glow from the north wing of the house where Kurt had his office. All three windows on the side of the office facing Adam were heavily draped, but narrow shafts of light were visible from each of them.

He was amazed to have made it this far without being challenged. He'd expected the area around the house to be closely guarded, even at this late hour, but the gunfire he'd heard a few minutes ago could have distracted whoever was supposed to be standing watch.

Gulping huge mouthfuls of air, Adam felt his way along the stone wall of the house, through lush flowerbeds, over ornate planters and past exotic shrubs. Now he was only a few feet from the office windows and the narrow strips of light. His right hand closed over the butt of the Luger. Even if it wouldn't fire, the pistol might at least throw a momentary scare into someone. It just might cause a challenger to hesitate long enough for Adam to jump him.

He froze as he heard a sudden sound behind him in the driveway, then slipped quickly behind a holly bush and flattened himself against the wall.

A car was coming up the drive – coming fast. He saw its lights flickering through the trees. It was all Adam could do to keep from breaking and running. He was almost sure he'd been spotted, but the car streaked past without slowing down. It sped on toward the collection of barns, corrals and other outbuildings beyond the house until the red sparks of its taillights dissolved into the night.

When he was sure the car was gone, Adam moved quickly to the nearest window. He peered through the narrow gap at the edge of the drapes, but he couldn't see anything. The second window was open a foot or so, and the drapes covering it were partially open, too. As he eased toward it, he heard a muffled moaning sound from inside the house.

A second later, he reached the window and looked inside. Ellie was lying on a bearskin rug on the office floor with her hands and feet tied. Her skirt was around her knees, and Kurt was ripping savagely at it. She was squirming and trying to scream. But the only sound coming through the tape that covered her mouth was a low, agonized whimper.

Adam's whole body went tense, and he bit blood from his lip to keep from howling out his anguish. He reached out to rip open the window and hurl himself through it. Then he saw the skinning knife in Kurt's hand, its six-inch blade hovering inches from Ellie's bare breasts.

Adam's upraised arms froze in mid-air. If Kurt discovered his presence now, he could slash Ellie to ribbons before Adam could make a move to defend her.

EIGHTY-NINE

The Sheriff crouched low behind the steering wheel and kept his hand on the.38 Special in the seat beside him as he zoomed by the darkened ranch house. He half-expected to hear gunshots at any moment, but there was no sound from the house or grounds.

Streicher had been to the airstrip on the Radke Ranch several times in the five years since it was built, so he had no trouble remembering how to get there. It was only about a half-mile past the big tin barns and the horse corrals, and it should be within sight in another minute.

"You've got an urgent job to do for your country tonight, Sheriff," the Secret Service agent named Starling had told him on the phone. "I know Mr. Radke's an important man in your part of the world, but we've got overwhelming evidence that he's involved in a plot to kill the President. We're coming to get him one way or the other, but it'll be a whole lot easier if we can count on your help."

"I'll give it a try, but I can't make any promises," Streicher had replied. "Kurt's got what amounts to a small army of his own. If he gets wind of what's going on, there's no way anybody could do what you're asking."

"Okay, I understand. Just make the airstrip lights your main concern, but if you run into Adam Wagner or Elena Velasco, do whatever you can to protect them."

Adam was somewhere close by. Streicher was sure of it. He'd passed a '34 Ford coupe that fit Starling's description of Adam's car, but there was no time to search for Wagner now. It was five minutes past midnight. The plane could show up at any second.

Two horsemen suddenly loomed in front of the car.

"Hold it right there," one of them yelled. "Where you think you're goin'?"

The Sheriff hit the brakes. He was shaking inside, but when he recognized one of the riders as Slater Tillman, his brain manufactured an audacious lie.

"That you, Slater?" he hollered out the car window. "Damned glad I found you. Kurt sent me down here to give you a message."

"Oh, howdy, Sheriff," Tillman said guardedly. "What kinda message?"

"He's got some important friends coming in from Mexico in a light plane. They're due here in the next few minutes. Kurt wants you to turn on the airstrip lights to guide 'em in."

Tillman gave Streicher a dubious frown. "You sure about this?"

"Sure I'm sure. Kurt says to hurry it up. It's real important."

Tillman shrugged. "Well, okay, but I'll have to fuel up the generator first. Tell Mister Kurt it'll take a couple minutes."

"Just make it as quick as you can," the Sheriff said, shoving the car into reverse gear. "You should hear the plane circling anytime now."

NINETY

The final act of the nightmare was rapidly approaching. Ellie no longer prayed to be rescued or told herself that Adam would somehow save her. For all she knew, Adam was dead by now. There were no miracles left. She only prayed that Kurt would kill her when he was through with her. If she could do anything to provoke him into killing her, she would.

The heavy skirt lay in a wrinkled heap on the office floor, along with the remnants of her blouse. A few feet away, Ellie cowered on a white bearskin rug in front of the fireplace, where Kurt had deposited her after his triumph over the skirt. Except for her underpants and the cords that bound her, she was totally naked.

Even her plan to come up kicking when her ankles were freed was doomed to failure. Kurt sat across her lower legs with his full weight resting on them as he deftly cut the cords, and she had no chance to fight back. She felt the knife blade cold against her belly as he slit both sides of her underpants and tore them away. Finally, he laid the knife aside. He smiled in anticipation as he raised himself over her.

"You don't have to make this as unpleasant as it was the last time, little sister," he said softly with his face close to hers. "Promise you'll be good and I might take the tape off your mouth."

Just do it, she thought, *and I'll bite your face off!*

Steeling herself for his assault, she jerked her head instinctively to one side, and her eyes darted beyond Kurt's smothering figure in time to witness an incomprehensible sight.

A window suddenly exploded in the far wall. A large, booted foot crashed through the pane in a shower of broken glass. An instant later, Adam tumbled into the room. He fell hard on the glass-strewn floor and rolled over once, but he was on his feet in a split-second. A wordless cry of rage burst from his throat.

At that instant, Ellie drove her left knee into Kurt's groin with every ounce of force she could muster. She heard Kurt grunt in pain and felt him tumble away from her.

He went immediately for the knife, but she was able to twist around far enough to kick it from his reach with her bare toe at the last possible second. Then he whirled and grabbed for her, but she scrambled out of his grasp, propelling herself with her feet.

As she did, she strained with all her strength at the frayed cords binding her wrists. She jerked them again. And again.

She felt the last remaining strand give way. She jerked again and felt it snap. The severed bonds still hung from her wrists, but she was free for the first time in nearly twelve hours.

She felt Adam close to her, reaching out for her with one hand. He was holding a pistol in the other and aiming it straight at Kurt's head. Then she saw the pistol clearly for the first time, and her heart sank.

Oh, no, she thought. *Not* that *pistol! Not the Luger from the bottom of the pond! It's no good, Adam. It's no good!*

Adam watched Kurt get slowly to his feet. He clutched the knife in both hands, hardly seeming to notice the gun Adam held. His eyes burned into Adam's face like coals of fire. The look in them was wild and senseless, but Kurt's voice was amazingly calm when he spoke.

"You always have to play hero, don't you, Adam? Always the Boy Scout to the rescue – the eternal do-gooder."

"Shut up, Kurt," Adam said between his teeth. "Drop the knife or I'll kill you."

Kurt laughed harshly. "You're going to *have* to kill me, old friend. If you don't, I'm going to kill you. Then I'm going to make this wetback bitch wish she was dead, too. I'm going to make her wish it for a day or two before I slice her up for coyoté bait."

He leaped forward suddenly, slashing out with the knife. The blade missed Adam's throat by inches.

Adam fell back, raising the water-logged Luger. He pulled the trigger, but the pistol only clicked. He tried again with the same lack of results. Nothing.

"Oh, to hell with it," Adam muttered. He threw the Luger as hard as he could at Kurt's head, but Kurt ducked and the useless gun crashed into the wall.

Kurt lunged at Adam again. The knife barely grazed Adam's arm, but Kurt's body hit him with such force that he fell backward. Before he could move, Kurt was on top of him, stabbing furiously at his face and neck. The blade barely missed its targets, but it ripped a deep gash in Adam's left forearm. Blood spewed from the wound, but somehow Adam managed to roll away.

Out of the corner of his eye, Adam saw Ellie crawling across the floor. She was pawing at the skirt Kurt had torn from her body moments before. Adam couldn't imagine what she was doing, and he didn't have time to think about it, anyway. He clutched his arm with his hand, trying to stop the blood. He saw the rifles in Kurt's gun cabinet on the other side of the room. They were much too far away. He didn't have a chance of reaching them, but he had to try.

He stumbled dizzily toward the cabinet with Kurt close behind. He turned and saw Kurt raise the knife high above his head. As the hand with the knife started down, Adam's brain formed a final thought:

It's over. I'm dead.

Then he heard the explosion. He saw Kurt stiffen in mid-air as a blank, questioning look crossed his face. For a moment, Kurt stood as motionless as a statue. The knife fell from his fingers, and he half turned to look behind him.

That was when Adam saw Ellie standing there. Except for the strips of tape across her lips and the cords dangling from her hands, she wasn't wearing a stitch of anything. Eleanor Roosevelt's little silver pistol was smoking in her hand.

"You . . . bitch," Kurt said softly. "You bitches are all alike. Just like your sister." He looked down at the blood oozing from a gaping exit wound just above his belt buckle, and he took one faltering step toward her. "Just like . . . my mother . . . "

Then Ellie shot him again. The second bullet tore through the center of his chest and blasted him backward. He fell heavily and without another sound. Most likely, he was already dead when Ellie shot him a third time.

After a moment, she laid the gun on the edge of the desk and slowly peeled away the tape that had covered her mouth since sometime yesterday afternoon. Her whole body was shaking as she looked down at Kurt.

"Rot in hell, you bastard," she whispered.

It was the only time in all the years they would spend together that Adam ever heard her use profanity.

❋

Approximately two minutes later, six heavily armed Secret Service agents led by Colonel Edmund Starling smashed through the front door of the headquarters house of the Radke Ranch.

When Starling reached the office at the end of the long hallway, he found Kurt Radke's lifeless body lying on the floor in a puddle of blood. Adam Wagner was slumped in a large leather chair behind the desk. Wagner had a bloodstained towel wrapped around his wounded left arm. An almost-nude woman wearing only another towel was curled in his lap. Starling deduced immediately that the woman was Elena Velasco.

Wagner frowned at him. "Can't you people ever get anywhere on time?" he asked.

EPILOGUE

Arlington, Virginia
June 13, 1966

To Whom It May Concern:

Murder charges in the death of Kurt Radke were filed by Sheriff Wilfred Streicher against Paco Ortiz and Slater Tillman on Monday, June 15, 1936. Both loudly professed their innocence and posted bond of $10,000 each. It was never clear where the bond money came from, since neither suspect had ever been known to have more than $100 in his possession at any one time.

Ortiz disappeared within two days of his release and was presumed to have fled to Mexico. A week later, Tillman's bullet-riddled corpse was found lying beside Highway 4 six miles south of Leakey. No one was ever charged with his slaying.

The body of S.S. Major Ernst Dietrich, whose identity was established during a series of interviews with Karla Radke, was never recovered. It was probably eaten by coyotés, but in point of fact, nobody ever actually looked for it. Within weeks, all four of the other ranch employees who participated in the "deer hunt" left Réal County. One had his citizenship revoked and was deported to Mexico, where he vanished. One was jailed on armed robbery charges in Del Rio, Texas, and died in his cell of an apparent heart attack. One was struck and killed by a hit-and-run driver near Portales, New Mexico. Another committed suicide by jumping from a tenth-floor hotel window in Tulsa, Oklahoma.

With the death of her brother, Karla Radke became sole owner of the Radke Ranch. Within three years, she declared bankruptcy, and the ranch was eventually broken up and sold. She moved to a small apartment in San Antonio, where she was found dead of an apparent drug overdose in September 1941.

Sheriff Streicher resigned his post without waiting for his term to expire. He left Réal County and took a job as a prison guard at the federal penitentiary at Leavenworth, Kansas. In March 1946, he was killed by a deranged inmate.

Once they provided a detailed debriefing to the Secret Service about their roles in this bizarre case, Adam Wagner and Elena Velasco were, of course, released and allowed to go their ways.

After all, what else could we honorably do with two citizens who had done as much for their country as these two? They had singlehandedly saved the life of the President of the United States, not once but twice. They had personally taken out two of the five would-be assassins as well as the man who masterminded the whole plot. And they had somehow managed to do it all without touching off an international crisis of incalculable proportions. After our heads quit spinning, we had nothing but gratitude and appreciation for them.

In fact, a little later that same summer, the federal government quietly paid all their expenses for a return visit to Dallas and the Texas Centennial Exposition. By this time, Adam and Elena were married, and the trip was in the nature of a honeymoon for them. They stayed in the bridal suite at the Jefferson Hotel, and they had a great time. I understand they also enjoyed the fair.

The only thing their government asked in return was that they each sign an affidavit promising not to discuss any aspect of the case with anyone else for a period of thirty years. That was the same pledge exacted from each of us who had first-hand knowledge of the plot against Roosevelt. There were approximately thirty of us in all.

Details of the failed plot were withheld even from most high-ranking officials in Washington. Outside of Press Secretary Steve Early and

President and Mrs. Roosevelt themselves, the only key members of the Administration who were fully informed were Secretary of State Cordell Hull and Secretary of War George Dern. If it hadn't been for this policy of strict containment – plus the fortunate coincidences that kept the bodies of the plotters from being directly linked to the plot – we could well have been forced into a war for which we were woefully unprepared at the time.

From that moment on, however, FDR committed himself to preparing the nation for the conflict he knew would come with Germany, Italy and Japan. And because of questions about John Nance Garner's loyalty that FDR couldn't shake from his mind after learning that a Garner supporter had instigated the plot, he never fully trusted his vice president again. The two split permanently over Roosevelt's decision to run for a third term in 1940 – without Garner as his running mate.

After reading Adam Wagner's account of his telephone conversation with J. Edgar Hoover, Roosevelt never trusted Hoover again, either. He correctly recognized Hoover's capacity for deceit and deviousness, as well as his lust for political power. None of the information obtained by the Secret Service was ever shared with the FBI.

Despite Adam's lingering dream of greener pastures, he and Elena stayed on in Réal County, where Adam bought part of the former Radke Ranch and doubled the size of his family's farm, where he and Elena still live today. Their son, Adam Jr., was born in May 1938, followed by a daughter, Julia Luz, (named in memory of Elena's cousin Julio and her late sister) in October 1941.

Elena Wagner continued to teach at the Leakey school until her promotion to principal in 1949, then to school superintendent in 1962. She plans to retire next year to devote more time to playing with her grandchildren and traveling with Adam. I have no doubt that, if they were told about this written account of their long-ago heroics, both Adam and Elena would deny to their last breath that any of it actually happened.

As for other figures in the case, Gus Gennerich died of an apparent heart attack while accompanying FDR on a trip to South America in the spring of 1937. Ed Starling retired from the Secret Service in the summer of 1944, after several years of failing health, and died of pneumonia in New York City that December. Franklin Roosevelt suffered a fatal cerebral hemorrhage in April 1945, as America's war against Nazi Germany was in its final stages. Eleanor Roosevelt died in February 1962.

I've kept my vow of silence for thirty long years, and now it's over. The story has finally been told in full – assuming that anyone cares anymore.

But the most tragic aspect of this whole affair is that the truth wasn't allowed to come out earlier. If it had, it might have spared the nation untold grief. Revealed ten or fifteen years ago, it could have set new standards for executive protection in high-risk areas. Even five years ago it could have served as a valuable warning. An open, objective examination of the facts might have spurred us to increase and improve presidential security procedures – steps that might well have saved the life of another American President.

To me, it seems the height of irony that the assassination plot of 1936 reached its climax in the very city – and within a few blocks of the very site – where John F. Kennedy would be shot down twenty-seven years later. Both he and Roosevelt rode in open cars in motorcades through downtown Dallas, travelling several of the same streets, passing many of the same buildings.

For me, Kennedy's murder in Dallas on November 22, 1963, represented the most terrible kind of *deja vu*. Even beyond the geographical coincidences, the circumstances were hauntingly similar. Like Roosevelt, Kennedy had a Texan as his Vice President, and the relationship between FDR and John Nance Garner was every bit as thorny as the one between JFK and Lyndon Johnson.

There were distressing similarities in what happened *after* the Kennedy assassination, too.

When it became obvious that the FBI, the Secret Service and other elements of the federal government were covering up the truth about JFK's murder – just as we covered up the truth about the near-murder of FDR – it was harder than ever for me to hold my tongue. Now I don't have to keep quiet anymore. I've fulfilled my promise to the thirty-second President of the United States. I've completed my thirty-year sentence of silence and second-guessing. I've been retired from federal service for more than two years, and I have no intention of ever going back, so the time has come to let the chips fall where they may.

In defense of my colleagues and myself, there was no way that any of us could foresee the deadly parallels that lay ahead. In the late spring of 1936, and for many years thereafter, there seemed no reason to brief police and other local authorities in Dallas or anywhere else on the details of an obscure, unknown plot by foreign agents or to upgrade VIP security procedures in those cities.

As my friend and mentor Ed Starling innocently phrased it at the time:

"What chance could there possibly be that any American President will ever again be the target of an assassination attempt in Dallas, Texas, of all places?"

Simply speaking, we were all a great deal more naive then than we are today.

Respectfully submitted,
Nathaniel Grayson

16962610R00252

Made in the USA
Lexington, KY
19 August 2012